HORSEMEN UNITED

BENJAMIN S. HARTMAN

This is a work of fiction. Names, characters, businesses, places, events and incidents are either the products of the author's imagination or used in a fictitious manner. Any resemblance to actual persons, living or dead, or actual events is purely coincidental.

PART ONE

Prologue

Earth Core Inspection Report - August 19, 2482

Prior to terramorphing, planet was in possession of an atmospheric rating of 98 percent similarity to Earth. Therefore, terramorphing efforts have been minimal. Military sweeps show no signs of intelligent alien life despite planet's rich ecological diversity. Colonization efforts authorized to proceed.

Arthur C. Stockwell, Minister of Exploration

Exploitation to Extinction

"Sweetie, I've been picked!" Sulture said. "They're in need of a Chief biologist and say I'm perfect for the colony!"

"Adam, that's great news! I'm so proud of you!" Katrina says as she hugs him. She slides her hands through his slick, black hair, which sits atop his long face like a rooster's crown.

"Although moving to a colony is a big commitment, do you think Joey will be okay with it?"

"Adam, he'll be fine. He's six, he won't remember anyway. Besides, this is your chance to write your own Origin of Species instead of just reading it!"

Sulture knew that she was right. Cataloging the exotic plant and animal species of a new planet was what biologists lived for. Rather than drag out the talk about moving, Adam called Joey to the kitchen.

"Your father has something to tell you." Katrina said.

"What is it? Is it about when I asked if I could get a puppy?" Joey asked.

"No son," Sulture replied. "I've been picked to explore a new planet in space, and we're going to be moving there soon."

"So, we're not going to get that puppy?" Joey asked with a grin on his face.

"Well, we can't have a puppy where we're going," Sulture replied.

"Well, I guess if I can't get a puppy, I'll just have to be an

4

astronaut instead," Joey said, then ran off through the house.

"See? I told you he's got bigger problems than leaving the planet, he's really concerned about that puppy," Katrina said as she stifled a giggle.

"There is another issue."

"Oh? What's that?"

"The colony is stationed in the middle of a jungle. The planet is very warm and humid."

"If Joey can handle it, I'll think we'll manage to adapt."

Adam and Katrina kissed each other and started packing.

Three days later the Sulture family arrived at the docking station for the Angkor colony. There was a heavy military presence since colonization was kept close under Earth Core Military regulation. All housing, food, and defense would be subsidized by the Earth Core Government, until there were adequate resources discovered to invite industry. While standing in line, a man accidentally bumped into Adam.

"Oh man, I'm sorry sir," He said to Sulture.

"It's okay, we're all a little tense. I mean, we're moving to another star system," He replied.

"I'll say, I just canceled three month's worth of appointments. My patients weren't too happy about that, but they'll find a way."

"Ah. What do you do?" Sulture asked.

"I'm a medical doctor, Dr. Murph McGinnis," He said as he fumbled for a business card. "And you are…?"

"Dr. Adam Sulture, Chief Biologist. It's a pleasure Murph. This is my wife Katrina, and our son, Joey."

"Hi!" Katrina said politely."

"Since you're a doctor, do you have any suckers on you?" Joey asked with big, innocent eyes.

"No, I'm afraid not little man," Murph chuckled as he eyed the guards.

The guard in front of the ship asked the Sulture family for their identification papers. He checked their names against his list, and waved them by onto the ship. Murph was sweating bullets as he pulled out his papers, but the guard waved him along.

"So, what brings you to the colony Adam?" Murph asked, relieved to be aboard the ship.

"I've always wanted to leave my mark in biology. Planetary exploration, charting plant and animal species is the best way to do it. How about you?"

"I dunno. Don't have any family, and figured I could see the Universe. The Core doesn't like it when bachelors sign up for a colony assignment, but they said they'd make an exception because they were desperate for a medical doctor," Murph chuckled and slapped Sulture on the shoulder.

"Doctors have a hard time in colonies because there's no telling what you'll come across," Sulture said. "And, you wanted to see the Universe, this is a great way to do it."

"Huh. That's a good point. It'll look good in the medical journals," Murph replied.

The families strapped in for take off. Even with warp drive the trip would take three months to get to the new planet. Adam and Katrina socialized with some of the other passengers while Joey ran around playing 'spaceman' with a girl who was a couple of years older than him.

"What an adorable little boy," a balding man with gray hair on his temples said.

"Oh, thank you," Katrina said. "Seems like Joey may have a crush on your...daughter?"

"Yes, she was a surprise to us. A blessing indeed, but a surprise," the man said. "And now she's all I have."

"If you don't mind me asking, what happened to her mom?" Katrina asked.

"She died to cancer. Erica has been strong, and I believed that a fresh start for the two of us was what we needed. Plus, I'm an engineer, and the government was desperate to recruit me," the man chuckled.

"A fellow scientist?" Sulture asked. "They seem to be all over this ship. I'm Dr. Adam Sulture, Chief Biologist. And you are...?"

"Adar Toub. A pleasure to meet you Dr. and Mrs. Sulture."

After three long months, the ship finally landed on Angkor. The planet was far, even for deep space standards. The families inched off the ship, embracing the sun. The colony wasn't much more than a clearing in the dense jungle. The only shelter were some tents constructed of durable plastic that resembled the 'huts' the poor lived in back on Earth.

A nearby officer screamed an order: "All civilians please report for assignment. You will be given a plot and then lunch will be served."

As Sulture gave his name and position, the officer waved him over to the commander in charge, Sergeant Griffin. He was a thick man, with a square head, buzzed cut hair, and small eyes.

"Dr. Sulture, a pleasure," Griffin said.

"Nice to meet you Sergeant, this is my wife Katrina and my son, Joseph."

Griffin saluted both of them. "So, as Chief Biologist we'll be bringing you lots of alien specimens. We have a lab set up for you over here, it would be best if you provide us information on your findings right away."

"Oh, okay sir. We'll just go to our tent and unpack."

"My men can escort your wife and your son to the tent. I need you to start now."

Butterflies fluttered in his stomach. "Is everything alright?"

"Please, just come with me."

Griffin and Sulture headed into the makeshift lab he would be using. It was one of the only places that was solidly built. It had four walls but no temperature control. All of the basic equipment was set up and the fuel lines for bunsen burners were properly installed. It may have been basic, but it would work. Four soldiers opened and held the doors, while the stench of rigor mortis flooded out.

"What is going on?" Sulture demanded.

As soon as the words left his mouth, more soldiers came in

with a tarp-covered cart, the source of the stench.

The soldiers pulled back the tarp. Under it was a creature with limbs contorted in unnatural angles, and its white-gray flesh was peeling away. Bullet holes riddled the creature, and it's huge, lifeless eyes stared past Sulture.

"What is it?" He asked.

"That's what we need you to figure out Dr. Sulture. No reports during the initial terra morphing of Ankgor identify or even mention this creature. We have a physical description of everything else except for this thing," Griffin replied.

Sulture looked over the decaying alien. The flesh was still moist and was deteriorating rapidly in the humid environment. The skin and bones both appeared to be transparent, revealing the organs beneath. The creature's head was wide at the base of the skull and narrowed towards a crown, which made the head look like a shovel. There were two arms that were similar to humans but with only three fingers at the end of each arm. The torso was wide at the shoulders, but narrowed at the pelvis where a singular limb was attached to the hip and looked more like a third arm than a leg.

Sulture had the soldiers place the alien on a workbench and seized some measuring tape. The creature was slim and muscular, only about 1.25 metres from nose to toe. The wingspan was the same width across. Based on the shape of its skull it was possible that the species was sapient. He made detailed notes in a small handbook.

"I'll need to dissect it in order to have a thorough analysis," Sulture said.

"We'll leave you to it," Griffin replied with a nod.

The camera screen flickered to life. Sulture caught his reflection on the feed, but took his place behind the specimen. He cleared his throat and began his recording.

Colony Log: - November 26, 2483

I've started this log in an effort to record our experience of the

Angkor Colony in the name of science. We've come across a deceased alien that we have no record of encountering prior to settlement. My current theory is that these aliens were able to hide beneath the rampant overgrowth on this world and that our scanners were unable to detect them amidst the great biological diversity this planet holds.

I have dissected the creature and will present a full description of its anatomical makeup.

Sulture started with the chest cavity. He sawed through the creature's sternum, split open the rib cage and inspected the creature's organs. There was a heart, a liver, a stomach, a uterus, and several glands which he couldn't identify, but placed them in biohazard containers.

As Sulture worked, the heat began taking its toll. Sweat dripped into his eyes and fogged the goggles up since there wasn't any air conditioning in the lab. He kept working, lest he lose this specimen to decay. He described in his notebook every incision he made and every bit of flesh he sampled. The creature's reddish-black blood covered his pen and some of his notes, but he barely noticed. He was in his own world when someone came into his tent unannounced.

"Hey Adam I just wanted to see – Jesus! What is that smell?" Murph cried out, as he covered his nose.

Sulture turned and grinned. "You're a Medical Doctor, shouldn't you be used to this kind of thing?"

"Once a patient dies, someone else takes over at that point. Geez, what is this thing?" Murph asked as he peered over at the alien.

"It's an alien the soldiers want me to study. They've never seen it before and it was never mentioned in the terra morphing expedition."

"That's weird. Seems like they'd know if something like this was lurking around nearby."

"I know. It's a fascinating specimen. Based on the muscular development of its three arms it doesn't go to the ground much. The limbs are optimal for grasping tree vines and jumping. It's strong – very strong. Could easily rip a man apart if it wanted to."

"Damn. And these guys are the new neighbors."

"That's not all. The shape of its skull reveals that it has highly developed auditory and ocular sensory inputs. Combined with the developed prefrontal cortex, it's not outlandish to say that this species may be sapient!"

"So, a strong, smart tree hopping alien that can see and hear really well. Don't piss off one of these guys. What's with the blackish blood?"

"Oh, while it does have a red tinge similar to human blood which has a high iron content, I believe my blood tests will reveal that creatures on Angkor possess a high content of a black metal, most likely pewter or onyx."

"Hmm…interesting," Murph said.

"I know. It's fascinating!" Sulture replied. His wild fascination beamed through his sweaty face and the foggy goggles.

Murph donned a lab coat and assisted Sulture with the alien dissection. The two worked in sync with one another, both making observations on the anatomical structure of the creature lying in front of them.

As the afternoon turned to evening, the two men hit their limit. They had studied the creature as best as they could and the decay was taking its toll. Most of the vital organs and tissues were stored in the lab's freezers for further study. The two men looked at each other. They looked as though they operated a butcher shop since they were covered in blood, flesh and sweat.

"We need to get back to our quarters," Murph said. "Get some water in your system since you've been at this all day. Can't have our Chief Biologist getting heat stroke. He may turn out to be our savior," He joked.

"Yeah right. That'll be the day," Sulture replied, then looked down at the alien remains. "Well, we got most of what we needed out of the specimen. I'll have the military dispose of what's left."

Sulture and Murph bumped into Griffin as they were leaving the tent.

"Who're you?" Griffin grunted as he gestured at Murph.

"He's a good assistant," Sulture replied.

"Didn't think we approved of an assistant for you Sulture."

"What's the harm Sergeant?" Murph asked.

"The harm is that what you saw and studied in there is strictly classified with the Earth Core Military! Only authorized personnel are allowed inside of that tent!" Griffin growled.

"Shouldn't people know what we're cohabiting with?" Sulture asked.

"For the good of the colony protocol dictates that the military must establish first contact with the aliens. We don't need people to panic."

"Panic over what? You think the colonists here are a bunch of cowards? You need to trust in them more," Murph said.

"Look, all I'm saying is that the military knows what it's doing. Just stay out of our way," Griffin replied.

"Stay out of your way?" Sulture snarled. "You're the one who came to me for help!"

"Don't get a big head from this. Just keep those freezers full of that alien goo," Griffin said.

Sulture got nose to nose with Griffin. "That alien goo is key to understanding this planet's ecosystem and what we will need to do in order to survive here -"

"C'mon Adam," Murph interrupted. "Let's get home, get some water. Don't worry Griffin, we'll keep quiet." Murph pulled Sulture towards his tent.

"What did you do that for? He was being an ignorant meathead!" Sulture said as he shook Murph off.

"Look Adam, you may be brilliant, but the military is the law out here. Griffin is one of those who doesn't take shit from anybody. He'll lock you up even if you have a family to support."

Sulture gave an icy glare, but took a deep breath and

realized that Murph was right. The heat and humidity was getting to them despite it being past sundown.

Sulture walked into his tent and saw that Katrina and Joey were just sitting down to dinner.

"Daddy!" Joey hollered as he leaped up and ran to his father.

"Hey kiddo! How's my big spaceman?" Sulture asked as he picked up his son.

"Oh, I was starting to think that you got swept up by some alien," Katrina giggled. "What was so urgent honey?"

"I'm afraid the military won't let me say honey. Even though I want to," Sulture replied. He hated keeping secrets from his wife. They were always open and honest with each other.

"That means it's something cool right daddy?" Joey asked.

"Very cool." Sulture replied, and gave his son a tired smile.

Sulture noticed that the two were covered in sweat. There wasn't any air conditioning inside the hut. All they had was a fan they remembered to bring along for the journey.

Sulture walked over, set Joey down, kissed Katrina and sat down at the head of the table. Dinner was a set of military rations created more for nutrition than flavor...or texture for that matter. Sulture sighed as he looked around at the tiny, dismal tent, then turned back to Katrina. In her green eyes Sulture saw that although the tents weren't much they were all he needed as long as Katrina and Joey were by his side.

"So, what did the two of you do today?" Sulture asked.

"Oh, I got things organized here and Joey made a few friends." Katrina replied.

"He did? What'd you do with them Joey?"

"They taught me a game called 'Rebels and Core Soldiers' Daddy! It's a lot of fun!"

The idea of Joey playing that game made Sulture uneasy. He wasn't sure what to make of the war since he served in the Army, but never saw action. It set him back on his Doctorate three years and he always felt like he had to struggle to make up for it.

The family chatted idly for an hour, then Sulture and Katrina put Joey to bed. The two opened a bottle of wine to celebrate the new leap forward in his career. He found it ironic that the greatest way to get prestige, funds and lab space for a biologist was to spend months living in a tiny tent carving away at alien specimens. Still, colonization was his route to prestige.

"I won't ever forget the sacrifice you made for us to come here Katrina. I'll find some way to make it up to you."

"Just get tenure when you teach at a University okay?"

Sulture laughed. The two danced together despite the heat. Sulture gazed into Katrina's eyes, forever grateful of her support for his career. Her green eyes sparkled under the light, and Sulture remembered what it was like the first time he fell in love with her. The two embraced in a tender kiss that only soul mates know, and danced long into the night.

Blaster fire erupted in the middle of the night. Piercing screeches followed, not more than a mile away from the colony. The blaster fire was relentless, a suppressive wave meant to keep an enemy at bay. Two men screamed, then three. Screams of agony triggered another volley of blaster fire. Sulture looked in panic at Katrina as she held Joey who was sleeping in her arms. The screeches echoed across the valley until a blanket of eerie quiet descended on the colony.

A man howled through the darkness. "HELP! HELP! MY DAUGHTER!"

"That scream came from only a few tents away!" Sulture whispered as he scrambled out of the cot. He threw on a set of clothes while Katrina begged him with her eyes to stay.

"Stay with Joey. I'll go help." Sulture whispered. Katrina nodded, and clutched Joey tight.

Sulture ran out of the hut, and locked the doors behind him. He followed the crowd which had already gathered around the sobbing man who was on his knees.

It was Adar Toub.

Toub was disheveled, in his pajamas and looked hysterically

around him. "Why is nobody helping? My daughter! They took my daughter!" He screamed.

As he wept, the military wheeled in. Griffin stepped out from the roader and lead his men through the crowd.

"Who took your daughter sir?" Griffin asked, almost sounding annoyed.

"It was some kind of alien!" Toub screamed.

Murph and Sulture looked at each other. A murmur spread through the crowd, everyone wondering of what the military was battling tonight.

"Rest assured everyone we had some local wildlife trying to breach the perimeter, but nothing got through." Griffin said, trying to calm the crowd.

"Bullshit! An alien took my daughter! It went that way!" Toub pointed to the East, whereas Griffin and his men came from the West. The murmurs grew louder.

Griffin seemed baffled for a moment, then Sulture stepped in. "The alien, what did it look like?" He asked.

Griffin turned and stared daggers at Sulture, who ignored the glare.

"Its head was shaped like a shovel. Two arms and one leg. It ripped the lock right off my door, came in, threw me at the wall and ran off with my daughter!"

"I heard something rip off the lock!" A voice from the crowd shouted.

"I heard the little girl screaming!" Another voice from the crowd.

"Please Griffin, save my daughter! What are you waiting for?" Toub implored.

"We cannot leave this camp. Colony protocol states that the military must not cross the perimeter at night."

"Please! Please! My little girl!" Toub begged as he crawled up to Griffin.

"Stay back!" a soldier erupted, knocking Toub to the ground with the butt of his rifle. Toub covered his head, while blood flowed from his wound.

"Easy soldier," Griffin said. "We will look for your daughter tomorrow morning. We cannot leave at night." Griffin turned away.

"Aren't you supposed to protect us? What about my daughter? With a small search party, you may be able to find her!" Toub pleaded while on the ground.

Now Griffin was irritated. "Arrest this man!" He shouted.

Sulture was outraged. "For what? The man just wants to find his little girl!"

"Insubordination. Care to join him?" Griffin said as he puffed himself up. His soldiers were tense - they'd lost men but were doing their best to keep straight faces. Sulture backed down, the adrenaline for a fight surging in his veins. Fear overcame him and a growing resentment of Griffin settled in.

"That's what I thought," Griffin snarled.

Sulture clenched his fists. He wanted to strike Griffin down and put him in his place.

No. He couldn't do that to Katrina and Joey. There were counting on him staying free to support them.

Murph put his hand on Sulture's shoulder. "We'll help him. Not now, but we'll help. We'll find a way to save that little girl." Murph's confidence calmed him down. He was right. This was a time to be patient and develop a rational plan to save Toub's daughter.

"All right, disperse!" Griffin yelled. The crowd went back to their tents, while Toub was dragged off by soldiers.

"Can you track?" Murph asked Sulture as they walked back to their tents.

"No. You?"

"Yeah. Let's see what we can find without the crowd. I'll be back in five minutes."

Sulture went back into his tent. Joey was sleeping soundly and Katrina held him close.

"Is everything alright?" Katrina asked.

"An alien kidnapped Erica, Toub's daughter. Murph and I are going to see if we can track it."

"An alien?!" Katrina gasped. She squeezed Joey closer.

Sulture knew he slipped up. There was no point in hiding

the truth from Katrina. "Yes. Barricade the door and don't let anyone in except me."

"Adam, can't the military handle this? You've never dealt with aliens." Katrina said as she struggled to keep her tears at bay.

Sulture went up to his wife and cupped her face in his hands. "I want to help. Toub begged for someone to help him and I could only imagine how I would've reacted if Joey was taken."

"Okay," Katrina said. "Be careful."

"I will." Sulture held Katrina close, gave her a deep kiss and then walked outside. Murph was waiting with a pair of flashlights. Sulture locked the door, hoping Katrina would stay safe.

The two men started at Toub's hut, where the kidnapping took place. Beneath the flashlights, Murph noticed three-toed footprints left behind despite the trampled grass from the crowd. Murph followed the tracks out of the encampment, into longer grass. The soil was moist…but the footprints were at least three metres apart each time.

"Our alien friends are leapers," Murph said. "Just like you hypothesized. Good work Adam."

"Yeah, they'd have to be with only one hind leg. Where'd you learn to track?" Sulture asked.

"I'm a country doctor. Comes with the title," Murph replied.

The two men approached the perimeter fence, the lights shined down on the wet grass, and the low hum indicated the fence was active.

"Bastard jumped right over," Murph said as he pointed at the final set of prints pressed deep into the dirt.

The fence was split into three electrical line segments. While it appeared one could crawl underneath or in between the segments, the electrical current would catch anything that tried to go through.

The light from the flashlights caught the attention of two guards, who came running up to Sulture and Murph.

"Colony police. What are you two doing near the perimeter

this late past curfew?" A red-haired policemen asked.

"No sense in lying to them." Murph whispered. "We're out here tracking the kidnapped little girl."

"The military his handling this matter. Go back to your quarters." The blond-haired man ordered.

"Griffin said colony protocol dictates that the military cannot leave the perimeter after dark." Sulture said in a hollow voice while he gave an icy glare.

The two soldiers shared a confused look.

"So there is no protocol about soldiers going past the perimeter after dark?!" Sulture accused, unable to contain his outrage.

"Look sir, we lost several guys tonight. Griffin didn't want to risk any more of us," The red-haired soldier replied.

Murph stepped in. "Seems like you two would love to get a little revenge against these aliens. Why not see where they're hiding?"

"Yes, we can learn their behavior in their natural environment," Sulture said. "We can observe them and use what we find against them."

The two soldiers looked at each other and were almost convinced.

"What do you think O'Malley?" The blond soldier asked.

"I think Griffin would lock us up for disobeying orders Erikson. He has a reputation," O'Malley replied.

"A reputation for what? Being a dictator?" Sulture snapped.

"A hot head," O'Malley replied. "There's a reason why he's a Sergeant in control of a colony. He was demoted and is pissed about it. He gets...overzealous with colonial locals, and locks up anyone who doesn't do things his way."

"We've already seen that happen," Sulture hissed.

"As we said, we've already lost several men tonight," Erikson said.

"How many did you lose?" Murph asked.

"Ten," He replied in a defeated voice.

"That information is for military personnel only!" O'Malley hissed through gritted teeth.

"0.01% in one night isn't a massacre," Murph said. "However, I can see that you two are smart, resourceful men. If you help us, we'll help you. Doesn't colonial protocol contain a militia clause where you can draft civilians if necessary?" He asked.

"We never hope to use a colonial draft, but yes it exists," Erikson confessed.

"Then tell Griffin you drafted us and we can try to find that little girl. Tell Griffin you saw one of the aliens on the edge of the perimeter here carrying the girl and you needed to pursue. You also happened across two men on their way back to camp and desperately needed their help." Murph was going for broke. Sulture was impressed by his silver tongue.

The two soldiers looked at each other. "It would be nice to get a few of the bastards..." Erikson said.

"And it's not breaking protocol if we were in imminent danger..." O'Malley added. "Fine. We'll open the fence. But if we need to pull back, we do so. No questions, no arguments," He said.

"Done," Sulture replied, and offered his hand for a handshake. "I'm Dr. Adam Sulture."

Erikson shook Sulture's hand. "Fred Erikson."

Murph shook O'Malley's hand. "Murph McGinnis."

"Another Irishman? Tom O'Malley," He chuckled.

"Can we go now?" Sulture asked.

Erikson tapped on a small remote located on his chest plate. A quiet beep signaled that the fence was down.

"We have 15 seconds," Erikson said.

Sulture sprinted past the perimeter fence, while the others followed behind. Murph saw where the alien had landed, but the footprints had ceased. The alien got into the trees.

All four of the men stood dumbfounded. Erikson and O'Malley drew their pistols and offered one to Sulture and Murph.

"Ever use one of these?" Erikson whispered. Sulture took the handgun, cocked it and nodded his head.

Murph took a gun from O'Malley, but seemed shaky

handling the weapon.

O'Malley signaled everyone into a huddle. "Okay, we all know what these freaks sound like. They'll leap from tree to tree and will attack in a dive bomb against you. They will rip your limbs off without hesitation. Shoot to kill because they're hostile."

Sulture hoped to understand the habits of these creatures so that he could get a sense of their motives.

The four men marched in silence, O'Malley and Erikson in the lead while Sulture and Murph brought up the rear. A light mist snaked along the ground, and the jungle was pitch black. The lights from the colony were long gone, and the forest came alive with noise. Erikson stopped, and pointed out a robe on the ground. They stopped for inspection and discovered blood was on the inside of the small, pink robe.

"Sons-a bitches" Erikson whispered. Sulture used his flashlight to look around the area, trying to spot something, anything. Another 30 metres ahead was a child's slipper.

"Guys! Up ahead," Sulture whispered.

The four men moved forward to check it out. There was blood on the ground next to the slipper. An ominous grip tightened around all of the men's stomachs.

Sulture noticed something else less than ten metres ahead. It was some kind of device standing on three legs. Atop of the tripod was a container and gears made of wood. There were stones inside for grinding and what looked like the remains of a native fruit pod. Looking in the trees, Sulture saw that there were several simple machines along trees using gears, pulleys, and ropes - an intricate machine system made with nothing but wood, stones and vines! This native species was indeed sapient!

Just ahead of him, Sulture noticed movement. It was a little pod wriggling on the side of a tree. When he shined his light on the pod, it appeared to be a transparent, gray color. Wriggling inside was an alien just like what he had dissected earlier in its infancy. The infant recoiled as he flashed his light on its eye inside the pod. As he shined his light along the trees,

Sulture saw more pods...thousands more all attached to trees deeper within the jungle.

Sulture gasped, and was at a loss for words.

The other four looked towards his flashlight and stared in awe at the thousands of pods all over the jungle.

"Drip." Murph heard the noise first.

"Drip." Murph flashed his light to the left. The others turned to him.

"What is it Murph?" Erikson asked.

"I hear something...dripping."

"Well with this mist and humidity in the air that shouldn't be a surprise," O'Malley replied.

"No, it's something else..." Murph said as he ran off.

A few metres away Murph saw a crimson puddle at the base of a tree. He looked up the tree and vomited. The other men rushed over.

The three men stared in disbelief, mouths agape and recoiled in horror from the tree.

Erica's body was pinned through the chest ten metres high on the massive tree, blood dripping which formed the crimson puddle Murph discovered. Her skin on her chest was gone, the muscles on her arms and legs were torn out and thrown in all directions. The surrounding trees clutched to the gore that had landed on them, greedy for the foreign flesh.

"This...this..." O'Malley stumbled.

"It's a ward," Sulture said. "The aliens are telling us we're not welcome here."

Murph noticed movement out of the corner of his eye. It was an alien climbing down, a piece of human flesh in its maw. The alien saw him, dropped the flesh and prepared to pounce. He froze but couldn't stop shaking.

"Murph shoot it!" O'Malley ordered.

The alien opened its mouth and unleashed a piercing screech. It felt as though nails were being driven into the eardrums of the men, which stunned them and caused a splitting headache. Murph stumbled back, hands on his ears right as the alien prepared to pounce.

Sulture pushed past the pain, and raised his pistol at the creature. The alien didn't notice him. The other three men tried to recover from the sonic blast.

The alien leaped at Murph, but Sulture shot it right through the head in mid leap. The blaster bolt ripped through the creature's skull as it slammed into Murph, who was shaken out of his stupor as he hit the ground. Two lidless, black eyes stared at him, which scared him back to his feet. The commotion caused the trees to come to life, a voracious rattling on all sides. The branches echoed with low level screeching and clicking.

"They're communicating with each other...they may even be coordinating an attack!" Sulture said as he looked around the trees. "We need to get out of here...NOW!"

O'Malley, Erikson and Sulture grabbed Murph and sprinted back for the colony. The rustling in the trees became a thunderclap as the aliens darted from limb to limb overhead. The men were losing the race. An alien dropped to the ground in front, but Erikson shot it. The men kept moving as sweat poured down their faces. Their limbs were heavy and it was impossible to catch their breath with the air being as thick as clay.

Sulture felt his lungs burn as they raced through the jungle. Aliens leaped from the trees in erratic patterns, attempting to capture the intruders, but the men fired back.

After having sprinted for ten exhaustive minutes, the men made it back to the perimeter fence. Erikson keyed in the access code, and the fence went down just in time for them to cross. O'Malley dropped Murph and reactivated the fence while the others kept moving. He turned around and one of the aliens landed right in front of him. Others got rebuffed or fried by the electrical field. O'Malley didn't waste time. He drew his pistol and shot the alien, which wounded the beast, and he left it in the field to die.

Sulture felt waves of guilt wash over him for his desire to re-enter the jungle and conduct more research on the aliens. He knew a biologist's job was to study life, not destroy it.

However, he knew better than to let his scientific curiosity get in the way of O'Malley and Erikson's trigger fingers.

Two more leapers cleared the fence and landed in front of Sulture and Erikson. They prowled towards the men, itching to strike. A third alien landed. However this alien attacked the one on the right. The intruder snapped the creature's neck and tore off an arm. The second alien attacked the intruder, each wrestling the other to the death. Erikson and O'Malley took advantage and shot both aliens.

"Take that you miserable Tritops," Erikson grunted.

Everyone gasped for air, desperate to catch their breath through the humidity.

"Guys, will you help bring these to the lab?" Sulture asked. "I need to run some tests."

"Yeah? What kind of tests?" O'Malley replied.

"Well for one, why did the third one here attack the others?"

"Who cares? It stopped those two bastards from mauling us," Erikson said.

"Something's not right. Those…Tritops were coordinating an attack in there. This one here didn't just go rogue," Sulture said as he pointed at the intruder. "Tritops. Catchy name. Mind if I steal it Erikson?"

"Go for it."

The jungle erupted in screeches as the men watched the trees rustle and listen to branches snap. More screeches pierced the night.

"What's going on in there?" O'Malley asked.

"The Tritops coordinate attacks like pack animals. When one intrudes on the territory of another, they will attack him on sight," Sulture explained.

"Then why did they let us build a colony?" Erikson asked.

"They were watching…now they are testing our capabilities. They see us as competition for their environment and they intend to drive us out," Sulture said.

Murph finally snapped out of his stupor. "What happened?"

"We're collecting the bodies. You guys are going to examine these freaks," O'Malley said as he grabbed ahold of one of the carcasses and slung it over his shoulder.

"Oh. Sounds about right," Murph replied.

The men dragged the carcasses back to the laboratory. Dawn peaked over the horizon.

"Murph, please start dissection. I need to check on my family," Sulture said.

"You got it. You boys need anything?" Murph asked the soldiers.

"We need to file a report with Griffin. He's gotta learn that the Tritops breached the fence," Erikson said.

"Jumped over is more like it. But we'll see what he does," O'Malley said.

"Yeah, we'll see," Sulture scoffed.

Katrina was worried sick about Adam, but understood after he confided in her all that happened throughout the night.

"Please, keep this between us," Sulture said.

"But Toub," Katrina replied. "He deserves to know what happened to his little girl. Wouldn't you want to know if something like this happened-"

"Katrina, please don't speak of such things. I would do anything to protect you and Joey," Sulture said.

"I know you would and I would do anything to protect you," Katrina replied placing her hand on Sulture's cheek.

Sulture rose from the chair, grabbed a slip of paper and wrote a note.

"What are you writing?" Katrina asked.

"You're right! I've got to tell Toub what happened to Erica," Sulture said. "And I've got to go to the lab and dissect those aliens we recovered last night."

"Oh, please don't go Adam! I just got you back from those terrible creatures," Katrina begged.

"I have to."

"At least stay for breakfast. Joey is terrified over what happened last night."

"I'm sorry sweetheart. I've got to get to the specimens before they rot. You can talk to him. You do it a lot better than I do. I'm too...grim as you like to say," Sulture said with a grin.

Katrina sighed.

"Look, I'll talk to him at dinner tonight. Promise," Sulture said as he kissed Katrina on the forehead, took his breakfast rations and walked towards the lab. Along the way he spotted Erikson coming out of Griffin's station.

"How's Toub doing?" Sulture asked.

"Devastated and confused. He wants to know where his daughter is," Erikson replied.

"Can you give this to him? Discreetly?"

"I'm not sure if I'm allowed to…"

"Of course you're not allowed to, but the man has a right to know!" Sulture snapped.

Erikson hesitated, but he knew that Sulture was right. Erikson pocketed the note and went back into Griffin's station.

Inside of Griffin's station there were papers scattered everywhere, as well as two prison cells, one of which contained Toub.

"What is it now Erikson?" Griffin grunted.

"Didn't get any breakfast. Mind if I snag a bar sir?"

Griffin pointed to where he kept an extra supply of protein bars for the soldiers. It was right next to the prison cell. Erikson moseyed over, and placed the folded slip of paper in between the bars of the holding cell.

"Quietly," Erikson mouthed to Toub. He snatched the paper, and tenderly unfolded the note which read:

Mr. Toub: Do not react while reading this.
We found Erica and she is no longer with us.
The aliens took her deep into the jungle and...I think you know.
She is at peace with her mother now.
I vow that I will do everything I can to ensure
that this doesn't happen to other families.
Erica's passing will not be in vain.
I hope that peace and closure will come to you,
and I am truly sorry for your loss.

-Dr. Adam Sulture

Toub looked at Erikson and tears formed in his eyes.

"Thank you," Toub whispered. He carried the note to his cot, folded it up and stared at the floor. A pair of tears dripped down his face as he closed his eyes. Erikson's stomach twisted into a knot as he thought back to the grotesque nature of her death. Sulture must have left that out, because if he knew, he'd want Griffin's head. Erikson stood up, thanked Griffin and left the station.

Sulture and Murph worked in a feverish dissection of the new Tritop specimens. They were careless with their autopsy due to sleep deprivation and rattled nerves. Sulture noted that all of the specimens were female; however, his attention was drawn to the beeping of the computer analysis done on the pheromone mixture.

"This makes no sense," Sulture said.

"What's that?" Murph asked.

"These glands. Out of the three that fought each other last night, two of them have the same pheromone mixture, while the third has a different chemical composition."

"Is that why it attacked the other two instead of us?" Murph asked.

"Most likely that is the case. The Tritops operate under a pack mentality and this proves that we are dealing with more than one pack," Sulture said.

"Let's preserve these pheromones. With them we can make ourselves invisible to them with a camouflage spray," Sulture said.

Colony Log: November 27, 2483

"We've taken to calling the alien creatures "Tri-tops" due to the shape of their skulls. While a part of me wants to believe that these creatures are shy and beholden to us, they're instead quite bold and willing to attack. We suffered a kidnapping last night. Erica Toub, an

eight year old girl was taken from her home into the jungle where we discovered her…"

Sulture trailed off as he struggled to hold back tears. He cleared his throat and resumed.

"Her corpse was mangled. She was left to rot in the midst of the jungle to serve as a ward, to keep us out. We've asked the military to retaliate. I don't believe that these creatures mean to do this, but I cannot shake the image of Erica's body.

There is hope however. The aliens attack and fight each other, the primary difference being their pheromone makeup. Perhaps we could pit them against each other."

As the two men worked on dissecting the Tritops, another presence entered the lab. Both men looked up through fogged goggles to see Toub. His eyes were red and his palms open as if he couldn't comprehend why his daughter was taken.

"Mr. Toub my deepest apologies -" Sulture started to say, but Toub cut him off.

"Dr. Sulture, thank you for going into the jungle when no one else would," Toub said as he wrapped his arms around Sulture. He normally cringed when someone other than Katrina hugged him, but he let Toub have a moment to ease his despair.

"Mr. Toub, my condolences as well. I know it's hard, but we'll help you through it," Murph said as he wrapped his arms around Toub who turned and sobbed into Murph.

He composed himself. "I am a highly trained engineer Dr. Sulture and…?"

"Murph McGinnis. Call me Murph."

Toub smiled weakly. "I am a highly trained engineer, and if there is anything you need built, or anything I can do for the two of you in your quest to stop these monsters, let me know. I would be happy to be of assistance."

"We're not here to stop them Mr. Toub. My job is to research these creatures and report my findings to the authorities.

They're sapient after all."

"They kidnapped my daughter Dr. Sulture. You may be Chief Biologist of this colony and your job may be to research these abominations, but do not forget your role as a father. Especially, since that role was stolen from me by those monsters," Toub replied. "If you ever need my help, you have it." He turned and walked out of the lab, a frazzled, traumatized walk whose steps are haunted by his lost family.

"Poor guy," Murph said.

After two months of sleepless nights filled with the screams from both men and Tritop, Sulture began to wonder if there was more he could do than just research and report. He grew weary from the restless nights that he spent clinging to Katrina and Joey. The mounting causalities turned his scientific curiosity into disdain for the creatures.

Dissection revealed that the Tritops were nocturnal creatures based on their ocular design. The discovery didn't surprise Sulture, but this put the colony at a disadvantage. All of the attacks would be at night, when the colony was vulnerable. Sulture missed Murph, who'd been called off to run the medical ward due to the wounded soldiers as well as colonists succumbing to Yellow Fever, as well as a new virus that Murph hadn't categorized yet.

Colony Log: January 30, 2484

"The military brings me more Tritop bodies by the day. They're getting bolder, attacking our colony and kidnapping people from their homes. We lose between one and three after each attack. Considering we started with about two thousand people, it feels as though we're being bled dry. There is no pattern to who they take, yet I am continually asked why someone's family member has been taken. My exasperated response is an apology and a promise to continue my research. The worst part is we cannot find the bodies. We know they've been taken into the jungle, but the jungle is so vast we'd need to lead an expedition to explore it. Considering our numbers, we

can't afford to leave the colony for more than an hour, and this greatly limits our range."

"I've run a battery of tests from the latest collection of specimens and have discovered that all of the Tritops now have the same pheromone signature. When before we saw dozens of different packs, now we see all of the Tritops belonging to the same pack. This means that they've banded together to fight off a common threat...us."

Sulture closes his eyes, takes a deep breath and gives an exhausted sigh.

"We stand alone in the middle of the jungle against an entire planet of aliens, which seek to eliminate us."

Griffin was sitting at his desk when he received a notification of an outgoing video transmission to the Core. He clicked on the notification and saw the startling revelation of Dr. Sulture's work. As he watched, he felt a chill run down his spine. The realization that if the video transmission were to reach the Core, his career would be over. He couldn't handle another demotion, and the entire situation with the aliens was spiraling out of control. Now that they faced an entire planet of aliens united against the colonists he realized that he only had one option left.

Griffin stopped the video from transmitting and picked up his comm device.

"All military personnel report to headquarters before dark," He said.

There was a rumbling on the edge of the colony. The smell of ozone was rife in the air as the engines roared to life. Sulture looked around the tent, his face a mixture of confusion. He stepped outside and saw the lights of hundreds of shuttles rising into the sky.

Other colonists stepped out of their tents to witness what was going on. Their faces were mixed in confusion and horror as they realized that the military was abandoning them.

Murmurs through the crowd spread like a growing flame.

"Wait!" a woman screamed as the military shuttles lifted off into the sky.

"No! You can't do this to us!" Sulture screamed. Deep down he knew it was no use, but he was overcome with panic.

The shuttles blasted off into the sky, each ignition felt like a nail being driven into the coffin. Murmurs from the crowd turned to screams of panic as their only chance of survival flew away.

Members of the night guard treaded in through the grass, a look of shameful resignation on their faces.

"You!" Sulture screamed. He rushed to O'Malley and seized him by his collar. "How could you do this to us?"

"We didn't Sulture!" O'Malley snapped. "Griffin pulled the plug and took most of the military with him. He couldn't handle a failed colony on his record. According to the records, Angkor is uninhabitable and the people were dying from a mysterious disease. That's why the military pulled out."

"Who's left?" Murph asked.

"Volunteers only," Erikson said.

"How many?" Murph replied.

"Barely over a hundred." Erikson's voice is weighted by the gravity of the situation.

"My last colonist count was 1,536," Murph said. "That puts the ratio at thirteen colonists for every one soldier! How are the volunteers going to defend all the colonists?" He asked.

"We...don't know," O'Malley answered. "We hoped that more would've stayed, but when Griffin gave them the option to leave, they jumped all over it."

"Cowards," Sulture growled.

"Hey, we've seen a lot too." Erikson snapped. "More than any of you colonists have."

"I'll bet," Sulture replied. "Must be hard to watch people die from a distance."

Erikson lunged at Sulture, but O'Malley grabbed a hold of him. Murph held Sulture back and got in between the two men.

"Guys! Now is not the time to fight each other!" Murph screamed. "We have a colony to defend and we will not survive if we're at each other's throats!"

"He's right," O'Malley said. "The best course of action is to do our jobs. We have a man sending request for aid to the Core every hour on the hour."

Sulture returned to his laboratory a defeated man. He clicked on the camera, and saw in the preview screen the dark circles under his eyes growing with each recording.

Colony Log: January 31, 2484

The military has abandoned us. The Core military under the authority of Sergeant Griffin has lifted off from Angkor here on this day. We're on our own now. We have no idea how long we have out here in the jungle. We're desperate for aid. We've sent a constant stream of transmissions and requests for aid to the Core, but nobody is listening. Private O'Malley has taken charge of the colonial government and has been diligently defending the colony with what little supplies and men were left from Griffin's cowardly escape.

Colony Log: March 2, 2484

Sleep only comes three to four hours a night. All of the civilians are on edge. They can't sleep because they worry about members of their family being taken from them. Screams echo through the night when someone is taken from us. They beg us to help, and we try our best, but the Tritops are too fast.

We're being besieged on all sides. The aliens on this planet are openly hostile. These aliens attack unprovoked. I have used this video series to record everything I've learned about them to this point, but our future here on the colony remains in doubt. The aliens take at least three people a day, but they're growing bolder. They're attacking in broad daylight. They seek to eliminate our colony. I'm creating this video to plead with the Core authorities about our situation. Please send reinforcements, aid, and assistance. The colony is in danger, and while I am searching for a more peaceful solution, no act of peace appears to stave off the attacks."

Sulture stopped the recording and sent the video to the Ministry of Colonial Affairs, the Science Bureau as well as the Ministry of Alien Affairs, hoping against hope that someone would watch.

"Adam, wake up." Katrina whispered as she tapped his shoulder. Sulture was startled awake, having realized that he fell asleep at the dinner table.

"What is it Katrina?"

"I'm scared for our family. I'm scared for the colony. We uprooted our lives and everything we knew to come here and now we've been abandoned," Katrina said through tears.

"Katrina, I will never abandon you!" Sulture said as he pulled her close.

"Don't worry mommy, I'll protect you!" Joey said, while waving his toy gun in the air.

"We are doing everything in our power to defend the colony and protect what is left. I have been working on a pheromone spray that may allow us to go further into the jungle-"

"ADAM!" Katrina snapped. "This is no longer a scientific expedition! There is more at stake than your career!"

She buried her face into her hands. "I'm sorry sweetheart. I haven't slept in weeks and I know you're doing all you can for us. I know you watch over us at night and I hear you pace through the tent."

Katrina looked at the table and tried to put the pieces together. "What do you plan to do with the pheromone spray?"

"Ideally it will make us undetectable to the Tritops," Sulture said.

"I know if anyone can pull it off, you can," She said. "I'm ready for us to get off this god-forsaken planet."

"I have sent a video plea to the Core. However, a response

from it will take three months at least," Sulture said. "Until then, we're on our own."

Colony Log: March 27, 2484

Every night there are more kidnappings. Our current total of those lost is somewhere above 700, almost half of our civilian population. We have no recourse, no ability to defend ourselves. They attack us when we're most vulnerable. They're stronger than us, which is why we're overpowered and they carry us into the jungle. O'Malley is doing all he can, but the Tritops know we're on the verge of collapse.

The next morning, people gathered in the colonial square to voice their fears over the Tritop threat. O'Malley stood on stage, the strain of keeping the colony's morale evident on his face. He held his hands high to quiet the crowd.

"Colonists, my apologies for the loss of your loved ones. Rest assured, we're doing all we can to-"

"That's not enough!" A woman screamed. The crowd turned to her. "My babies were taken from me even though you claim to be protecting us!"

"Yeah!" Another man screamed. "Why haven't you armed us so we can defend ourselves?!"

"You bring up a great point," O'Malley replied. "Which is why we're invoking the emergency colonial draft protocols and-"

A bloodcurdling scream cut O'Malley off. The crowd searched for the source until they saw the grisly spectacle of a Tritop tearing a child apart. The crowd howled in fear as more Tritops swarmed in from all sides, a raging flood that couldn't be contained.

"All soldiers respond now!" O'Malley screamed as he opened fire on the incoming Tritops. Other soldiers joined in, but it wasn't enough to stave off the tide.

Sulture picked Joey up and seized Katrina by the hand. He led them through the mire of broken bodies and scattered limbs until they'd reached the emergency station.

"Take Joey and hide under here!" Sulture ordered as he handed his son off to Katrina. She crawled under a desk and held him close while Sulture tinkered with the emergency beacon to get a signal out to the Core.

"Angkor Colony under attack! I repeat: Angkor Colony under attack! We're being overrun by hostile aliens! Send help! I repeat, send help immediately!" Sulture screamed into the mic.

The screech of sheared metal rang outside until the satellite crashed into the ground. Sulture stood frozen as he realized that his only connection with the Core had just been severed like a vital artery. He walked outside in a dumbfounded state and looked at the crinkled dish.

"Adam!" Katrina screamed behind him. But it was too late. As he looked to his wife he was thrown away from his family by a Tritop. Two more dived into the shack and took Joey and Katrina. They screamed in horror as they were carried off through the colony.

"NO!" Sulture howled. He dived into the shack, grabbed a can of pheromone spray, an assault rifle, two clips of ammo and sprinted off to the East.

Murph and Erikson heard Joey and Katrina call out Sulture's name as they were being carried across the field outside the colony. The Tritops easily leapt over the fence and ran into the jungle. In a mad dash, Sulture shot the terminal, which shut down a section of the perimeter fence. Murph and Erikson shared a look, then sprinted after them.

The Tritops leaped from tree to tree, and Sulture couldn't keep up. The roar of a hoverbike whipped past him. The soldier on top stopped a few metres ahead.

"Take it. Save them. We'll follow on my tracker," he said. Sulture thanked him and tossed the can of pheromones to him.

"Makes you invisible," He said as he revved the bike and took off in pursuit.

The trees ahead were adorned in a gruesome display of human bodies. Pods which contained infant Tritops clung to the trees by the thousands. The pods were beaded over with human blood, a crimson blanket made possible by the gruesome sacrifice committed by these demented creatures. The jungle reeked of death from the bodies in various states of decay.

Sulture pushed the throttle as hard as he could, and wished the hover bike would go faster. Katrina and Joey begged him to save them through the trees in a hysteric plea for life. The Tritops split off in different directions.

"Adam! Save Joey! Promise me that you'll save him!" Katrina screamed.

The creatures finally made it to a pair of trees which didn't have any bodies crucified to them. Bile swirled in Sulture's stomach as he looked at his wife and his son being split apart.

"I promise I'll save him! I promise you Katrina! I love you!" Sulture screamed.

"I love you too," Katrina said as the beast pinned her to the tree. Sulture saw the alien draw a knife with its leg and slash Katrina's throat.

"MOMMY!" Joey screamed in despair. Sulture shot at the Tritop that was holding Joey, but missed.

The Tritop then drew a wooden stake and stabbed it through Joey's chest. The poor boy coughed up a mouthful of blood before the Tritop slashed his throat and silenced his pleas.

Both Tritops leaped down to the ground in front of Sulture. They growled and sniffed the air but were confused. They couldn't smell the intruder.

Sulture shot and killed the Tritop which killed Katrina. He aimed at the second one, pulled the trigger, but his clip was out of ammo. He threw the gun away from him and charged at the alien.

He unleashed a deep, guttural howl that echoed for miles. It was a bellow for the departed, an outcry that sacrificed his humanity upon an altar to a cosmos that had forsaken him and so many others. It was a roar overcome with bloodlust, a thirst awakened that could never be satiated.

Sulture struck the Tritop with a left hook which stunned the beast. Tritops may be strong and able to rip a man apart, but they were also small and a fit man could easily lift one of them. He unleashed a flurry of blows against the alien's cranium, each strike elicited shrieks of pain from the creature and he backed it to a tree. He grabbed the alien's face, his maniacal fingers searching for the beast's eyes, not noticing the sharp edge it used to slit his son's throat. The Tritop pierced him twice in the thigh and slashed across his chest.

Sulture stomped on the joint which connected the hip to the leg bones. There was a loud crack, followed by a shriek in pain. The Tritop dropped its primitive knife, which he grabbed. The alien's eyes betrayed fear, while he gritted his teeth in anticipation of the bloodletting to come.

Sulture hacked and slashed at the muscles to stop the Tritop from moving, stabbed its vital organs, all in the hope of inflicting as much pain as possible. To stop the awful shrieking, he grabbed the top of the Tritop's mouth and slowly dragged the knife across the its throat. Blood erupted through the slit, and the screeching finally stopped.

Sulture let the body drop to the ground, and he heard a cough nearby.

He dropped his knife and ran over to Katrina. Her body was covered in blood, and he kneeled before his wife, covered in gore himself.

"Oh God, Katrina. I'm sorry I couldn't save you two. Please...I'm so sorry," Sulture whimpered as the tears flowed from his face. Katrina's lips moved while she stared at her husband. He leaned in to hear her last words.

"It's okay, we'll be together again," She whispered. "Please, save the colony."

"They will pay for this...all of these god damned aliens! They will pay! I swear...on my life!" Sulture said.

Katrina gave her last breath as Sulture helplessly watched her life leave her body. He wailed in agony, until he noticed movement out of the corner of his eye.

Another Tritop.

Before Sulture could react, the Tritop dragged Joey's body into the trees. He rushed over and climbed the tree. The Tritop stabbed Joey with a hose at the base of his neck, then leaped away.

He followed the hose as it drained the blood from his little boy. It led into a primitive irrigation network, which sprayed blood over the infant pods.

Sulture watched as the Tritops grounded human organs into food which they devoured like ravenous wolves.

The chirps from the Tritops echoed, the stench of putrid flesh ingrained within the jungle filled his nostrils. His mind swirled as he realized that the native species on this planet sought to devour all of the colonists.

Sulture leaped down from the tree and kneeled in the dirt. His hands were covered in a brackish mess of blood and gore. His foe's lifeless body was on the ground next to him. It's clouded, listless eyes stared into the distance, and its tongue dangled from its maw. Katrina's and Joey's screams still echoed in his ears. His spine rattled as he heard his family in their death throes, taken from him by the alien species of this world.

Sulture felt the pillars of his humanity collapse and crash down upon him. All desire for discovery had vanished. It was as if some ancient demon had baptized him, tore his humanity out of his soul and exchanged it with the bloodlust of extermination. A strange calm nestled into his mind. His brilliance would bring about the apocalypse of the Tritops. They had made a crucial mistake: they didn't kill him. If the Tritops had killed Dr. Adam Sulture, the Angkor colony wouldn't survive. Now, it was the Tritops who were in danger, for Sulture would never rest until these jungles fell silent and the Tritop species were driven into extinction.

Sulture felt Angkor's mantle being placed upon his shoulders, like Atlas being tasked to burden Earth. A small knife lied on the ground. It too was covered in the blood and gore from its former master. He reached for the knife, the handle slicked from the intermingled blood of both species. He seized the dead alien barely a metre away, and a low screech left its body. He jerked the knife up to protect himself, but realized the cry was only air escaping the Tritop's lungs. He dragged the corpse in front of him, placed the knife on the neck and carved with unholy fervor.

"Adam?" Murph asked nervously. Sulture turned and faced the group. His eyes no longer held the spark of scientific curiosity. They'd become hollow and savage, revealing a shattered soul inside. Sulture leaped to his feet and the guardsmen raised their guns in a reflex.

"I finally understand. I realize what I need to do here," Sulture said with demented inspiration as he looked off into the distance. An evil grin creased his lips. In one hand he squeezed the knife, and in the other was the decapitated head of the alien that killed his family. His arms were covered in blood, and his black fingers pressed against the eyes of the alien head.

Murph was the only one without his gun raised. "Shh. It's okay Adam. Mind uh, tossing that knife away?"

"Huh?" Sulture looked up. "Oh, yeah," he said as he forced a grin. He tossed the knife away from the group. Murph turned and gestured to the other soldiers to lower their guns.

"Now, uh what were you saying bud?" Murph asked.

"I finally understand how we need to deal with these… things," Sulture said as he raised the alien head to the group.

"Conquer them?" Murph asked.

"No. Conquest is not enough," Sulture replied. "We need to drive them to extinction."

"Extinction? How are you going to do that?" Erikson asked.

Sulture's icy glare pierced Erikson into the depths of his soul and for the first time, Erikson was uncomfortable around the biologist.

"Billions of species in this universe have gone extinct. What makes you think these can't be terminated?" Sulture asked as he raised the head.

"So you're going to play God?" Erikson asked.

"No," Sulture replied. "God had mercy."

Two soldiers climbed into the tree and took special care to retrieve Joey's body. They gave Sulture his lifeless boy and he wept while the other men remained silent out of respect.

"C'mon boys, let's give 'em a proper burial," Murph said to the guard.

Sulture kissed his little boy on the forehead. He gently placed Joey next to Katrina. The men toiled in the midday heat, digging a grave with short military-issued folding shovels. The Tritops were oblivious to the intruders, but kept investigating the smell of Tritop blood. After half an hour, Sulture's wife and son were laid to rest.

As the men walked into the colonial square, dismembered bodies littered the area. Huts had been decimated while people pulled each other out of the wreckage. Most were in mourning, devastated from the attack the Tritops had unleashed. O'Malley was directing soldiers where to go, but he held his head in shame. Sulture approached him.

"I'm taking over the colony," Sulture whispered. "I'm going to erase the Tritop species from the historical record. If you want in or out, it's your decision, but make it quick."

"You sure about this?" O'Malley asked.

"It's the only way we'll survive," Sulture replied. He walked to the middle of the square. A crowd had gathered around the man who was covered in Tritop blood and carried one of their heads in his hand. He turned to face the crowd and held the head high.

"Communication with the Core was knocked out during the latest attack. We're on our own now. These things...we cannot coexist with them - I saw them drain the blood of my son to spray on their infants. I witnessed them grind and consume the organs of humans they captured today! I have the means to exterminate these monsters, but in exchange I'm going to need absolute authority to wipe this threat out. The guard is with me, I hope you will be too," Sulture said as he dropped the alien head and walked towards the Command Station.

As the crowd rushed in, one man grabbed the Tritop head and mounted it on a pole. He staked the pole into the ground, and raised the decapitated head for all to see. People murmured, even cheered about someone who was going to fight back against the Tritops.

On his way to the station, Sulture came across Toub. He looked upon Sulture with a gaze that only another man who lost his child would know. Toub placed his hand on Sulture's shoulder. Sulture blinked his tears away.

"Can you make some earplugs for the soldiers?" He asked. Toub forced a smile and nodded.

Sulture entered the Command Station, where Murph, Erikson, and other members of the guard were waiting for him.

"First thing I need to do is clean up. Murph, will you dress my wounds?" Sulture asked.

"Yeah bud, but we have to make it quick. We just suffered a massacre and I got at least 30% of the people who're still alive to tend to out there. Kinda violated my Hippocratic Oath by running off with you," Murph replied.

"Of course," Sulture replied. "Do we have any idea of how many we lost today?"

"Too soon to tell," O'Malley replied as he walked through the door. "Projections of deceased are in the four hundreds, number injured are about the same."

"That would put the total of able bodied colonists at-"

"Just over six hundred," Murph said.

"Jesus Christ," Erikson said. "That's all we have left out of the combined three thousand civilians and soldiers who arrived here?"

"Yeah, it's bleak," Murph said.

"An understatement," Sulture said. "However, we can make their numbers account for nothing, but we need time in order to execute my plan."

"Which is…?" Erikson asked.

"I'll explain in a moment," Sulture replied. "First, we need to develop a plan of retaliation against these beasts. We should widen the colony and create a buffer zone in the jungle."

"That'll leave us even more acreage to defend!" O'Malley said.

"We don't have to defend it, we just show the Tritops what happens when they wander into our midst. We send a message to them. If they come here, they will die."

Sulture felt the warm water cascade over his shoulders and bring a sense of relief. The blood and gore rinsed off of his body, and flowed down the drain. He walked out and gazed at himself in the mirror. His eyes looked hollow, a husk of a man staring in the reflection.

"Help us!" Katrina screamed.

"Daddy!" Joey cried.

Sulture hissed as he felt the blood rush to his temples.

"I promise I'll save him!" Sulture said. He saw Katrina lying on the ground, covered in blood. She turned her head up to him, her cloudy eyes fixed on his.

"You failed us Adam. You failed to keep your promise!"

Sulture howled in anger and punched the mirror. A spiderweb crack was etched along the surface, with blood smeared along the edges of the inner circle. Blood trickled down his knuckles and into the sink. He grabbed some glue, sealed up his wounds, and got dressed. He grabbed a map of the colony and brought it to his new desk. As Sulture unfolded the map, Erikson walked in.

"Sir, I've rounded up the remaining members of the guard. They're at the laboratory now."

"Excellent," Sulture said as he looked at the map.

"What're we going to do?" Erikson asked.

"Erikson, we have an enemy that uses guerrilla tactics to fight against us. They hide in our jungles, attack us at night and have sought to bleed this colony dry. We cannot confront them head on because they have numbers on their side. Phase one of my plan is simple: We burn the jungle surrounding the colony."

"What good will that do?" Erikson asked.

"It allows us to see them coming," Sulture replied. "Come, I'll show you." The two men left the command station and went to the laboratory.

The entire remainder of the guard stood outside of the laboratory. As they saw Sulture approach, Erikson ensured that the men saluted him. Sulture returned the salute and took them to the back of the lab which contained several drums.

"What's all this?" Erikson asked.

"I've tasked Toub with mass-producing the Tritop pheromones. Our goal is to make the colony invisible to the savages. Within a few weeks the pheromones will wear off and the Tritops will change their scent. However, we may as well use what we have. Spread the pheromones around the fence. Can you assemble five teams of six men each Erikson?"

"Yes sir," he replied. "This will keep the Tritops out right?"

"Only for a few weeks until they change their scent, but since I know how to harvest and grow cultures, it will be much faster next time. Ideally the Tritops will see us as one of them, and therefore leave us alone," Sulture explained.

"I thought you said you had the means to eliminate these freaks," a soldier said.

"I did, which is why we're moving onto the next phase of my plan," Sulture replied. "Can one of you give me access to the colonial weapon stores? I need to see what we have to work with."

"It's locked sir. Griffin sealed it up before he left," one of the soldiers said.

"And none of you have the pass code?" Sulture asked.

They all shook their heads no.

"Does anyone think they can change it?" Sulture asked.

"I believe so," one of the soldiers said.

"Excellent. What's your name?"

"Brooks, sir."

"Excellent," Sulture nodded. "Erikson and Brooks, with me."

At the weapons stores, Brooks struggled with the access panel. He attempted several passwords, all to no avail.

"This is pointless!" Brooks growled. "I can't reset the access codes without the original set! Some military safeguard, and we don't have the software which will decrypt the password. We need someone who can run the numbers and figure out what Griffin's pass code would've been!"

Sulture thought for a moment. "I know just who to call," he said.

O'Malley and Murph arrived at the weapons stores. "What is it guys? I got a lot of patients I gotta tend to."

"He's a medical doctor!" Brooks said.

"Just tell him," Erikson snapped.

"Okay, we need to figure out what the pass code to the weapons stores would be, and I can't reset the access codes until I know the original. The problem is that Griffin took them with him when he ran with his tail between his legs," Brooks said.

"I'm guessing you've tried the big ones?" Murph asked. "12345678, password, etc.?"

"Yes, we've tried them. We're at the point now where if we fail, the system will shut down and deny all access," Brooks replied.

"Whoa! No pressure right?" Murph chuckled. "How many numbers is the access code?"

"Five," Brooks replied.

"Okay, that gives us 90,000 possibilities," Murph said. "Was there ever anything personal on Griffin's desk? A picture, a date, anything?"

"I once saw a picture of him with his ex-wife," Erikson said. "Would he have used her name?"

"Not likely," Murph said. "Only 5% of men use their partner's name, and that's if they're still happily married. Was there anything else?"

"He had a picture of his dog on the desk," Brooks said.

"That brings it up to 21%. What's the dog's name?"

"Scout," Brooks said. He punched in the numbers 72688 into

the access panel. The lock in the doors clamored open, the haunting echo music to the ears of the desperate men.

"Seems like you would've been a mathematician with a talent like yours Murph," Sulture said.

"Well, Epidemiologist doesn't have the practical application that a medical doctor does," Murph replied. "But it's still an interesting field of study," he grinned.

Behind the steel door was an elevator, where the men climbed aboard and descended into the darkness.

Sulture flipped a switch, where the fluorescent light buzzed to life from the generator, and through the dim room there was an impressive cache. Every weapon required to wage a small war was here: artillery guns, shells of every caliber, machine guns, assault rifles and canisters full chemical and biological agents.

"All of this held here for months while the people of Angkor were getting slaughtered," Erikson hissed.

Brooks got to work on the security systems, changing the access of who could come and go. "Who do you want to be able to get in Dr. Sulture?"

"All of us in here. Ideally, anyone we draft if we have to," Sulture said, absent-mindedly looking over the weapon crates.

"Okay, I'll change the input code," Brooks said.

"That's fine. You can pick the numbers. Everyone memorize it," Sulture ordered, still exploring the weapon stocks. He hadn't been around this many weapons since the Unification Wars.

"Where have we seen the most activity from the Tritops?" Sulture asked.

"The Western jungle has had a lot of activity, but there's also been a lot of movement to the South as well," Erikson replied.

All of the other men confirmed what Erikson said.

"South and West it is then. Retaliation is in order," Sulture said as he lifted a cannister off the ground and placed it on the table. "Since the attack today came from the West, we'll start there. Does anyone know what this does?"

Erikson looked at the label on the canister. "Yes sir, it will melt their skin," he said.

"Exactly," Sulture replied with an evil smile.

Erikson lead the six teams and covered the perimeter with Tritop pheromones. The colony was still recovering from the morning's raid, but Sulture was more concerned about devising a counterattack. He watched the colony and assessed his priorities, trying to get a feel for his next move. Murph walked up next to him.

"How're you holding up Adam?" Murph asked, concerned for his friend.

"Planning the counterattack. You?" He replied, his gaze fixed on the surrounding jungle.

"Got everyone we could save bandaged up. Look Adam, you need to rest. Everyone's getting concerned and-"

"Murph, I need someone here I can trust in charge of civil affairs. I'm not known for my people skills, and I'd much rather have someone more...charming talk to the people. I need you to run civil affairs."

"Yea, of course," Murph replied. "But Adam I think you should rest. You lost your fa-"

"Excellent! I'll put you in charge, and I will deal with the Tritop situation," Sulture said, ignoring Murph's advice. "We have a batch of chemical weapons I intend to use to wipe out the Western nest."

"When do you plan on doing that?"

"Tomorrow. I'm also going to begin a new project, and I could use your help Murph."

"What is it Adam?"

"I want to begin a genome mapping project of the Tritops."

"Ambitious program. Do we have the technology to do it?"

"We do. We just need the time. I think I can get some software to scan and record the Tritop's genome automatically."

"From where?"

"Off site source. If we can get a signal, I can download the software. Then we can begin the final phase of my plan."

"What's the final phase Adam?"

"It will all become clear in time Murph."

The sweltering day descended into a sticky night where the air hung heavy over the freshly dug graves. O'Malley approached Sulture, not having spoken to him since the transition of power between the two men.

"Report," Sulture grunted.

"No attacks sir. It's as quiet as...well...midnight sir," O'Malley replied.

"We've seen a couple, but they don't approach because of the pheromones," Erikson said.

"Or they ate their fill for today. Regardless, a night without an attack hasn't happened since we landed on this God-forsaken waste," Sulture hissed.

"Sir, you should get some rest. It's been a long day...for all of us," O'Malley said.

"Now would be the perfect time to retaliate against them," Sulture said.

"No, sir," Erikson pleaded. "Please let everyone rest. The colonists need it. You need it."

"What about you guys? You've been up all day, still on night watch," Sulture said.

"We're used to it sir," O'Malley replied. "It's a quiet night, and with luck, it'll stay quiet."

"If we move now, we'll make damn sure that it stays quiet!" Sulture hissed. "Now let's go!"

Murph, Erikson, O'Malley and a few others joined Sulture as they delved deep into the jungle to snuff out the nest. The men covered themselves in pheromones and plugged their ears with Toub's specially made ear buds. Sulture lead the men single file into the jungle, the fading lights of the colony becoming a dim reminder of the civilization they sought to protect.

As the men approached the nest, Tritops walked right past all of them, paying no mind. They noticed the squad's movement, but after a quick sniff they meandered along as though nothing was out of place. Sulture pressed on, leading the men deeper in, but the others were in awe that they'd traveled this far into the jungle unhindered.

Three miles from the colony, the squad came across the Tritop nest. Tritops leaped between the branches, chirping to each other as they cared for the thousands of infant pods which clung to the trees.

The men pulled four canisters of chemical agents from a duffel bag and primed them to detonate. Sulture set the timer personally.

"Alright, masks on. Hazmat suits too," Sulture ordered.

The men sealed up their gas masks and suits. The seconds counted down. Once the countdown ended, the top half of the canister rose up, and belched a sickly pea-green colored gas from the interior pores. A pair of soldier Tritops descended from the trees to inspect the canister. The gas was supposed to be odorless, but Sulture suspected the Tritops had a much finer sense of smell than humans based on their nasal cavity.

One of the Tritops screeched in horror and clawed madly at its arm. As it clawed the skin literally fell off, and formed a puddle of goo on the ground. The other Tritop screeched as its skin fell off, exposing muscle, bone, organs and other tissues to the hazardous gas. The creatures collapsed, helpless against the hazardous vapors, and died a slow, agonizing death from melted organs. Something splashed behind the squad. The pods on the trees containing Tritop offspring peeled away and exposed the fetuses to the harsh gas which caused them to melt even faster than the adults.

Pods high up in the trees fell, splattering like water balloons as the infants become an indistinguishable slime. The strike team doesn't flinch as they observe the effects of the gas. Low screeches and squeals filled the air as the offspring either suffocated or dissolved. More Tritops came to see what was going on, but they dissolved immediately. Within two minutes, the entire nest was a scene of gore and decay from the liquefied bodies of the Tritops.

"That was a good counter strike," Sulture said. "Split up and deliver one of these to the nests even deeper in the jungle. No one more than 20 metres apart. Clear?" He asked. The team nodded in agreement. The six men separated, each carrying one of the canisters containing the deadly gas. One of the men set the timer and watched again, while another activated the timer and rolled it away. The end result was that for at least three miles into the jungle the ground was saturated with Tritop blood. The strike team headed back to the colony, rinsed off any poisons, and began to discuss their next move.

"What's next sir?" Erikson asked.

"We're going to be clearing out an additional five kilometre perimeter of jungle that surrounds the colony," Sulture said. "Our goal is to give the colony a buffer in case the Tritops attack.

"That's ambitious," O'Malley said.

"Yes, but the areas contaminated by our chemicals must be burned or we risk the possibility of poisoning our own colonists.

"What do you want me to do Adam?" Murph asked.

"Two things. First, I've reached out to a contact who will secure us genome scanning software. I don't want anybody knowing that communications are live again. Second, tell the colonists to gather all of the lumber inside the colony. We're building a wall."

The ships screeched overhead as they unleashed payloads of Napalm on the Angkor jungle. Once the contaminated area was cleared, colonists began to assemble a second fence beyond the perimeter. The wooden planks from the homes of fallen colonists were sharpened and positioned to Toub's calculations. Designed to stab and spear any Tritop that leaped over, the artillery guns were positioned to cover any gaps left between the two fences. The entire colony was put to work, grateful that Sulture was taking action for their defense. The fence worked too: for three weeks, not a single person was kidnapped or killed from a Tritop attack.

"Everyone's relieved. Hasn't been a single Tritop attack in weeks," Murph said.

"Not only have there not been any attacks, but nobody's seen them," Erikson added.

"Maybe those freaks got the hint that we can fight back," O'Malley said.

"Not likely. We wounded them, but this planet is covered with Tritops," Brooks replied.

"But not much else..." Sulture said with a pause. As he rummaged through a pile of papers a particular note caught his eye. "What do we know about the Tritops so far?" He asked.

"Seriously?" Erikson asked. "We know they eat us."

"They're savage," O'Malley said.

"They travel in packs," Murph said.

"Yes, but that's all rudimentary," Sulture said. "Every time we've encountered them, they're near a nest of some kind."

"So what?" O'Malley said.

"All the Tritops we've ever faced have been female," Sulture said. "How would the eggs get fertilized?"

"You can't have a kid without a dad," Murph said.

"Exactly," Sulture said. "We haven't come across any males to date. What if these packs are led by an alpha male, like a lion in a pride or a band of gorillas?

"If those were females we were encountering, can you imagine what the boys will look like?" Erikson asked.

"The only way to find out is to go deeper into the jungle and find them," Sulture said.

"Wait, we have to go into the den?" O'Malley asked.

Sulture looked up at the men. "Find it. Get someone in the air and find that den!"

The soldiers rushed out of the station. Only Murph remained.

"How you holdin' up?" Murph asked.

Sulture sighed. "I barely sleep. When I close my eyes I'm haunted by images of Katrina and Joey being ripped from my arms."

"I know. You look exhausted Adam. You're headed for a crash from sleep deprivation," Murph says.

"I don't care. I lost Joey and Katrina, no one else in the colony should suffer," Sulture said.

"I think this is more about revenge than saving the colony," Murph replied.

"So what?! Because of me there's no more traumatic injuries right?" Sulture asked.

"No there aren't, just a stuffy nose now and then. Common cold," Murph responds.

Sulture turned to Murph. "Why haven't we seen any Tritops catching our diseases? The influenza virus must be new to them, they shouldn't have an immunity."

"Now that you mention it, that is strange..." Murph trailed off, lost in thought.

"The blood!" Sulture exclaimed.

"They were using it to expose the young to our diseases, make themselves immune," Murph said.

"Then let's find a disease they're not immune to," Sulture said.

The two men explored the weapons depot for biohazard containers. Most of them would kill humans just as effectively as they would kill a Tritop. It was a dead end.

"Damn," Sulture exhaled.

"I know. This is definitely the harder stuff. Nothin' here we can use that won't kill us too," Murph said.

"That leaves us with one option," Sulture said.

"What's that? Murph asked.

"Ever heard of a Chimera Virus?" Sulture asked.

"Oh, no, no, no, no, no. You can't possibly be suggesting..." Murph said.

"Of course I am Murph! We create a virus that wipes them out!"

"Adam, chimera viruses are like opening Pandora's box! Once unleashed, they cannot be contained! They wiped out that Colony on Neferteri - 6, a place humans still can't inhabit! You can't guarantee the safety of Angkor's people from your modified virus," Murph snapped.

"You're right Murph. I can't. However, this is the best chance we've got to destroy the Tritops once and for all!"

"At what cost?!" Murph screamed. "I will not risk the lives of our people so recklessly!"

"Then we don't do it recklessly. We document everything, step by step. We will know where we went wrong. We're scientists after all," Sulture argued.

"We won't know until it's too late!" Murph snapped.

"Immunization. If I can prove that I can immunize people from my virus, then-"

"How? How are you going to do that Adam?" Murph asked. Sulture stood there, unable to answer. "That's what I thought! You know as well as I do that all it takes is one mutation and your immunization is worthless!" He hissed.

"Look Murph. The colony is on the brink of collapse. We're not getting any relief from Earth. We're on our own. If I don't do this, then the entire Angkor colony will be devoured by the Tritops."

"Adam, your defenses are working!"

"For how long though Murph? How long before those ravagers break through?"

"If the defenses weaken or collapse and the colony is exposed, I'll give you the go-ahead," Murph said.

The following morning, Erikson and Brooks came into the command center and saluted Sulture. "What do you have for me?" Sulture asked.

"Photographs of a strange clearing within the jungle," Brooks said. "There is a large concentration of pods along the rim, even more so than the nest we eliminated two days ago."

Sulture glanced over the picture. "Jesus Christ, looks like a breeding ground. Do we have global positioning coordinates?" He asked.

"Right here," Brooks said.

"Excellent. Now we can go after-" An alarm cuts Sulture off. His radio crackled with hysteric voices. "Sulture here. What is it?"

The static cleared up. "Movement sir," the voice replied. "Huge wave of Tritops coming from the East. Thousands of them are about to storm the walls. Immediate action suggested."

"What do we have on the bombers?" Sulture asked.

"Three payloads of Napalm sir."

"Wait until they're out in the open, then blow them all to hell. Command on the way, over and out," Sulture said as he tuned the radio to the megaphones. "Angkor colony, massive Tritop attack coming in from the East. All able bodied fighters flock to the eastern wall immediately!" Sulture dropped the microphone, cocked his rifle, and grabbed a machete.

"Let's move!" He said.

"Yes sir!" both men replied as they cocked their rifles.

All three ran out of the command center and rushed through the crowd. When they got to the eastern wall they met up with hundreds of colonists ready to protect their homes. As the colonists took their positions the guard aligned the artillery guns for the impending assault.

The Tritops rushed through the charred forest and leaped the first fence. A quarter of them were speared or electrocuted, but the rest made it through the first barricade.

Sulture walked through the crowd of defenders and took the helm. "Earplugs on!" He ordered. Toub's new earplugs blocked the high frequency of the Tritop's screeches, but allowed them to hear one another just fine.

As the Tritops closed in on the colony, three jets roared overhead. The open fields erupted in flames and the Tritops were swallowed up in a lake of fire. They screeched in agonizing pain, and 90% of them were consumed in the pyres of vengeance.

The artillerymen signaled they were in position. Sulture called out for them to fire.

As he gave the order, another wave of Tritops spilled out of the jungle.

The artillery guns roared to life, cracking like thunder. The machine guns erupted in a torrent of blaster fire, cutting down the Tritops in droves. The infantry was determined to hold the line at all costs.

However, the Tritops wouldn't stop coming.

Sulture turned around, and spotted Toub. He was standing next to a side project he'd built for the colony's defense.

"Now Toub!" Sulture screamed.

"See you bastards in the depths of Hell!" Toub hissed as he pulled a lever and watched his wooden trebuchet launch a chemical weapons canister into the oncoming crowd of Tritops.

As the canister struck the ground, it split open and released the sickly pea-green gas contained within. Dozens of Tritops waded into the noxious plumes before they realized what they had done. Some melted on sight, others slipped in the gore of the fallen. The exposed had limbs fall off, but the beasts were undeterred. They were driven forward in a possessed state, hellbent on wiping out the colony once and for all.

A dozen Tritops closed in on the infantry defenders. Sulture's gun jammed, which forced him to abandon the weapon, but he remembered that he grabbed a machete. He drew the blade and walked out into the fray. He carved his way through the crowd of aliens, some of them stopped to unleash a sonic blast but it had no effect. They shared looks of confusion before Sulture hacked them to pieces. He watched the Tritops in the field crawl along the ground to get to him, but they were disfigured beyond recognition.

Sulture watched another canister fly deep into the jungle, and the Tritop screeches of torment was a symphony to his ears. He couldn't quench his thirst for the blood of these monsters. He walked into the line of fire, unconcerned with his own life. These creatures took away the only people he ever loved, and it didn't matter the cost, they had to die. Finally, the great tidal wave of Tritops slowed to a trickle.

"Sir! The Tritops have rerouted to the South because of the

gas!" A voice crackled over Sulture's radio.

"All available units to the South! I repeat: all available units to the South!" Sulture screamed over the radio. He sprinted for the incoming wave of beasts. The rest of the soldiers abandoned the Eastern wall and flooded to the South, which was on the verge of collapse.

Sulture waded into the fray, hacking and slashing at Tritops in a grisly ritual of primal rage. The soldiers opened fire, and drew attention to themselves. The aliens unleashed their sonic blasts, but to no effect. Upon realization, the Tritops leaped at the soldiers, tearing limbs off and bit them like ferocious jackals. One Tritop leaped onto Sulture's shoulders and tried to break his neck, but he flipped the creature down and buried his machete in its chest.

An airship floated overhead and breathed streams of fire across the valley at the incoming Tritops. The artillery guns played an anthem of carnage as they tore apart the stragglers who were lost in the confusion. Sulture felt the oppressive heat from the Napalm as he smelled the burning flesh of his foe. The final attack had broken the Tritop's resolve, and they stopped flowing out of the jungle.

Sulture gazed upon the ruin all around him. He witnessed tear-lined faces of broken families who wandered aimlessly to collect the fragments of their loved ones. He saw the shock in their eyes and how their resolve hanged by a threat. He even saw a little boy kneeling behind his fallen father, who was still armed and protecting a man he thought could never die.

"Adam, Erikson, you need to see this," Murph said over the comm.

The men arrived on the scene, right as Murph placed a sheet over the body. He saw them arrive and lifted the sheet, straining to hold back tears. They saw the O'Malley's pale face, and his neck contorted in an unnatural angle. Erikson sobbed as he kneeled next to O'Malley's body.

"Dr. Sulture, we need you back at Command," Brooks said over the radio. Sulture turned his device off.

"How bad is it?" Sulture asked while staring at Murph.

Murph sniffed, and tears slid down his cheeks. He closed his eyes to stop them from stinging.

"Murph…?" Sulture asked.

"A hundred and three," Murph replied. "One hundred and three people left on this fucking, worthless, shit hole of a planet!" He screamed as he kicked a rock, then fell to his knees.

"Build it," Murph said. "Build the Chimera virus Adam," He sobbed, knowing that he may have condemned the entire colony to death. Sulture stared at the ground. He got his answer, but he still felt hollow. He inched forward and embraced Murph. Murph wailed in anguish as Sulture held him tight.

"This will end," Sulture whispered. "I am the flood that will cleanse this world."

Sulture called Toub and Erikson into the Command Center. They were disheveled and ragged, but more determined than ever.

"I have the means to destroy the Tritops once and for all, but I cannot do so while running military affairs here on the colony. I also need Murph's help, and he cannot run civilian affairs while helping me. I would like to ask you Erikson if you'd take over military and you Toub to handle civilian."

"How do you plan to wipe out the Tritops?" Erikson asked.

"It's a dangerous plan and it will put the lives of the colonists in danger. However, we believe the less you two know, the better. If something goes wrong, persecute us," Sulture said.

"But this will for sure wipe out the Tritops?" Toub asked.

"I believe so, yes," Sulture replied.

"Then I'm in," Toub said.

"Yeah, me too," Erikson said.

Inside of the laboratory, Sulture found Murph staring at the Tritop genome, hoping to decipher the genetic code for a breakthrough. "Our roles have been delegated out. People may wonder why the switch, but Erikson and Toub will be fine," Sulture said.

"The colony's in good hands. What were you thinking of using against the Tritops?" Murph asked.

"What is the one virus that has a 100% fatality rate when exposed and untreated? A virus that is not communicable through the air, but through saliva."

"No, you can't possibly mean-"

"I do Murph. Rabies."

"How do we acquire a sample? It's not native here."

"Investors hope that the local fauna on a new colony holds the possibility of a new medicine being discovered. Every colony ship is outfitted with a strain of viruses that require treatment on Earth. All of these are to be watched over by the Chief Biologist."

"And you have a sample of rabies aboard the ship?"

"I do. We can modify the virus so that the Tritop hosts will only attack each other and alter the pheromones they produce. We make them more aggressive and prone to attack those that are not infected."

"And we can limit the risk to colonists since we already have rabies medicine," Murph said.

"Exactly," Sulture replied with an evil grin.

The two men worked day and night, splicing the rabies virus and created a sinister variant of the brutal disease. They utilized the genome they had on site and adjusted the virus so that it could only infect other Tritops as a failsafe. The two men recorded every step of the process which Sulture used to compile a scientific paper on the subject. Just before he could send the paper out, Toub and Erikson came into the laboratory.

"Gentlemen, sorry to interrupt your experiment, but we just received word that the Core will be landing here by the end of today," Erikson said. "They were concerned by the communications blackout and sent a relief force."

"Why're you telling us this?" Sulture asked.

"Because Sulture, the Core believes it's illegal to kill aliens like these, especially on the scale you intend to. You'll be the first man tried for Xenocide!"

"I'm not running," Sulture said. "I'm going to finish this! And I'll start by submitting this paper, my declaration of intent."

"Adam, no journal will approve of your paper. It'll be blacklisted by every scientific community in the galaxy," Murph said.

"People need to know what happened here on Angkor! Besides, I'm not sending it to any journal. I have another source. He'll get it into the right hands."

"Same guy who got you the genome scanning program?" Murph asked.

"The very same."

"He got a name? Guy like that may be useful," Murph asked.

"Never met him in person. He just goes by Hacker," Sulture replied.

"Seems convenient. What're you calling your paper?"

"Exploitation to Extinction."

"Catchy title."

"I thought so too."

Sulture uploaded his paper, sealed the virus canister and Murph grabbed the anti-viral medicine.

"Here Toub, we need this mass produced. Make sure all of the colonists get a dose," Murph said as he handed over a box of syringes. Toub smiled and took the box.

"Good luck," He said to the two men.

"Sulture, I just received word that Griffin is leading the Core to our front door," Erikson warned.

"Of course he is," Sulture said. "That way instead of being tried for cowardice he can be hailed as a hero for leading the rescue mission."

"He won't get that satisfaction from us," Erikson said. "Anything else I can do for you?"

"We need a handful of soldiers and to get into the air. Volunteers only," Sulture said.

"I can do that for ya," Erikson said.

Brooks and the others greeted Sulture and Murph outside the speeder ship. "Erikson said you needed volunteers to wipe out the Tritops?" He asked.

"High risk mission," Murph said. "We're opening a can of worms on this one boys. We have no idea what the fallout from the Core will be."

"It's alright," Brooks replied. "I want to see these freaks gone. Don't care what happens to me."

"Our pilot. Can he be mobilized?" Sulture grumbled.

"Yeah, where do you want him to go?" Brooks asked.

"This clearing," Sulture replied, as he pointed to the map.

"Alright Collins get us to these coordinates quick!" Brooks said.

"Yes sir!" He replied as he ignited the jet's engines.

Sulture explained his plan and intent, that this mission would likely end in the deaths of the soldiers either at the hands of the Tritops or the Core. He explained that since the planet was one giant continent, this virus was going to spread quickly.

"What does this virus do, give them the sniffles?" One of the men asked.

"It's a modified rabies virus which makes them devour each other," Sulture said.

"Holy shit!" One of the soldiers cheered.

"Here's the anti-viral," Murph said as he passed a box of syringes to the squad.

"We're with you 'til the end, Dr. Sulture," Brooks said.

"Good, because we're going into the belly of the beast," Sulture replied. The men all held the anti-virals in their hands and plunged them into their veins at the same time, a silent oath that they were going to finish this mission no matter what.

As the squad approached the clearing, the stench of mold and decay filled their nostrils. The bones of all of Angkor's native species, including humans, littered the landscape.

"Earbuds!" Sulture ordered. "Collins! Drop us off anywhere

you can and stay in the air! If something happens to us, just get the hell outta here!"

"It was nice knowing you fellas. Good luck!" Collins replied. He spun the ship around, opened the cargo hatch, and the squad ran out.

"Adam, what are we looking for?" Murph asked. A guttural bellow echoed through the clearing. The trees shook and branches snapped as their new foe came for them.

"The alpha male," Sulture replied.

A massive, gunmetal gray Tritop burst into the clearing. It was ten times the size of any of the Tritops they'd encountered before. The beast slammed its fists into the ground and bellowed in Sulture's face. The air pulsed and rippled from his cry, but Sulture stood his ground. The roar was deafening, and wasn't a high enough pitch for the earplugs to block out.

Tritops swarmed in from all directions, furious over the intruders who'd wandered into their midst. The squad huddled back to back, completely surrounded.

The alpha slammed his fists again and roared out at the Tritops. They stood in a circle around the squad, eager to attack, but remained in place. The alpha pawed at the ground, raking the earth with his jagged fingers.

"What is he doing?" One of the soldiers asked.

"He's challenging us," Sulture replied. "I'll go after him, you guys take the rest of 'em. Remember, spread the infection." He unsheathed his machete and coated it with the viral serum. The rest of the men followed suit.

All of the men howled their battle cry as they charged at their foes, the last stand of the Angkor colony coming to a head.

The alpha bellowed back and charged for Sulture. Sulture dived and slid in between the massive fists bearing down on the ground. He leaped up and sliced at the alpha's abdomen, exposing him to the virus. The alpha turned around, his sinister black eyes boring into Sulture.

The others hacked wildly at the female Tritops, seeking to maim rather than kill their enemy. They weaved and dodged the leaping beasts, cutting at them and spreading the contagion.

One of the soldiers howled as a Tritop landed on top of his shoulders and ripped off his arms. The man collapsed from the pain. There were too many Tritops, and it seemed that the squad would be overwhelmed in the middle of the jungle.

The alpha traipsed up to Sulture. He backed away slowly, brandishing his bloody machete for the beast to see. The alpha growled as it approached, each step taking an eternity.

"Why isn't the infection taking hold?" Sulture cursed to himself.

The lumbering behemoth swept the ground with his arm, but Sulture leaped over the arm and slashed at the beast's bicep.

Sulture struck a nerve on the beast because before he could react, the creature slammed him to the ground with its other hand. Sulture struggled to breath as the multi-ton colossus squeezed the life out of him. It growled as it neared him, the stench of rotting flesh flowing from its maw.

A screech pierced the air. Sulture and the alpha both looked at the source. Two Tritops were interlocked in combat, fighting to the death. More joined in. They snarled and growled as they tore each other apart, blood splattering everywhere. A feral look settled into the eyes of the Tritops as they encircled the alpha. All of those that encircled him were unmarked, and they were no longer paying attention to the humans.

One of the females leaped onto the alpha's shoulder and bit him. He reached up, grabbed the female and threw her far into the jungle. Another attacked him, while he bit her in half. The more the alpha fought back, the more savage the females became as they dog piled on top of him. Those that were marked with lacerations charged into the jungle, a telltale froth covering their mouths.

The entire nest descended into a frenzy as the alpha crushed and bit every Tritop that attacked him. The rabies virus was taking hold and the monsters were tearing each other to pieces. He gazed at Sulture, an unnatural fury in his eyes, but was too restrained by the attacking females to charge him.

"Collins, get us out of here," Sulture ordered.

"Roger that. One minute out," Collins replied.

Collins descended through the edge of the clearing as the alpha was being torn to shreds. "What did you boys do?" He asked.

"We finished them off," Sulture replied.

As the jet rumbled for take off, the alpha leaped to his hind leg, throwing the female Tritops off. He was covered in bite marks and lacerations, with froth dripping out of his mouth.

"Go now!" Brooks screamed.

The jet hovered a few metres above the ground as the alpha closed in. As the jet rose, the alpha made one last desperate attempt annihilate the intruders that brought this disease upon him. He leaped and swung to bat the jet out of the sky, but missed only by centimetres. Sulture watched as he fell, and savored the sight of the Tritops leaping onto him for the kill.

It was a quiet trip on the way back home. They questioned whether or not this disease would take root and exterminate the Tritops, or if it would burn itself out within the next few hours and doom the colony.

As the jet descended to the landing pad, Core warships dominated the scene, and soldiers swarmed like locusts in a wheat field. An entire squad surrounded the jet within seconds.

Collins lowered the cargo ramp, and Sulture could hear Griffin's obnoxious voice scream obscenities and other curses. As Griffin came into view he pointed at Sulture.

"That's him!" He screamed. The soldiers drew their rifles.

Sulture dropped his gun and raised his arms in surrender.

One by one, the squad followed suit. They were escorted to Griffin, who was flanked by members of the Core elite.

"Dr. Adam Sulture, Dr. Murph McGinnis, you're both under arrest for conspiracy to commit xenocide and the murder of sentient aliens," Griffin said as he placed the cuffs on Sulture.

"That's 'sapient' you shard-born mongrel," Sulture hissed.

"Get this asshole outta here!" Griffin shouted. Erikson

walked up to escort the prisoners to their holding cells.

Erikson leaned in next to Sulture.

"Did you succeed?" He whispered.

"We'll find out soon enough," Sulture replied.

Over the course of the next three days, all of the men were interrogated. Sulture confessed his plan to exterminate the Tritops and how he planned to do so in excruciating detail. Sulture and Murph bargained for the freedom of the soldiers who accompanied them during their final mission. In return for their freedom, Sulture and Murph took full responsibility for their plot.

The two men were locked in neighboring cells. New teams of scientists were brought in to study the Tritops...except that no live specimens could be found.

Anywhere.

The military scoured the planet and all they could find were mauled corpses. It was as if they were wiping themselves out.

Two more weeks passed. No live Tritops were ever found. The Core authorities signed off on having the species officially declared extinct. Erikson walked up to Sulture's cell.

"They're adding Xenocide to the list of charges against you. I'm forced to tell you to consider your last meal," He said.

Sulture formed a slight grin. It wouldn't ever bring his family back, but they could rest in peace. Soon enough he would join them.

A ship landed on the edge of the colony. A black man walked out, wearing a gray suit and a black tie neither of which seemed to fit quite right. Core soldiers led by Erikson rushed up, wondering why this civilian was entering a military installation.

"What can I do for you sir?" Erikson asked.

"Oh, I was in the area and wanted to meet Dr. Sulture and Dr. McGinnis. Their names have been thrown around a lot lately," the man said.

"Can't let your do that. Sir, are you aware this is a military installation?" Erikson asked.

"Oh, I'm quite aware and between you and me, Ionics owns a lot of the technology here on Angkor which made colonization possible," the man replied as he flashed his Ionics badge.

"Even for an Ionics manager I can't make an exception…"

"Well son, I'm afraid you must make an exception. Ionics is very interested in acquiring these two men as advisers for a special project," The man said with a wink.

Erikson nodded, a grin forming on his lips. "You heard the man. Let him through!"

Four guards came in and retrieved Sulture and Murph, and lead them to the interrogation room.

The man walked in and sat across from the duo.

"You two are the most talked about men in the galaxy. 'The Xenocidalists of Angkor,'" He chuckled. "Rumor also has it that you guys were the ones who killed all of those colonists."

"How dare you come in here and-"

"Relax, Dr. Sulture," the man said. "I believe in one of the other stories, the one the colonists are telling. That you guys are the ones who saved this colony, that you're heroes."

"Hey man, that's great and all, but we're goners in twenty hours and thirty eight minutes," Murph said. "Are you a lawyer or…?

The man chuckled again. "No, my name is Colonel John C. Henry, and I'm putting together a team."

--The End--

PART TWO

Forrest and Sujay: On Top of Your Mom!

"MAYDAY! MAYDAY! The *Dreamweaver* is in rapid descent! We're going to crash!"

"You always say that Sujay! Just remain calm and I'll land this ship safely."

"Forrest, the engine is on fire! I told you that you were cutting the atmosphere too hard! But did you listen to me? Nooo! Apparently instincts trumps a Doctorate in Astro Navigation!"

"Of course my instincts trump your piece of paper!" Forrest said.

"AUGH!" Sujay howled.

"As for the engine being on fire that's just Aurelius Prime," Forrest said as he waved off Sujay's concern. "There's so many particulates in the atmosphere that one of them was bound to get caught in the filters."

"Clogged filters don't cause the engine to burst into flames! We need to activate the engine extinguisher systems!"

"Funny how after I activated my engine extinguisher system, your mom begged me to put out her fire -"

"You leave my mother out of this you scrap wrangler!"

"That the best you can do curry peddler? That ain't nothin'. Just you watch: I'll land this ship safely, on an skydock no less."

"Ahhh, Aurelius Prime, my second home! I love this

planet!" Forrest said in triumph. Several dock workers rushed in to extinguish the *Dreamweaver's* engine fire.

"Eww, I hate this planet! Can we just get our replacement parts and get out of here please? I always feel like I'm going to get mugged, kidnapped, an STD or worse," Sujay replied.

"Don't worry slick, I got your back."

"Last time we were here you tried to peddle me off saying that their crew wasn't diverse enough. 'Just outsource your navigation to the Indian' you said."

"That was only to settle a debt, which we did by the way," Forrest said.

"By taking a loan from a crime lord who will break our knees if he even *thinks* we'll default on him! I swear Forrest, you never think things through!" Sujay replied as the two men stepped into a crowded elevator.

"That's what I got you for Sujay."

"But you never ask for my opinion!" Sujay shrieked. The onlookers stared in silent disbelief while Sujay's face burned bright red.

"We're rehearsing a play!" Forrest said to the onlookers. The elevator door dinged. Forrest and Sujay shoved to be the first one off. The onlookers also shoved the duo out into the street and were relieved to be rid of them.

"Y'know, this place has come a long way since the Core Invasion."

"That's what you're calling it now? When we were in the service we referred to it as the 'Unification Wars.' The Core was trying to bring the planets back under one civil governance. Remember all that?" Sujay asked.

"Well I remember resigning when the Admirals thought it was justifiable to start bombing civilized worlds into compliance. Left a bad taste in my mouth, just like the bad taste I left in your Mom's -"

"Finish that joke and I swear upon Vishnu I will strike you down Jack Forrest!" Sujay said as he held up a wrench.

"Oh, dear Sujay has finally learned to stand up for himself...eight years too late! Wish you would've had that backbone when you were in the service," Forrest said as he picked up a few parts, inspected them, and then tossed them back onto the table. "Where would a thruster modulator be in this market?" Forrest asked the merchant.

"Thruster modulators are down towards the end. These are components for the warp drive you nebbie," the vendor croaked. He was greasy and had a carpet of fur underneath his tank top.

"Uhh, I know how to fly, and I know what parts these are. I was just feelin' my way around. Not my fault you have them scattered around like some crazy junk dealer. I mean trying to sell this capacitor in the condition that it's in..."

"Alright Forrest, let's go get that modulator. The last thing we need is another enemy on this planet. Seriously, you need to learn when to keep your mouth shut," Sujay said as he shoved Forrest towards the modulators. The furry vendor gave an evil eye and crossed arms. He made a mental note to never deal with them again.

"If I recall correctly, it was this mouth here that caused us meet in the first place my dear Sujay."

"Oh, sweet, merciful Vishnu, do we have to hear this story again?"

"We certainly do," Forrest said as he pointed towards the sky.

14 Years Earlier...

"Hey you! Scrawny ass Indian guy!" Mason howled.

"Ye...yes?" Sujay stuttered, as he tried to carry his stack of textbooks back to his room. Three blond fraternity brothers approached Sujay.

"Mason, Green, Myers! What brings you gentlemen along?" Sujay asked the most respected flight duo in the academy, backed by their lone henchman."

"Prof in Aeronautics said that you wanted to be an Admiral. Is that true?" Mason asked, unable to contain a snicker.

"Why, yes I would like to be an Admiral one day," Sujay

replied as he hid his face behind the stack of textbooks.

"Didn't you know that you had to be sponsored in order to be an Admiral? What makes you think that you'll be able to get a sponsor since you don't actually know an Admiral?" Green asked.

"Maybe one of the professors will sponsor me," Sujay muttered.

"Maybe one of the professors will sponsor me," Mason mocked.

Sujay's books weighed on his arms, getting heavier by the moment. The strain caused sweat to bead on his brow and tickled his neck.

"How are you going to get a sponsor when you can't even get a flight partner?" Myers asked Sujay as he towered over him. "I don't know of anyone who wants to partner with the whiny nerd kid."

"Guys, guys, guys! We're all friends here, airmen on the same side. Let's not pick on the Indian guy just because his junk may be too small," a skinny, curly-haired man said as he waltzed down the hallway with a swagger that rivaled a cowboy. The blond kids snickered at the pasty cadet's joke as he put himself between the blond trio and Sujay.

"Um, actually my genitals are the appropriate size," Sujay replied softly.

"Yeah, sure kid. Anyway gentlemen, there's no reason we can't all get along...HI-YA!" the curly haired kid screamed as he sucker punched Myers in the gut. He barely flinched as his eyes ignited in a blaze of fury.

"Wait a minute, why did you punch him when you were just telling about how we can all get along?" Sujay shrieked.

"To help you out moron! Why aren't you running?" the curly haired kid wailed.

"You never said to run!" Sujay screeched.

"Well, run now!"

Sujay turned, dropped his textbooks and ran. The curly haired kid turned to run, but Myers grabbed him by the collar of his uniform. The three cadets wailed on the him but he didn't scream once. They left him with a black eye, a cut on his lip and barely conscious on the floor. After the fighting was over and the cadets left, Sujay returned to retrieve his books. He approached his protector.

The guy had been laid out on the floor, with a gold medallion dangling from his neck. Sujay reached down and picked the medallion up.

"No! Hands off!" The guy screamed. He shoved the medallion inside of his shirt and made sure to hide the chain beneath his collar. Sujay stared wide-eyed.

"Sorry," He said. "It's...a lucky charm."

"Oh, okay. Sorry about what happened there," Sujay said as he gathered his books.

"Nah, nothing to worry about. Happens all the time," the curly haired cadet said as he climbed up the wall.

"It's just...no one has ever stood up for me before. Didn't care for the comment about my genitals though," Sujay said.

"That was just to get those preppies to lower their guard," the guy said with a wave.

"Well, anyway, I'm Sujay," Sujay said as he offered his hand to the curly-haired man.

"Jack Forrest, but everyone calls me Forrest. Is it true about what those guys said? That you can't get a flight partner?" Forrest asked while he shook Sujay's hand.

"It's not my fault! I..."

"No, no, no. I didn't mean it like that. My flight partners are all super lame and cannot keep up. They don't have the proper team spirit. You seem like a cool cat, if you're half as good as you claim, I'd be willing to partner with you."

Sujay eyed Forrest with suspicion. "Is there a catch?" Sujay finally asked.

"I just took a beating from some bullies for you, offered to be your flight partner and you still don't trust me? I mean, what more do you want?"

"I'm sorry. I'm just slow to trust. I've been blown off by so many people, I was just unsure of how to take it," Sujay said as he offered Forrest his shoulder to walk on.

"Ha! Your mother blew me off right after I made her take

it!" Forrest said as he stumbled onto his new friend's shoulder.

Sujay erupted in laughter. "That was great! I loved that! I could never get tired of 'your mom' jokes!" he said as the two walked down the hall together.

"Alright cadets, it's time to train you for dog fighting. You've had enough 'practice' with all of the droid simulations, now it's time to fight actual humans," flight instructor York said.

"It's only because we beat all of the droid combatants on the hardest settings. Even the ones deemed 'unbeatable,' " Forrest said as he snickered to Sujay.

"And thanks to Forrest's big mouth, I believe that we have our first volunteer!" York said as he pointed at Forrest.

"You sure do big guy!" Forrest said as he stepped forward and gave a salute. Sujay sighed, but saluted and stepped forward as well.

"Let's see, Forrest and Sujay against...Mason and Green!" York said as he practically cheered out Mason and Green's names. They were the two dynamic pilots who knew every strategy in the book and wielded it to great efficiency. It was also no secret that York once belonged to the same fraternity as the two boys during his cadet days.

"POW!" Forrest said as he finger-gunned the competition. Both men kept tight lips and raised their noses high in condescension.

"We're so going to crush these snot-nosed punks," Forrest said.

"Into the sky!" York howled as the teams ran to their fighter ships. Everyone else went into the command center to watch the fight.

"I want recordings and transcripts from this flight simulation. These cadets need to learn how to communicate with one another," York said to Byron, the operator of the flight simulation within the command center.

"Flight simulation active. Recording in progress," Byron said.

All four ships launched into the sky and each team went

opposite ways. Forrest and Sujay were flying together when Forrest veered his ship wildly off course as he made a hard right.

"What are you doing? Where are you going?" Sujay shrieked into the comm.

"I got an itch, one that only your mom can scratch," Forrest replied. All of the cadets roared in laughter as they listened to the transmission.

"Is it always like this with those two?" York asked.

"Sir, you have no idea," Byron replied.

"You leave my mother out of this! Always with the 'your mother' jokes! Can't you be original?" Sujay screamed. His warning lights flickered.

"Oh, sweet Vishnu, they're on my tail. Forrest?" Sujay said. There was no reply. "You're leaving me alone to fight with these men by myself?" He shrieked. His sensors indicated that the enemy ships had acquired a lock.

Sujay jammed down on the thruster to accelerate. "Defensive maneuvers initiated! Deploy flares!" He said to the computer as he toggled the controls. Flares erupted from the rear of his ship as Sujay dived down. He was able to get out of the target zone, but Mason and Green closed in. They were steady fliers and once someone was in their sights, it was damn near impossible to escape them.

"Forrest I could really use your help here!" Sujay said. He looked all around his ship as he weaved back up. He searched the skies for the curly-haired joker that seemed to have abandoned him.

"Where is Forrest?" York demanded as he flipped through the screens.

"He's not in any of our viewing ranges, but the computer indicates that everything on his ship is working fine," Byron replied.

"Well, his partner is going to be taken out if he's doesn't do somethingl," York said.

"That's why nobody wants to be Forrest's partner sir," Byron replied.

Sujay's sensors indicated that Mason and Green were locked onto him. He scrambled at the controls like a mouse as he tried to find a way out. The only counter maneuver he could safely execute were flares, and those wouldn't hold Mason and Green off for long. Still, Sujay reached the point of no return and had no other choice.

"Deploy flares!" Sujay said. "Where are you Forrest?" He cried as he pounded against his ship's terminal. The flares forced Mason and Green out of their steady flight path, but they still tailed Sujay.

"Dive down buddy," Forrest said calmly.

"Where were you?" Sujay demanded.

"Banging Mason's mom, since Green's is about as ugly as he is!"

"You worthless, selfish, derpy idiot! You can go straight to hell!" Sujay yelled.

"Dive down buddy, it's the only way my maneuver is goin' to work," Forrest said.

"What in God's name is he doing?" York yelled at the screen. The computers showed Forrest's flight trajectory moving towards a head-on collision with Sujay.

Sujay grumbled and relented. He dived down, while Forrest cheered and headed directly for Mason and Green. The two were forced to split apart in order to avoid a collision.

"You didn't fire at them!" Sujay screamed.

"Uh, you deployed the flares, cow worshiper," Forrest replied.

"Oh that's original. Just because I'm Indian doesn't mean-"

"Sujay! Go after Green! Geez, maybe you'd do better at charming a cobra."

"Cobras are dangerous beyond all reason you moron! How original that the white guy makes stupid jokes all day long!"

All of the cadets at the Command Center keeled over from laughter. York pinched the bridge of his nose in frustration.

"Are you sure it's always like this?" he asked Byron again.

"During the last fight we printed off over fifty pages of transmissions like this sir," Byron replied.

"Good God," York said as he held his face in his hands.

Sujay turned his ship around and set his sights on Green. Now that he was separated from Mason the two were easier to outmaneuver. It was only when they were together did they seem unbeatable.

"Oh you didn't..." Sujay said as he finally caught on to Forrest's plan.

"Took you long enough. Saddens me how I could've counted all of your Gods before you figured it out," Forrest said.

"I hope you crash your jet and come back reincarnated as a worm!" Sujay said as Forrest flew next to him. The two locked on to Green's ship, but Forrest rolled and dived his ship below Green and Sujay.

"Stay on Green!" Forrest ordered. Sujay followed his instructions, and stayed close. Just as Sujay was about to fire on Green, Green deployed his flares, which scrambled Sujay's targeting sensors. However Forrest flew past the flares before they rained down on him. Forrest got a lock and fired on Green. Green's ship indicated that he'd been hit and he veered off back to base.

"Sons a bitches can fly," York said.

"Oh yeah. They're the best we've got," Byron said. "Those drones we put out, the AI can't compete with Forrest's creativity.

"Now for Mason!" Forrest cheered.

"I'm still mad at you," Sujay said.

"And why's that?" Forrest replied sweetly.

"You used me for bait."

"Only because I knew you could handle yourself!" Sujay groaned.

"Whoop! Mason's on our tail!" Forrest turned his ship upside down, cut the thrust, and went soaring backwards. His jet hurled through the sky, which forced Mason to dodge him and give up his lock on Sujay. The move didn't give Sujay time to react. He noticed that Forrest activated the comm line to communicate with the opposing team, which was strictly against the rules.

"Now I'm chasing your tail Mason! Just like I did to your mom! Too bad you're into boys like our pal Sujay up there!" Forrest goaded. "Oh, and your blond besties mean to tell you what a failure you are without them."

"You sorry sack of shi-" Mason growled before Forrest muted him.

"Well this is for you being a potty mouth!" Forrest said as he shot at Mason. Mason deployed his flares, but Forrest scored a partial hit. Mason dived, but Forrest kept steady in pursuit. "Finish him off Sujay!" Forrest hollered.

Sujay flew up in an arc until he was able to circle around and point guns his at Mason's ship.

"Atta boy Sujay! Swoop him! Show this bully that nobody can stand against the maniacal genius of Forrest and Sujay!" Forrest whooped. The rush of charging through the clouds towards the surface was indescribable. Sujay realized why Forrest pulled so many stunts and why he was so reckless. It was all about having fun. Sujay felt his organs press against his spine as he locked onto Mason and opened fire. Mason was gaining speed, but Sujay pressed down on the trigger so that his guns could 'lead' Mason and end the fight. Mason's screen went red. The simulation was over, Forrest and Sujay were the winners.

Forrest and Sujay became an unbeatable duo against all other combatants. Every cadet was challenged to shoot them out of the sky, but the two outmaneuvered everyone. They acquired (and still maintain to this day) the most successful flight record in the history of the Space Corps. A record of being the only flight duo in the history of the corps to never lose in a dogfighting.

"So, what do you want out of the academy Forrest? What do you hope to achieve?" Sujay asked.

"All I want is to save enough to buy my own starship and fly across the galaxy. You?" Forrest asked as he tinkered with a thruster modulator.

"I want to become an Admiral of the Core Navy," Sujay said as a dreamy gaze which blanketed his face.

Forrest laughed, "No you don't."

"Why not?"

"You don't have the pompous, arrogant nature to be one of those buffoons," Forrest said absent-mindedly.

"I could be an Admiral if I wanted to!" Sujay said with a sneer.

"Look Sujay, you're a great strategist, but the Admiralty is bought by rich guys. Rich guys who will only sponsor the frat boys, ergo, having more rich guys bribe each other for the position. You're too valuable as a fighter pilot," Forrest said.

"I'll be an Admiral one day! I'll show you! I'll show everyone!" Sujay said as he pointed his finger angrily at Forrest.

"Sujay, if you get sponsored to be Admiral, I will never make another 'your mom' joke ever again."

"You mean it?"

"Cadet's honor."

"You have no honor."

"Oh right! Let the guy who carves his guts out with a butter knife if he dishonors his family make the call about what's honorable!"

"Wha...that's the Japanese you chutiya! You can't even get your stereotypes right!"

"Ahh whatever! My point is, the Admirals won't sponsor a no-name Indian guy. But if you get sponsored, I'll keep my promise and never make another 'your mom' joke...ever."

"You're serious?"

"Of course I am caramel-sauce."

"Deal," Sujay said as he extended his hand. The two shook on their agreement.

Forrest and Sujay fought bravely throughout the Unification Wars against the Coalition of the Outer Realm or more simply, the "Rebellion." Forrest went on to become a Quintuple Ace since he had brought down over twenty five rebel fighter ships over the course of three battles known as the Melpomene skirmish. Sujay got promoted to Lieutenant as a result of the Melpomene battle, since Forrest let him have the credit for masterminding their daring missions during the raid. Forrest didn't care about rank, he just wanted the war to be over so that he could explore the galaxy. Sujay could have the promotions.

"Sir! What is it you wanted to see me about?" Forrest asked.

"Ah Forrest, hero of the Melpomene skirmish. I have a special mission for you," Captain Ransom said

"Aww shucks sir, you'll make me blush."

Ransom shook his head. "I'm going to need you back in the air Forrest. The Melpomene skirmish was a turning point for us in this war against the rebels. Command has ordered us to begin a preemptive bombing run against Calliope."

"But sir, that's a civilian world!" Forrest protested.

"You're right Forrest. But Intelligence reports indicate that Calliope helped, housed and aided the Melpomene traitors. We must make an example of them. Our orders are no quarter, no mercy, no surrender, and I would like my bombers into battle."

"Sir...it's a civilian world!"

"Do you have sympathies for the rebellion Forrest?"

"I'm starting to because you keep telling me to bomb women and children!"

"It is because of this attitude that the war has dragged on for longer than it should have."

"Sir, I won't bomb a planet out of existence...there's gotta be bad karma in there somewhere."

"Forrest, lead the bombing run or I will court-martial you!"

"You know what? NO! I'm not going to bomb a civilian target just because you guys can't stand for liberty, free speech and all that junk. I'm not a political man captain, but I won't stand for this. I'll run."

"Do so Forrest and we will hunt you down," Ransom

hissed.

"Yeah? Well, start with your mom's house Ransom! Uunngghh!" Forrest said.

"Soldiers! Seize him!" Ransom shouted.

"Uh-oh!" Forrest said, and scurried off.

"Forrest what is going on?" Sujay asked through the comm.

"Minor disagreement with Captain Ransom! No need to panic!"

"Really? Because there's a warrant here for your arrest."

"Sujay! They want us to bomb a civilian planet to smithereens! I won't do it and now they're going to kill me!"

"Hold on Forrest, I'll help you get out of here."

"Don't! You'll be demoted or worse!"

"Go left up ahead. I've unlocked the hangar bay. In there you can take one of the fighters and run as far as you can from here. Best of luck out there Forrest," Sujay choked as he stifled a cry.

"Thanks buddy, I owe you. Remember that these guys believe it's okay to bomb civilian worlds. They think it's okay to execute a man for standing up for what's right. Remember who you're fighting for Sujay. Remember what you want to be an Admiral of..." Forrest pleaded. Sujay put him on mute and awaited the Captain and his guard, while Forrest slipped away in one of the fighter jets.

"Oh yeah, I remember that warning. Then you went and smuggled for the rebellion," Sujay said as the two walked down the street. The streets were nothing more than pounded dirt since few companies were willing to invest in the infrastructure of Aurelius Prime for citizen benefit.

"Uh, the word is 'blockade runner.' Much cooler and less criminal-ly sounding than 'smuggler.' Smuggler makes me sound like a mule who's willing to put drugs up my bum," Forrest replied.

"You take these remarks so out of context it's a wonder anyone can understand you at all," Sujay said.

"Yeah well, the rebels paid better for contraband goods,"

Forrest said. "Their desperation gave me a few years of some nice tidy profits."

"Which you completely blew that and then some by acquiring the *Dreamweaver*," Sujay snorted.

"Hey! I needed a bigger ship. You were so good at leaving me breadcrumbs to get past all of the blockades because you were vengeful about being passed over for promotions...which is exactly what I told you was going to happen!" Forrest said.

Sujay turned away. He knew that Forrest was right. The two stayed in touch while Forrest was on the run, and Sujay was just as guilty about helping the rebellion as Forrest was. However, Sujay saw it as more helping a friend who believed in him rather than hurting the Core who kept passing him over for promotion.

"I give you this though Sujay: dogged persistence. Even when the Admiralty had given up on you, you still went on to Titan University, acquired your Masters in Astrophysics and started your Doctorate after the war was over. You also failed to have sex with...how many women?" Forrest asked.

"What does that have to do with anything?" Sujay demanded. "...And there was only one."

"Oh yeah. What was her name?" Forrest asked.

"Maya Helmirra. She was beautiful, but some snot nosed asshole named Richard got to her first. I'd punch that guy's lights out if I ever met him face to face."

"Yeah, sure, mm-hmm," Forrest replied. "Look on the bright side, at least I busted you out and provided you with a life of fun, adventure and nookie."

"Hookers don't count."

"Since when?" Forrest screamed.

"And I would hardly call what you did at Titan 'busting me out,' " Sujay replied.

"Oh come on! Yes I did! I even personalized a message just for you!"

"An announcement over Titan's comm system saying: 'Sujay Malak, there is a man in the docking station who claims that he is your son,' is so immature."

'Aww c'mon, that was hilarious!" Forrest said as he laughed to himself.

"I wasn't old enough to have a son, especially when people saw your pasty white face! All you want to do is humiliate me!" Sujay shrieked.

"True, but I still managed to convince you..." Forrest said.

"Are we going back down memory lane?" Sujay asked.

"We certainly are!" Forrest replied with excitement.

"Was that really necessary to tell everyone that I was your father?" Sujay screamed. He couldn't believe the difference in Forrest's attire. Instead of the crisp, proper gray uniform of the Core, Forrest wore leather boots, a satchel/bandolier with several clips, pilot goggles to block out the UV rays, and a long leather coat which looked two sizes too big on him. He symbolized the look of the rebels, a ragtag outfit composed of whatever clothes a person could find, and focused on utility instead of fashion.

Forrest stood outside of his starship the *Dreamweaver*. "How else would you know it was me?" He asked. "Besides, I've got a job for you."

"Really. And what would that be?" Sujay asked.

"I am here to take you under my wing as a blockade runner. I'm feeling so generous I'll cut you in for half since I need a partner," Forrest said.

"I would much rather be a carrier pilot, I could even make Admiral," Sujay argued.

"Please? Come run blockades! Live a little! The pay is way better than being a carrier pilot," Forrest argued.

"My understanding is you regularly struggle to get paid," Sujay said as he glared at Forrest.

"Yeah...uh...well...I still manage to get by..." Forrest said as he avoided Sujay's gaze.

"I'll finish my Doctorate program ahead of schedule. Of course I'll be a shoo-in for Admiral. They'd be crazy not to." Sujay said

"Have you ever seen an Indian Admiral with a Doctorate?"

Forrest asked.

"I could easily be the first," Sujay argued.

"I don't doubt your smarts Sujay, but with a Doctorate, you'll be stuck behind some desk, stonewalled from advancement, the life slowly oozing out of your ears from boredom," Forrest said as he wriggled his fingers next to his ears.

"I really doubt that my brains will ooze." Sujay said .

"Just run blockades with me for two months. If we don't make any money, I'll let you go, no questions asked, no hard feelings. Just two months Sujay. I know you want to explore the depths of space, to see the forgotten worlds of the Core. You'll be the most beloved Admiral ever with all of the contacts you'll make."

Sujay hated to admit it, but it was a reasonable offer. A part of him knew that with Forrest, he'd never be able to leave, but he thought he could always try again with the Naval Academy…

"You made that offer eight years ago and I still haven't made much money!" Sujay said. "Nooo, I got up to my eyeballs in debt with some of the lowliest mobsters in the galaxy! Because of you I'll never be able to get back into the naval academy!"

"Oh please! You love the adventure Sujay! You were bored stiff at school,and at the naval academy. Tell me you don't love the freedom!"

Sujay stared off into the distance, and refused to admit that Forrest was right.

The eight years of running blockades made the two infamous smugglers…and risky businessmen to deal with. Since Forrest was reckless with his money and Sujay was helpless to stop him, they were always cash poor, and got deeper and deeper into debt looking for the big score. However, the two did have the reputation of being very reliable smugglers. Thus, people were willing to trust them with their cargo, but not their money.

"Why don't we go see Brocker? He'll give us some pointers on our next big score!" Forrest said as he pumped his fists in excitement.

"You just want a plate of his fries," Sujay said. "That's a lot of fuel we're going to burn for a plate of fries."

"Well, who wouldn't burn all their fuel for a plate? They're fantabulicious!"

"Brocker's place smells like tobacco and B.O."

"Nero's Cove is an Aurealian establishment! May be a little low-brow for the 'Admiralty' folk, but for those of us with simpler tastes it's perfect."

"It's also where Kingsman and his underlings spend their time. You have a payment ready for them?" Sujay asked.

"Oh, that could put a damper on things. But I really want a plate of those fries..." Forrest pleaded. Sujay rolled his eyes and sighed.

"I know! Why don't you use your mad Sujay-negotiation skills to convince Kingsman to give us an extension?"

"He's already given us an extension - twice! You keep losing our profits at the casinos and buying parts to make repairs to the *Dreamweaver* because you have something to prove with your flight capability. Have you even paid Kingsman off for the *Dreamweaver*?

"Uhh..." Forrest muttered.

"You haven't even paid off Kingsman for our ship?" Sujay shrieked. "Where has all of our money gone?" Sujay screamed.

"You already said it. Casinos and repairs. All we need is that big score and we'll be able to pay off *all* our debts, which is why we go directly to Brocker."

"So your plan is to see Brocker and hope he has info on a big blockade run while at the same time trying to avoid Kingsman's goons from capturing us and either extol payment or break our legs?"

"No, but that plan is *genius*! I knew there was a reason why I wanted you as my partner!" Forrest screamed in excitement as he charged off for Nero's Cove.

"That's not what I meant!" Sujay howled as he chased after

Forrest.

In front of the door to Nero's Cove, Forrest adjusted his collar and then kicked open both swing doors to the diner. He sauntered in with the slow and confident swagger of a mob boss. He even gave himself a stone face, and looked down on the patrons who ignored the curly-haired man. Brocker waddled out of the kitchen, his white tank top covered in grease and sweat stains. His face was also covered in a black scruff that didn't fully cover his second chin. The air changed when Brocker stormed out of the kitchen and unleashed a tsunami of body odor into the dining room.

"You've got serious balls comin' back here," Brocker growled at Forrest and pointed at him with a spatula. The diner air was lacquered with greasy hamburgers which tickled Forrest's nose. He noticed how the cooks scrambled in back over the grill as the burgers sizzled and crackled in fat.

Forrest inhaled deeply through his nose, waved his head around, and then puffed out in joy. "Reeks of grease, tobacco and sweat. Smells like home," Forrest said with a grin.

"Forrest my boy! Good to see you!" Brocker said as he held his arms open. Forrest wholeheartedly embraced the greasy cook. "I swear, you're the only one who actually likes this dump," Brocker croaked.

Sujay ran into Nero's Cove, and scanned the patrons in the restaurant to spot any of Kingsman's goons. He didn't see any and they weren't a group to hide who they worked for. Sujay breathed a sigh of relief and then immediately regretted it.

"Sujay! Can't believe you still hang around with this deadbeat," Brocker said as he slapped Forrest on the back.

"I can't either some days," Sujay said with scorn as he glared at Forrest. Forrest placed his hands on his chin, blinked and gave Sujay big Bambi eyes.

Forrest turned back to Brocker. "Mind if we get a plate of your famous fries?" He asked. "And a blockade tip if you have the time," He whispered

"Depends on whether you'll actually pay for either this

time," Brocker growled.

"We have enough!" Forrest replied, then turned to Sujay. "Right?"

Sujay rolled his eyes, pulled out a credit chip and tossed it to Brocker. Brocker took the chip and eyed it with suspicion. "Booth's over there," He grumbled and waddled back into the kitchen.

Forrest and Sujay grabbed a booth, and sat on opposite sides. Forrest danced a little jig to an unsung song in his head while Sujay sat with his arms crossed and stared daggers at Forrest.

"What?" Forrest asked.

"Would it be so hard to actually be productive and y'know, save some of the money we earned instead of always trying to make the big score?" Sujay asked.

"Ah posh! I'm a lucky guy. I was born lucky," Forrest cheered.

"Then why are we always in so much debt to underhanded criminals and rely on grease covered cooks to find us big scores?"

"Hey! Grease covered cooks are people too!" Forrest said as he pointed his finger in indignation at Sujay.

"Don't change the subject! Why don't we consider getting actual contract work? Get a steady paycheck working transport for one of the legitimate enterprises?" Sujay asked.

"Listen to you! 'Lee-jit-ah-mitt!' Where's your sense of fun? We'll just go the same routes over and over. I became a pilot to fly across the galaxy, not go around in circles. I'm free out here!"

"Now you're making fun of my accent you inbred hick? The contract work doesn't have to be permanent. All I'm saying is we do some honest work and get out of debt with Kingsman."

"I like being a free man. I don't want my soul sucked out through the air intakes inside of some corporate ship working for a bunch of goons we don't know."

Sujay rolled his eyes. "It will be temporary. Contract work only. It's too late anyway, I've sent out feelers to a guy I trust."

"Traitor! Judas! When Kingsman finds us, I'm going to give you to him for some debt relief."

"You've already tried that! Besides, I trust who I asked for help from. He won't give us work we don't like, plus we've worked and secured parts for him before."

"Which guy? There's like a million of them."

"He works for the *Grid*, and he's their second in command. His name is Rick and he's given a lot of work to us in the past. He'll come through."

"Well we may as well call him "Ricky Tricky Dic-""

"Fries are here," Brocker grunted as he slid the massive steel platter across the table. Brocker jammed himself into the booth next to Sujay, the smell of his body odor wafted through the air and the stench of sweat made Sujay gag.

"Boo-yah!" Forrest cried for joy as he mowed down on the crispy golden fries in front of him.

"Does he actually like them that much?" Brocker asked Sujay.

"You have no idea how much he loves them," Sujay said with a sour tone. While Sujay was hungry and the fries smelled fantastic, he couldn't bring himself to eat any because of Brocker's stench. The man was as greasy as his fries and in desperate need of a shower.

"Alright, so yer' lookin' for a big score eh' Forrest?" Brocker said.

"Always! Debt with Kingsman is making me nerfus," Forrest replied with a full mouth as he dipped some of the fries in ketchup.

"No kiddin.' That's why I was so surprised you'd come here. Kingsman has put a bounty on both yer heads," Brocker said. Forrest and Sujay looked at each other, and their eyes flashed panic. "Now, I don't intend to collect because I like you two boys, but it's getting high. Ye need to do somethin'," Brocker said.

"That's why we came to you Brocker!" Forrest replied. "You're always tuned into the comings and goings around here! We need your help of finding some decent paying work.

None of those pointers where we're collecting scraps. I want a real treasure trove!"

Brocker sighed. "You an' everyone else Forrest. I may have one tip, but it's going to be dangerous."

"Oh boy, here we go again," Sujay said. He tried to squeeze against the wall and get away from Brocker's stench, but every time he got closer to the wall, Brocker scooched closer to him.

Brocker leaned in between the two, and lowered his voice down to barely above a whisper. "There's trouble on the planet Alcyone. Some Admiral wants to conquer the planet and sell it off for vacation estates, but the locals are holding him up. They're resisting," Brocker croaked in a subtle glimmer of admiration.

"Do you know which Admiral it is?" Sujay asked.

"Couldn't tell ya. One of the greedy ones."

"That's all of them," Forrest said in a bitter tone.

"But the guys on Alcyone who're standing up to him, they've got balls! Balls the size of Jupiter!" Brocker said as he erupted with laughter, slapping the table and rattling the silverware.

"So what are we supposed to do?" Sujay asked.

"The Admiral running the show has the planet embargoed. Completely blocked off. Wants to force the locals into compliance. One rumor says he's preparing an invasion force. Another says he'll bomb them with those microbes that make ye sick if he has to," Brocker said.

"Okay, so it's one of the more abrasive Admirals," Sujay said as he looked at Forrest.

"Which again, is all of them," Forrest replied as he shoveled more fries into his mouth.

"Anyone who is willing to run the blockade to help these rebels with supplies will earn themselves a tidy profit," Brocker said as he gestured the money sign.

"That's us!" Forrest shouted as he held his hand up for Sujay to high-five. Sujay folded his arms and glared at Forrest.

"C'mon Sujay, where's your sense of fun? Wouldn't it be nice to pay Kingsman off and have a chunk of change left over?"

"It'd be nice, yes, that is if you can guarantee we would have some money left over."

"Well, whatever the case may be, ye better make a decision, and quick," Brocker said as he eyed the doorway. "Two of Kingsman's goons just came in, and I'm sure they ain't 'ere for the fries."

Forrest's eyes grew wide and he shoved as many fries into his mouth as he could.

"I'll go distract them. You two get out of 'ere. Go through the kitchen. Gus! Jagger! So good to see you two fine gents 'ere!" Brocker said has he held his arms up high for Kingsman's goons.

Sujay bolted for the door to the kitchen. Forrest got out to leave the booth, but then reached behind to grab one last handful of fries. He followed Sujay as the two booked it through the back door, but the goons caught on to their escape. Forrest and Sujay ran down the stairs and into the streets of Aurelius Prime. They separated in an attempt to lose the goons who pursued them.

"I think we lost them," Sujay said as he gasped for breath.

"Yeah, but that was close. About as close as I was to your mom…"

"Now is not the time for that!" Sujay shrieked. "What are we going to do?" He asked.

"Alcyone keeps sounding better and better," Forrest replied.

"With what? We don't have any supplies or parts to run through the blockade and I doubt anyone will extend us credit with Kingsman on our tails," Sujay said.

"Use your mad negotiation skills to get us a consignment deal!" Forrest shouted as he waved his hands in the air.

"They'll demand credits up front you fool!" Sujay shouted.

"Go all gorgony stone faced and talk them out of it you curry peddler! I swear, you could sell that slop to an Indian!" Forrest said as he slapped Sujay.

"That's because it's delicious you uncultured hick!" Sujay

screamed as he slapped Forrest back. A slap fight between the two erupted in the middle of the street. Onlookers wondered what was going on, and even cheered as the two waged their little slap war.

"Fine! I'll go see if I can get us a deal! Go get the ship!" Sujay said as he shoved Forrest away.

"About time you came to your senses!"

"Just get the ship ready so we can leave this smog pit!" Sujay shrieked, and then stormed off.

"With what parts?" Forrest screamed.

"Oh you pasty mop-haired doofus!" Sujay said as he reached inside of his coat pocket, pulled out a credit chip and threw it at Forrest.

Back aboard the *Dreamweaver*, Forrest made the repairs needed for the ship to become space-worthy again. He was covered in grease and grime when Sujay walked in and slapped down a paper contract, signed and ready to go.

"Hey! You got one!" Forrest said.

"It was from some greenhorn who's hoping to make big a score like we are," Sujay said on a sour note.

"Wow, he must be green if he made you sign a paper contract out here," Forrest replied.

"He wouldn't do the deal without it. I'm pretty sure they're stolen parts," Sujay said in a shaky voice.

"Are there really any ship parts circulating on this planet that are completely legit?" Forrest asked.

As Forrest and Sujay made repairs to the ship, a blast slammed into the ship and dislodged it from the jacks. The ship slid and rocked and both men slid on their backs in a desperate rush before the ship crashed onto the floor. "Please tell me that was our new friend being rough with loading the parts onto my ship," Forrest said from the floor.

Sujay looked out the window. "Nope, it's Kingsman's goons firing regulators to keep us from flying away," he said.

"Screw 'im!" Forrest screamed, as he jumped into the cockpit. "He can take my ship over my cold, limp noodle of a body!" Forrest started the ship, which groaned and sputtered, but roared to life despite the regulators shorting her circuits.

"Nyah nyah!" Forrest chanted. "Too bad I installed a little something here…" He said as he pressed a button. Bolts of electricity surged through the regulators, and the devices flew off of the *Dreamweaver*.

"Now let's go get those parts!" Forrest wailed in victory. The duo flew across the shipyard, however as Forrest landed in the dusty street where the shop was supposed to be, Sujay's face turned to sheer panic.

"That bastard sold us out!" Sujay shrieked as they closed in. Dozens of soldiers waited for Forrest and Sujay's arrival. As the ship landed, the men fired their regulator bolts, but Forrest's electrical shield deflected them off with coordinated surges of electricity.

"Why did you land?" Sujay screamed.

"We'll get out of this! Kingsman is perfectly reasonable and trustworthy! I've always said so!" Forrest said as he rushed for the back of the ship.

"No you haven't! You've said for I don't know how long he's a degenerate mob boss who preys on those in perilous positions and is a bloodsucker of their profits!"

"Don't put words in my mouth Sujay!" Forrest shouted as he put his finger in Sujay's face. "I've never once used the phrase 'perilous positions,' " Forrest said.

"Those were your exact words!" Sujay shouted as he jumped up and down. The cargo ramp groaned as it lowered, and revealed a heavily clothed trader swarmed by men who carried an array of firearms all pointed at Forrest and Sujay. In the middle of the armed men was a tall, freckled, redheaded man whose hands were clasped on his belt.

"Kingsman! My favorite dealer!" Forrest said with his hands held up high, like he was going to hug him.

"Got my money Jack? It's about time you paid me back for my ship," Kingsman grumbled.

"I will. We just heard about Alcyone and we're here to pick up those parts to fly them out so that we can sell them and pay you back."

"Can't have these parts Jack," Kingsman said.

"And why not? Are you against trade? I thought we were free men! Isn't that what we fought for against the Core Invasion?" Forrest asked as he tried to appeal to the Kingsman's sense of pride having fought for the Coalition.

"Y'know Jack, there's a saying here on Aurelius Prime: In the end, we're all just kings and thieves..." Kingsman grumbled.

"Come to think of it, I never really understood that phrase," Forrest said as he walked forward, and put his arm around Kingsman's shoulder. "Perhaps you could explain it to me. Did you think of it since your last name is Kingsman because I think that would be appropriate," He said as he turned everyone so that their backs were to the ships.

"It means you're either the big dog, or you're a scoundrel who can't make his payments. And guess which one you're leaning to Jack?" Kingsman said as his grip tightened around Forrest's collar. Forrest began to panic as Kingsman lifted him off the ground.

"Forty percent extra bonus! An extra late-please don't break my knees late fee! You know Sujay and his negotiation skills - he'll get us a great price! Give us the parts and we'll pay you all we owe plus the forty percent bonus!"

"Y'know I really hate dealing with the thieves of Aurelius Prime," Kingsman grunted. Something captured the corner of his eye and Kingsman turned to look. Fury ignited on his face as it turned beet red and he realized he'd been double-crossed. Sujay had taken advantage of Forrest's distraction to load the parts they needed onto the ship.

"You son of a bi-" Kingsman growled, but Forrest punched Kingsman in the face with a hard right hook. The crack echoed through the street, and Forrest knew that if he didn't escape he was a dead man. Kingsman dropped Forrest, who scrambled backwards, and drew his pistol right as the goons drew their rifles.

"I'm not a violent man Kingsman, but you're leaving me no

choice. I mean really, how can a man pay you back when his legs are broken?" Forrest implored to the soldiers around him.

"Kill them!" Kingsman roared as he drew his pistol and fired. Sujay pressed the button to close the cargo hold.

"Shoulda known that would happen. You just can't reason with some people..." Forrest said to himself as he weaved through junk piles to the *Dreamweaver's* cargo hold. Forrest barely crawled over the closing door amidst a torrent of blaster fire, which left an acrid smell of smoldering metal in the cargo hold. Forrest bolted through the ship to the cockpit, jumped into his seat and ignited the *Dreamweaver's* engines.

"Okay baby, show papa how much you love him, because if you don't daddy is gonna die," Forrest said as he rubbed the dash. He pushed on the thrusters which lurched the *Dreamweaver* forward. She sputtered and coughed, but finally left everyone in the dust.

"Think I wouldn't be ready for your getaway Jack?" Kingsman growled through the commlink as two fighters swarmed in to pursue the freighter.

"Sweet Vishnu is there no escape from that crazed ginger?" Sujay shrieked. However, now that Forrest was behind the controls of an aircraft, he wasn't phased. Whenever Forrest piloted a ship, an eerie calm overtook him, which made the wiry and mouthy man into a model of focus and concentration. Forrest covered his furrowed brow with his flight goggles to block out the bright Aurelian sun. He studied the sky and calculated his options to outmaneuver the fighters in pursuit. Forrest's instincts guided him during times of turmoil and he always seemed to know exactly what to do when behind the controls of a star ship.

"Deploy flares," Forrest ordered. Sujay nodded and activated the controls.

"Think I wouldn't be ready for those?" Kingsman said.

"These ain't your normal flares fire crotch!" Forrest replied. Rumbling explosions detonated behind the *Dreamweaver*, which disrupted the flight patterns of the pursuing ships and gave Forrest and Sujay the chance they needed to break orbit.

"We're going to make it! We're going to make…" Forrest said as the engine screamed and the controls rattled until everything came to a sudden stop.

Sujay looked at Forrest, trembling with fear. "What did you do?" Sujay screamed.

"It wasn't me I swear! It was…that!" Forrest said as he pointed at a large frigate overhead. The frigate floated leisurely through the sky just beyond orbit, and drew the *Dreamweaver* in with her tractor beam. A small shuttle flew past the *Dreamweaver* and into the frigate. Kingsman's voice broke through on the comm.

"Told you that you wouldn't be getting away Jack," Kingsman's raspy voice said in triumph. "My tractor beam will pull you in before you have a chance to destroy my ship."

Forrest looked at the controls. He knew there was a way to escape the tractor beam, there had to be. He pressed down on the accelerator, but met stiff resistance which stopped the ship from lunging forward.

"Can't do it Jack, not without killing yourself. Although it'd save me the trouble with you and the cheapskate," Kingsman croaked.

"What did he call me?" Sujay demanded as he pounded on the controls. Forrest watched Sujay's hand, which landed right next to the missile firing controls.

"That's it! Atta boy Sujay! I remember what to do! Deploy the chaff!"

Sujay snarled as he deployed the chaff which would scramble the sensors on the frigate, and made it damn near impossible to detect the ship's presence. At the same time, Forrest leaped across the console and launched two torpedoes from the *Dreamweaver*.

"You fired our only two torpedoes!" Sujay screamed.

"It was either them or being caught by Kingsman!" Forrest replied. "Besides, when I fired my missile at your mother…"

"Now is not the time for a 'Your Mom' joke!"

"There is always time for a 'Your Mom' joke!" Forrest screamed as he jammed the accelerator as hard as he could.

The tractor beam locked onto the torpedoes as they flew past the chaff, which set the *Dreamweaver* free. Forrest activated the gravity well boost, which was only to be used on planets with a stronger gravitational pull to break through the atmosphere.

Forrest slammed his fist on the button, and jammed the accelerator. A horrendous roar came from the engine chassis, but the ship broke free of the gravitational grip and the pair escaped. However, Forrest didn't head for deep space. He arced the ship and skimmed along Aurealius Prime's Atmosphere.

"Why aren't we getting away?" Sujay asked in panic.

As the ship arced around the planet, a monstrous fortress just outside of the planet's orbit came into view. It was an ivory white, mechanical moon designed to house millions of droids. It was also very hostile to trespassers.

"Freighter ship, you are trespassing in private air space. Leave now or prepare to be fired upon," a mechanical droid voice warned over the comm.

"All shields at full power!" Forrest ordered. Sujay weaved his fingers through the controls and watched as dozens of Kingsman's ships pursued the *Dreamweaver* while hundreds of ships spilled from the Ivory Moon and headed right for them.

"Please tell me you have a plan," Sujay said.

"Yup," Forrest replied.

"Are you going to tell me about it?"

"Nope."

"Why not?"

"You're a negative nancy. You'll panic and tell me how we're going to die!"

Sujay rolled his eyes, but Forrest's plan was coming to fruition.

"Freighter ship! This is your final warning! Leave now or prepared to be fired upon!" The mechanical voice repeated over the comm.

"Ignore them," Forrest said as he looked over to Sujay. "And get ready for a jolt to starboard!" Sujay understood the plan and tightened his harness. Both men held steely gazes as the ship veered a hard ninety degree turn, and made the calculations to jump into hyperspace.

As the ivory ships closed in upon the *Dreamweaver*, their sensors warned of a band of incoming onyx-colored fighters.

"Kingsman!" A voice shouted over the comm. It was a voice that Forrest and Sujay had only heard rumors of, and belonged to a reclusive being whose exploits bordered on legendary.

"Neuron!" Kingsman spat.

"I knew that you'd try to invade me!" Neuron shouted.

"Keep your hands off of my prize! Men! Fire at will!" Kingsman ordered.

The scene behind Forrest and Sujay erupted into a massive battle between Neuron's and Kingsmen's fleets. Missiles and blaster bolts streamed on the edge of space, the clash even drawing Kingsman's personal frigate into the fray.

"Boy, it sure is a good thing that the droid pirate Neuron and Kingsman hate each other" Forrest said with a sigh of relief.

"What would you have done if they maintained peaceful relations?" Sujay asked.

"We would have been royally screwed. Just like your mom was-"

"I knew it! Just shut up and make the jump to hyperspace!"

Alcyone was a tranquil world, and one of the few that the Core could credit as being an overwhelming success through terramorphing efforts. One of the only planets free from disease and an atmosphere that didn't collapse, Alcyone was a lush, green temperate world with massive, pristine freshwater lakes, crisp air and only one major city, Alcian. The lakes of Alcyone were formed during the terramorphing process when the planet was heated to a liveable temperature which forced the massive freshwaters glaciers to melt.

The planet was encircled by a massive Core fleet blockading the planet. Embargoes were expensive business, and contraband would be valuable.

There were six battleships, eighteen destroyers, twenty nine frigates, and thousands of individual fighters, all flying in a swirling vortex to ensure that no one could get in...or out.

"We've got to run that?" Sujay asked.

"I can run it."

"You always say that!"

"Because I always run the blockade! Name one blockade I've never run!"

"Mathis."

"That doesn't count! You distracted me!"

"What? You were the one downloading those pictures of half naked-"

"What matters is that we made the delivery alright?"

"After hiding inside of that asteroid!"

"It worked, that's what matters! Now, calculate my trajectory, while I go find some fresh pictures of your mom."

"Ugh, you and those stupid jokes..."

"Do we have any intel on why there's such a heavy blockade?" Forrest asked.

Sujay used his military credentials on the Core mainframe and pulled up the dossier of Alcyone. Since Sujay made it to Lieutenant, he had access to the Core's military database, but after he left the military his credentials and logins were revoked. Sujay merely hired a couple of computer guys to restore his access.

"According to the official report Alcyone's trade has been shut down because they refuse to export any more freshwater, Sujay said.

"And what kind of booty are they calling for?" Forrest asked.

"Uuuhh, not much we're carrying...oh, here we go. They want ship parts. Big orders too. Wow, these are Core military-level volume orders. Almost like they're getting replacement parts for an aerial fleet. We could dump all those engine fuselages in the cargo hold..." Sujay suggested.

"And tack on a minimal 600% hazard pay fee," Forrest said as he clapped his hands together like a grinning monkey.

"We'll be able to pay off Kingsman for the *Dreamweaver* and finally become free men!" Sujay said as his eyes glimmered.

"Try to find out who the Admiral is. See if it's one of our old chums," Forrest said.

"It's Ivanov running the blockade. He always sticks to the basics. The old fashioned Chinese Wall technique. Crude, but effective," Sujay replied.

"I can run it," Forrest said.

"You already said that!" Sujay replied.

"Well, when I find a blockade I can't run I'll say so. Calculating trajectory," Forrest said.

"You never take the care and attention to plan your trajectory right. You always rush in, fly fast and break my ship in the process."

"*Your ship*? How *dare* you Sujay Malak?!

"I take far better care of her than you do Jack Forrest!" Sujay mocked.

"That is simply not true! I take great care of-" Forrest was interrupted by a green light that blinked on the dashboard. "Oooohhh! The propulsion jets are ready. Here we go!" Forrest screamed as he slammed down on the accelerator.

"Oh yeah, you take such good care of the *Dreamweav-*" Sujay said as he was thrown back into his seat when the ship launched forward. He pulled himself to the dashboard to project flight patterns for their path through the blockade using his revised star map. Sujay tapped in a frantic pace at the projected map as he created and dismissed dozens of courses for the pair to take.

"Destroyer is on top of us! We're marked!" Sujay said.

"Whoooo!" Forrest screamed as his hands spiraled around the controls, and forced the cargo ship into a barrel roll, which brought him within centimeters of colliding into an incoming frigate. The maneuver proved unbelievably frustrating to anyone who was tracking the pair, since the Core ships couldn't acquire a lock.

The destroyers and frigates were too large to move in such small confines, which was how Forrest liked to best outmaneuver them. There was always the risk that they would be blown out of the sky, but the Core blockade fleets almost never fired on a little cargo ship on the chance that they'd hit one of the other Core ships. Once they'd weaved outside of the destroyers and frigates though, they would have to run like hell. This blockade however, had a different setup.

"Fighters have spotted us," Sujay said. He braced himself for another run of Forrest's insane flying maneuvers. While Sujay was used to Forrest's erratic piloting, and his air sickness had long been cured, Sujay strived for a little less excitement in his life. Forrest loved the feel of rising and falling in the midst of the stars and believed that the adrenaline rush made him a better pilot. His senses and reflexes became sharper. The needs of the moment damned the needs of the future. It was all about living in the present, pure and simple.

Five fighters pursued the *Dreamweaver*. Given its status as a small Manta Class Freighter ship, the fighters thought taking down the *Dreamweaver* would be like shooting a fish in a barrel.

"Are we in a hurry?" Forrest asked.

"Nope, our schedule is clear," Sujay replied.

"Good, because I felt like taking the scenic route!" Forrest said as he activated the secondary thrusters. The ship screamed forward, and arced along the atmosphere towards Alcyone's North Pole. The Northern regions of Alcyone were lined with imposing mountain ranges, which enhanced the planet's aura as a tranquil paradise.

"Fine place for a ski resort. No wonder why the admiral want's-" Forrest was cut off when the fighters opened fire. "Scuffords! Divert all shields to the rear!" He ordered.

Sujay swiped at the controls, lowered the shields in front and raised them in the back. A couple of the blasts hit home, but the shields deflected the full brunt of the blast.

"Now for a little boost!" Forrest said as he triggered the emergency (and illegally modified) thrusters.

"We're about to enter orbit!" Sujay screamed.

"We'll skid the atmo, and hopefully lose a few of them," Forrest said.

"That's your plan? Skid the atmosphere, increase drag along the belly of the ship and hope that the Core fighters dip one degree too much against the planet's atmosphere, which tears their nose off and blows the ship to smithereens?" Sujay asked.

"Sure! I've done this thousands of times!" Forrest replied in a vibrant cheer.

"This is suicide," Sujay whispered to himself. He increased the shields on the bottom of the ship as well, which stretched the power core to the limit as the ship's engines teetered on the edge of collapse.

Each bump along the atmosphere felt like skidding across concrete. The two were tossed around in their seats like rag dolls, but Forrest never lost control of the ship despite the turbulence. The shields on the bottom of the ship took most of the beating, but each time Forrest struck the atmosphere, he risked one of the engine's parts being knocked out of place. However, Forrest knew that the cargo ship just had to hold out longer than the fighters. One of the Core ships dived under the *Dreamweaver*, but the heat proved too much and the ship erupted into a fireball.

"That's one!" Forrest screamed.

The debris from the first fighter flew into the face of the third fighter. Pieces of shrapnel sheared off the wings which caused the ship to dip into the atmosphere and tear the nose off, while the pilot sealed inside plummeted planetside. "That's two!" Forrest screamed again.

"They're not breaking pursuit! We can't hold on much longer," Sujay said as he watched the thermostat rise.

"Yup! Let's cool things down a bit," Forrest said as he calculated another trajectory. This one arced into the polar ice caps below. Forrest shifted gears, and prepared to veer starboard towards the surface of Alcyone. He arced the ship, ignited the gravity well boost and braced for the polar mountains that were up ahead. Three more fighters followed, which left Forrest at a disadvantage since the fighters were more maneuverable than the *Dreamweaver* was.

"They have a lock on us!" Sujay said.

"Deploying flares," Forrest said as he keyed in the command. The back of the ship erupted a series of bright red lights, which jammed the targeting sensors of the pursuing fighters. Their launched missiles exploded behind the *Dreamweaver* and the sonic blast bounced off their shields.

"Preparing to level off," Forrest said as they approached a snow-capped mountain range.

The red warning light flashed again. One of the enemy fighters had a lock on them.

"Forrest...?" Sujay asked.

Forrest focused on the controls, almost oblivious to what was going on around him.

"FORREST...?" Sujay screamed.

"I got it," Forrest muttered. It didn't persuade Sujay.

Forrest dived into the deep valley between two mountain ranges. The pristine beauty of the mountains was spectacular...if the two had the time to enjoy the view.

The alert signaled that missiles had been fired. They closed in on the *Dreamweaver*.

"FORREST!" Sujay screamed.

"Right. Deploy flares on my mark," Forrest ordered as he grabbed the gravity well throttle.

Sujay moved his shaking hand to the flares control. Beads of sweat trickled down his brow as he hugged the dash of the *Dreamweaver*.

"NOW!" Forrest screamed as he jerked down the gravity well throttle.

Sujay deployed the flares. The ruby lights attracted the heat-seeking missiles and the incoming fighters were helpless to stop Forrest's bait.

The explosions from the rockets triggered avalanches on both sides of the *Dreamweaver*. Forrest held down the gravity well throttle, weaved through the canyon in short, sputtering bursts to avoid the massive avalanche. The incoming fighters weren't so lucky as massive sheets of snow and ice buried them in a tidal wave of snow. The pristine mountains became the final resting place for those three unlucky fighters.

"Wooooo!" Forrest screamed in excitement, as he raised his hands in triumph. Just then, the engine to the *Dreamweaver* sputtered, choked and belched black smoke. Forrest's maneuvers may have saved their lives, but his antics overwhelmed the ship's engines.

"That's not good," Forrest said.

"Not good? We're stranded up here in the arctic! I don't even have a coat for this kind of environment!" Sujay screamed.

"Relaaax Sujay. We're out of danger now. Most likely blew one of the lines that carries oil through the engine. Black smoke is almost always oil being leaked. We'll just set the ship to autopilot and wait to get to Alcian," Forrest said.

"You literally blew a gasket in there! A piston may be destroyed or the reactor was cracked! Alcian is thousands of miles away! How will we ever make it there in one piece?" Sujay asked.

"Fine. I'll use the emergency channel and see if we can get it towed. Just know that *you're* cutting into our profits!" Forrest accused.

"Me? You're the one who had to weave and twirl in the sky, skid across the atmosphere and keep your hand pressing on the gravity well throttle!" Sujay replied.

"Oh, I'm so *sorry* that I saved your life Sujay! If it wasn't for me, we'd have been blown to smithereens! I'll bet if I told your mother of what happened today, she'd get down and thank me properly..." Forrest said as he pressed the emergency beacon signal.

"Don't you bring my mother into this!" Sujay screamed.

"Oh! Oh! Ooohhh! Yes, Mrs. Malak, I did save your son. Your gratitude and enthusiasm certainly shows! Be careful when talking, you might choke!" Forrest said with his eyes closed and his hands resting on his thighs.

"You son of a bitch!" Sujay screamed as he slapped Forrest across the face.

The autopilot landed the *Dreamweaver* softly on the ground

while Forrest and Sujay slapped each other inside the cockpit. The two were locked in such an equally matched struggle that they nearly missed the response to their emergency beacon.

"*Dreamweaver*, you have requested a tow? Repeat, *Dreamweaver*, you have requested a tow? We have received your emergency broadcast," a static male voice said over the comm.

"Yeah, we have a faulty engine..." Forrest said while panting.

"That you broke," Sujay said.

Forrest stared daggers at Sujay, then continued over the comm. "We have a faulty engine which seized up here in the arctic on our way to deliver parts and we cannot risk the flight to Alcian. Please provide assistance."

"Blockade runners," The voice on the other end said. "Sit tight, we'll have a pair of tow ships come get you. Expected waiting time is twelve hours," The man said.

"Twelve hours?" Forrest exclaimed.

"Every available resource is tied up at the moment. You'll just have to wait like everyone else," The man said, clearly irritated.

"Fine," Forrest replied.

After fourteen long hours, a pair of tow ships descend to the site. "Alright, *Dreamweaver* please turn your ship on and set it to Neutral. We can take it from there," one of the pilots said.

"Roger that," Forrest replied. "You're a lot friendlier than the other guy."

"It's a stressful time for all of us, what with the embargo of the planet. Thank you for requesting a tow, the fee would be a lot less than the fines you would've had to pay had you flown in with a belching ship."

"I do what I can," Forrest said as he kicked back in his pilot chair. Sujay rolled his eyes. The tow ships connected their cables to the *Dreamweaver* and sealed off the engine's exhaust.

"Sealing up the exhaust, won't that cause carbon monoxide to flow back?" Sujay asked.

"Nah," Forrest replied. "The engine's in neutral and since we're being towed, there shouldn't be a lot of exhaust. Plus, the filters inside of the cap they put on the exhaust system will draw out most of the carbon monoxide."

"Ugh, why are you so smart about the ship, yet so dumb about everything else?" Sujay asked.

"Well, your mom thought I was real smart about how I got her off when I-"

"Are you really going to spend fourteen hours making 'your mom' jokes?"

"Well, I gotta find something to do! Not like you brought cards!"

"Oh sweet Vishnu, give me strength," Sujay said.

Alcian glimmered like a jewel against the surrounding pristine lakes. It was a sprawling, clean metropolis. The buildings gleamed in the morning sun, and gave a warm, saffron glow to the cityscape. The tow ships were cleared for landing and pulled into a docking port with the *Dreamweaver* attached. The two men looked at the city below, but it wasn't a bustling hive of activity. The city had a strange feeling of abandonment, like an orphan whose mother was forced to give her up. A small entourage waited to greet Forrest and Sujay.

"By the stars..." Forrest gasped.

"What?" Sujay asked.

"Tim Riley!" Forrest screamed in excitement.

"Who is...?" Sujay asked.

"Jack Forrest, scum lower than what I scrape off of my boots! C'mere!" Riley said as he embraced him.

"Who is...?" Sujay asked again.

"Sujay! This is my old smuggling partner Tim Riley! He's one of the few guys in the galaxy who thinks he can fly as good as I can!" Forrest said.

"Old smuggling partner?" Sujay asked.

"Yeah. C'mon Sujay, I've told you about him," Forrest said.

"You've never once mentioned -"

"So Tim, what is the deal with the armed guards here? Are

you really worried about little ol' me?" Forrest asked.

Riley chuckled. "Nah Forrest, just a precaution. With the war over, blockade running only attracts the daredevils and the psychos. Can't be too careful around here anymore."

Tim Riley possessed the same love of flying as Forrest and seemed to live in the air. He was also a very skilled fighter pilot on behalf of the Coalition, and earned Triple Ace for bringing down fifteen ships. Having fought until the bitter end of the Unification Wars Riley became a smuggler after the war, and sought to bring supplies to the oppressed peoples of the Core. Riley was one of the few who trusted Forrest after he'd defected, since people to him mattered more than politics. Riley also taught Forrest everything he knew of the smuggling trade. He knew that Forrest was a more than capable flier, what mattered was his loyalty and ability to deliver. Forrest completed Riley's "tests" such as flying reconnaissance in the midst of a Core/Rebel clash and proved his loyalty to the smuggling ring. The two remained friends and each brought plenty of business to the other. Over the last year, Riley was suddenly absent in the smuggling circles, and Forrest thought he had settled down. What struck Forrest as odd was Riley's crisp, blue military garb.

"So, what brings you to Alcyone Riley? The sky-high smuggling rates?" Forrest asked.

"Forrest...Alcyone is my home now. I'm here to organize the defense force against Ivanov," Riley replied.

"Whoa, settling down? You?" Forrest asked.

"Yeah, I have. It's peaceful here, and I don't want that greedy Admiral to get his hands on our land here," Riley growled. "We've settled here, and we cannot allow those greedy bastards to steal the land where we've spilled our blood building our homes!" Riley's tone made him appear like he was preparing his men for bloodshed.

"Hey buddy, I'm just here to deliver some parts…"

"Do you like it here Forrest?" Riley asked.

"Yeah...it sure is pretty…" Forrest replied. He looked around. Riley and his men had the fire of zealots burning in their eyes. "...But I just came here to deliver parts."

"Ah, right. You should be paid for your efforts since you took the risk of bringing us these vital supplies," Riley said as a thought cascaded into his mind. "You know, if you're looking for some more money I am in dire need of some mercenary pilots. It's not like Ivanov will wait forever with this Embargo. He's tested our defenses a lot lately but there isn't a pilot good enough to challenge him here."

Forrest got a glint in his eye, and a grin spread across his face.

"Nope. No no no no no no no!" Sujay interrupted. "We're just here to deliver our parts, get paid and get out of here. We need to go. Now!" Sujay said as he shoved Forrest aside.

"Well, based on the damage to your ship's engine, I'd say you don't have much more than a really expensive hovercraft. Doesn't look like that'll be breaking orbit anytime soon," Riley said.

"Aww, I can fix it," Forrest replied, as he waved his hand in the air.

"With what parts? The city needs every last component they can get for the coming airfight. Now, we could provide you with a fighter ship that would be yours to keep if you help us defend the city..." Riley said, as he turned to walk away. He continued: "You see gentlemen, the cityscape here is well developed, but we're not an armed people. We don't have a proper fleet to defend against an Admiral. We're desperate for fighters who can match the skills of the Core," Riley said, as he lead the group to his command center.

"What we need is to get paid," Sujay whispered harshly to Forrest. "Get paid, scrap or fix up our ship, and leave. We have debts to settle Forrest," Sujay explained as he tugged at Forrest's arm.

"Scrap the *Dreamweaver*? Are you nuts?" Forrest screamed at Sujay.

"If it gets us out of here with credits, then yes. Paying to get that ship to break orbit again will cost more than it's worth!" Sujay snapped.

"You shut your dirty whore mouth! The *Dreamweaver* is an icon! A hero of our time!" Forrest said as he waved his finger through the air.

"...It's a ship," Sujay said.

Riley and his men watched in amusement as Forrest and Sujay argued about what to do with the *Dreamweaver*.

"...That's your offer?" Forrest asked the scrap dealer.

"I feel like I'm going to be sick just thinking about it," Sujay replied.

"Take it or leave it," the dealer said.

"But...you...you can't expect me to..." Forrest muttered as he struggled to hold back tears. "Sujay you can't make me do this!" He cried.

"Do it or I will," Sujay said. "So help me Jack Forrest I will pay for those computer geeks to steal your title and sell this ship myself!"

"You're a monster!" Forrest screamed. As he ran away he saw the Alcyone fleet parked and sparkling in the sunlight. His eyes lit up like Christmas.

"No, too soon. Can't forget about my baby just yet..." Forrest whimpered.

"There, it's done. I managed to get a little more out of him, but it's the best we can do," Sujay said as he tossed Forrest the credit chip.

"That's what all of this came to? My beloved ship for a teensy wheensy little piece of plastic?" Forrest said as he burst into tears.

"So Riley, what's Ivanov's plan with this blockade?" Sujay asked.

"He's become a renegade Core Admiral who bombs and conquers 'troublesome' planets by force, then acquires or resells their assets, which has made him one of the wealthiest men in the galaxy. The blockade is a trumped up charge to justify his embargo," Riley said. "Let me ask the two of you this. I've known Forrest for a long time, and I think I've got a good grasp on you Sujay. Are you saying that you don't want to dole out a little bit of punishment to the Core? Could you live with yourself knowing that hundreds of Core Admirals will be resting on their fat asses here in their cushy resorts and mansions? Will you be able to rest knowing that they bulldozed over every citizen who ventured out and settled here?" He asked.

"Yes because of what you're doing to my ship!" Forrest shrieked as he held up the credit chip.

"I don't have any property here, so I don't have any attachment," Sujay added.

Riley sighed. "Then what if we hired you on as 'consultants' for your expertise? I'll make it worth your while..." He said as he tossed a credit chip at Forrest which showed the amount he was willing to pay.

"We need to help them," Forrest said, as he turned to Sujay with big, puppy dog eyes..

Sujay rolled his eyes and sighed. "No. Half your city is abandoned. This is for all intents and purposes a lost cause. Do better."

"What are you doing?" Forrest pleaded in a whisper.

Riley pulled out another credit chip and tossed it to Sujay. Forrest looked over Sujay's shoulder. "That's a lot of zeroes!" Forrest giggled as a glob of drool dangled out of his mouth.

"Okay, I'm convinced," Sujay added.

"Excellent. I'll take you to our fleet." Riley gestured to the others, and lead them to the flight bay.

"These are some of the saddest looking pilots I've ever seen!" Forrest shouted. The men standing in front of their ships were haggard and tired. Nightly bombing runs have kept the civilians awake, but these men still mustered the strength to stand at attention in front of their ships.

"Their ships are just as bad, if not worse," Sujay said. "A ragtag fleet with all kinds of different makes and models - makes setting up some kind of repair system damn near impossible!"

The pilots themselves were as diverse as their ships -

ranging from civilian militiamen to mercenaries from every corner of the known regions.

"So what do you two think?" Riley asked.

Sujay sighed. "Forrest, don't get any wild ide-"

"Admiral Ivanov is going *down!*" Forrest shouted. "He's going down on me harder than Sujay's mother-"

"Really? At a time like this?" Sujay screamed. The pilots struggled to contain their laughter at Forrest's overconfidence.

"One more condition Riley," Forrest said as he turned to the Commander.

"Name it," Riley answered with his hands behind his back.

"I want the codename Dawn Leader," Forrest said. Sujay groaned and rolled his eyes.

"We can do that. However, there's still the matter of your ship to attend to. Yours too Sujay," Riley said. He led the duo through the shipyard.

"You didn't think we'd have fine men such as yourselves fighting in pieces of slag did you?" Riley asked.

"Well based on the ships your men were using..." Forrest replied.

"Oh, those ships are sturdier than they look. The men here are great mechanics, doing incredible things you wouldn't believe with their machines," Riley said. "There's yours Forrest."

Forrest stared, dumbfounded. It was a Nebular Scuttle class fighter ship, the sleekest, fastest fighter ship in the galaxy. It was equipped with rapid-fire twin blaster cannons on the nose. The wings spread out in the back like two golden plumes that channeled the fire of the engines and gave the ship her speed. The Nebular came into production right at the end of the Unification Wars, but Forrest saw one of them in action with his own eyes. The Coalition didn't have a chance in the skies.

"How did you...?" Forrest stuttered.

"We found it here, abandoned. It's been modified too. Goes faster than anything I've ever flown, I can tell you that," Riley said. Forrest didn't respond, he just walked over and hugged the ship.

"Did you just…? Okay. Yup.That is happening. Sujay! Let's go look at your ship," Riley said as he waved Sujay over.

Riley showed Sujay one of the more classical Core fighter ships. Known as the "Stingray", these ships were wide across the front, but the body was sleek. They had great lift and speed, but they couldn't maneuver as well as other fighters. Thanks to their heavy plating and shield tech, these ships could take a serious beating and could fly in every environment. The blaster cannons were on the wings and had been modified to deliver ion blasts, which would fry the circuits in enemy ships. Riley could tell that Sujay wanted this ship and turned to his fighter pilots.

"Atten-tion!" Riley shouted. The fighter pilots fell in line.

"I have here two men who have agreed to help us defend against Ivanov's invasion. These two are some of the best fighter pilots the Core has ever produced…and they let them slip through their fingers! I introduce to you *quintuple* Ace Fighter Jack Forrest!" Riley said as he riled up the haggard defenders.

"Welcome Ace Fighter Forrest!" The men shouted and saluted in unison.

"I like the sound of that. Good call Riley," Forrest whispered to Riley.

"Just wait for Sujay's intro," Riley replied. "And I present to you men, one of the best Naval Officers the Core has ever produced…a man they didn't believe fit to command their skies…a man we know will send Ivanov and his fleet riling back for the Core…your Starfleet Commander Sujay Malak!"

"Welcome Starfleet Commander Malak!" The men greeted and saluted in unison.

Sujay couldn't believe his ears. All his life he'd wanted to be commended for his abilities as a Naval Commander. Sujay felt a warmth in the depths of his soul. He remembered all of those long nights studying tactical maneuvers, star maps, and understanding how to calculate the gravity of a planet's influence on the battlefield. He felt his pride swell deep within, a rising tide of confidence that made Sujay believe these fighters had a chance against Ivanov.

"Let's give them Hell!" Sujay screamed in excitement, and raised his fist in the air.

"YES SIR!" The men replied to Sujay and saluted.

"Oh Starfleet Commander Sujay!" Forrest said as he bowed before him. "We're not worthy! We're not worthy!" He chanted, then rose to his feet.

"Well, that was fun," Forrest said. "Okay guys we'll call you when we need you. Dismissed." The pilots dispersed and returned to working on their ships.

"Yes! We sure will!" Sujay said.

"Right, now we have an aerial assault to plan out," Riley said as he slapped Forrest with some written battle plans.

Riley escorted Forrest and Sujay to his command center. Sujay noticed that it was housed in the old "Hall of Justice" building. As they entered the building there were about fifteen armed men in full black body armor and heavy weaponry, geared to fight a small war. Forrest seemed oblivious, but Sujay felt a little tense about the presence of these soldiers here. Especially for such a peaceful planet.

"Out of curiosity Riley, how did you become the organizer of Alcyone's defense force?" Sujay asked as he tried to sound nonchalant.

"Oh, once the embargo started, people were given a chance to leave. Many of the people who lived here and the city's leadership simply got up and left. The ones who stayed are those who've built their lives here. They needed a defense leader, so I volunteered," Riley explained as he poured himself a glass of brown liquor.

In Sujay's mind, this explained why the streets seemed abandoned for such a large city. Still, there was something off about the city streets. They felt haunted with an unnatural chill in the air. There was also something different about these men in the Command Center. They weren't makeshift militia fighters like the pilots were. These men had vicious weapons, armor and a professional demeanor. Their lips were tight, as though they'd been welded shut. Sujay wanted to help the pilots. Their eyes were warm and engaging. These men had an iciness in their stares, as if they were waiting for him to die in the skies.

Forrest, Sujay, Riley and his command team debated for hours on an adequate battle plan. The fighters would take on the bombers, and the primary goal was to last long enough for Riley to arm his 'secret weapon' to use against the frigates and the destroyers.

"So uhh...what's the weapon?" Forrest asked.

"What? It...it doesn't matter..." Riley replied.

"Like heck it doesn't matter!" Forrest shouted. "If you expect me to fight up there in defense of your city, you can't be all secret mastermindy and keep secrets about a secret weapon that will bring down the Core battleships! I need to know what this thing is so we can fight around it!" Forrest said as he drew circles in the air above the city map.

"Alright, fine. It's a cannon," Riley confessed.

"Ooh a cannon! Thbbbt! Big whoop!" Forrest replied.

"It's an ion cannon! Capable of delivering three exajoules at a target-"

"Oh yawn, I'm bored listening to this lecture!"

"Damn it Forrest, you asked!" Riley shouted as he slammed his fist on the table.

"True, I did. Although telling me that you have a massive ion cannon at the ready to blow Ivanov out of the sky would've sufficed," Forrest replied.

Riley pinched the bridge of his nose. "What is the tactical capability of your fighters Riley?" Forrest asked.

"They're good pilots. They just need some synchronization. We were hoping that you and Sujay could provide that. That is what I'm paying for...can you deliver?" There was an undercurrent of harshness to Riley's voice. A voice that wouldn't tolerate failure.

"Yup, we can do it. Sujay here is the one who can do all of the synchronization right buddy?" Forrest asked.

"We sure can," Sujay replied as he forced out a grin.

"This is where you'll be staying," Riley said as he slapped Forrest and Sujay on the shoulder. Both men gazed up in amazement at the massive luxury hotel, which was only half-lit and even showed blaster scarring.

"What happened here?" Sujay asked.

"The Core attempted to acquire a foothold under my watch, but we were able to drive them back. This place is one of the safest in the city," Riley said.

"I love it! Very accommodating for a man such as myself," Forrest said as he adjusted his coat.

"Well, there are provisions inside, but our food is limited due to the embargo," Riley said.

"Can't you...y'know, grow stuff?" Forrest asked.

"We've tried, but the soil here on Alcyone is laced with nickel. Every soil sample comes back with enough nickel to be considered contaminated. We've had to rely on imports for our food source," Riley said. "Alas, once the Core realizes that they can't steal this planet from us, she will send us machines to extract the nickel out."

"Certainly hope so," Forrest said with a dinner roll in his mouth.

"At least our fish is edible, and thanks to the fishing guilds there is plenty here for you," Riley said. "Enjoy your stay gentlemen, I shall come for you in the morning." Riley bowed and took his leave.

"Something is fishy here," Sujay said.

"No kidding. Does this mackerel smell right to you?"

"Forrest! I was talking about the situation!" Sujay hissed.

"Oh, bad word choice then buddy."

"Doesn't something seem...off about the situation here, with Riley?"

"The man is giving us a huge payment, two fighter ships *and* letting us stay in the ritziest hotel ever! What can possibly be off about this?" Forrest asked.

"Gee, I don't know. Perhaps it's too good to be true? There's an eerie chill to this city. I don't think Riley is telling the truth.

Why would he need to hire so many mercenaries to defend his city? Where is he getting the money from?"

"Sujay, Riley is one of the good guys. True you may have fought against him in the war, but you don't see him rubbing your nose in it do you?"

"Forrest! I'm more worried about getting out of this city alive! Something is very off here. This city feels...haunted."

"We'll be fine. After all, I was born lucky," Forrest said.

Since Riley hired Forrest and Sujay as aerial battle consultants, they outlined several maneuvers and plans of attack against Ivanov. The Admiral hovered in the sky, an indomitable leviathan that circled the skyline and patiently waited to devour its prey.

That night, Sujay was restless. As he gazed at the ceiling he jumped when his comm beeped from an incoming call. He looked over and Forrest was still snoring in his bed. The call was on an encrypted line, so it's message was meant to remain secret.

"Hello?" Sujay asked as he answered.

"Hello Lieutenant Malak," a man said in a thick russian accent.

"Admiral Ivanov! I...I will...I..."

"Relax Lieutenant," Ivanov replied. "I wished to speak with you in private. It is my understanding that you have studied interstellar navigation have you not? It seems that your studies ended rather abruptly."

Sujay glared over at Forrest who was snoring with his mouth wide open. "Yes my studies did end abruptly," He replied.

"I also see here that you were in good standing here in the Navy and that you aspire to become Admiral. What if I were to tell you that I was willing to sponsor you Lieutenant?"

"Wha...? What?" Sujay stuttered.

"Think about it. Your peers at the naval academy didn't respect you for your study skills or diligence. Your flight partner belittles you in public and I suspect that your position granted to you by Riley is a ruse."

Sujay stayed silent, only because he was worried that he'd break down into tears.

"I on the other hand have reviewed your doctoral work as well as your history within the military Lieutenant and I like what I see. I see diligence, a keen strategic mind and incredible talent for interstellar navigation. I believe you're one of the most qualified men in the military Malak and I would like to sponsor you for the Admiralty."

Sujay gasped.

"There is a condition however. You must defect and abandon those rebels on the ground. Defense Minister Reynolds is asking me too many questions about this embargo, and I find myself in need to put an end to the resistance on Alcyone sooner rather than later."

"I'm still not sure about this, I mean-"

"Lieutenant Malak. Consider how proud your parents will be for all of the prestige and the influence you'll acquire. I'll even cut you in on the spoils once I conquer this world. You'll be richer and more powerful than ever. I'm feeling generous, so I'll give you time to consider my offer. Your actions tomorrow will tell me everything I need to know," Ivanov said as he cut the feed.

The comm went blank and the room was dark again. Forrest was still snoring, but now Sujay had to wrestle with Ivanov's offer. Sponsorship for the Admiralty and all he had to do was help put down the rebellion. Sujay lied down and mulled over his options.

On their sixth day at Alcian, a ball of energy slammed into the hall of justice. Everyone dived for cover as they felt the electrified air stir their stomachs in a cauldron of nauseating bile. Ivanov and his dark fleet descended on Alcian. A hornet's nest of fighters spilled from the battleships. The militia pilots watched in amazement and horror as these ships plunged their way towards the city.

"We can take them! All squadrons assemble!" Forrest

shouted. The fighter pilots rushed to their ships. The first three pilots to climb aboard their ships were incinerated as a chain of bombs was unleashed on the runway. The searing heat melted metal on contact, and threw their tools and slag in all directions. Forrest and Sujay made it to their ships just in time, and they were able to get out of the airbase just as bombers began unleashing their payload in their attempt to wipe out Alcian's air defenses. The anti-air turrets were activated, but there was significant damage to the runway. Still, enough fighters made it into the air to mount a defense.

"The bombers! They're going after the civilians!" A voice crackled over the comm.

Forrest realized that the few fighters that made it into the air had to compete against thousands. They'd be swarmed and annihilated before they even had a chance to fight back.

"All squadrons to me!" Forrest said. He flew through the streets and weaved his ship between the buildings. Dozens of fighters trailed behind until Forrest was able to get ahead of the Core's bombers.

"NOW!" Forrest screamed as he came to a stop, pointed the nose of his ship towards the sky and opened fire. His faithful starship hovered only a few metres above the ground, but his guns breathed a torrent of blaster fire at the bombers.

The other fighters followed suit, and blaster fire rose from the planet's surface. The slow bombers were like floating balloons in the air for the picking of the Starfleet's guns. Sujay noticed the destruction from the falling bombers as they crashed into the surrounding buildings.

"Forrest, we're going to kill a lot of civilians if we keep fighting like this!"

"The buildings provide cover for us!"

"If we stay here, then we'll destroy the city!"

"Fine! What's your idea then Mr. Starfleet Commander?"

"Send a squadron to dogfight between the frigates and the battleships," Sujay ordered.

Forrest gasped. "Wait! You're suggesting that our fighters swarm around those ginormous ships where we'll be totally helpless against their cannons and are very likely to be blown to smithereens?"

"Yes," Sujay replied.

"That's my boy!" Forrest screamed. "Silver squadron, you're with me. Delta, defend our Starfleet Commander."

"Roger that. Silver squadron en route," the leader said. Silver squadron charged into the sky, and sought to bring the dogfighting to the crème of Ivanov's fleet.

Forrest pushed his thrusters hard as he charged the oncoming fighters at near breakneck speed. Such reckless disregard for the g-forces left most pilots feeling sick in flight, but Forrest lived for it. The maneuver allowed him to take out two fighters before they even realized he was upon them.

Forrest rushed at the oncoming starships, and the buildings became blurry on the edges of his vision. He could feel his organs shift in his chest cavity and the gravity push against his chest. It was the thrill that any one moment would be your last, the idea that the slightest wrong push of the handles would send your ship flying into the enemy was all Forrest ever wanted. The rush of knowing that one small slip meant death allowed Forrest to feel more alive now than he ever could growing up.

Silver squadron kept on Forrest's tail, and covered him from oncoming fighters. It was only a matter of time before Riley's secret weapon was unleashed.

"Riley, we need an ETA for that care package of yours," Forrest said over the comm.

"We just need a little more time. Hold off the frigates if you can!" Riley ordered.

"Sujay want to give them the ol' whirlpool maneuver?" Forrest asked.

"You can't be serious…" Sujay replied.

"Oh come on! Where's your sense of fun?!" Forrest asked as slammed down his accelerator and charged at the frigates.

"Blue squadron, arc and go for the frigate's shields," Forrest said. "The weak point is near the engines. Seriously Sujay, I have no idea why you wanted to command those guys!"

Sujay growled, but followed Forrest as he flew like a lone crazed fighter against the frigate. Scores of enemy fighters tried to swoop in and take him out. Forrest weaved and dodged, and happily served as a distraction, while Sujay finished them off. Delta and Blue squadrons struggled to keep pace with Forrest as their worn engines roared and screamed through the effort of dogfighting.

Forrest made a hard turn to port, then arced his ship into a tight crescent. The g-forces pressed hard on the pilot's chests as the two squadrons followed suit. The pilots held tight, but Forrest's heavily modified ship eked further and further ahead. Even the hardiest fighter pilots felt a knot in their stomachs as they watched him arc directly into the line of fire in front of the frigate's cannons. He was oblivious to the cannon blasts that whirled past him, the silent ghosts which have sent thousands of pilots to their doom. Forrest dived down for the belly of the frigate. As he coasted underneath the ship, his daring plan came to fruition.

"Follow my mark boys!" Forrest screamed, as he launched a stream of blasts near the engines of the frigate ship.

Sujay continued firing at the weak spot, while Forrest covered the other fighter pilots.

"Is this really going to work?" Sujay asked. "Firing on the rear engines of the ship to break its shield?"

"Of course it's going to work! I thought of it!" Forrest said beaming with pride.

"Your plans rarely work! You're lucky we manage to pull any of them off!" Sujay argued.

"Your mother's lucky I managed to get her off!" Forrest replied.

"Why do you always bring my mother into this? She has nothing to do with our missions!" Sujay shrieked.

"I like a little curry on my white rice, and your mom is my favorite flavor!" Forrest said.

"I hope you get shot and go down in a pile of flames! I hope you get reincarnated as an eel to be baked into some British pastry you lousy rotten-" Sujay paused.

"Say it! Say it boy! Finish that insult! Prove it to us that you're a man!" Forrest shouted.

"AUGH!" Sujay screamed. "When this is over, I'm going to kick your skinny, dimwitted ass all over this planet!" Sujay overcharged his cannons and fired at the ship. Delta and Blue squadron did the same, and the last of the fighters finally broke the frigate's shield. The electric tendrils faded and Forrest screamed for joy, but he wasn't done yet.

"Let's whirlpool 'em, boys!" Forrest said.

"Uhh...Dawn Leader?" One of the fighter pilots asked.

"Just stay on me!" Forrest screamed.

The ships started flying in a circle around the frigate. Fighters in all directions swarmed in, but the Alcyone defenders were able to keep the Core ships at bay.

"This is borderline suicide!" One of the pilots screamed.

"It's going to work!" Forrest replied. "It has too," he whispered to himself.

The "whirlpool maneuver" cost the squadrons a few fighters, but it allowed them to keep firing on the frigate's turrets. One by one, the turrets were disabled, until the frigate was nothing more than a lumbering starship, dead in the sky.

"Dawn Leader, we managed to hack into their comm network -" One of the technicians said through the comm.

"Hey Core scumbags in frigate two! Shoot me the down! I dare you! I'm the guy in the golden ship!" Forrest screamed at the Core pilots.

"Greetings Dawn Leader, this is Admiral Ivanov. You are in direct violation of Core authority and have no prior affiliation with this insurgency. Disengage my fleet," Ivanov said. Forrest felt a wave of shock wash over him as he realized that the commline the techs hacked went two-way.

"I'm not a political man Admiral, but this planet is not a rebel stronghold. You're just hoping to score an easy win since you think your paycheck is too small," Forrest replied.

"You have nothing to gain by fighting for these people Commander Forrest. Join my fleet, and I'll cut you in on the spoils. I know of your debts," Ivanov said.

"You need to learn a few things about motives Admiral. I love being a fighter pilot and I wouldn't dream of taking your dirty, contaminated, syphilitic spoils!" Forrest said.

"That's quite a shame because I believe your friend Lieutenant Malak has already accepted my offer," Ivanov hissed through a gleeful smile.

"You stay away from him!" Forrest yelled.

"You've mistreated the poor boy quite enough Mr. Forrest," Ivanov replied. "All he wants is recognition for his skill which I'm more than willing to provide. He gave his answer when he ordered your pilots to attack my battleships and frigates."

Forrest watched as the battleship shot a fighter out of the air, which plummeted to the city below. He felt his heart sink. The attack on the heavier ships was a suicide mission.

What's worse is that Ivanov would turn around and kill Sujay the moment he had the chance, and Forrest knew it. He patched Sujay through.

"How could you?!" Forrest screamed, as he pushed down on the accelerator.

"How could I what?" Sujay asked.

"You took Ivanov's bait? You're willing to trade all of us in for a cushy desk job?"

"It's better than dealing with deadbeat cooks and constant threats from mobsters!"

"What? I thought you loved Nero's Cove!"

"I hate that greasy bee-oh factory!"

"Since when?!"

"Since *always*!" Sujay shrieked.

"I...I had no idea..."

"That's the problem Forrest! You're so self-involved that you don't know anything about me!"

"That's not true! I know-"

A rumble from the ground cut Forrest off. He looked and saw a massive cannon barrel rise through the roof of an old warehouse. Riley and his cannoneers adjusted the sights as their platform rose into view. They were protected by a blue shield from the fighters in the air. The barrel arced into the sky, took aim at Ivanov's battleship, and fired.

The monolithic barrel recoiled as a massive orb of ion energy slammed into the battleship. The energy short caused a sonic pulse which decimated all of the fighters in the immediate vicinity and knocked hundreds of others away. Forrest and Sujay's fighter ships were washed away from the battleship as a result of the sonic wave.

"Maybe that'll knock some sense into you Sujay!" Forrest screamed. He looked over at the smoldering battleship. One more shot, and it would be destroyed. No other cannon during the Unification Wars had this kind of punch.

The cannoneers prepared to fire again, and Forrest noticed that Sujay's ship was floating idle in the air.

"Sujay?" Forrest asked. The cannon was charging for another volley.

"Sujay! Get out there!" Forrest screamed. The battleship's cannons rotated and Sujay was in their direct line of fire. His comm was offline.

"Well, what a shame you lost your Starfleet Commander," Ivanov chuckled. Forrest gripped the steering controls, and felt his blood boil. He pushed forward as hard as he could, and felt his stomach slam into his spine.

Ivanov's cannons fired back. Right before Sujay was hit, Forrest intercepted the blast. His shields were crushed, but he was still able to fly. As he was knocked away, he saw that he'd knocked out Sujay's wing.

Forrest grabbed ahold of the cable gun in the rear and fired it through the good wing of Sujay's ship. As Forrest fell, he steered his ship towards the water, dragging Sujay behind him.

"Thank...y-...Forr-" Sujay said over the comm.

"What? You're conscious?!"

"Comm...knocked…"

"Knock on what? Knock on wood? Knocked up?"

"OUT!" Sujay screamed.

Forrest watched as Ivanov's battleship decimated Riley's shield, while the second bombardment brought down the brick warehouse.

His heart sank as he watched the rubble crumble on top of the men. Riley and his men's screams went silent over his comm. He felt sick to his stomach. This wasn't supposed to happen. These men were defending their home. They didn't want to fight. They were given no choice.

Forrest glared at the battleship overhead. He pulled Sujay into the water, who was able to eject safely. He retrieved his cable and hovered above the ground for a moment.

Thousands of fighters buzzed around the massive battleship, while hundreds of bombers released their payloads on the peaceful city. Riley's cannon lied at the bottom of a smoldering pile of rubble and people were running for cover throughout the city.

Forrest typed in some calculations into his computer and tightened his grip around his steering handles. He pulled on a golden chain wrapped around his neck and opened the clasped disc on the end. Inside was a picture of a curly haired woman who had a smile that would never fade.

"You always said I was your lucky charm momma. Let's see how lucky I am," Forrest whispered to himself. He closed the clasp and tucked it back into his shirt.

"What are you doing?" Sujay asked over the comm.

"Taking out your boss," Forrest said as he pushed as hard as he could on the accelerator column. He knew he only had one shot to take down Ivanov's battleship. It had to be done with a level of precision that left no room for error, otherwise he'd end up in a pile of slag. This would require nerves of steel.

"You know I wasn't going to join him right?"

"Only because I saved your sorry butt!"

"No, but it was touching to see how much you care."

"Plus you can't lead even this tiny outfit. How do you expect to run a section of the Earth's Navy?"

"You really know how to kill the moment don't you?"

Forrest's navicomputer ran a series of calculations. The computer told him this was far too dangerous and kept trying to override his commands. He circled around, and pointed his ship right at Ivanov's battleship.

"Shut up you stupid computer! I'm smarter than you!" Forrest screamed as he pounded on the dashboard.

"You sure about that?" Sujay asked.

"You shush!" Forrest hissed as he jammed down on his accelerator to the edge of warp speed. He flew over an incoming bomber and released his drag cable at the unsuspecting heavy ship. His ship's engines howled in rage as he pushed his ship to her limits, and forced her to drag the bomber by cable.

The pilot inside the bomber didn't have a chance to react. He witnessed a golden ship fly overhead, and then was jerked violently off course. His controls locked up. Every command he issued into his ship didn't work. He was helpless behind the golden Nebular fighter.

Ivanov looked out through the ship's front window. He noticed that a golden starship was flying directly for the bridge.

"Hey! Ivanov! Want to play a game of chicken?" Forrest asked.

A lone bead of sweat crept down Ivanov's neck. His thoughts swirled inside his mind: *What is this man doing? Who would charge a battleship? Is this man crazy?*

"So Ivanov," Sujay said over the comm. "I see that your loyalty is quite...flimsy since you were willing to shoot me out of the sky. I don't think I'll take your offer to defect."

"Sir, the auto turrets can't get a lock. What do we do?" One of the officers on deck asked Ivanov.

Ivanov stared blankly out the window in stunned silence.

"AUGH!" Forrest screamed.

"GET DOWN!" Ivanov bellowed to his crew.

At the last second, Forrest pulled up, and scraped against the bridge. He slammed his fist on the button which cut the cable. Gravity carried the bomber into the bridge. The sound of metal's shrill screech as it tore against more metal felt like a nail driven into the ears of the onlookers. People on land panicked as the bomber ripped through the bridge, and smothered the officers in an infernal fusion of smoke and fire. Streams of sheared metal, debris and molten slag pour from the bridge onto the city below.

"She's blind! Let's bring this battleship down! All squadrons concentrate firepower on the engines!" Sujay screamed into the comm.

"Roger that, Starfleet Commander," Forrest replied.

A flock of fighters swirled around the engines of the battleship. They fired and pummeled the engines with everything they had. The barrage triggered a series of explosions in the engines, which left the battleship a smoking mass that slowly descended towards the water.

"Tow ships! Drag that monstrosity to the water!" Sujay ordered. Dozens of tow ships rose from the surface, extended their cables and pulled on the lumbering battleship towards the lake.

The battleship descended into the water. The resulting wave crashed into the city against the crystal-colored skyscrapers. Most of the water flowed into the sewer systems and left only a slight trace on the streets. The remnants of Ivanov's fleet retreated back to the heavens in search of reinforcements.

"We beat them," Forrest said in a breathless whisper as he watched the Core fighters retreat.

The Alcyone squadrons touched down, and most of the fighter pilots howled and cheered from their victory. The pilots ran and hugged each other as they celebrated their victory over a Core embargo fleet. Forrest climbed out of his ship, walked over and hugged Sujay.

"Great job out there Starfleet Commander," Forrest said to Sujay.

"Yes sir. I think your mother will reward me nicely for shooting down those three fighters that tried to take you down. Put some of my curry on her white rice," Sujay replied with a grin.

Forrest burst out laughing. "Oh, you're such a necrophiliac! You're not the only one who likes to be stiff eh Sujay?"

"What?" Sujay asked.

"Uh, my mom's gone you sicko. Six feet under."

"Oh my goodness Forrest I'm so sorry! I didn't know-"

"Just leave the jokes to me m'kay?"

"Fine," Sujay replied. "And Forrest?"

"Yea buddy?" Forrest replied.

"Thanks for...thanks for saving me up there," Sujay choked out.

"Yeah...there's no way Ivanov was going to let you become Admiral," Forrest replied.

"I could be Admiral!" Sujay snapped.

"Eeehhh," Forrest replied. "I did most of the work up there and you were only a Starfleet Commander which is mostly an honorary title and..."

"Oh you son of a-" Sujay said.

"Mind if I cut in?" Riley said.

The two paused their argument and stared at Riley. He was covered in dust from the collapsed building. "Thank you to both of you for your help. Without you, this planet would belong to Ivanov and the other Admirals," He said.

Riley's armored guards stormed in, and seized the surviving Core officers as they crawled out of the water. "Where should we take them sir?" one of the men asked Riley.

"To the prison. We'll prepare a ransom. Show the Core what happens when they trifle with me," Riley said.

Forrest and Sujay exchanged a look. This wasn't the Riley they were talking to a few days ago...

"And this one?" Another soldier asked, as he dragged a badly bruised Ivanov from the water. Ivanov stumbled out of the lake but the soldier kicked him behind the legs so that he kneeled before Riley.

"I've defeated you Ivanov," Riley said.

"Yes, I can see that Riley. You won't get anything by ransoming me. The Core doesn't deal with terrorists," Ivanov replied.

Riley drew his pistol and pointed it at Ivanov's head.

"Whoa, whoa, whoa!" Forrest said as he stepped between Riley and Ivanov. "I'm not one for saving the stereotypical

Russian bad guy, but there are at least a dozen or more fleets the size of what we faced up there. The Core will surely retaliate Riley," Forrest said.

"No they won't Forrest. No one from the Core is coming," Riley replied.

"Why not?" Forrest asked.

"Jesus, you really are dumb," Ivanov said as he snorted and spat on the ground.

"What's he talking about?" Forrest asked.

"The embargo is a ruse," Ivanov said. "A ploy I used to get my agent here to surrender what is mine. I sent Riley here to infiltrate the Alcyone government, convince them to sell, and when they wouldn't, he killed all who resisted. I made up the story of them not exporting water to provide cover. Except Riley here wanted a bigger finder's fee for his troubles," He explained.

"What? Riley is this true?" Forrest asked, his voice hurt.

"Of course it's true!" Ivanov shouted. "Riley came to me to make a deal, start the rumors of an embargo, but turned all of his mercenaries against me and-"

Forrest and Sujay jumped when they heard the shot fired. Ivanov fell over, lifeless. Riley stood, holding the smoking pistol. All of the Core soldiers were in shock from the sight of their Admiral's execution.

"What did you get us into...?" Sujay whispered to Forrest.

"I had no idea! I had no idea! I swear! How was I to know that Riley would go all ...violent!'" Forrest whispered back.

"What are you looking at Forrest?" Riley snapped as he turned and pointed his pistol at him.

"I...I don't get it. That's all. I mean...you hate the Core..." Forrest stuttered.

"The smuggling trade is on the verge of collapse Forrest and Ivanov made me the offer of a lifetime. All I had to do was instigate a little overthrow of the local government and-"

"In what Universe is that the right thing to do Riley? All those people you hurt and killed...there...there be some bad ju-ju for you!" Forrest hissed.

"So what? Once the Core pays me off, I'll be one of the wealthiest men in the galaxy. And with the head off of the snake, they may be more willing to negotiate," Riley said.

"You're not going to get paid off you idiot!" Sujay screamed. "You'll be lucky if those ships up there don't turn this city into a fused ball of glass!"

"Not as long as I got you two here," Riley said as he pointed his pistol at the duo. Riley's mercenaries also raised their guns at Forrest and Sujay. Forrest looked into Riley's eyes and witnessed the gaze of a man who'd gone mad with greed. There would never be enough credits to satisfy Riley's lust for money.

Forrest and Sujay stood shoulder to shoulder, and were surrounded by heavily armed men itching to exercise their trigger fingers. Several ships descended along the edge of the sky until they came into view.

"What are they?" Riley grunted.

"Core ships sir," One of the men replied.

"Ah, maybe they finally came to their senses-" Riley said right before the back of his head burst out in blood. Riley collapsed onto the ground, followed by an array of oppressive fire that was determined to eliminate his guard. One of the ships broke off and flew down to the ground. It was a freighter ship, not one used by the Core military.

"Oh sweet Vishnu, what now?" Sujay asked.

The ship touched down, and a black man who carried a briefcase walked off the ramp to the loading bay. He wore a gray suit and a black tie neither of which seemed to fit quite right. He adjusted his necktie twice before he made it off the ramp.

The man approached in a calm, confident stride. "Jack Forrest and Sujay Malak. You two gentlemen have a moment?" He asked. Several Core ships landed and soldiers burst out, who were determined to end Riley's coup once and for all. Forrest and Sujay both gave a silent nod.

The man lead the two over to a nearby piece of building rubble, and motioned for Forrest and Sujay to sit down.

"Now, I'm sure that you don't need to tell me that the both of you are royally screwed," the man said. "But I also know that you weren't part of Riley's deal-gone-wrong here. Ivanov was every bit the greedy Admiral that Riley made him out to be, but his first mate is a stand-up guy who owes me a favor. He's going to right this situation as best he can."

"Are we going to die?" Forrest asked, a forced innocence wrapped within his question.

"Not if I can help it," the man replied. "I'm here to make sure you live. Y'see boys, I know that the two of you are some of the best pilots in the galaxy. I also know that the two of you are in a very bad position both here and with the mob boss Kingsman. However, I'm really good at getting men out of bad positions."

Forrest sniffed the air. It was a familiar scent. Rich and oily. It came from the man's briefcase.

He noticed Forrest's infernal sniffing. He opened the briefcase and pulled out a brown paper bag littered with grease spots.

"Brocker sends his regards," the man said as he tossed the bag into Forrest's lap.

Forrest's jaw dropped and he shivered in delight as he plunged his hand into the bag and mowed down on the golden fries. He moaned in euphoria.

"I don't know which is more gross those fries or the way you eat them," Sujay said.

"Anyway," the man said."My name is Colonel John C. Henry and I'm building a team. I need some pilots as skilled as you two to fly my ship. As far as I see your options are-"

"Where do we sign?" The two asked at the same time.

—The End—

PART THREE

Africa's Deadliest Son

"Ooh!" The crowd screamed as Warrens stumbled from the hard left on the cheek. He grunted, and shook the blow off. He bounced on the edge of the ring made up of cheering men, and sought out the weaknesses in his opponent, Mac McGee. The men encircling the boxers hooted and hollered, the room an echo chamber of cheers for both Jackson Warrens and Mac. The two were the best boxers in what became known as the "Veterans League," a social club created to help survivors of the Unification Wars adjust back into civilian life. Every Friday night the club met and held sparring matches to compete in. The testosterone-fueled match ups lured in the men of Beckwell Defense, which turned white collar veterans back into warriors.

Warrens studied his opponent, breaking down his moves. Mac may have been nothing more than a glorified brawler, but he was a hard hitter. He'd knock his opponents out quickly in the ring, a lesson Warrens learned the hard way when the two first sparred. He had never faced an opponent who hit so hard, but realized that Mac's strength was his biggest weakness.

Warrens took the calculated risk and moved within Mac's striking distance. He threw a hard left, which Warrens dodged. Warrens countered with a series of small jabs which rippled against Mac's torso, but the indomitable Scotsman didn't seem to notice. Mac went into overdrive by throwing his weight behind another left, but Warrens shoved himself away before the hit could land. Mac followed up with a right hook and a left uppercut, but he hit nothing but air. Warrens dived in and pummeled his opponent with another series of small jabs to the chest and torso. Mac shoved him away, and he used the break in battle to take a few deep breaths and steel himself for the next round.

Mac caught on to his strategy. He knew that he was slow compared to Warrens, but all he needed was distance and to land a hard blow in order to finish his opponent off. The room was filled with grunts from the two men as they sparred back and forth. The place reeked of sweat as it flew off of the boxers and onto the men in the crowd. The primal display drove them into a frenzy, and their cheers echoed across the halls of the building. Many of the men even placed wagers on the fight, the room evenly divided between who they rooted for.

Mac took a defensive stance as he closed in on Warrens. He held his hands clutched in front of his face, and was tired of Warrens' surgical strikes that were wearing him out.

Warrens studied Mac as he approached him. The Scotsman's body was drenched in sweat which betrayed the position of every gnarled muscles on his frame. He watched Mac's lungs fill as he drew in precious air. He noticed his eyes growing weary and frustrated. Mac's stance was off by only a degree, but his legs were too far apart, which leaked his secret of another charge. He saw that Mac was tired. Put together Mac revealed that he wanted the match to be over and given that the two boxing titans had fought for fifteen rounds, Warrens couldn't blame him.

The men around the boxers roared and cheered, and their cries became deafening. Warrens was tired himself, but he kept to his disciplined regimen to rebuild his stamina. Warrens was obsessed with fitness and lived for the arena.

Mac shifted his legs and lowered his arms. Those knotted vines that he called muscle tensed up like coils. He was conserving his energy. His breathing had slowed, and he regained his composure.

If Warrens was going to win this fight, he needed to goad

Mac into attacking, to get the infamous hard hitter to overextend himself so that he could defeat him.

Warrens charged in like a bull. He unleashed a flurry of blows on Mac, but the Scotsman had braced himself. He'd reversed the roles now, with Warrens expending energy while Mac waited for the right time to strike. Warrens launched a hard right, but Mac deflected the blow and delivered a hard right of his own into his opponent's gut, which stunned him. Mac unleashed his own assault and his fists became battering rams as they struck Warrens in the gut.

Warrens stumbled backwards, while the men shouted for him to recover. Mac delivered a vicious left hook which sent Warrens reeling into the crowd. The men shoved him back into the ring, demanding that he fight back. He stumbled back, and could barely stand upright. The match seemed over.

Mac howled like an a barbarian and charged forward. He threw wild punches and sought to eliminate Warrens once and for all. Mac's bullrush was the technique that brought Warrens down the first time, but he was determined not to let this be a repeat performance.

"Bullseye," Warrens whispered to himself right as Mac got centimetres away from him.

Warrens ducked and threw a devastating uppercut onto Mac's jaw.

"Ooooh!" The men in the crowd shouted as Mac stumbled backwards.

Warrens lunged forward and delivered a hard right directly to Mac's solar plexus. The blow echoed loudly while the crowd gasped as they felt his pain. Warrens pivoted left, and dealt a hard left hook into Mac's temple.

Mac stumbled backwards with his arms at his sides. Warrens closed in, unleashed a hard right to the gut, and drove home a left hook which knocked Mac to the ground. The referee dove in and counted as he struggled to get up. Between exhaustion and having the wind knocked out of him, he made two attempts to get up, but his arms gave out beneath him. Every man in the crowd leaned in.

"...Eight, Nine, Ten! Warrens wins!" The referee shouted as he seized and held his arm up, while the crowd went wild. Warrens had just handed Indomitable Mac his first defeat. The battle between the giants left both with a record of 12-1, which made them tied for the best in the ragtag league.

Mac crawled up off the floor, gasping for breath and drank his water as though he'd thirsted for years. The men around him slapped him on the shoulder, and congratulated him on a good fight. Mac approached Warrens and held his hand out.

"Tidy fight in there laddie," Mac said in his thick Scottish accent. "Thought you were a bit radge for gettin' aggressive, but it was pure barry to lure me in like that."

"You didn't make it easy Mac. I need to fix myself up real good from all those blows you dealt me in the ring. You're a real killer," Warrens replied with his big, infectious grin.

Warrens held his arms up in triumph, then grabbed Mac's wrist and held it up alongside his. The two titans relished in the cheers from the crowd as the referees shooed them out and readied the men for the next match.

Warrens threw his boxing gloves and hand towel into the locker. He picked up the special metal case that he'd had since he was a young boy which prominently displayed two pictures inside. One was his father Earl (Bud) Warrens in full uniform while in service to the Earth Core Army. The other was a picture of him as a baby with his mother Ruth and father, a family of three who couldn't smile wide enough.

He thought back to when sat starry-eyed on the floor and his grandmother Gladys would read Bud's transcriptions of his service during the "Skirmishes," at a battle called Arasha Valley. The skirmishes were a series of battles triggered by the secession of the fringe planets in which Core forces were deployed to maintain peace and stability. The skirmishes led to what became known as the "Unification Wars," but Bud never saw the war declared. He lost his life by throwing himself on top of an antimatter mine to save his platoon.

"That fool," Gladys would always snap as she grasped his

picture in between her delicate fingers.

"And your poor mother Jackson," She always said. "I loved Ruth, but that dear girl fell apart after your father passed. The two of them were so deeply in love that I swear Shakespeare wrote *Romeo and Juliet* as a premonition of them. It was then that I was blessed to bring you into my home and raise you myself. While I do mourn the loss of your parents Jackson, I have been blessed with raising the Da Vinci of our time in my household." She wiped away a stray tear from her eye.

She glanced over at a case on the wall which displayed Bud's Chancellor's Medal of Valor as well as the Phalanx Stars of Courage. These were the two most prestigious medals of the Core. They also lionized him in his son's eyes and set the path Warrens would take nine years later, when he enlisted in the Core Army after turning seventeen. He served over three years during the Unification Wars, earning the Distinguished Service Cross, as well as the same medals his father earned.

A beep from his tablet brought him back to the present. Warrens grabbed the device that was on top of his reptile field guide and scrolled through his files. Inside was hundreds of sketches of weapons, armor and war machines that he'd compiled over the years. There was also a message from Beckwell Defense's Human Resources Department:

ATTN: Transfer

Dear Mr. Warrens,

This is to notify you that we're transferring you to our South African division to help with our stabilization efforts.

Thank you for your understanding during this time of need.

Sincerely,

Lori Anderson, Director of Human Resources

"Grandma I'm home!" Warrens shouted as he walked into the house.

"Where have you been?! It's almost midnight!" Gladys asked as she shuffled into the kitchen.

"I was working late, making notes for future designs."

"Always working late. Need to find you a woman!" Gladys stopped in her tracks when she looked up at her grandson. "Dear lord my boy, your face is all scratched up! You were out boxing again weren't you?! I don't know why the Da Vinci of our time insists on getting his head knocked around every Friday night! It would seem to me that he would put that noggin to use!"

"Well, I won't have any boxing opportunities anymore. Beckwell is transferring me to South Africa."

"Like hell they are! I'm not going to that hole!"

"Grandma, this company has given us everything."

"And they're asking too much! They can send somebody else to that war zone! You barely came home from that decade-long war, I don't need you goin' into another one!"

"Grandma, I'm one of their best engineers."

"Why'd you have to go into defense?! Why couldn't you have designed...speeder engines or something?!"

Warrens chuckled. "I do design engines for tanks and-"

"You know what I mean!" Gladys snapped.

Warrens wrapped his arms around his grandmother. "Someday I will wield the armor that would've saved Dad. Until then, I'll do what the company asks. And that means moving to Africa and taking you because I promised I'd take care of you."

"I *really* wish those other boxers would knock some sense into you!"

"This just in from Global News Cast. The violence in Africa continues to escalate as the three warlords bid for power. Atrocities such as beheadings are committed on a daily basis. Accusations of infanticide, genocide, and rape are commonplace while the Core authorities do nothing to alleviate the suffering of civilians. Each warlord claims that he's the better humanitarian, however the ever-growing scope of desolation reveals that none of these warlords desire to appease their potential followers. The devastation has purged the African continent into a devastating civil war, with no end in sight."

"Deebs, turn that damn newscast off," Warrens ordered as he entered the testing lab.

"You and your stupid nicknames. It's DeBoer meathead!" His lab partner snapped. "What's your deal?!"

"Hate the news. Can't fix anything when savages run a war like this one. I like my machines because I can fix 'em."

"It's good to be informed. I'd like to know if I should buy an insurance policy on you in case you get kidnapped and killed."

"Oh, don't give me that crap or I'll lay you out flat dutch boy."

"Damn yanks, think you can always wrangle us to get your way?"

"Guess I don't share the morbid South African sense of humor."

"Damn straight," DeBoer said as he shut the news off. The two men put on their safety equipment and approached the Lepton Forges, which were drawing in particles and assembling them into armor plates.

"What've we got?" DeBoer asked.

"We're gonna test the armor against some shieldbreaker rounds," Warrens replied. "But first we gotta clean the guns." He shoved a rifle into DeBoer's chest and placed a pistol on the work bench. Within seconds Warrens had disassembled the pistol, ready for cleaning while DeBoer watched in amazement.

"That is incredible!" He said. Warrens moved to the other side, took the rifle and disassembled it before his partner's eyes as well.

"So we're removing the energy cells and converting these

into ballistics since the shieldbreakers are a projectile ammunition," Warrens explained. "Real easy to do, just gotta switch the cells for a hammer and the barrels."

DeBoer gathered the new parts and tried to install them in the guns, but they wouldn't fit. He tried over and over, but only found frustration.

"These ballistics parts don't fit! Are you sure these are meant to convert?"

Warrens grabbed the barrel and looked down both ends. He measured it, then took out a micron laser torch.

"It's a few microns too big. Just shave a bit off, and we're all set. Won't be enough to harm the structural integrity," He said as he positioned the barrel within the assault rifle and had it assembled in 30 seconds.

"It's scary how good you are at doing that, even if you are some kind of war hero," DeBoer said.

"Too bad we can't use *these* to defend ourselves," Warrens said as he sighted in the rifle.

"Good luck with that plan. Core won't allow civilians to carry the very weapons we make for them. They think we're too unstable and dangerous."

"Real shame," Warrens said as he fired off a few rounds into an armor plate.

"Armor plate holds up good," DeBoer said.

"If anything we're the *most* qualified to handle these weapons. The Core's laws only punish the lawful. I'll do whatever it takes to protect my family."

"Don't you just have your grandma?"

"Watch it Deebs."

"Was only askin'. Hear about that consultant they're bringing in in a few weeks? Maybe he'll make you feel better about going outside."

"Yeah. Maybe I'll bore my captors to sleep," Warrens said as he fired off another volley.

"Thank you everyone for attending this meeting today," Greg Hoffberg, the Regional Manager said. "Not sure what you guys have heard, but the situation here in Africa is deteriorating."

"That's an understatement," Warrens thought to himself. He kept his hands folded in front of his face, waiting to hear the proposed solutions. Kidnappings were rampant across South Africa. Murders occurred daily. Firebombs were being set off without a clear target. There was an uprising that simmered beneath the dark continent's shell, and none of the men in the room knew how to handle it.

"We've brought in an expert who will advise us on the political climate here in Africa. Nigel Harris, thank you for being here with us today," Hoffberg said.

"Thank you Mr. Hoffberg. Now, I'm not sure how much history you gentlemen know, but to make it easier on everyone, I'm going to start from the beginning. Two hundred years ago, on the rise of Earth's prominence within the Core there was a man of Nubian Descent who believed in Africa's unification: Enai Kharakoum. Enai was a brutal warlord who ravaged Africa, but he successfully unified the continent while the rest of the world clinged to their false hopes of independent states. For two hundred years, Enai's lineage has ruled Africa in a pseudo-monarchy tolerated by the Core Authorities due to Aluminum Isotope - 26," Nigel explained.

"What's that?" DeBoer asked.

"Really DeBoer?" Hoffberg interrupted. "Iso-26 is what makes our warp drives create and manipulate magnetic fields which allows us to pass through the space-time continuum."

"Doesn't that isotope only have a half life of 750,000 years?" Warrens asked.

"Normally that is correct," Nigel said. "However, inside the African deep mines, they found that our magnetic field and a proximity to uranium kept the Isotope active."

"What about the Earth Core Government? Why don't they get involved?" DeBoer asked. "If this stuff is that valuable…?"

"That is far more simple," Nigel said. "Who wants to be on the receiving end of ethnic cleansing charges? The powers that be have always left Africa to her own devices since most of her wars are ethnic in nature. Enai Kharakoum was a sadistic, bloodthirsty dictator, but he united Africa under one regime. The Core gave him everything he wanted to develop the continent in exchange for unhindered access to Isotope-26. The Core is holding back to see who holds the most promise of controlling Africa, by that I mean who owns the Isotope mines. When they see a clear leader emerge, their retribution will be swift, and they will annihilate the competition."

"So how many millions have to die before that happens?" Warrens asked.

Nigel looked at Warrens with remorseful eyes. "As many as it takes I'm afraid. The Core is war weary. The Ministry of Internal Affairs will negotiate what to do over the civil war, but nobody will make the first move. We need to be ready for whatever happens on our end should things escalate…"

"And by that you mean we need to be ready with weapons and armor?" Warrens asked. "Do we need to sell our 'merchandise' to the warlords or be ready if they try to come and take it?"

Hoffberg sighed. "Nobody builds weapons and armor to fuel conflicts like these unless they're sadists. Warlords aren't good business because they're volatile, they turn everyone against them, and are always looking for something on the cheap. These guys are buying leftovers on the secondary markets from the Unification Wars, not in the primary market where we're at," He explained.

"Right," Nigel said. "The main concern here gentlemen is how much this firefight escalates. Beckwell Defense will need to begin taking measures of securing personnel to prevent kidnappings and ransoms from occurring."

"What happens to us if we're kidnapped? Will the company help us out?" DeBoer asked.

"Beckwell Defense will do everything in their power to secure the safety of their personnel," Hoffberg replied. The answer relieved the fears of no one. There was a tension in the air which loomed like a thundercloud.

"I can start a self defense class," Warrens said. "Teach you boys how to box should anybody come lookin' for trouble."

"I would strongly advise against such measures. Hostility will only breed hostility in this environment," Nigel said.

"Just leavin' us as sheep for the slaughter," DeBoer whispered to Warrens.

"Yeah. Good luck tellin' a soldier to lie down when he's about to be kidnapped."

Warrens shoved the door to Hoffberg's office open. The meeting had left the normally rational mechanic full of bile and the desire to use the consultant as a punching bag.

"I want a transfer," Warrens said. His tone was harsh and dismissive.

"Look Warrens, I can tell that just because the consultant didn't like your fight club idea…"

"He was telling us to lie down and get taken Hoff! How are we supposed to protect others when we're hiding under our desks? Why not arm us? Allow a program where we can lease the weapons we build and use them to defend ourselves. You have pull with the Ministries, have them issue us special permits to bear arms!"

"Even with my pull Jackson, they'll never allow our weapons in the hands of private civilians. You know the law, only military and police are allowed to possess a weapon."

"So we're supposed to let those 'soldiers' come by and shoot us while we do nothing?" Warrens asked. "Give me the transfer Hoff. This isn't what I signed up for!"

"Actually, per your contract Jackson, it's exactly what you signed up for. You agreed to come here to South Africa, regardless of the risks, and you accepted the hazard pay. You wanted to be a part of the action, remember?" Hoffberg's cocky attitude was wearing on Warrens' nerves.

Warrens snorted, and resembled a bull brandishing his horns. "I will not risk my family's life here. You either put me in for a transfer, or I quit!" He said as he pointed his finger in Hoffberg's face. He glared at the imposing mechanic, whose gnarled muscle intimidated everyone within the company.

"You quit on us, and I'll see you blacklisted from the defense industry!" Hoffberg hissed.

"You *really* think I can't go somewhere else?!" Warrens roared. "I'm one of the best engineers alive! I can get work *anywhere* I want!"

"How about this?" Hoffberg asked as he tried to compose himself. "We get a security detail for your grandma. We also provide escorts to and off company grounds. Would that help?"

Warrens didn't like the idea of two grown men watching over his frail grandmother. He saw it as his job to protect her, but he understood that it was the best deal he was going to get.

"Fine," He said as he relented to Hoffberg's attempts at a truce. He turned and stormed out of the office.

Warrens flinched as cracks of thunder echoed through the alleyways. It was hard to tell whether it was gunfire or fireworks. Sirens followed, and the alleyways became deserted in the midst of the maelstrom. He felt the chill in the air as he gazed at the graffiti etched around the concrete block. He thought it was such a shame for those kids to waste their incredible talents using concrete as their canvas. The way their colors danced along the walls was beautiful, but ultimately, wasted talent. He shook his head and his thought was interrupted by a short man in a brown leather trench coat. The guy looked like a fool with a baseball cap and large sunglasses, and he reeked of suspicion.

"Fancy meeting ya here," The man said in a thick South African accent. "What're your wares?"

"You know what I came here to get," Warrens replied.

"Oh, right. The hard stuff. Well, here ya go," the man said as he slipped a pistol to Warrens while watching the alleyways.

Warrens dismantled the pistol in front of his 'vendor' and inspected each of the parts with a discerning eye.

"Hey! What are you doing man?" the guy asked.

"Relax. I'm an expert. And your wares are shit," Warrens

said.

"What you expect? No genuine holdovers from the Uni Wars."

"The barrel is caked with carbon, the energy cell is corroded and the trigger is flimsy. What are you peddling?"

"Whoa-oh man! You gotta cut me some slack here. Between the Ministry of Internal's troops and those jungle soldiers, pickins are slim 'round here. We gotta use what we can get."

Warrens put the pistol back together. "Here. I don't need this. This was a bad idea." He said as he turned and walked away.

Just as Warrens was outside of earshot, the 'vendor' pulled a communication device out of his pocket.

"Hey it's me. Yeah, he just left. He's northbound. Tried to buy some wares off of me, but he's got a good eye. It's him alright. Never seen a man take a pistol apart like that. Alright, we'll do that," the vendor said as he pocketed the comm device and walked off.

"Hoff, something is wrong," Warrens said as he burst into Hoffberg's office.

"Good morning to you too Warrens," Hoffberg replied.

"DeBoer hasn't come into work for the past three days. Is there a meeting or a convention you sent him off to?"

"No, not that I know of," Hoffberg said as he leaned back in his chair. "Maybe the guy needed a vacation."

"Hoff, you know that you have to force DeBoer into going on vacation! And he hasn't called in for the past three days!"

"Relax Warrens. I'll give him a call this afternoon, see where he's at. We haven't received any calls from a doctor or mercs looking for ransom money. There's hope."

"Maybe for you there is. It just keeps getting worse out there and you sit around here like nothing's wrong!"

"Listen Warrens!" Hoffberg said as he rose from his seat. "What good will come if I worried about every single threat to my employees huh? We get threats all the time, I'd need a full time person just handle them! Relax. It may be getting worse out there, but you're safe here."

"It's not my safety I'm worried about. It's theirs," Warrens said as he pointed outside.

"Wrong time to be a humanitarian, especially when working at a defense company," Hoffberg replied.

Warrens stormed out of Hoffberg's office without saying a word. His decision had been made for him. All he had to do was be the last man out of the office, a common occurrence for him.

Warrens looked both ways down the hall. The coast was clear, there wasn't another soul left in the building. He had free reign of the safe. "I don't care what happens," He whispered to himself.

The beeps from entering the safe's combination thundered through the hallway. The vault's lock banged open like a shot. The door opened in silence, and the treasure trove of weapons gleamed under the fluorescent light.

"I can't believe it's come down to this," He whispered to himself.

Warrens pulled out a picture of him and his family from his wallet, then looked at the picture of his grandma. He promised his father when leaving for the army that he'd take care of her no matter what. He took a deep breath as he entered the vault. Guns of all makes and models sat in silence as he debated in his head which one he'd take to defend his family. He ran his fingers against their black stocks, and savored the smooth surface.

With the situation in Africa deteriorating, Warrens had to pick something that would take down anyone who threatened him or his grandmother. He eyed the shieldbreaker rounds.

He chose a pair of pistols, a pair of assault rifles and several ammunition clips. "I survived the Unification Wars, I will survive this," he said to himself.

"I'm sorry Hoff," He mumbled as he cocked the assault rifle. He tossed the guns he'd picked into a bag, hoisted the bag over his shoulder and shut the door to the vault. He keyed in the code, and the lock in the door slammed like the gavel that sentenced his fate.

As Warrens walked home that night, he noticed it was a sunny evening. The light became a relentless stream of gold yet dusk began to show her shy silhouette on the horizon. He smelled grilling meat in the air as people prepared their dinner. A few echoes of gunfire rippled through the streets, but Johannesburg wasn't being ravaged by the civil war. At least, not yet. Warrens looked around. An encompassing void surrounded the neighborhood that still basked in the afternoon light.

The quiet before the storm.

There were four men standing in front of his apartment building. All of them in dark suits and sunglasses.

Sentries on the lookout.

Warrens got a sinking feeling in his stomach. He was suspicious of these strangers who were dressed far too nicely for the neighborhood.

Then Warrens felt his heart fall into his gut.

A man walked outside and escorted an elderly woman towards their parked speeder.

"GRANDMA!" Warrens screamed as he tore a rifle out of his bag. One of the men behind her slid a black bag over her head, and threw her into the speeder. Two men hopped in while the other two drew their pistols and opened fire on Warrens.

Warrens fired a volley of bullets at the first man, who went down while the second recoiled from the spray of blood.

"Whoa, whoa, whoa!" A man screamed, breaking the chain of conflict. "There is no need for violence here, not when a grandmomy be in danger," A slight, impish man said as he stood up from the back of the speeder. His accent was a thick African one. Incapable of saying the letter "R", his words always expressed the "ah" sound instead.

"Come now, lay down your gun, or grandmommy die. Is that what you want Mista Wahhens?" Warrens was used to his name being butchered throughout Africa, but there was a slithering element to this man's voice which made him feel like he was dealing with the traitorous angel Lucifer. Warrens threw down his rifle and let the blood-spattered goon come up and tie a zip tie around his wrists.

The goon escorted Warrens to the speeder and eased him inside.

"Come! Make room for our guest! Get this bug outta the way!" The impish man ordered. They pushed another person whose head was covered with a bag to the other side of the car. The man under the bag gave a stifled groan, and held his covered head down in despair.

Warrens looked around. They were packed like sardines inside the speeder. There was the driver, a man in the passenger seat, and a man on each side of him. Across from him was the impish man with Gladys on one side and a man with a black bag over his head on the other.

The imp pulled the black bag off of the man next to him. It was DeBoer, who sported a bruised face and a bloody nose. He jerked around in panic, his eyes adjusting to the blazing sun outside.

"Are you alright?" Warrens asked.

"Is this him?" The imp asked as he pointed at Warrens with his pistol.

"Deebs, are you alright?" Warrens pressed.

"You shut up!" The imp snarled. Warrens got a good look inside his mouth. Two rows of filed, dagger-like teeth, enhancing his devilish image. "Is it him? I won't ask again."

"Sean don't - "

Warrens was cut off by the pistol's hollow eye glaring at him. There was a hesitation in the imp's eyes, but there was a darkness there. This man had not only killed before, he enjoyed it. He savored every kill. Warrens stayed silent.

"Yeah, it's him," DeBoer said. There was a defeated look in his eyes. His face begged for Warrens' forgiveness. Warrens could see that DeBoer endured unimaginable tortures, and would never hate him for giving up his secrets to a bloodthirsty enemy.

"Good," The imp said as he rolled down the car window. "No more use for you," he said as he shot DeBoer through the side of his head. Gladys shrieked, while the imp opened the car door and dumped DeBoer's body out into the street. Warrens felt more bile swirl in his stomach. He wanted to vomit but he couldn't give in. Gladys kept screaming, but the imp wrapped his arm around her and put his hand over her mouth.

"Quiet now, or I make you quiet," the imp said. Warrens prepared to lunge himself at the cretin.

"Relax Mista Wahhens, she is safe for now. It is you we need," the imp said. "Allow me to introduce myself. I am Iboee, Mista Wahhens and I am one of your biggest fans."

Warrens felt guilt and adrenaline flood his bloodstream. A venomous rage welled within, a volcano on the verge of eruption.

"You're lucky I don't kill all of you for what you've done," Warrens spat.

"You are in no position to threaten me Wahhens," Iboee replied. "Just calm down and we'll get through this without any trouble."

Warrens fought to calm the storm within. Lashing out would only get his grandmother killed, and that was the last thing he wanted to happen. He closed his eyes, breathed in deep, and braced himself for the long fight ahead.

"Who do you work for Iboee?" He asked.

"I work for the great Diallo. Our informant back there tells us you can make weapons. Great weapons. We need them to help Diallo secure his kingdom," Iboee explained. His accent made him hard to understand and he spoke at a snail's pace.

"Leave my grandmother out of this. I'll do anything you want, but please leave her out," Warrens pleaded.

"Don't beg boy. Makes you look weak. Besides you is a son of Africa. This is your fight too," Iboee said to Warrens as they watched street gangs fight outside.

"My grandmother and I are from the American Provinces. I

only moved to Africa for my job."

"All black men are sons of Africa. The women her daughters. White men steal Africa's sons and daughters and sell them as slaves."

"Like what you're doing now?" Warrens asked.

Iboee gave his trademark impish grin. "Black enslave white, white enslave black, and sometimes black enslave black. It is the way of life in Africa. The strong conquer the weak. Diallo the strongest amongst us, he will give Africa life again," Iboee said.

"By bringing death millions?" Warrens hissed.

"Like you can talk merchant of death. You Mista Wahhens known as a spirit of death here in Africa. You bring death to all you gaze upon. You bring death to Diallo's enemies now. If you don't I dismember your grandmommy right in front of you. Piece by piece am I clear?" Iboee asked as he brandished a machete along Gladys' neck.

"Yes, very clear," Warrens replied.

"Then welcome to the African Continental Government! Ooy-aayy!" Iboee shouted in celebration.

Warrens watched out the window. Pillars of smoke rose on the edge of the horizon. There was violence everywhere. Soldiers hacked limbs off of villagers with machetes. Houses burned while soldiers screamed in celebration of another village taken. Men seized innocent women, pinned them to the ground and raped them in broad daylight. Seven year olds held assault rifles and fired on other children. Bodies and limbs lied everywhere. Alleyways and roads were blocked off by oil barrels and gateways made of human intestines.

Warrens looked to the floor. He couldn't take the torment outside. His family believed that there was honor in war.

Brotherhood.

Valor.

Duty to one's home.

War was hell, but there was no honor in such tribal butchery. Even if the skies split and blood rained down it wouldn't quench the thirst of this ancient bloodlust.

The speeder closed in on the city of Pretoria, home of the Trans-African Railway, a railroad that extended almost 9,000 miles North to South through Africa. It was one of Enai Kharakoum's pet projects to "unify" the continent. The railway was built under the premise of increasing trade, but it instead became his own personal means of travel throughout Africa. If Diallo had managed to seize this railroad, he would have an unmatched edge to transport men and materialé throughout the continent.

"Ah! The Trans-African Railroad! Quite glorious wouldn't you say Mista Wahhens?" Iboee asked.

"Yeah, it's a knockout," Warrens replied without enthusiasm. He thought it was a good sign that the railway still looked like a means of luxury transport rather than a converted military railroad.

The speeders pulled up and parked just behind the caboose of an electromagnetic bullet train. Warrens felt another round of bile slosh around in his stomach as the car came to a stop. The speeder had stopped on the edge of the Serengeti, a golden ecosystem kept in perfect balance. Despite all the centuries, no one could ever tame this wilderness.

"Now you get to prove yourself Mista Wahhens," Iboee said as he climbed out of the speeder and pulled Gladys out with him. Warrens was escorted out and his handcuffs removed. Why would the captors risk releasing him? The trunk of the speeder popped open and Iboee pointed inside.

"What is this?" Warrens asked.

"That's what you're here to do. Figure it out," Iboee ordered as he pointed inside the truck.

Warrens saw the remains of an armor gauntlet scattered in the trunk. Next to the arm was an energy cell for propulsion used on speeders. There were two worn out rifles scored with carbon. Finally there were two boxes of tools sitting towards the back of the trunk next to a glass case with an orb inside of it.

"A'ight. Now we need proof that you is as good as they say Mista Wahhens. Take those parts and make me an arm which can fire some bolts. Should be easy for you," Iboee said. Warrens looked at the pieces and tried to figure out how he could use them together.

"And just so you don't get any funny ideas Mista Wahhens," Iboee warned, he pulled out his machete and held the edge right next to Gladys' neck. She squealed as the blade dragged across her skin, and a thin trickle of blood leaked down her neck. "There be much more if you do anything stupid."

Warrens peered inside of the trunk. "Iboee, what is this?" He asked as he pulled out the case which held the metal sphere. The metal appeared to vibrate, a constant shimmer rippling across the silvery surface.

"Ahh! Even bettah! Make that into a weapon!"

"I...I don't even know what this is!" Warrens stuttered.

"You better try, or Grandmommy bleed!" Iboee snarled as he pressed his machete to Gladys' neck.

"Jackson!" Gladys cried.

"Iboee wait!" Warrens howled. "Where did this come from?"

"We dug it up. Found it in dem Isotope-26 mines. Workers say it be the weapon of a Kibuka," Iboee said, as though that explained everything.

"What does it do?"

"Said to be the weapon of the Gods! You here to figure out how to wield it!"

"I don't know what this is...how can I turn it into a weapon if..."

"If you cannot give Diallo the weapon of Kibuka, then you useless! Your grandma be the first to go!"

"Iboee wait!" Warrens shouted. "Wait. I'll...I'll try..." He said as he opened the cover of the glass case. Something about this sphere unnerved Iboee, Warrens could see it in his eyes. He lifted the sphere out and held the vibrating metal in his hands. The metal pulsated, as if it had a heart.

"How am I supposed to wield-" Warrens asked as he felt the sphere become weightless. He recoiled in terror, dropping the glass case while the sphere melted like mercury through his fingers.

"What did you do?" Iboee screamed.

"I don't know I-"

"Figure it out! Now!" Iboee howled. The metal collected back into a sphere right before it crashed onto the ground. It lied like a vibrating ball bearing on the ground, creating tremors which made the sand all around it dance in an erratic pattern.

"Pick it up! Now!" Iboee screamed. He kept digging the machete into Gladys, and Warrens gave her an agonized stare. Tears glided down Gladys' cheeks.

Warrens reached down and grabbed the sphere, the vibration rattling across his fingers and up his back.

"Stop stalling!" Iboee hissed.

"Iboee. Relax. There's nothing I can do with this unless I have the chance to analyze and inspect this...whatever this metal is," Warrens said.

"Then your grandmommy -"

"Iboee. If you cut my grandmother one more time, I won't help you build the weapon you want. Let her go, and I will build you a weapon of incomprehensible destruction. Diallo will have Africa in the palm of his hand by the time I'm done." Warrens said. An air of confidence swelled in his being, and bought some time to figure a way out.

"Fine. Have her," Iboee said as he shoved Gladys into Warrens' arms.

"It's okay Grandma, you're safe now," Warrens said.

"Jackson, why did you promise my life for millions of others?" Gladys whispered as she wept.

Warrens felt ice flow through his veins. His stare hardened on Iboee. "I'll need a workshop. Not some cheapskate tool shed where you store the acetylene tanks. I need a lab to test and to experiment. I have never seen a metal like this before."

"How dare you make demands from me!" Iboee snarled.

"You wanted a weapon out of this, a weapon of the gods right? Then I need the proper tools!" Warrens snapped as he held out the vibrating sphere. Iboee eyed the sphere, and his lip curled up into a sneer.

"Git into the railcar," Iboee ordered.

Under the leering, beady eyes of Iboee and his guards, Warrens studied the sphere. At times as he passed the sphere back and forth in his hands, it would 'melt,' pass through his fingers and reform wherever it landed. He noted in the back of his mind the mercurial properties of this melting orb. He wondered if he was handling a ball of mercury, which would explain why Iboee and his men dare not touch the substance.

"Why does it do that?" Iboee asked.

"I don't know. I need to experiment with it," Warrens replied, lost in thought. Iboee referred to this as a weapon, but there was nothing inherently dangerous about it in Warrens' mind.

"We approach our first stop in the provinces of Zimbabwe. I need to check on our factories. You help us here Mista Wahhens, make our shields stronger."

"Pardon?"

"The Dutch boy say you can make shields resist the shieldbreaker rounds. Teach my workers to do the same," Iboee commanded.

Iboee's guards escorted Warrens across the factory floor. His gaze froze as he saw girls as young as seven operating volatile Lepton Forges which churned out armor plates, ammunition and even assault rifles at such a dizzying pace. Warrens calculated they could manufacture as much in a week as what any Core factory could produce in three months at the height of the Unification Wars.

There was a trade off for such furious churning of war machines. Warrens inspected the quality of the armor plates and the rifles. They were slipshod at best. The weapons couldn't possibly handle the dramatic differences in climate throughout Africa. Therefore, it was better for the factories to produce vast quantity over high quality. Produce a lot of older, cheaper models rather than the fewer, more expensive designs which could last the duration of the war.

"Impressive yeah?" Iboee asked. "Diallo's empire make more weapons than any other! With you here Mista Wahhens, we will be unstoppable!"

"How many factories does Diallo have like this one?" Warrens asked.

"Twenty at least. All up the Trans-African railroad. Our enemies will be buried beneath steel while we conquer all we see!"

"Dear God," Gladys gasped under her breath. "Those poor children..." She reached out as though she wanted to help, but Iboee waved his pistol at her, signaling to keep her distance.

Warrens looked around and realized that this factory wasn't much different than Beckwell. His office was cleaner, and their machines sturdier, but at the root they were the same. This wasn't a legacy he wanted. He wanted justice, not slaughter.

"Where is a place I can work on this?" Warrens asked as he held out the orb in his hand.

"In da back," Iboee said with a nod of his head.

Warrens rolled up the filthy sleeves of his dress shirt, ignited a blowtorch and covered his face with a mask. The orb vibrated with such intensity that all of the tools nearby rattled against the workbench. He took the blow torch and held it against the sphere. The torch breathed its flame against the shimmering metal. A red glow simmered at the mouth of the torch, then spread through the middle and across the surface. The entire sphere became a small, twinkling star until it popped and spread into an orange pool of molten metal. The table and floor sizzled from the searing heat.

"Damn it!" Warrens screamed as he jumped back to avoid the spilling molten metal. It pooled and collected back into a sphere on the floor. Warrens held his hand just over the metal, it was still fiery hot to the touch. He put his briefcase on the ruined table, pulled out a notebook and opened to a blank page. Inside he wrote:

Experimentation Log Day 1

Substance: Unknown

A sphere of unknown metal and origin has come into my possession. My captors are scared of whatever this substance may be. Tested how to break by applying heat to the sphere. Sphere melted, but not due to heat. It has a habit of 'melting' at random intervals into a mercurial-like substance. Still managed to retain molten-level heat temperatures. Due to lack of carbon scores and burning of the metal, I believe that most of the impurities have already been burned out. My new sphere won't rust.

Warrens put the orb on the table to test when the orb would 'melt.' He grabbed a hammer, struck the orb on the table, and grunted in frustration as he felt a wave of pain shoot up his arm. The orb held completely intact without so much as a dent. Warrens grabbed his pencil:

Damn thing is solid as a rock now! My hammer didn't damage the sphere at all yet it melts into a pool of mercury. I need to see what makes this thing so...unstable.

Warrens picked up the orb and inspected it closely. His bones rattled as the orb vibrated in his hand.

"They all fear you, but I don't see how you can be a weapon," Warrens said. The orb vibrated until it melted down his arm.

"Gah!" Warrens screamed as he stumbled backwards and tried to shake the liquid metal off of him. The metal clung to his skin, molded into shape and hardened into a gauntlet on his arm that moved as elegantly as though it were a part of his flesh.

The gauntlet gleamed in the light. Warrens looked at the front and the back of his hand. The metal had molded itself into an intricate armored gauntlet and still bore a slight shimmer rather than a full-fledged vibration. He stared in amazement, until the gauntlet 'melted' off of his arm and reformed into a sphere on the ground.

"Damn it!" Warrens howled. He glared at the metal orb.

"C'mon, do it again!"

The orb vibrated like an idle engine on the floor.

Warrens picked up the sphere. "Please! Do it again!" The shimmering orb rattled in his hands.

"DAMN YOU, DO IT AGAIN!" He roared. His bellow echoed across the lab, and the orb melted in his hands and streamed down his arms.

"Finally!" He watched as the metal swirled around on his forearms and hardened into a pair of glistening gauntlets. He went to his journal.

The metal seems to respond to...thought. Wish I could explain how, but I'm not sure. If this thing breaks, I don't know if I can figure out how to fix it. Would I have to imagine it being fixed? So many questions.

"This stuff is incredible. It moves as fluid as water, yet it's as hard as..." Warrens paused. "I wonder how hard this stuff is..."

"Aauuurrrggghhh!" He screamed as he fell to his knees and pounded at the concrete floor with his fists. The gauntlets held, and there was a damning crater in front of him. He heard the door's locks on the outside being unlocked one by one.

"Oh no," Warrens whispered to himself. He willed the metal off of his skin. The metal released its form, dripped down his arms and pooled within the crater before re-forming into a sphere. He turned and grabbed his hammer right as the last lock was unlatched.

"What is going on in here?" Iboee screamed. His face was contorted into a mixture of confusion and anger as he glared at Warrens on the floor.

"Just tried to break it is all," Warrens said breathlessly.

"Don't break it, turn it into a weapon! Melt it down!" Iboee snarled.

"Yes sir. I'll try that," Warrens replied. Iboee turned and left, locking the ladder of locks behind him. Warrens looked around the room and noticed a small camera watching his every move. Or at least, made to look like it was watching him, otherwise Iboee would have noticed what Warrens did and eliminated him outright.

Warrens looked at the hammer in his hand. He placed his palm on the sphere and watched as the sphere melted into a pool of metal and reformed into a hammer that was a carbon copy of the one in his hand, save a metal handle instead of a wooden one.

"Incredible," He whispered. He heard a vicious clatter outside of the door. With his concentration broken, the hammer inverted back into the vibrating sphere. He stood up and went back to his notebook.

Appears that the substance requires concentrated will. Otherwise, it becomes liquefied. Don't think I'll have to worry much about fixing it or melting it down.

Terror spread like ice through his veins as he realized that he wielded an object that could mold into any form from a mere thought.

"If this got into the hands of Iboee or Diallo..." He whispered to himself. He looked around the room in panic. He couldn't break the metal, or cut it with a torch. For all intents and purposes, it seemed indestructible. The idea of a warlord getting their hands on this made Iboee's claim true: that this was a weapon of the gods.

And Warrens needed to learn how to wield it.

Warrens arranged his new laboratory to have a small area hidden from the prying eyes of the cameras. If these butchers were going to keep him alive, then he needed to make it look like he was churning out new devices for this factory to produce. Easy part was, they wanted the same technology that he produced while in service to the Core and employed at Beckwell. This gave the weapons master time to experiment.

He slammed his notebook on the table. A hollow echo rippled across the room which reminded him of how alone he was. His grandma was locked up in a cell, isolated from anyone who could help her. Sealed in a place where he couldn't protect her. His eyes burned in anger. He should've done more, he should've fought...

"No! Now is not the time!" He whispered to himself. "Now I need to figure a way out of this."

Warrens placed the sphere on the table. He watched the orb as it hummed against the steel. "If the metal could resist the impact of a hammer, maybe it can resist..." He trailed off and ran to the door. He pounded against the steel slab until he heard the locks click and stepped back.

The door screeched as it swung open while Iboee waltzed in with a pistol in one hand and a rifle in the other. Warrens held the sphere up and placed it on the floor.

"Iboee, I need you to shoot that thing," Warrens said.

"You learned what it made of?"

"Not yet. But with your help, this will further my research."

"Fine," Iboee replied. "Bullet or blaster?"

"Both. Bullet first." The moment the words left Warrens' mouth Iboee raised his pistol and fired at the sphere. Then he raised his blaster rifle and shot the sphere with a blaster bolt.

"Anything else?" Iboee asked.

"Yes, is there a chance you can get me a physics or quantum mechanics textbook?"

"What? Why?"

"This...metal has very strange properties that I as a mechanical engineer have never seen before. Although I have an idea, but I need one of those books to be sure. Or you can get me a computer that I can research on-"

"NO!" Iboee snapped. "You are here to make me weapons, not read! You work, make my shields better!"

"Iboee, I can fix anything, but in order to make this metal work I need to -"

"You figure it out soon Wahhens or your grandmommy not going to look so good. Dinner coming soon, but if you keep talking, dinner for her may not show up."

Warrens swallowed hard. He knew deep down that with one hit he could knock Iboee out. Hell, if he hit hard enough he could kill the imp outright. However there were other men just outside the door, armed and willing to shoot him if he so much as gave them a funny look. His grandmother was in imminent danger as well. No, Warrens needed to bide his time and strike when the moment was right.

"Do you think you can find a handheld metal spectrometer so that I can analyze what this orb is made of? It'll help me replicate it for you," Warrens said.

Iboee glared at Warrens. Those dark, impish eyes pierced through the fiber of his being. He could feel the malice leak through, the urge to kill, the unquenchable bloodlust. Iboee's eerie silence lingered like a bloodthirsty specter in the room, but Warrens didn't utter a word.

"Very well, I'll see what I can find," Iboee finally replied. He turned and left the lab without uttering another word. The door slammed shut and the locks sealed Warrens in.

He ran up to the sphere. He looked at the humming orb on the floor which didn't possess an indentation or carbon mark of any kind. The lead slug lied only a couple of metres away, pancaked by its effort from attempting to damage the sphere. He picked up the bullet, the sphere and placed both on the table. There was a slight burn mark from the blaster bolt, but that could be wiped away with ease.

Substance seems borderline indestructible. Bulletproof, blasterproof, but retains the heat from the blaster bolt. Don't believe this will fare well if I wear it as armor. Wouldn't wanna be roasted alive.

Warrens held a magnet next to the sphere. The magnet flew out of his hand and latched onto the orb.

Substance is magnetic. This leads to one of three possibilities of what it's made of: Iron, Nickel or Cobalt.

Warrens looked up at the flickering fluorescent lights. His eyelids were heavy and his eyes were strained. He needed to rest. The day had been long, but he worried about his grandmother. In his mind he reasoned that if they hurt her, they had no leverage against him, but Iboee and his ilk weren't reasonable.

Warrens crawled onto a steel slab that was acting as his bed for the duration of his captivity. His thoughts dwelled on his grandma. He wondered how she was doing, how the guards were treating her, whether they were feeding her. He tried to sleep, but it remained as elusive as the spirits of his parents. He prayed to all the heavens and appealed to the ghosts of his parents to protect Gladys.

Experimentation Log: Day 5

I received the spectrometer and have run the orb through a battery of tests. It appears that the sphere is composed of not only of titanium and nickel, it also contains gold, silver, mercury, lead, silicone, carbon and a variety of other alloys. What's also curious is the range of materials are contained within. There's plastic polymers so sophisticated, we haven't even begun research into them. What I can't understand is the random melting of these assorted materials.

Perhaps the vibration is the key...

Iboee stormed into the laboratory. His eyes betrayed fury. They were glassy, drug-crazed and malicious. Warrens willed the sphere into a shield which could be worn on the shoulder.

"Mista Wahhens you lazy piece of -"

"Iboee, I am so glad you're here!" Warrens cheered. "I was able to figure out the composition of the sphere and replicate it into this shield for you to produce." Warrens tore out a sheet of paper from his notebook and scribbled down a list of metals and their amounts.

"Here are the materials you'll need to produce your own. They're mostly carbon, which is what a majority of that orb is made of," Warrens lied to his captor. "I'll get the instructions to produce these with the printers."

Warrens watched those bloodshot eyes. Iboee's drug-induced haze had him teetering on an edge. He would either praise Warrens as a genius, or shoot him on the spot. Warrens readied himself in case the imp was feeling violent.

"About time you produced something. Next time, give us guns," Iboee said as he snatched the materials list out of Warrens' hand.

Iboee turned to leave.

"Can I see my grandmother...please?" Warrens asked. Iboee whipped around, his glassy eyes on the verge of shattering.

"You make demands from me?" He snapped.

"No sir! I just want to know if my grandmother is okay!" Warrens realized that he had pushed too far. Making requests from a drug crazed man, what was he thinking?

Iboee held up his pistol.

Warrens hid behind his shield.

Iboee fired a round which struck the shield with a dull echo. He fired, again and again, laughing maniacally until his pistol clicked from being emptied.

Warrens looked around. There were pieces of lead scattered nearby, bullets which failed to pierce his shield.

"Oyyya-yyaaayyy!" Iboee screamed. "Your shield work perfectly Mista Wahhens!" He laughed as he sauntered out of the laboratory.

Warrens felt the harsh sting of defeat well within. He wished he could be near his grandmother. Help her. Comfort her. Instead he had been shot at by his captor while hiding behind a shield.

Warrens walked to his workbench. "Let's see what you can really do," He muttered to himself. He placed the shield on the table and held his hand over the metal. When he opened his eyes, the metal had morphed into a pistol. He grasped the pistol on his hands and searched for an ammunition clip. The empty clip he found slid into the pistol perfectly. He pulled the trigger, and recognized the sound of an empty hammer immediately.

"Maybe I do have a prayer," He said to himself.

Experimentation Log: Day 8

Been able to "call" the pistol for three days in a row now. Just need a loaded clip to test if my gun will actually fire. I've also noticed that the metal never vibrates while in a form other than the sphere. There we also limitations to what it can change to. I've been able to make this metal into a shovel, armor plates, a gun, bullets, a spear and a few other simple machines, but that is all. I cannot explain what causes this. Need to analyze the orb in depth to knock out this problem.

"Okay. Different tact, time to switch things up this match," Warrens said to the throbbing sphere in front of him. He reached to the sphere and pictured an engine block and all of the components contained within. The amorphous metal separated and formed into the differing components, creating an engine block before his eyes.

The sound of the clicking locks broke Warrens' concentration, and he released the metal back into its primary state.

The door opened, and Iboee walked in. His eyes were clearer now, but his brow was covered in sweat.

"We're moving out. Pack up. I've got more factories for you to inspect."

Warrens nodded, picked up the sphere and walked out with Iboee. The guards were holding Gladys, who didn't look like she'd eaten well.

"Jackson!" Gladys screamed when she saw her grandson. She tried to break away from the guards, but they restrained her.

"C'mon Iboee. Let me see her. She can't hurt them," Warrens

argued. Iboee flashed a look of irritation, but nodded for the guards to let her go. She ran over, still in her nightgown and hugged her towering grandson.

"Alright, enough. To the train," Iboee ordered.

The train was as Warrens remembered it. Wood paneling, gold trim, crystal glassware, all the fine trappings reminding someone that they're inside the railcar of a lost King from a lineage praised for enslaving a continent.

"Did you serve in the Unification Wars Iboee?" Warrens asked as the group took a seat.

"We all deed," Iboee replied. "Diallo and I were part of the 721st, the Africa Corps, and this one time, we were ordered to ambush this group of rebel scum and they poopoo themselves when we attack!" Iboee cackled. "They begged for mercy, but Diallo order us to hack them to pieces!"

Warrens felt his stomach churn. He also felt Gladys pushing against his shoulder. "Excuse me," She finally said. Warrens slid out of the seat to let her by. She covered her mouth and rushed into one of the bedrooms on the railcar. Warrens tried to follow, but one of the guards blocked his path.

"Let me go to her. Please!" He pleaded.

"Aye, let him go. Nothing he can do here," Iboee said. The guard stepped aside and Warrens went into the bathroom.

"I can't stand it! I can't stand these savages any longer!" Gladys cried.

"Grandma, I'm getting you out of here as soon as I can."

"No! I don't want you working for these monsters a minute longer!"

"Grandma, they will hurt you if I don't follow orders."

"I don't care! Better my life than the countless millions they're killing all in the name of some dictator!"

"Grandma, I can fix this. I can make everything right."

"HOW?!"

"I am making a weapon. One that will-"

"What good is another weapon, even against them? You're no better than they are Jackson!"

"But Grandma-"

"But nothing Jackson! I can't even look at your right now! Get out of here!" Gladys screamed as she waved her hand. Warrens' heart felt as though a burning dagger had plunged through and was being twisted. He'd never seen his dear grandmother so upset. He wanted to fix the situation, but he didn't know how. Humans weren't like an engine with gaskets that you could pull out, clean or replace. The intimidating mechanic sheepishly turned around, exited the bathroom, and left his grandma to cry in peace.

Back on the train, the wilderness outdoors turned from savannah to jungle within minutes. Warrens stared out the window, trying to admire the scenery. There was a deafening silence aboard the train. Iboee leaned back and rested his eyes while the guards stood on silent watch over Gladys' in the bathroom.

The skies split and sheets of rain hammered against the train. The brakes squealed and the railcar began to slow down. Iboee jumped from his slumber and looked around in panic. "Go find out why we stopping," Iboee ordered one of the guards. He walked in the stride of a disciplined soldier into the sleeting rain.

The guard talked to a man in civilian clothes, who brandished an assault rifle and made choppy gestures in his attempt to portray a warrior. Their conversation was brief. The guard turned around and marched back onto the train. His heavy boots clicked against the laminate and he stopped before Iboee, his face a neutral canvas.

"Well?! Out wit it!" Iboee yelled.

"Dey's want tribute," the guard responded

Iboee became infuriated and jumped from his seat. "S'cuse me Mista Wahhens," Iboee said as he barged through the aisleway. He drew his pistol, marched outside and screamed in an ancient tongue at the armed civilian. He waved his gun around, and got right in the man's face.

The man mouthed a string incoherent phrases, which only ignited Iboee's short fuse. He stepped forward and shot the man under his jaw. Warrens' heart erupted in his chest.

Iboee came back in, and stomped his way through the train. He stopped to speak with the guard. "Tell the engineer not to stop if there are any more jungle bandits demanding money!" He hissed. "Tell him to run dem over!"

As they rode through the villages, Warrens recoiled at the carnage that ravaged the landscape. Diallo, Okafor and Akiloye's forces had left a visceral wound on the psyche of Africa. People walked with crutches on only one leg, and children cradled bloody stumps where their hands used to be. As far as the eyes could see there were innocent people maimed and disfigured by the brutality of this new civil war. It was as if an ancient hatred had been suppressed beneath the surface for centuries, and the fall of Enai unleashed this monster upon the continent.

Warrens tried to close his eyes and sleep, but he couldn't shake the images of the maimed from his vision. This was what building weapons had gotten him. Companies like Beckwell Defense may not have made weapons for warlords such as the three, but he couldn't stem the flow into the secondhand markets. He realized that he had a new mission: to root out the cancer that infected Africa's heart. He had to do what the Core wouldn't. He had to eliminate all three African warlords and allow the Core a chance to install a more peaceful leader.

Warrens felt the familiar vibration in his pocket from the mysterious orb. He knew deep in the marrow of his bones that this was the weapon which would end Africa's civil war. How this would be done, he had no idea.

After countless hours on the gilded train, the bell whistled, and the train started to slow.

"Ah! The next factory! Come Mista Wahhens, you can build me some real guns here!" Iboee said as he flashed his impish grin.

The guards escorted Warrens and Gladys to a small saffron house. It was a grimy building where the concrete walls were painted a nauseating yellow. Those same walls glowed as the sun set behind them. Warrens notice the sand around the house, which to him meant they must be on the edge of the desert.

"Ah, New Nubia! Homeland to Enai Karakhoum our greatest King!" Iboee screamed with the glee of a child. "Now we reclaim it for Diallo." Iboee waved to the Southeast where a warehouse belched smoke into the sky. The guards unlocked the door to the yellow house and led each member of the Warrens family into a holding cell.

"I will go check an' see if they is ready for you Mista Wahhens," Iboee said, his words full of needles. He turned and left the two guards inside to watch over Warrens and his grandmother.

A wall of bars separated the two of them. Warrens slumped as he walked burdened with shame over to his grandmother. "Grandma, I am so sorry about all of this," He whispered.

His grandmother walked over, put her hands through the iron bars and cupped his face. "Jackson, none of this is your fault," she said as she gently stroked his cheek.

"Yes it is. If I keep working for them...thousands...millions will die," Warrens choked out as tears streamed down his face.

"You my dear boy, are the Da Vinci of our time. You will come up with something to save us. I know you will. I have total faith."

"What do you think Dad would do in this situation?"

"He'd bide his time and wait for the right moment. Bud was very patient, just like you need to be. Your time will come Jackson." Gladys sounded frail, but her voice became steel whenever she praised Warrens or his father.

Iboee waltzed into the house. "They say they be ready for you in the morning Mista Wahhens."

"What about a lab where I can work?" Warrens asked.

"What's wrong with here?"

"Well, I don't have a bench, tools, my workbook-"

"Oh, that alright. We brought your notebook here," Iboee said as one of the guards held up Warrens' notebook. A chill scattered up his spine. Iboee and his men now had access to his notes on the weapon. If they had discovered how to wield it...

"Iké read through these notes. Why you record so little?" Iboee asked.

"I suppose I-"

"Don't matter. What I need to know is can you make more of dat weapon?"

"I gave you instructions Iboee."

"You gave me a list of materials. Now we need assembly instructions."

"I'll need to test for proper assembly. If you give me a lab-"

"All this testing! Test this! Test that! Why you need to keep testing?"

"Because it's unstable! The vibration is something I can't replicate unless I do more research! If I'm to rebuild this weapon for you Iboee, I need to know everything about it, not just what it's made of."

Iboee stared hard at the notebook. "What is your theory?"

"What do you mean? I -"

Iboee pulled out a pistol, cocked it and held it to Gladys' forehead. "What do you think make it vibrate? Unless you think I'm stupid."

"No! Never Iboee! I wonder...I wonder if it's fourth dimensional metal."

"Hmm...interesting. How do you know this?"

"I'm not certain, but I remember hearing about this concept in a physics of metal lecture. To be certain, I need access to a computer."

Iboee thought for a moment. "Iké go with you. He watch all you search."

"Fine. Done," Warrens nodded. He may have made a deal with the devil, but he needed to know what he was dealing with.

"Good. First thing in the morning then," Iboee said as he holstered his pistol inside his jacket. He and the guards left the small house in solemn silence. Warrens looked to Gladys, who was still rife with gloom as she took a seat on the metal bench.

"Go, get some sleep. Don't worry about me Jackson, I'll be fine," Gladys said. Her voice was flat and empty. Warrens held his head down in shame and mourned for all those soon to be lost at his hand. He pulled the orb from his pocket. He noticed the lock on his cell door. He walked up to the door and willed for the orb to transform into a key.

The orb didn't change its shape.

Warrens willed even harder and gave his full concentration. The orb remained stagnate in his hands.

"Guess even you have your limits," He said to the orb as he walked back to his bench. He felt his eyelids grow heavy from the day. He was far more tired than he realized. He lied down on the bench and tried to sleep.

Iboee opened the rusty door the next morning with his usual escorts. "Iké, take Mista Wahhens to the computer. Let him do his research."

"What about breakfast?" Warrens asked.

"When you work, you eat. Dat is the deal," Iboee replied with a chill in his voice.

Iké escorted Warrens to an office with a computer inside. The office reeked of oil and had jet-colored streaks all over the walls. To Warrens, this was home.

He sat down at the computer as it prepared for his search query. Iké slapped Warrens' notebook down in front of him, along with a pen, then took a defiant stance behind him. As the computer loaded, Warrens reached into his pocket, pulled out the orb and placed it on the desk. The computer's projection shimmered and became unstable.

"What did you do?" Iké asked.

"I...uh...nothing. Shouldn't these computers be..." Warrens gazed at the orb. He opened up his notebook and took out his pen.

Experimentation Log Day 10

Substance is electromagnetic. Interferes with electronics. That means it interacts with electronics. I wonder if I could rig something up where the computer and the substance can 'speak' to one another.

"Cut it out!" Iké hissed. He grabbed the orb and pulled it away. The computer screen immediately stopped flickering.

"Where you gonna search?" Iké asked.

"There's a place which holds a massive database of scientific discoveries and other black market data. Known as 'The Grid.' Is that alright?"

Iké cracked his knuckles. "Yeah, it alright." Iké was about the same size as Warrens, so his intimidation ploy wouldn't work on the boxer.

Warrens researched and read one scientific paper after another regarding metals and physics until he found one which dived in depth about the theory of metals and substances from the fourth dimension. He got out his pen and scribbled in his notebook.

Incredible! According to the description here, this metal is constantly vibrating because it exists in multiple dimensions at once! It also vibrates due to the fact that fourth dimensional metal is apparently in all states of existence at once. That means the metal will take the form of everything it has ever been throughout its entire span of existence. It also states in here that the fourth dimension removes all "effort" from the equation, which explains how I can "think" an item into existence. The only thing I'm not finding is how I can create-

Warrens' pen stopped in the middle of the page. He sat there, frozen in fear. He could feel the poison from when he'd bitten the apple of knowledge circulating through his blood. This substance, this orb, the great weapon couldn't possibly be replicated. It was an object from another dimension, one that he couldn't accurately experience, let alone replicate. The sphere existed in every state at once.

"It's like energy. Can't be created or destroyed. It just...exists," Warrens whispered to himself.

"What?" Iké asked.

"Oh, nothin' just solving a problem out loud," Warrens replied. He kept a cool front, but inside he was collapsing. If Iboee found out that the orb couldn't be replicated...Warrens would be executed on the spot. He needed something, anything to save his hide.

Warrens looked to a nearby cord on the desk. It was a standard plug, one used for the most antique machines. Cords meant communication, and he'd already discovered that the orb could interact with computers. He took the cord into his hand.

"Iké, may I?" Warrens asked as he motioned for the orb.

Iké looked confused, but he held the sphere up to Warrens. He touched the sphere with his finger, and a dock formed before his eyes. He plugged the cord into the sphere, and waited to see if the screen would change. The screen flickered for a moment, but then a window flashed open. Thousands of lines of code spilled down the window, a waterfall of instructions being uploaded to the device.

"What did you do?!" Iké screamed.

"It's...uploading data," Warrens replied.

"Make it stop!" Iké screamed as he ripped the cord out of the sphere. The screen froze in place. Warrens looked at the screen up close, the coding language as foreign to him as the thousands of indigenous languages across Africa. He took his pen to his notepad.

Confirmed: the device can communicate with computers. It's...programmable.

Iké seized Warrens by the arm and dragged him out of the office. Warrens was so transfixed by what had happened, he barely noticed Iké dragging him. As Iké dragged Warrens through the complex, the orb melted through his fingers.

"Damn it!" Iké snarled as he tried to pick up the sphere. His fingers couldn't grasp the metal in its liquefied state. "What is wrong with dis?!" He screamed.

Warrens reached down and touched the metal. It hardened back into the orb, which allowed him to grab and carry it. Iké rolled his eyes in frustration as he dragged Warrens back to his holding cell. In his haste, Iké threw Warrens into his cell, and slammed the iron gate shut without confiscating the notebook or the orb. He stormed off to find Iboee.

"What happened?" Gladys asked.

"I discovered a way to fix everything grandma. We'll be outta the ring in not time. Baloo out there was too dumb to take these away, and I know what I need to experiment with this little devil," He said as he held up the orb.

The door squealed as it opened, like a stuck pig. Iboee, Iké and the second guard stood in the doorway, shadows that displaced the sun. "Bring him," Iboee ordered to Iké.

Iké waltzed in, opened the door and dragged Warrens out. Any sense of fair treatment to Warrens before this point had been lost. There was a new anger rooted in his captor's movements. They led Warrens to a warehouse stockpiled with weapons, armor and other vestiges of the Unification Wars.

Inside the warehouse there were benches, a welding station, a mobile fabricator, even an eyewash station. The warehouse was grimy. The oil smeared walls combined with poor lighting gave the warehouse a sinister feel. One lone ceiling fan spun lazily, and did nothing to alleviate the stifling heat.

"We...treat you quite well wouldn't you say Mista Wahhens?" Iboee asked.

"Sure. You threaten my grandma hourly, kill anyone who offends you, you-"

"I asked about you Wahhens," Iboee said with his impish grin.

"I suppose I'd say that I've been treated fairly," He replied.

"Then why do you communicate with the outside world? Why do you give away your position when I do everything in my power to make you as comfortable as I can? Do you not like my gifts?" Iboee asked.

"Iboee, what are you talking about?"

"I talking about the data you uploaded onto that server. Iké saw what you did. You take my kindness and spit on it!"

"I did no such thing! I didn't know the device would upload data! I didn't know that it had data to upload!"

"Then why do you think it do this?"

"I have no idea Iboee! That's what I've been wondering! It's like any file drive, you plug it in and data is uploaded!"

"Still, my security has been breached! You have given the location of my munitions factory away, and you've failed to produce the weapon you promised to me."

"It's been ten days Iboee!"

"And I thought a genius like you could figure it out in seven. Normally I would kill for such failure, but you still have value Mista Wahhens. I still put you to work. Welcome to your new home!" Iboee said as he held out his arms.

"What?" Warrens gasped.

"Take the weapon from him. We figure it out on our own," Iboee ordered the guards. Warrens couldn't believe what was happening. He was going to be forced into slave labor. The room began to spin, and the air became hazy. Warrens shook his head and tried to regain his bearings.

"What about my grandma?" Warrens yelled as his notebook and the device were confiscated.

"You work, she live. Best deal you going to get," Iboee said, his words laced with ice.

"You can't do this!" Warrens howled. He struck his captors who were seizing his property. Iké recovered, removed a syringe from his jacket and plunged it Warrens shoulder.

The lumbering mechanic felt his legs grow weak. He collapsed right as his world faded to black.

Even with his indomitable strength, the chains felt heavy on Warrens' wrists and neck. For the past eighteen months labored in chains and was forced to assemble weapons of mass destruction with his bare hands. He dragged a nuclear core encased in lead from one end of the warehouse to the other while Iké just stood and watched. Warrens glared at the guard but his eyes were covered by sunglasses which protected him from witnessing the cruelty of Warrens' captivity. His clothes were tattered rags, oil was a permanent fixture to his skin and his skin had been worn raw from the chains.

Once Warrens secured the nuclear core inside of the missile, he approached Iké. His chains only allowed him to make it halfway to the door.

"We're going to need a motherboard for all of the missiles. A nuclear arsenal isn't much use if you can't control where they go," Warrens said. Even he heard the echo of defeat in his voice.

"I'll tell the boss," Iké replied.

The door squeaked open and Iboee walked in. "Oyyy-yaaaayyy!" He screamed as he held his arms up again in triumph. Diallo's forces must've won another battle. Whether he liked it or not, Warrens had shifted the tide of the war into Diallo's favor.

"Mista Wahhens, yah workin' hard?" Iboee asked. Iké leaned over and whispered something into his ear. "Yah, we can do that," Iboee replied. Mista Wahhens, are you ready for another boxing match?"

"Iboee, I've been moving missile cores all day, I'm in no shape for-"

"That is why I feed you so good! I don't feed other workers as good!" Iboee snarled. "You entertain de soldiers! Fight is tonight!"

Warrens stumbled across the floor the following morning. He was tired, bruised, and bloody. A shadow of his glory days. Forced to fight soldiers before they shipped out, Iboee had bets placed on all the fights, which only resulted in the soldiers using Warrens as a punching bag. He didn't care though. His mind was focused on how he was going to escape, on how he was going to right all the wrongs done by these savages. He didn't know how, but he had faith.

For three days Warrens' wounds healed as he built the war machines which fueled Diallo's armies. On the fourth day, Iké came in with an envelope.

"Parts you wanted. Hard to get. Don't screw it up."

Warrens glared at Iké. Not like it did him any good. He took the envelope, tore it open and spilled the contents on the table. He reached for the instruction manual which described how to solder the motherboard together. However, there was a small computer in the midst of the chips. There was also a note:

Mr. Warrens,

Came across your upload at The Grid. This should help you with your...device and grant you exclusive access. Best of luck setting yourself free.

-A Friend

Warrens' heart nearly burst through his chest. If he was caught with a small computer such as this one, Iboee would execute him for certain. He crumpled the note and shoved it into his tattered pocket. He took the circuit boards and installed them into the nuclear missiles. He could hardly believe that he was helping Diallo develop a nuclear arsenal, but he had no choice. The Core wouldn't see things the same way, but he figured that he'd deal with the authorities once they actually got involved.

"Tell Iboee it's done," Warrens said. Iké nodded his head and left the Warehouse. Warrens inspected the handheld computer. It didn't look like much more than a small pane of glass, but he had to believe it would give him a fighting chance. He turned the computer over, and noticed the word "Coeus" inscribed on the back.

The glass screen flashed to life. "Please place thumbprint here," a humble, robotic voice asked. Warrens looked at his thumb, but did as the computer asked.

"Thank you...Jackson...Warrens. You are now the exclusive wielder of Coy-us," the device said. "Ready for synchronization."

"Synchronization?" Warrens asked himself. He heard the

door and pocketed Coeus before Iboee and the guards came in.

"Mista Wahhens, Iké say you finished my missiles?"

"Yes I have," Warrens replied. He stood straight and defiant despite his muscles begging him not to.

"Good. Now that Diallo have nucleah ahsenal, he can sue for peace!" Iboee screamed.

A searing whistle outside made Warrens dive for the floor. An explosion rocked the warehouse and flames engulfed the roof. The spectre of war had descended upon the supply camp through artillery fire and rocketry.

"It's Akiloye and the South African Liberation Front!" Iké howled. Gunfire erupted across the camp as a wave of soldiers clad in jungle green camo descended like jackals for the kill.

"The missiles! Get them out of here! Wahhens too!" Iboee screamed in the midst of gunfire and smoke. The fire was consuming the building, a ravenous beast that wouldn't stop until everything was ash.

"Iboee, I can help! Give me a gun!" Warrens pleaded. Iké ran up and unlocked Warrens from his chains. The pair ran for the door to the warehouse, while Iboee and the other guard opened fire against the SALF forces. The grinding sound of tanks followed as they opened fire on the nearby warehouses, where innocent civilians poured out in a mass of hysteria to escape the guns of the enemy.

"Iké I can help! I was a soldier too!" Warrens growled.

"It's not your ability to fight Warrens, it's your loyalty," Iké replied. Behind them, Warrens heard the men inside load the tank's main gun.

"Get down!" He screamed as he pulled Iké to the dirt. The train car that Iboee had been using as refuge exploded in an encapsulating fireball of wood and gilded metal. Fireballs fell from the sky, until Warrens recognized one of the items that landed in front of him. It was the orb, still pulsing like he remembered it. He crawled forward and reached out to seize the sphere into his hand. Once he made contact, the metal melted and slithered across his skin.

Iké came to and looked up in stunned horror at the fully

armored figure that rose in front of him.

"My turn," Warrens said from beneath the gunmetal gray armor.

"Synchronization initiated," the robotic voice said. Warrens looked beneath his forearm. There was Coeus, his handheld computer synchronizing with the fourth dimensional metal.

Warrens reached down, grabbed Iké by the throat and held the giant aloft. Iké slapped at the metal arm as hard as he could, but couldn't break the grip. Warrens didn't feel a thing.

"This is for holding me hostage!" Warrens growled as he snapped Iké's neck. The man went limp, and Warrens discarded him like a rag doll.

Multiple SALF soldiers saw Warrens and opened fire on him. The bullets bounced off the armor, while Warrens reached down, snagged a gun from a fallen soldier and opened fire on them. After three soldiers fell, their resolve broke, and they turned tail. One by one Warrens used the ferromagnetic material within his armor to pick up the discarded guns. Then he placed them on his armor, while the fourth dimensional metal fused itself to the rifles and created a seamless immersion between armor and weapon.

The two tanks turned their guns on Warrens. They fired their shells, but he kept walking, unfazed by the display of aggression. One of the soldiers had left behind an energy blaster. Warrens picked it up, and merged it with his armor underneath his right arm. The fourth dimensional metal seemed to swallow everything it touched.

He held out his palm and fired the energy blasts at the tanks, dislodging their treads. They were dead in the sand. More soldiers charged for him, but he kept shooting from the more than half a dozen guns embedded in his armor.

As the soldiers fell, the tanks whirred up to fire again. Warrens heard the soldiers load the main gun, the all to familiar clank echo across the battlefield.

"Drones en route," The robotic voice said.

"Can't you take control of them?"

"My programming was to help you secure control of the

armor. I could access the utilities of your armor and make *you* take control of the drones sir."

"Yes! Do that! Coy...uh..."

"It's pronounced 'Coy-us' sir."

"Too complicated to remember. I'll call you Cal. Yeah, Cal." Warrens felt a new presence in his mind. It was as if he could detect new sensations on the edges of his vision. He felt light headed for a moment, but then his perception was greater than ever before. He realized the airlessness was him feeling the connection of the drones overhead.

"Sir, you're now in control of drones overhead."

"Holy shit," Warrens said. "Locking on to two Rommel Series tanks..." He saw the targeting systems appear through his eyes and as he glared at the tanks, the systems locked on.

The battlefield grew silent as everyone held their breath. The lead tank fired at Warrens. He blocked with his arms and was launched backwards from the explosion, but he was unfazed. Two missiles rained down from the sky overhead, one for each tank. The tanks were engulfed in a devastating fireball as two more missiles screamed through the sky and obliterated whatever remained.

As the dust settled, all of the warehouses were either in flames or leveled. Bodies littered the landscape. Innocent workers lie massacred, their only crime having been working for the wrong warlord.

"Synchronization complete. Congratulations Mr. Warrens, you are the only human who can now wield this weapon," Coeus said. Warrens wasn't sure what the computer meant by that.

"WAHHENS!" A voice screamed behind him. It was Iboee and his other guard who were holding Gladys at gunpoint. Tracks from their eyes revealed their tears since both of the men were covered in ash. Warrens recognized the gaze from one he'd seen in Gladys' eyes as well as his own. It was an emotion imposed on the two by Iboee: fear.

Warrens thought long and hard to himself. He could end this. End Iboee and his guard, take Gladys and fly away to safety. It would be so easy to kill the two men.

No.

That wouldn't end the war. That wouldn't protect the people of Africa. If Warrens was to accomplish his end goal, he'd have to surrender to the imp one last time.

"Thanks for your help Cal, but I'm going to need to eject you," Warrens mumbled. The armor popped his computer out and slid the device into the palm of his hand. The guns fell off of his frame and the metal retracted from his body and reformed itself into the vibrating sphere.

Warrens slid the computer into his pocket, hoping against hope that neither Iboee nor the guard saw it. He walked up to them slowly, holding the orb in front of him.

"Please, don't hurt her. I beg you," Warrens said as tears formed in his eyes. He was both anguished and relieved that his grandmother was still alive.

Warrens approached Iboee and handed him the orb. He shoved it into his pocket, while a sadistic grin spread across his ashen face.

"Abdul, go help him load up the nucleah missiles. We're taking them to Egypt, as well as this weapon here. Diallo will be able to sue for peace now," Iboee said.

Warrens held his grandma close for three days as the convoy closed in on the pyramids. The separation had been hard on her. She looked frail, tired and weak. Gladys spent most of the trip asleep in her grandson's arms.

Iboee hung up his comm device. "Diallo be pleased! He would love to meet the man who made it all possible. You get to meet Diallo Mista Wahhens! Oyy-yeeehhhaaayyy!" He held his arms up in triumph.

As the convoy closed in on Cairo, a massive, ornate palace came into view. It was a vibrant palace, lush with color. A gift from the Russian Federation to Enai for allowing the Russians to come in and mine his continent for resources. Since then, the Palace has been the heart of African authority and the home of Enai's lineage.

It's also the palace Diallo had claimed for himself.

The three day trip through Africa left its mark: devastated villages, maimed innocents, and razed landscapes. The plight of these innocent people steeled Warrens' resolve to end this Civil War once and for all.

Cairo was a city burgeoning with industry. Cranes towered the skyline, factories churned out machines, all a ploy to showcase Diallo's grandeur as the leader of Africa.

Gladys and Warrens were escorted into a plush bedroom within the palace. Their tattered clothes made them stand out in the midst of luxury, the opulence of their surroundings threatened to overwhelm the senses.

The room had a televisor, which displayed looped feed of the fighting between the three African forces. Images of the dead, the wounded, the displaced, the vicious, the hopeful and those who'd lost everything filled the screen. Warrens felt a blanket of grief overcome him. The despair boiled over, and for the first time since his capture, he wept.

He mourned for all of the deaths he'd caused. All the men, women and children. Sons and daughters, mothers, fathers, aunts, uncles, brothers, sisters, grandparents, all who died on the continent from this ravenous civil war. Gladys shuffled over, put her hand on his shoulder, and rubbed it gently.

"I killed them Grandma. I've killed so many…" He said in between sobs.

Gladys' misty eyes looked at the screen. She tightened her lips together, a gesture she used when she had something to say, but didn't want to say it.

"What is it Grandma?" He asked.

"Jackson...none of those people would've died if you'd just let me go!"

"Grandma! How can you say that? I would do anything to protect you! You raised me!"

"Jackson! My time is over! I have seen enough carnage wrought by these savages! And it tears me apart watching you build weapons for those animals. All because you had to be selfish and only worry about yourself!"

Warrens recoiled in horror at his grandmother's words. He'd never heard her talk like this before. He'd thought he'd been doing the right thing by protecting her.

Gladys rubbed Warrens' shoulder again. "I don't mean to hurt you sweetie, but it tears me apart to see one of the greatest minds of our time toiling as a slave to protect me. You were supposed to launch us into a new technological age, not slaughter innocent people."

Warrens sat in quiet contemplation, mincing over his grandma's words. He rose to his feet and towered over his grandma. "I will protect them grandma, no more innocent people will die, including you."

"Don't worry about me Jackson. Save the people of Africa from these brutes. You said you have a plan didn't you?"

"I do grandma, but I need to get ahold of the fourth dimensional metal. It's my only chance to knock them all out at once."

"What does that thing even do?" Gladys asked.

"It's metal that exists in all states at once. It can become anything it ever has been or ever will be through thought. And it makes other machines become a part of me. It can control every device in its presence and they all become an extension of my being."

"Huh?" Gladys asked. "I'm a simple woman Jackson, you'll need to explain it better than that."

"Sorry grandma," Warrens replied. "Let me put it this way. With Cal here, I can program the metal to become anything I need it to," he said as he pulled the computer out of his pocket.

"How does that work?"

"To be honest, I have no idea, but someone's out there watching over us."

"They need to do a better job since we've been locked up for over a year and a half."

The bedroom door squeaked open, and Iboee slid in. "Diallo would like to meet the man who made peace possible. Mista Wahhens, get yourself cleaned up, help yourself to some clothes and be ready. Dinnah is in thirty minutes." Iboee sneaked out and closed the door as quietly as he came in.

"I can't stomach the idea of you dining with that beast! I won't have it!"

"Grandma, if my plan is to work, then I need to dine with the devil."

"Doesn't mean I have to like it!"

"No grandma, you don't."

Iboee escorted Warrens to the Presidential Hall, the seat of the African Continental Government. Diallo seemed to have all of the assets necessary to begin rule under a new family dynasty. Warrens felt a chill run up his spine, he could almost hear the screams from both elephant and man with all of the ivory and gold trim that blanketed the walls. The floor was cut from marble which made their shoes click.

In the main dining hall, there was a lone figure who feasted on smoky meats and bright fruits, and was flanked by two guards. His hands labored under the weight of his rings and decadent cuts as he sliced the tender flesh and brought it between his lips. He noticed the two men approach, wiped the juices off his chin and stood up to greet the pair.

"Please forgive me. The food was growing cold and I couldn't resist," Diallo said in a velvet voice. It was pleasing to the ears, full of charisma that could entrance the most stern men. Warrens couldn't believe that a man with such a luscious voice could be a brutal warlord who razed an entire continent. Three scars on his cheek wriggled like worms as he spoke, which broke the spell for Warrens. He had to concentrate on the scars.

"Mighty Diallo, the next leadah of a United Africa. Peace be upon you," Iboee said as he embraced the dictator. Diallo noticed Warrens standing behind Iboee.

"And is this the man who made a United Africa possible?" Diallo asked.

"He be. Diallo, meet Mista Wahhens," Iboee said as he extended his hand.

"I cannot praise you enough Mr. Warrens. If it wasn't for you, peace wouldn't be possible in Africa," Diallo said as he extended his hand for a handshake. Warrens felt like a hot knife had been stabbed into his guts and was being twisted. The last thing he wanted to do was shake the hand of this monster, but he needed Diallo's trust.

Warrens gripped Diallo's hand tight. "I did it to protect my grandmother, the woman who raised me."

"My apologies for resorting to such tactics Mr. Warrens, but I have an empire to rebuild and I needed to ensure that you would work. A technical man such as yourself understands that we need to know how to make things tick. I do the same thing, but with people. I knew that your grandmother would make you work, that you would push yourself to new limits, and create the weapon that will bring me total victory," Diallo said as he pulled a metal orb Warrens knew all too well from his pocket. He felt like molten steel was being poured into his stomach.

"You two must be hungry. Come, sit and eat," Diallo motioned to the chairs at the table. The three men sat down to the table, which had a gold trim along the edges, and a spotless white tablecloth. Waiters marched like a civil army from the kitchen, and brought trays of glassware, wine, coffee, flaky pastries and other decadent foods to eat.

"Iboee, please tell me about how Mr. Warrens repelled the Akiloye's forces," Diallo asked.

"Ah it was magnificent Diallo! He walked out like a bull elephant, using that metal there as armor. It pick up the guns and shoot all the soldiers! He even seize control of their drones which bombed their own tanks!"

"A man who can build nuclear missiles and wield alien metal. Is there anything you can't do Mister Warrens?" Diallo asked.

"Program computers," Warrens replied. Diallo and Iboee broke out in laughter, while Warrens played with his food.

"So tell me Mister Warrens. How do I wield this thing?" Diallo asked as he held up the orb.

Warrens pondered whether or not he should lie to his captor. Diallo was much like this palace. Beneath the gilded exterior, one cannot hide that the they were both built atop blood and bones. Try as he might behind his bright, charming eyes, Diallo couldn't hide the malice that slithered beneath the surface.

"You just...will it into existence. The metal becomes what you think it can become. There are limits, but that's about it," Warrens explained. He tried to be vague with the hope that Diallo wouldn't figure out how to wield the weapon.

"So...if I imagine a gun," Diallo paused as he looked at his hand. The orb shifted into the shape of a pistol. He flashed a menacing smile and pointed the pistol at Iboee. He laughed along, but got nervous and grew silent when Diallo wouldn't point the gun away.

"BANG BANG!" Diallo screamed out, which made Iboee jump. Diallo cackled madly, and the metal shifted back into an orb. Iboee cackled nervously as well.

"You should have seen it Diallo, Mista Wahhens not only wield it as a gun, he make it into an armor that wield many guns! I cannot get it to work as well," Iboee confessed.

"That is quite impressive Mr. Warrens. You know, I could use a man like you in my government. Would you consider a position as a technical adviser? Your current conditions will be vastly improved, I can assure you. Same with your grandmother," Diallo said. He was bold, asking Warrens if he wanted a job in a dictator's regime. However, Warrens knew in the back of his mind that Ministers and Advisers didn't tend to last long in their positions.

Warrens lied. "I would definitely consider it. Thank you Diallo."

"Fantastic!" Diallo stood up, and took a final sip of coffee. "Well, the others will be here shortly. Once I've dealt with them, we will address the details of your advisor position alright Warrens?" Diallo asked as he extended his hand.

"Works for me," Warrens said as he stood up and shook Diallo's hand. It took every ounce of restraint to stop Warrens from striking Diallo as hard as he could. Amidst all the torture, all of the agony, he walked with his God complex and believed he was making a better world.

"Perhaps, I can use you in the peace talks. Let the others know just who I have as my new technology advisor," Diallo snickered as he nudged Iboee.

"Very good sir," Iboee replied.

"Now, go rest up you two. Tomorrow is a big day. Peace will finally reign over Africa once again," Diallo said.

Iboee escorted Warrens back to his bedroom. The two walked in silence, but Iboee had a question.

"So Mista Wahhens, you take Diallo's deal? Technical advisor make you a powerful man," Iboee said.

"Will my grandma will be used as a bargaining chip against me?"

"We can update the the agreement if you wish. Soon you work to get paid rather than keep her alive."

Iboee and Abdul came back the following morning to escort Warrens down to where the negotiations for peace were to be held. Warrens and Gladys were already dressed by the time the other two arrived.

"Personal escorts. Y'know, some people pay really good money for this," Gladys said.

Outside the main gate, a trail of black limousines rolled through and up the driveway. Servants flooded to the cars, releasing the tuxedoed warlords and their colonels in full military regalia and decorations.

"Okafor, peace be upon you," Diallo said with a wide grin. In the flash of a smile, it seemed that all the horrors, all the tortures, all the hatred instilled from one side to the other vanished.

"Diallo, peace be upon you," Okafor replied as the two warlords embraced one another. "I am glad that you have called for this peace conference. This destructive war has gone on long enough, it is time that Africa heals."

"I agree. Once Akiloye arrives, we can discuss our terms."

"I am curious Diallo. What is the superweapon that you claim to possess?" Okafor asked.

"Ah, It is right here," Diallo said as he pulled the orb out of his pocket. Diallo noticed Iboee and Warrens walking down the stairs. "And here is the man who mastered this great weapon for me. Solomon, may I present to you Mr. Warrens, my new technology adviser."

Okafor forced himself to smile as he held his hand out to Warrens. Okafor was a man of pride forced to heel thanks to Warrens' machinations. The resentment in his eyes couldn't be concealed, and Diallo introducing Warrens was like rubbing salt in the wound.

"And this is Mr. Warrens' grandmother, Gladys," Diallo said as he turned Okafor to introduce her. Okafor's eyes flashed in understanding of Warrens' compliance and he bit back a silent curse that he didn't think to steal Warrens for himself.

A rumble like thunder echoed in the distance. Everyone's heads looked around in a daze of confusion until reality settled in.

"JACKSON!" Gladys shrieked as she lunged forward, snatched the orb out of Diallo's hand and pressed it into Warrens' chest. The metal stretched outward, enveloping Warrens into some kind of cocoon.

Explosions burst on all sides of the Presidential Palace as man and tank descended upon the compound. Bullets flew in all directions as Diallo's Continental Guard charged out to rebuff the invaders, while the South African Liberation Front sought to destroy both of his rivals in a tsunami of soldiers. Thousands of SALF soldiers spilled in, while the artillery and tanks laid siege upon the palace.

The metal hardened into armor around Warrens' skin. He looked around him and saw the alabaster walls blown out and shards of glass everywhere. In front of him Okafor and Diallo lay dead. Iboee was face down and covered in dust. Down in front of him, one hand still on his shin, the other holding the cracked Coeus computer. Warrens saw his grandmother lying motionless on the floor. Her eyes were closed and she had the look of peace on her face.

Warrens unleashed a guttural howl of anguish, one that chilled even the souls of the hardened soldiers who were invading the palace. He'd failed his role as his grandmother's protector, and allowed these monsters to take her from him. What's worse is that this war was so close to being over, so close to being finished, yet one last monster sought out to prolong the bloodletting and seize the mantle of ruler for himself.

"If death is all you want, then that is what I will give you!" Warrens cried as he felt himself take over every machine with a microchip. He could see through the drones and tanks, and hear the voices of soldiers relaying their positions through their comm devices. Every machine around him became an extension of his consciousness, as though they were integrated into the fabric of his being.

"Time to kill all communications-" Warrens was cut off as he felt his body become wracked with pain. Electricity surged across every vein while he was encased within the armor.

As he looked around, he realized in horror that it was Iboee wielding an electric stun blaster.

Warrens found no means of escape from the continuous circuit. He let his concentration go, which caused the metal to shift back into an orb and his pocket computer to fall on the floor. Warrens collapsed, helpless against the electrocutor.

Iboee bent down, picked up the orb and stared at it as though he was entranced.

"Now I shall become ruler of Africa!" Iboee screamed in his mesmerized state. The metal unfurled and draped Iboee head to toe. The metal hardened into an armor, and an evil cackle echoed inside. He reached down for the Coeus computer and slapped it into the forearm.

"Thank you Mista Wahhens for helping me become ruler of Africa," Iboee said as he drew a pistol and aimed it at Warrens.

"You foul little imp," Warrens snarled. "That armor is mine!"

Droplets flowed from the armor towards Warrens. They

pooled on his arm, reforming a gauntlet.

Iboee fired his blaster, but the droplets ripped through the blaster bolt, and made it evaporate in the air. He looked at Warrens in horror as the last of the great metal floated onto him.

Warrens held out his arm towards Iboee. A gun barrel took shape and molded around his hand.

"This is for my grandma," Warrens said as he fired at Iboee. A red mist sprayed from the back of his head and the imp collapsed.

"Now, let's knock out the rest of these bastards," He growled. A circuit board-like pattern emerged from his armor, metallic veins etched across his body.

Soldiers on both sides of Warrens opened fire, and their bullets bounced off of his metallic body. He lunged for the soldiers in front of him and struck as hard as he could. The sickening crack from their caved-in skulls made Warrens' stomach lurch, but he seized their rifles and integrated them into his armor.

Warrens marched into the fray and executed every soldier that stood in his path. He would grant no mercy to these battle-crazed veterans unless they laid down their arms. Warrens collected more rifles, until he was firing from rifles on his arms and shoulders.

Warrens walked through the breach in the wall where the SALF soldiers had stormed the palace, only to find the entire city of Cairo aflame in violence. Akiloye was making one final bid for a United Africa under his rule.

An envoy of metal was rolling right for the palace with the fervor of conquerors. Diallo's soldiers surrendered en masse no doubt hearing of their leader's death, but Akiloye's forced executed all without discretion. Many units picked their guns back up and resumed fighting with a resolve that annihilation be their only option.

Warrens had a gut feeling that Akiloye was in the midst of this envoy, as well as his chance to end the war once and for all. Helicopters hummed in the distance, all forces converging on the palace.

He felt the tanks all around him. He sensed the signals from satellites overhead, armed with missiles that would rain armageddon from the skies. Through his will, the metal was taking control of everything, turning Warrens into a mobile war machine.

Warrens saw through the cameras of more drones that were closing in. He could feel in the prickling of his skin that he had control of the tanks too. He could see in the eyes of the soldiers that they hadn't realized any of this yet.

Warrens willed the tanks guns to turn around. They were a fully mechanized force, one that Akiloye spent many credits acquiring on the black markets.

"Fire!" Warrens screamed, and his two tanks unleashed their firepower at the oncoming envoy. The armor in front absorbed the brunt, exploding into a mass of fire. He could hear the unit reloading for another volley while the helicopters were closing in.

Through the drones Warrens saw that helicopters were closing in, but he willed the missiles to be launched and end that aerial assault.

The tanks in front of him unleashed another volley against Akiloye's envoy. This time, his soldiers fired back with anti-tank missiles. Both tanks exploded and rained fire down on Warrens. The searing heat threatened him out of his armor, but he pressed on.

A gun speeder leaped over the ledge, and the machine gun spewed bullets like a dragon. The bullets failed to penetrate Warrens' armor, but each impact felt like a savage blow from Mac McGee. Warrens fired back and killed the gunner. He charged the speeder, but the driver abandoned their game of chicken. Warrens grabbed ahold of the machine gun and tried to rip it off.

"Too bad this thing doesn't give me super strength," Warrens groaned. He willed his arm into a blade, sheared off the bolts and attached the machine gun to his shoulder.

The helicopters fired their machine guns at Warrens, but

four smoking missiles sent the helicopters to the scrap heap when they rained down as giant fireballs from the sky.

Warrens knew that he had control of the satellites since he could see himself from space. At a thought the missiles were activated, and the envoy was targeted by the laser guidance systems.

He walked to where the remains of his tanks were and stood before them. Soldiers charged up a sandy hill, while he fired against them the machine gun mounted on his shoulder.

"AKILOYE!" Warrens howled into the wind.

The envoy came to a stop, and a man stepped out from one of the speeders. He was a tall, muscular man wearing a maroon beret. His eyes burned with the same intensity as what Warrens saw in Diallo and Okafor, except his eyes burned with pride over taking Cairo once and for all.

"You must be Jackson Warrens. The man who stopped my forces in the South. Africa's deadliest son," Akiloye said.

"The Core authorities are on their way. Surrender to them, or I will knock out you and your entire army!" Warrens screamed from the top of the hill.

A smile spread across Akiloye's lips. He let loose a hideous cackle, which erupted into all of the men on the ground howling in a chorus of laughter. "How does one man defeat me?" He asked.

Warrens already knew the answer as he felt himself let go of a missile through the satellite.

Warrens dropped the machine gun, leaped down to the ground and willed the armor to recede. He stood face to face with the final dictator who sought to bring a continent under his bloodthirsty rule.

"This for all those you've hurt," Warrens said as he raised his fists. He unleashed all of his fury into a right hook which drove Akiloye into the ground. He stood up, blood flowing from his lip and raised his fists against Warrens.

Akiloye swung wildly, while Warrens let loose his anger and rage, each strike a defiant blow for all of the people of Africa whose lives had been ruined in this reckless war.

Akiloye's soldiers fired upon Warrens, but he willed the armor back on, which protected him from the bullets. His final blow landed against the side of Akiloye's skull, a sickening crack that echoed across the battlefield. The last dictator collapsed to the ground, a gaze of shock buried in his eyes. Warrens turned to face a stunned army, all guns fixed on him.

Just as Akiloye's forces were about to retaliate, a missile from above rained down and brought ruin to the entire envoy. Hundreds of men were caught in the ensuing blast, and the scorching heat threatened to roast Warrens alive. The army was broken, and another missile rained from above to finish the job. Two more missiles streaked across the sky and decimated the Presidential Palace, reducing one of the most opulent symbols of African Monarchial rule to dust.

Warrens could hear that Core soldiers on their way, the violence too much for them to ignore any longer.

As the dust settled, Warrens gazed upon the wasteland all around him. Scores of vehicles were now fused and twisted metal. Sand was burned to glass, the dust of a palace blew across the desert.

Hundreds of Core soldiers swarmed the remnants of the battlefield. They looked around in disbelief at Warrens, the only man standing. They screamed for him to surrender, and threatened to shoot if he didn't.

"Can't let them have the metal. It's too powerful. Nobody should have this weapon, not even me," Warrens said to himself.

The Core soldiers continued to threaten him to surrender.

"The metal...exists in all states at once. Then...that must mean..." Warrens raised his hands in surrender. The Core soldiers watched his every move with their sights trained on him. As the soldiers watched, the metal armor Warrens was encased in oxidized and rusted away, the remnants of the deadly weapon scattered in the wind.

For four long days, the Core didn't know what they were going to charge Jackson Warrens with. Because of his involvement, the entire political infrastructure of Africa was in disarray, and the Core was forced to get involved in peacekeeping efforts to keep the area stable. The continent was no longer unified under one banner, the violence wrought by the civil war created hundreds of new governments in the continental dissolution. The Core wasn't pleased with having to deal with all of these new governments.

The clear offense was Warrens "hacking" into Defense satellites, as well as the murder of hundreds of "civilians" despite the fact that they were armed to the teeth. For the time being, Warrens was placed in isolation until the authorities could figure out what to do with him.

Outside a freighter ship descended to the facility that held Warrens. A man carried a briefcase, one who was able to navigate the maze and bureaucracy of the military prison system. He was escorted to Warrens' holding cell and left alone with the indomitable boxer.

Warrens stood face to face with a man in a gray suit and a black tie neither of which seemed to fight quite right.

"I'll be damned, the infamous son of Bud Warrens," the man said. "My name is Colonel John C. Henry. Glad to see that you put that little care package of ours to use Mr. Warrens. Took my computer guy months to rig up that device you smashed," He said.

"If he wants it back, I can fix it," Warrens replied.

"Nah. Destabilizing a continental government, ending a three way civil war and eliminating three despots in one shot. I'd say you put it to good use," John said.

"Why are you here?" Warrens asked.

"Well Mr. Warrens I'm creating a team and I'm in need of a mechanic..."

—The End—

PART FOUR

The Anarchist of Ophridia

"Fire in the hole!" The Foreman screamed. They leaned down, plugged their ears and opened their mouths so their eardrums wouldn't burst as the explosion rocked the entire mine. The debris fell like a heavy rain, men filled in the gap and hammered away at the rich vein of coal with their pickaxes as though they sought revenge against the body of a fallen god.

Lee sighed as he heaved at the coal vein in front of him. "Stay strong and do your time," He whispered to himself in the English common tongue.

"Did I ever tell you boys about the origins of Ophridia?" Deng asked.

"Nobody wants to hear that stupid story again Deng," Zao said.

Lee turned. "Aww c'mon Zao. Let Deng tell it, makes the workday go faster."

"Thank you Lee," Deng replied. "They say that before the Beijing astronomers found this little gem here, Ophridia was actually a serpent deity named Ophie who slithered through the ground on this planet. Wrangled and murdered by his celestial father, Ophie's remains became the coal we dig from the soil."

"Beautiful story Deng, really," Bai said. "What about the fact that above ground all we see is black rock, while down here we find all this coal? Doesn't that mean there was life down here at one point?"

"Yeah, the great serpent Ophie!" Deng said. Lee laughed at his infectious smile. Deng wiped the sweat from his bald scalp.

"What I mean is, if there was life here before, where is it now?" Bai asked.

"Ask the Botanist here. At least, he was back on Earth," Zao said.

All of the men looked at Lee for his input on the conversation. His face grew flush and he gave a grin of embarrassment from all of the attention placed on him.

"Well a planet this rich in coal would mean that it used to teem with life, but given how barren it is now due to constant cloudcover it would signal a massive die-off of plant and animal life-"

"Ha! Told you Deng!" Bai said.

"But the life on this planet could've been the great serpent Ophie," Lee said with a grin. Deng burst out laughing and slapped Bai on the back.

"Get back to work!" the foreman screamed in the native mandarin tongue. The men lowered their heads and dove back into mining the rich coal vein they'd struck. The remaining hours of their shift were spent in silence until the whistle blew.

"Who's up for a drink at the Eternal Dragon?" Zao asked.

"I'm in," Lee said.

"Me too. I gots more stories about the great serpent Ophie," Deng said.

"Why don't you let that go?" Zao asked. "We're a planet full of people the Chinese Governors exported to help with Mother China's overpopulation problem." Zao couldn't contain the bitterness in his voice over being a displaced civilian.

"It's alright Zao, just keep your head down and work hard. We're bound to get out of here sometime," Lee said. "Ai ya! I'm tired. What I wouldn't give to see the sunlight again."

Zao turned and flashed a disgusted sneer. "It's Ophridia, the sun never shines here. It's as gray as the coal we dig from the ground." A string of cursing in Mandarin erupted nearby. A miner was being dragged by three guards dressed in scarlet red, the colors of the Emperor Yiu Mei's Elite soldiers. The man pleaded for his life, while the guards only seemed interested in beating him with their clubs.

"Another victim of Yiu Mei's 'Xiongbu,' his policy of terror to keep us in line," Bai said.

"Somebody should help him," Deng said.

"No! There's nothing we can do! Get in the tavern!" Lee hissed. He didn't want to watch this poor man get beaten in the streets and knew that onlookers were targeted next.

"Somebody should've helped that poor guy," Deng said as he sat down to a table and ordered a round of rice liquor for the four men. Lee tried to shake the image of the poor man from his head and deep down he knew there was nothing that they could do to help him. Intervention on the man's behalf would've meant death.

As the men drank the string music being played on the stage up front was soft and low. The bar filled with smoke from the cigarettes the miners smoked. Lee took a few puffs, and coughed from the harsh smoke as it constrained within his throat.

The music came to a close and a white man took the stage. White men were few and far between on Ophridia, even moreso since Yiu Mei had shut down all trade and travel to the planet. The man wore commoners clothes, along with the insignia of the Coalition, a shield with a cluster of planets on the front.

"Think he'll start with how Yiu Mei kept us out of the Unification Wars to make us miners weak?" Bai asked the table.

"Oh hell, I'd rather Yiu Mei kept us away from those desperate dogs," Zao said. "We had no business bein' in that war."

"He'll also say that when the Core was too focused on the outer worlds during reconstruction, Yiu Mei closed off Ophridia, and seized the planet's wealth for himself," Deng said as he pointed at the Englishman.

"Fuck that!" Zao hissed. "We have work to do, rice liquor to drink, what more do we need right Lee?" Zao asked.

"Right. We just do our time, drink up and listen to the Brit's fay hwa," Lee said with a forced grin. He raised his drink in a mock toast and the others followed suit.

The man fumbled with his papers and began to speak. "It is the dark times that try men's souls..." he paused. Zao and Bai were whispering harshly in Mandarin, their words slithering like snakes from their lips. The englishman continued: "It is through leaden indifference that allows the rise of tyrants!"

Bai threw his glass at the Brit. "Bee-jway! Your words are as worthless as Elephant shit! You don't work in the mines you chu shie fook! The Tingchia will haul us away and beat us or worse if we look at them wrong!"

"Bai, stay down! You're going to draw the tingchia in!" Lee said in a harsh whisper.

"The police should exist to protect! Not suppress," the Brit said.

"We've been paralyzed by fear for four years! We can manage a few more!" Bai screamed. The entire bar froze in silence and stared at Bai. His face was red from anger, and when he realized that all eyes were on him, he swallowed hard, but refused to back down.

"You've had enough to drink," Lee said. "The tingchia will come now for sure." Lee grabbed Bai's collar and escorted him through the back of the Eternal Dragon into the street.

"Get your hands off of me!" Bai screamed. His eyes burned into Lee, his blood simmering below the surface.

"Bai, it's okay," Lee said. "We'll get through this."

"When?" Bai snapped. "We've been trapped here for four years! How will we get through this?"

"Someone will come," Lee said. "We serve here and soon we'll be able to start a new life."

"Or die to the Emperor's Xiongbu!" Bai snapped. He gasped when he heard the tingchia voices echo through the streets on their patrol. The two men turned and ran for their homes. Both of them dived through the door of their humble hovels while the tingchia continued on with their patrol.

Lee slumped against the door of his hut granted to him by

the Mining Council upon his arrival on Ophridia. He heard a rattle in the kitchen, but his mind eased as he watched his daughter Ju stumble into the main room clutching her doll.

"Da-da!" Ju said as she approached her father. Lee scooped her up and his eyes met the brown gems that belonged to his wife in the doorway.

"Ai Fen, how are you my tin-ren?" Lee asked as he kissed his wife.

"Out drinking with the boys?," Ai Fen asked playfully.

"They only wanted one. I'm sorry," Lee said as he looked to the floor. Ai Fen cupped his face in her hand and looked into his eyes.

"It's okay, just be back before curfew," Ai Fen said as she went into the kitchen. "I made you your favorite sweetie. Even with the ration cards, I was able to mix up that soy chicken and rice you like so much."

"Great, thank you tin-ren," Lee said.

"When are you going to stop calling me that old mandarin nickname?"

"When I get tired of using it."

"Oh! Ju, show daddy his tree," Ai Fen said. Ju hopped off of her daddy's lap, went over and pulled a small curtain aside. Inside was a small spiral-trunked tree that reached for the solar lamp that constantly shined on it. There were also a few herbs which were growing in the pots underneath the nourishing light.

"Wow! Look at that! You've taken such good care of it Ju! I'm so proud of you!" Lee said as he held his daughter tight. She giggled in his arms while he blew a raspberry on her tummy.

"She sure did! I'll use some of this lemongrass for our dinner," Ai Fen said as she took a sprig.

Lee thought back to his home on Earth. He lived in a small house with a vast rice field behind and a tiny side garden that he loved to care for. He savored the smell of the soil, the warm sun and the sea of green that surrounded the countryside. Each breath was like a drink from a fine wine, luscious and full bodied.

Then the Tingchia came. Crimson police soldiers who descended upon the valley, armed to the teeth. An arrangement between Mother China and her new Colony of Ophridia saw the exportation of millions of her children. Ophridia possessed untold wealth in coal and devoured China's sons and daughters, creating the lore that Ophridia was the great snake which sought to devour all of her children. Initially there was an indenture work period, where if people labored long enough, they could buy their freedom. People of certain professions could buy themselves out faster, but that list grew shorter every year. Lee thought back as he watched the crimson soldiers descend, he let his gaze linger on the sea of green all around him since he had no idea when he'd see his fields again. At least Lee was able to keep his family close and remain with them.

A knock erupted from the door. Men on the other side screamed in Mandarin and commanded Lee to open up. His entire body grew tense. He rose from the floor, but the pounding was incessant, urgent.

Lee approached the door. He reached out and noticed that his hand couldn't stop shaking. Before he could reach the knob, the door burst open and three Tingchia filed in. The lead soldier slammed the butt of his rifle into Lee's stomach who collapsed to the floor. Ai Fen and Ju screamed out in terror. Ai Fen begged and pleaded with the soldiers in Mandarin, demanding to know why they were here.

"Xing Ming Lee, you have been accused of conspiracy to commit treason against the Emperor Yiu Mei. You are under arrest," one of the soldiers said.

Ai Fen screamed at the soldiers and pleaded Lee's innocence. The soldiers surrounded Lee and grabbed his arms. Ai Fen lurched forward and tried to pry the men off of her husband. The officer leading the squad drew his pistol and fired at Ai Fen.

A red mist burst out of her chest, her face contorted in a mixture of surprise and fear. She collapsed, while Ju shrieked in terror.

"Shut that baby up!" The officer screamed.

"Ju! It's okay! We're just playing see?" Lee pleaded. Ju didn't believe Lee's lie and continued crying. "Ju please! It's okay sweetheart, please stop crying!"

"She's going to wake the whole neighborhood," the officer grumbled. He raised his pistol, shot Ju through her head and her doll flew out of her hands.

"NO!" Lee wailed. He lunged against the soldiers and dove for the officer, unleashing a river of curses and insults in Mandarin. The soldiers pulled Lee back and struck him down with their clubs.

"Chùsheng xai-jiao de xiang huo!" Lee cursed. He sobbed and wrestled against the soldiers so that he could hold his daughter one last time, but each time he escaped their grasp they struck him with one of their clubs. Lee became hysterical and broke the grip of the soldiers, but they struck him behind the knees where he fell and landed with Ju just outside of his reach. The soldiers grabbed his ankles and dragged him out of his house, while the officer kicked out the light that fed Lee's plants.

Lee watched the officer as he was being dragged away and chiseled every physical feature of his into memory. On the officer's face there were three lines next to his right eye, four next to his left. He had a ridge halfway up his nose, an antique scar from being broken in the past. There was also a faint scar on the left side of his chin and Lee saw the final mark. The name tag on his jacket said "Quan Sito." He looked around with an air of indifference, wiped his hands and continued his patrol while the Tingchia dragged Lee to the nearest station.

At the station the Tingchia struck Lee with their clubs and tied him to a chair. Lee never knew what happened inside of the police stations, only that once someone was dragged in, they were never seen again.

The soldiers threw ice water at Lee to get him to list off the names of other "conspirators" to feed to the Xiongbu.

"Only one way out miner, and that's to confess your crimes

and co-conspirators. Besides, one of them ratted you out anyway. What's the point in defending traitors? Confess and we'll see to it you can get out of this alive," the guard said. Lee knew better. As long as the police held him, he wouldn't leave alive.

Lee held his head low and mumbled something under his breath.

"What's that?" the policeman snapped as he rose from his chair and held his club up.

Lee mumbled something again. The policeman waltzed up and brandished his club.

"What'd you say?" He asked.

"I'll give you names. Come closer," Lee whispered.

The policeman leaned down, his ear right next to Lee when Lee lunged forward and bit as hard as he could at the man's neck. The policeman howled in pain, while Lee felt his mouth fill with salty and grimy flesh before the iron blood flowed in. The policeman instinctively pulled away, the chunk of his flesh still in Lee's mouth. The policeman grabbed his neck in horror, but he was too late. His jugular had been severed.

The other policeman charged forward with their clubs. Lee jumped and kicked the policeman into the door, landed on his chair and shattered it into a thousand splinters. His hands were still bound behind his back but as the policeman came at him again, Lee spat the flesh into his face, and headbutted him which drove him to the ground.

Lee pressed his boot onto the man's throat as hard as he could. His arms flailed everywhere in a desperate bid for one last breath. He watched the man's face glow red and his eyes bulge out. He pushed harder while the policeman clawed at his leg. The man gurgled and weeped until his flailing limbs ceased and collapsed to the floor.

Lee grabbed a knife and cut the rope that bound his hands. He looted the pistols from both of the policemen, dived out into the street. Lee fell to his knees and sobbed, the reality of never being able to see Ai Fen and Ju again crashed into him like a tidal wave. What's worse is he killed two of the Tingchia, an executable offense if he wasn't already for the Xiongbu. Either way Lee was a dead man and he needed to escape.

Voracious whispers of more Tingchia signaled they were on their way. He searched the city for an escape, but he knew there was nowhere within the capital he could hide given the prominence of cameras. The eyes of the Emperor were everywhere. Lee's eyes fell on the mountains outside of the city. The mountains whose spires were hidden above the clouds, never seen by anyone.

Lee knew the mountains were his only chance for survival. He ran through the streets, weaving and dodging the Tingchia patrols as they combed for traitors in their midst. He feared that some of them may have heard him, but his focus was on the mountains in the distance.

Lee made for the gates that towered over the city. Their concrete faces were smeared with streaks of coal dust from the hands of miners who sought to leave their mark. The road snuggled between the gates was the only route in or out of the city. The gates opened for the behemoth-sized trucks that belched thick, black smoke. They lumbered in with their hundreds of tons of coal which strained even the industrial-crafted thrusters. The titanic vehicles passed through, and Lee made a sprint for the gate. After only fifty metres, the trucks passed through, and the gates closed.

Lee watched in terror as his only chance to leave the city closed in front of his eyes. He saw something glide across his hand. It was a red dot of light, which flowed across his torso and came to rest on his chest. Two more just like it lit up and marked him.

Lee turned and sprinted as fast as he could, the scorched dust singing the back of his neck. He could hear the Tingchia soldiers on the gates scream into their comms, feeding his position to the soldiers on the ground.

Lee weaved through the shacks and the streets. He could hear the Tingchia screams echo as they searched for him across the city.

A truck roared to Lee's right as it bounced across the

makeshift road. He had no choice but to attempt an escape, since remaining in the city would spell death. He could hear the truck's engines roar as the driver gunned for the gates. As it bounced on the road, Lee swallowed hard. One savage bump and he'd be crushed.

Lee ran for the truck, and dived for the dirt. He rolled right as the first axle cleared, grabbed ahold of the drive shaft and lifted himself as high as he could from the ground. The truck engines grumbled above him, while the drive shaft was covered in grease. His hands slicked and slurped against the metal which made him slide. If it wasn't for his legs, Lee would've fallen off the truck immediately.

Lee watched the world from beneath the truck as it sped along the outskirts of the city. There were no roads out here, only stray rocks which pockmarked the earth. He watched the towering walls of the city become a faint line along the horizon and when the world seemed quiet, he released his grip from the drive shaft.

Lee's back slammed against the ground which knocked the breath out of him. He searched out the mountain that rose into the clouds and ran for it. As he neared the base, he could hear the night shift miners striking with their pickaxes and carving at the rock with their laser cutters. He smelled the oily fuel of the coal mixed with the sulfur that ruled the air in Ophridia.

He scratched at the mountain and began to climb. He climbed day and night, never stopping despite the cold, the hunger or thirst. He climbed for his very survival, as if the whips of the devil himself drove him up the mountain. He figured that at least in the mountains he could survive whereas in the city he wouldn't have a prayer.

The mountain proved an indomitable foe. The jagged face of the mountain sliced at Lee's hands and he left hand prints of blood in his wake. The frigid air left his fingers numb, while the growing layers of snow made the mountain slick. For days he battled his way up the mountain, fighting numbness in the extremities. He ate the snow in a desperate bid for water, which only made him colder.

On the third day, when Lee put his weight on a rock, it launched out, and sent him tumbling down the ledge. He skidded across a realm of razors, and stopped on a ledge that was only slightly wider than him. Waves of wind battered him on the side of the mountain, and the icy snow in his belly threatened to coax him into a sleep that he wouldn't wake from.

On the fourth day of climbing, Lee noticed that the clouds glowed. He saw a glimpse of the heavens, which spurred him onward. He knew he'd reached the cloud layers when he could hardly see in front of him, but as he rose above the clouds, he was aghast.

Sunlight. It was only on the edge of the horizon, but it was here.

The clouds on the ground were so thick that the sun could never pierce through. Above the clouds, weak orange rays radiated the landscape, as if the realm was in a constant dusk, always waiting for the next sunrise.

Lee clawed at and dragged himself over a ledge. He looked around, but was nearly blind with the bright light surrounding him. As his eyes focused, a large temple came into view. He forced himself onto his feet, walked up the steps and threw himself at the front door.

The door opened, and an old man gazed down at Lee.

"Water...please..." Lee gasped as he stumbled onto the sloped steps.

"You want water? Come in here," the old man grumbled. He turned away and walked into the temple. Lee forced himself to his feet and placed one foot in front of the other and made his way up the steps for the temple. The cold wind howled as he tried to close the door. The door thundered in contempt of being shut while the lock squealed as Lee sealed himself inside.

Lee turned and felt the warmth of the room on his skin. The old man tended to the coal fires, then pointed to a pitcher of water with a glass next to it. Lee's hands shook as he grasped the pitcher, which clattered against the glass. He spilled the water into the glass without care and drank like a man who had thirsted for a hundred years.

"Drink up friend. It is a long trek here," The old man said.

"Who are you?" Lee asked.

"I house runaways like you who escape from Yiu Mei. What is your name?"

"Xing Ming Lee. Yours?"

"No name from me. If you're captured and tortured, the Emperor learns my name. Call me the Hermit," the old man said.

"Fair enough. How long have you been up here?"

"Since before the Xiongbu. I knew Yiu Mei was trouble when he was a Senator on Earth. I fled the moment he became Colonial Governor."

"I see. How do you survive up here?"

"Solar cells. Long since abandoned when they notice the sun doesn't touch the ground, but up here, they're worth more than gold."

Lee looked out at the cloudscape. The sun's light glimmered in the distance and created a carpet of gold and white as far as the eye could see.

"Shame since we will never know midday. The sun only rises as high the eyeline, then holds there for a few hours until she sets, and night sweeps in once more. Scientists said it had to do with the position of the planet."

"I never thought I'd see the sun again," Lee said. His mind wandered to when his family walked without a care through his garden. They loved the vibrant emerald green all around and the intricate ornate petals of a single flower. His time as a botanist was reflected in a vast greenhouse, which contained thousands of different species of plants, but his livelihood was snatched away from him through China's aggressive expatriation program. All it took was the unlucky draw of the lottery where families were forced to uproot their lives and were shipped off to Ophridia.

"Come, you must be hungry," the Hermit said as he escorted Lee to his table. The Hermit ladled a clear liquid into a bowl and slid the bowl in front of Lee with a spoon inside of it.

Lee smelled the hot liquid. The scent of lemongrass, onion and garlic filled his nose. His stomach growled as he realized that it'd been days since his last meal. He took a spoonful and shoved it into his mouth. He didn't care that the scalding liquid burned his tongue. The soup tasted even better than it smelled, and he devoured it right as the Hermit sat down to enjoy his own.

The Hermit chuckled. "Good to see that I haven't lost my ability to cook. Let me get you some more," he said as he took Lee's empty bowl from him.

"How...how did you make that?" Lee asked.

"Oh it was quite simple really. You know cooking is nothing more than a mixture of ingredients. A basic premise of chemistry, but the real trick is in the correct application of heat," the Hermit said.

"No, I mean the ingredients. Where did you get them?"

"Ah. Up here where there is some sunlight, a few plants and herbs grow. They endure the cold quite well. Wild onion and garlic, lemongrass, thyme, just wait until you try the wild pigeon," the Hermit chuckled.

"There's plants up here?" Lee asked.

"Not many. A shrub here, a bush there."

"But there are plants up here?"

"Yes, why?"

"In China, I was a botanist. I studied plants for a living."

"Ah, fascinating. What was your life like? Before all of this?" the Hermit asked.

"I collected and studied plants for medicine. I loved my work, but my family and I were forced here."

"It is like that with many families. What happened to yours?" the Hermit asked.

Lee's lower lip quivered. He felt something dry cracking against his chin and realized that he still had the dried blood of the soldier whose neck he'd bit days ago.

"I...killed the men who killed my family. All except one. The officer," Lee said as his fingers dug into the wooden table. The Hermit stared in quiet contemplation.

Lee snickered. "Wood? Up here? Are there trees?" he asked as he blinked away his tears.

"There is a forest nearby. I'll take you tomorrow. Too late now."

The rest of the dinner was eaten in silence between the two men. The Hermit showed Lee to his bed and left him there alone.

In the midst of the darkness Lee broke down into tears as his thoughts wandered to his family. He tossed and turned as his mind replayed Ai Fen's final screams when her life was stolen followed by the sight of his daughter being shot again and again. No matter how hard he tried, he was never able to hold her one last time within his dreams.

The nightmares stirred in Lee's mind, twisting his thoughts into insidious demons that tormented him in his sleep.

The morning sun couldn't come soon enough as it pierced through the curtain into Lee's bedroom. He walked out to see the Hermit tending to his fire. He flashed Lee a grin.

"Good morning. Trouble sleeping?" the Hermit asked.

Lee gave him a glare which gave the obvious answer.

"I'm sorry," The Hermit said. "When one loses their family, the dreams become nightmares that we cannot escape." As he spoke, small embers wafted through the air and up the chimney.

Lee looked down at the dirt floor and shuffled to the chair closest to him. He felt like a lost soul, without purpose. A man stripped of identity or meaning, his very existence snuffed out before his eyes.

"Come, you wanted to see the forest," the Hermit said as he hoisted a basket onto his back. Lee looked up and the Hermit tossed him some robes along with a basket to strap onto his back.

The two men trekked through the snow and the faint sunlight into the mountain range. As Lee crested over the ridge, he saw the face of the mountain covered in pines. They swayed in the breeze, a hypnotic wave that signaled peace and tranquility.

"Tell me about your family," the Hermit said as he thrust his walking stick into the snow and made his descent towards the pines.

"Ai Fen and I met through a friend. She was the most beautiful woman I'd ever seen. I knew the moment that I saw her I wanted her as my wife. Within the year, we were married. Then we had our baby girl Ju who cared for my tiny herb garden while I worked in the mines," Lee explained.

The only sound between the two was the trampling of snow underfoot as the two men sought out edible plants. The plants here reminded Lee of thistles. Their stalks were woody and aligned with tiny barbs that would blister and infect any who dared to grab the plant. Typical for plants that grew high in the mountains. He also found several spruces whose needles could be used to make a potent tea that would stave off infection. It was an hour before the Hermit spoke again.

"Why do you accept the burden of mining here on Ophridia?"

"What choice did we have? It was either come here or get arrested by the Chinese Government."

"Which resulted not only in your arrest here, but the death of your family did it not?"

Lee didn't answer. He let the question hang in the air like a ghost that refused to leave its haunting place.

"There is always a choice!" The Hermit shouted. His voice echoed throughout the mountain valley, but Lee didn't say anything.

The two men worked in silence for hours into the afternoon collecting plants and wild root vegetables. Lee felt the sides of his head threatening to burst from the altitude, but he pressed on.

"You make a great mule you know that? Take all of your beatings in stride, press onward, stay quiet-"

"Bee-jway!" Lee snapped. "I am no mule. I am no dairuomu ji hiding in the mountains either!"

"HA! You most certainly are a crazed chicken! You hide up here from the Tingchia rather than die like a man! You let your wife and your daughter get killed-"

"Bee-jway duh liou mahng! Ni tama de tianxia suoyou de ren duo gaisi!"

"Calling me names won't get you anywhere. Why did you run when the Emperor killed your family?"

"The Emperor did not kill my family. It was a hwoon dahn named Quan."

"Who did so on the Emperor's orders."

"It is not like there was anything I could do. I couldn't save them. I am not armed, I couldn't fight, couldn't-"

"Make enough excuses, I know."

"Ai ya! What was I to do? Please tell me!"

"That is for you to decide. Fight the Emperor or hide out here."

"You're a frustrating old hundan."

"So I've been told." The two men spent the rest of the night in silence. After dinner, Lee tried to rest and ease his headache, but each time he went back to sleep, the nightmares resumed. They chaffed and attacked his mind, threatening a madness from either sleep deprivation or the constant exposure to such gruesome detail.

The two men spent the next day in silence. They gathered more plants for food and the Hermit hunted pigeons that dared fly over his house. Lee's mind swirled with rebuttals and insults, all meant to put the Hermit in his place. He stewed in anger until dinner time when he finally broke the twenty-four hour silence between the two.

"I am just one man. How can I possibly fight the Emperor?"

"The Emperor is just one man. One man who rules millions and doesn't hesitate to kill them. One man who spreads terror like wildfire."

"What is your point?" Lee asked.

"I'm saying that he is only one man like you, yet you hide here in the mountains while he enjoys the fruits harvested from the labor of millions. Strange is it not?"

"Then why don't you do something?"

"Oh, I cannot. I can hardly walk, let alone try to bring down the Emperor. You however, a man in his prime, could do much...that is if you can endure the mountains," the Hermit said.

Lee gave a puzzled look.

"The cold is savage, heartless. It grips you at your very bones and draws your life away a little at time, lulling you into a sleep that you will never wake from," the Hermit said. Then he erupted into savage laughter, as if he told the best joke of his life. Lee didn't even crack a smile.

"Not a joker are you? The cold suits you then. Let the ice take you mister serious."

"What am I to joke about? I just lost my wife and daughter!" Lee hissed

"Nonsense. They were not your possessions. They were returned to the spirit world from whence they came. This is where they belong, not here, trapped in this crude matter," the Hermit said as he pinched a piece of his arm.

"They were shot in cold blood!"

"A gruesome sight, that is certain. Yet they're relieved from the sufferings of this world. Would you rather they suffered in torment at the hands of the Emperor?"

"Chur ni-duh ben tiansheng de yidui rou!" Lee cursed.

"Such anger...misplaced. You burn at the sight of me for being honest, yet you show no resentment against the man who took your family from you!"

"How do I get justice then? What good is my resentment against an omnipresent Emperor?

"Those are not the questions you should be asking!" the Hermit snapped.

"Then what is the right question?"

"The right question is: How can one man bring fear to a man who should know none?"

"I don't know! Your fay hwa questions are as useful as to gen houzi bi diushi!"

"Lee I am not asking you to engage in a feces throwing

contest with a monkey! Here, drink this tea and meditate on what I've asked you. Put that overactive mind which gives you nightmares to use."

Lee glared at the beige liquid, but he gulped it down in one swallow and stormed out. Outside, the sun prepared to set, while the clouds lulled in a listless wave of cotton along the horizon. He was desperate for an answer to the Hermit's question, to dole out justice to the Emperor and his men. Still, Lee only thought of himself as just one man.

He closed his eyes. He felt the icy mountain air claw his neck and slither down his back. He felt the crispness in his lungs as he inhaled one breath after another. Images began to unfold, hidden truths revealed before his eyes.

Lee wondered for a moment if he'd drank a hallucinogen, but his thoughts bloomed like a garden of wildflowers. He saw the crimson Tingchia march through the streets of Ophridia like an omnipresent draconic overlord. They beat people, shot them, and dragged them through the streets. Through all of this Lee watched, and the oppressed eyes all fell on him at once. He watched and let all of this happen, like an ancient guardian who had abandoned its post.

Next came Ju being dragged through the streets. Lee tried to grab ahold of her, but his limbs were as heavy as lead. He screamed, although nobody heard him.

The world flashed and Lee was brought before a crowd that gathered to watch the Emperor Yiu Mei decree his policy of the Xiongbu in an effort to provide stability. Yiu Mei was giving a rallying speech, but as Lee turned to look at the crowd, he only met the gaze of frozen lead statues.

"It is through leaden indifference that allows the rise of tyrants!" A voice said through the void. Lee looked around, but all he found was a knife in his hand.

A rumble of thunder echoed across the cloudscape and Lee felt a shiver rattle his bones. The crimson coats of the Tingchia began to bleed. Then the soldiers themselves began to bleed. They screamed and howled like wolves. Their cries echoed across the landscape, but an encroaching ice muffled their pleas.

There was an explosion on the first floor of the Imperial Palace, which caused the Tingchia to panic. The Emperor sent his soldiers to march on the populace and open fire. The hardened faces of the miners turned to revolt as a dark cloud of terror filled the palace. More blood was spilled between the Miners and the Tingchia as they clashed, while Lee felt himself become lighter than a feather.

He had become a wispy, smoke-colored creature that glided across the ground in search of prey. He could see the terror in the hearts of the Tingchia as he approached, an infected black cyst that was spreading. The Tingchia recoiled in horror at his presence. Bullets and knives went through him, and only moved wisps of smoke. He lashed at the soldiers with his claws, and savored the sight of the gashes in their chests. Anyone with a cyst was an abomination, a creature of terror that needed to be snuffed out. There would be no mercy, no forgiveness, no escape from the wraith that Lee had become.

Yiu Mei's heart became infected and he retreated into his elaborate palace. Lee glided across the ground, followed by a handful of other wraiths, who mercilessly cut down Yiu Mei's ranks. One by one Yiu Mei's soldiers, Generals, and Ministers all collapsed from the wraiths until Yiu Mei found himself locked away from the world in a prison of his own making. The ornate palace had become his tomb, where Lee could finish him off once and for all. As he made his approach, a blinding light covered his vision...

Lee gasped for air and his lungs felt the chill from the mountain. He had the answer he needed, the key to ending Yiu Mei once and for all. He would have to become an apparition, a wraith who would strike terror into the heart of the Empire the way Yiu Mei had done to the people of Ophridia four years ago.

"What did you see?" the Hermit asked as he approached.

"Visions of Terror. Terror in the heart of Yiu Mei," Lee replied

"Now you see how one man can bring down an empire,"

the Hermit said.

"How? How do I do this?" Lee asked.

"Too many questions. Fortunately, I have an entire library of books which will teach you everything. Now your training will begin."

Lee didn't notice the passage of the next three years where he immersed himself in the history, the philosophy and the methodology of revolutionaries from eons past. He acquired and studied specimens of plants for the purposes of poison. He learned how to manufacture explosives, trained in hand to hand combat and even taught pigeons to carry messages. The Hermit pushed Lee through his studies, prescribing texts that he acquired and were long since destroyed by the Emperor.

"Today, you take your leave," the Hermit said. "I will confess that I've forgotten how to make soup for one."

"Thank you for all of your help," Lee replied. "I must know one thing before I go: Why did you push me so hard to fight the Emperor?"

"I hope you will succeed where I failed Xing Ming Lee. I failed to stop the Xiongbu."

"How?"

"I was a personal advisor to the Emperor. I fled when it became obvious that he would slaughter anyone he perceived as a threat. Then I came here where he'd never find me."

"Seems to have worked well for us," Lee said.

"Indeed. Down there, they won't recognize you. They won't understand. You will be a ghost."

"Perfect. I'll be able to move freely."

"Go, and ju ni how ying."

"Good luck to you too," Lee replied.

For three days, Lee endured the cold as he traversed back down the mountain. Below the cloudscape, he couldn't tell day from night anymore. On the ground, he came across a group of miners and claimed that he'd been separated from the day shift. They gave him a lift back into the city and dropped him off in front of the Eternal Dragon. Lee peered through the windows inside to see if he could spot any of his old friends. Zao and Deng were enjoying their traditional after-work drink and the Englishman was poised to take the stage.

"Some things never change," Lee said.

"Hey! What are you doing there?" A mandarin voice snapped through the air. Lee looked over. Two Tingchia ran to him with a glint of ferocity in their eyes.

"What are you doing out here? It's almost curfew! You are not to wander the streets! Show me your papers," one of the officers ordered.

Lee nodded and he reached inside his robe. He feigned a look of surprise, then reached out and snapped the soldier's neck. The other one was about to scream, but Lee seized the man's throat and cut off all attempts to cry for help. He broke this soldier's neck as well, and his body made a dull thump as it collapsed to the ground.

Lee checked his surroundings for any more soldiers. None were coming and he noticed the uniforms on the dead men at his feet.

He swapped the uniforms of the soldiers for the clothes on his back, and discarded the bodies into a nearby trash unit. He plugged the comm piece into his ear and a world of communication opened up to him, the movements of the Tingchia unveiled through the entire cityscape.

"All units converge on the Eternal Dragon. Suspicious activity reported." Lee froze. His heart thundered in his chest. He forced himself to take deep breaths and steady himself for the oncoming squad. Four Tingchia ran past the alleyway in front of Lee. They marched into the Eternal Dragon and in an instant the cheerful laughter and ruckus ceased. The bar became eerily quiet as the Tingchia marched around the patrons to determine who was under arrest now.

Two of the soldiers surrounded Zao and Deng. Zao hunkered down and tried to ignore the soldiers while his hair covered his face. Deng tried to relax and look nonchalant. A soldier reached down and pulled Zao up by the hair and dragged him outside. The other soldiers followed.

"Why are you dragging me, I've done nothing wrong!" Zao said in his native tongue.

"Zao Qin you're under arrest for conspiracy against the Emperor as well as the murder of two Tingchia. You have been named as a conspirator against the Empire and shall be tried for your crimes against Ophridia," the Captain said.

"Fate has a strange way of bringing us back together," Lee whispered to himself.

Zao whimpered in the darkness on his knees before his accuser. This was how it was going to end. A faceless accuser, then the Tingchia arrest him and place the black bag over his head and make him disappear forever. Zao's lip quivered in terror as he realized that he was going to be made into an example, another victim of Yiu Mei's Xiongbu.

"Stop! Leave that man alone!" Deng screamed as he burst out of the Eternal Dragon.

"Oh, a wise man hmm?" The lead soldier asked. "Arrest him too!"

"I'll...I'll fight you!" Deng said as he raised his fists in a half-hearted gesture.

"No you won't," Lee said from the shadows. He drew and hurled his knife at the soldier in front of Zao so that he could stay hidden. The soldier gurgled a sickly groan as he collapsed, while the other stunned soldiers fumbled with their rifles. Lee slid behind and sliced the throats of the three remaining soldiers.

"C'mon!" Lee screamed at Zao and Deng. They followed as though they were trapped in a haze and couldn't believe their own eyes.

Lee stopped under a bridge and held his gun close. "The eyes of the Emperor are always watching..." He whispered in Mandarin and pointed to the cameras which lined the streets. He paused for a moment and realized a flaw in his plan: he didn't have one. He was moving on instinct and didn't have a safe house, an out or anything.

The whistles blew on the buildings lining the streets. "Curfew in ten minutes! Curfew in ten minutes!" The announcer blared. Lee's heart quickened, but a grin spread across his lips. This was their out.

"Follow my lead," Lee grunted to the other two. All of the bars and shops exploded as people flooded into the streets to make it back to their homes before curfew went into effect.

Lee waited until the street was full of people before he went behind Zao and Deng and forced them to walk forward. The three men maneuvered through the streets while Lee's comm was still full of chatter from the Tingchia searching for the men who shot and killed the others.

The patrons in the Eternal Dragon were stunned to find three dead Tingchia at the doorstep, and they were retelling what they saw to the soldiers investigating the matter.

"No place is safe. Not sure if you've figured that out yet," Zao hissed to Lee. "Hundan," he added.

"Gunkai ben tiansheng de yidui rou," Lee hissed back. "Perhaps I'll throw you back to the Tingchia. Turn left here."

"Thank you for saving us," Deng said. "I don't know why you did, but thank you."

"Bee-jway Deng!"

"And we're here," Lee said.

"The Brit's house?" Zao asked.

"Yeah. He's still got diplomatic immunity right?" Lee asked.

"He still gives all of them speeches. I'd say he does," Deng said.

"Perfect. Keep a lookout," Lee said. He pulled out a set of lockpicks and manipulated the door handle until it opened.

"You understand there are cameras everywhere and that everywhere you go, everyone you talk to is going to die right?" Zao asked.

"You two were dead either way. I gave you a second chance," Lee said.

"For what?" Zao snapped.

The door creaked open. Lee slipped inside while Zao and

Deng followed close behind. Lee ripped off the Tingchia uniform and searched Jay's place for a set of spare clothes.

"What did you save us for? They're going to torture us until they find you, traitor!" Zao said.

"Not very grateful are you?" Lee replied as he ignited a candle. The light shone on his face and Zao and Deng both gasped.

"Xing Ming Lee, is it you?" Deng asked with joy. He walked forward and gave Lee a big hug. "Lee! It is you! Back from the dead! Back from Ophie's belly!" Deng screamed in laughter as he swung Lee around.

Deng had squeezed all of the air out of Lee, who patted Deng on the back. "I love you too buddy, but you gotta be a little quieter.

"How...how did you survive?" Zao asked.

"I lived in the mountains outside of the city," Lee replied.

"In the forbidden regions? Oh, you're sure brave Lee," Deng laughed.

"I saw the sun you guys. The sun. It shines here, but the clouds keep it hidden away."

"You...you ruined it!" Zao screamed as he shoved Lee away.

"Ruined what?" Lee snapped.

"I had a quiet life. A life where I worked in the mines, returned home and could afford a drink of rice liquor every night. A simple life where I had all I needed."

"And look where it got you!" Lee snapped. "Arrested at random by an Emperor who does so to keep his people terrified. You didn't have a life. You were complacent, hiding until the day you died in either a mining accident or by the Emperor's hand."

"Well thanks to you, I'm going to be hunted like an animal!" Zao said.

"If it'll make you feel better, I'll take you to the station myself!" Lee said.

Zao gasped. "You'd let them take me?"

"I have work to do. If you slow me down, I will leave you behind," Lee said icily.

Zao glared at Lee with eyes of fire. They were interrupted by the jiggling of the door handle. The door opened, and the Englishman came in. He stared at the three men inside his home as he closed the door.

"Oh I'm sorry. Did I interrupt you blokes hiding out in my home?" He snapped.

"Apologies sir. We needed a place to hide since it's after curfew and we needed to lie low from the Tingchia," Deng explained.

"Well that's a bloody relief. A Tinger killer and his buddies hangin' out 'ere in me loft all looking to avoid capture from curfew. Usin' my diplomatic immunity as protection from the Tingers. Fat load a good it'll do ya," the Englishman said.

"Correct me if I'm wrong," Lee said as he approached the Englishman. "You're the man who gives rallying speeches trying to instigate rebellion."

"Sure am. People deserve freedom. Even you blokes. Can't say I agree with the trespassin' but I'm sure you're good folk," he said

"It won't work," Lee said. "Your rebellion. China gives into oppression because of their belief in the deification of their Emperor. We focus on the collective, not the individual freedoms you preach."

"Sure does explain a lot."

"If you want change, we must choose a different tact. The miners won't rebel. They're afraid. We must make the Emperor feel fear."

"How do we do that?" He asked.

"Through acts of terror. We attack Yiu Mei and his ministers at random. We bleed the Empire of their best and brightest. We sow chaos. We unbalance the system and cause him to overreach to the point where the miners snap and fight back. And finally, we kill Yiu Mei," Lee explained.

"No. I won't do it," Zao said. "We can't win against the Emperor. I won't end up like Bai, who was taken the same night you were and didn't come back," he said as he sneered at Lee.

"Then what would you do?" Lee asked.

"I don't know, maybe hide in the mountains for three years while all of this blows over."

Lee lunged forward while Deng wrapped his arms around him. "Hwoon dahn! Dairuomu ji!"

"You blokes certainly got a way with the filthy language eh?" the Englishman asked.

"I'm not going to deal with this. I've got work to do!" Lee snapped as he broke Deng's grip and beelined for the door. The Englishman stepped in front of it.

"I like your style friend and I think your plot will work. Bob's your uncle-consider me part of your plot. Name's Jonathan Jay," he said as he extended his hand.

"Xing Ming Lee, back from the dead," Lee said as he shook Jay's hand.

"Now, I'm certain with all the ruckus you caused getting your pals here, the streets will be crawling with them Tingers."

"I don't care. Let me go," Lee said. His eyes became as hard as steel, and Jay saw a face that he knew he shouldn't trifle with. He stepped out of the way to let Lee cool down. He left the house and wandered through the streets. He kept to the shadows as best he could, but in the back of his mind he knew that the Emperor's cameras would catch him, there were just too many. Lee's saving grace was that they wouldn't be able to identify him since he'd been labeled as 'deceased' for three years.

He made it to a house that had haunted him for years. It was his old home which had long since been occupied by another family. There was a dim light inside, but a quick look through the window revealed that the husband and wife were asleep in their bed.

Lee picked the lock to his old home and creeped inside. The rickety floorboards groaned in protest, despite his effort to tiptoe through the house. He looked over at the couple who were still fast asleep. He searched for something, anything that could serve as a memory of his family.

He noticed that there were seeds buried between the

floorboards. He drew his knife and scraped them out, the only remnants of his past life which remained.

There were less than ten seeds which could be dug out, but they would do. A groan came from the bed and Lee leaped into a defensive position, and held his knife pointed at the couple in bed. He looked into the eyes of a frightened man who was more afraid than he was.

"Forgive me, I mean you no harm," Lee said in the native tongue. "This was my home before you, but the Tingchia came, killed my family and I only seek a token to remember them by."

The man listened, and then nodded. "Perhaps I can help," he said. He crawled out of bed and retrieved something from a box on a shelf next to Lee.

"We were going to give this to our first born, but you should have it back," the man said as he handed Lee a small doll.

Tears welled up in Lee's eyes as he held the doll. It had big black eyes, long black hair and fit in the palm of his hand. He clutched the doll tight and held it to his heart as a tear rolled down his cheek.

"Thank you for this," Lee said.

"You're welcome. I'm sorry about your family. We were taken from the homeland and I know the pain of having your home taken from you. We all do," the man said.

Lee felt his anger grow like a rising flame. He tied Ju's doll to his belt, nodded to the man and left his house. The night air was humid, like you were stuck inside of a cloud. Thunder rumbled in the distance and the skies were preparing to unleash their fury. Sprinkles of rain turned to a cascading downpour and Lee collapsed onto his knees.

Through the rain Lee saw the police station. The cystic infection that had rotted the heart of Ophridia, Lee knew that he was the one who needed to cleanse his world.

"It's time the Empire felt terror," Lee said as he rose from the ground. He walked up to the police station and knocked at the door. As the door opened Lee took his knife and thrust it into the throat of the soldier who opened it. He grabbed the soldier's gun and shot the other Tingchia one by one as they screamed in alarm over the intruder.

"Backup! We need backup!" One of them screamed over the comm. Lee shot him and kicked his corpse away from the controls. He saw that more units were on their way, which was perfect since a police station under duress would result in the death of more Tingchia.

Lee took the grenades off of the soldiers and stockpiled them inside the armory. He heard the sirens of the approaching Tingchia coming, grabbed two guns, some rope and loaded the bodies of three soldiers onto a dolly. The thrusters kept the dolly afloat without any signs of strain or effort. He pulled the pin to a grenade and tossed it into the armory.

Right as Lee left through the back door a squad of Tingchia stormed through the front. The soldiers paused at the sight of the dead bodies before the grenade exploded. The city rumbled as the police station erupted into a pillar of flame. The rain continued to douse the city streets below, but the Tingchia scrambled to the station to investigate the bombing.

With the distraction, Lee tied a rope around the necks of the three soldiers and hoisted them up on the streetlamps for all to see. He knew that he was on camera, but he didn't care. Jay, Zao and Deng ran up and caught Lee in the act.

"What the bloody hell did you do?" Jay screamed.

"I attacked the police station!" Lee hissed.

"You chùsheng xai-jiao de xiang huo! The Tingchia will hunt us! Like dogs!" Zao screamed.

"The gate is that way. Let's see how far you make it," Lee snapped. "As for me, I'm going to melt into the populace, they'll never find me."

The three men stood silent for a moment. "Count me in Lee. It's about time somebody stood up to the Tingchia," Deng said.

"Glad to have you buddy," Lee replied. Deng helped Lee hoist the soldiers on the lamp posts for all to see.

"May as well," Jay muttered as he ran over and helped the

two men out. Zao was standing alone. He looked towards the gates of the city. He heard the screams of the soldiers marauding around the city and witnessed the growing crowds around the fiery station. The soldiers shot into the air to scare the people back to their homes, but he felt the winds change. There was something in the eyes of the Tingchia that Zao had never seen before...fear.

Zao shuffled along and helped the others string up the final soldier. They heard another shot from the station and the screams of soldiers who caught onto what they were doing.

"Do you have a safehouse?" Lee asked Jay.

"A safe house? Why do you think that I've got a safe house?" Jay asked.

"You're an importer-exporter here on Ophridia. You either own a warehouse or know of one. Plus you're a revolutionary wannabe," Lee said.

"Well you're certainly a charming chav. Course I got a safe house."

"You better lead us to it if we're going to survive," Lee said as bullets whistled through the streets. The Tingchia were cracking down on anyone breaking curfew and didn't hesitate to bludgeon or shoot civilians on the spot.

"Right. This way," Jay said as the four men ran through the streets. Jay weaved through the alleyways and brought the men into the warehousing districts where Yiu Mei's coal was waiting to be shipped to Earth.

"Needn't worry 'bout the cameras out here. All belong to private corps that even Yiu Mei can't risk pissing off."

"Why not?" Deng asked.

"Because he needs Earth to buy all his coal, otherwise he'll be a very poor world leader," Jay said. "Anyway, I've got all the necessities here to survive. Food, water, communications-"

"Anything that requires a signal?" Lee asked.

"Of course."

"We can't use them. Can't use anything wireless, Yiu Mei's forces will hack in," Lee said.

"How're we to communicate then?" Zao asked. As he posed

the question, a pigeon fluttered down and landed on the roof to the warehouse before them.

"The pigeons here are quite tame," Lee said. He stepped forward, cooed and held his arm out. The pigeon leaped off of the roof and flew down onto his arm.

"Pigeons?" Jay asked. All three men stared in confusion until a smile formed on Deng's lips. He held out his arm and the pigeon hopped off and fluttered over. He giggled in delight as the bird walked along his arm in.

"The more basic we remain, the harder it will be for Yiu Mei to counter us. In-person meetings, messages relayed by pigeons, dead drops, the works. The Empire will never suspect it," Lee said.

The pigeon cooed, flew away and walked along on the roof of the warehouse.

"Pigeons?" Jay asked again.

"You'll get used to it," Lee said.

Five weeks passed with the Tingchia breaking down doors and arresting people in a maddening search for the terrorists who strung up their fellow soldiers on streetlamps. The Tingchia retaliated by hanging those who were even suspected of being connected with Lee's terrorist network.

"Why are we hiding down in here?" Zao asked. "I thought you wanted to attack the Emperor, not hide from him!"

"Patience Zao. Our attacks must be random to cause fear. If they're predictable, then the Emperor can respond. We need to draw him out," Lee explained.

"How're we going to do that?" Deng asked.

Lee placed a bowl of berries on the table. "With these," He said.

"I didn't think there were any plants down here," Zao said.

"There aren't. I found these up in the mountains. They're like the Rosary Pea on Earth. You get these into the bloodstream, and the victim is eliminated."

"Devious. How does a berry draw the Emperor out?" Jay asked.

"We move throughout the populace with poisoned blades or barbs and stick soldiers throughout the city. They'll fall over one by one and the Emperor-"

"Will hide inside of his Palace while his guard dies," Jay said. "It's a decent plan, but you need to get his attention. You need to strike somebody close to the Emperor!"

"Any suggestions on who?" Lee asked.

"What about Diang Xia, the Minister of Mining? He uses the Foremans to spy on the workers to find people for the Xiongbu," Zao explained.

"Brilliant target. Diang is supposed to be touring the mines tomorrow. We can strike while he's in public," Jay said. "Now all we need is a delivery system for the poison."

"I would suggest knives, but none of us will ever get past the guards," Lee said.

"What about acupuncture needles?" Deng asked. "We can get them right in the market."

"That's brilliant!" Jay screamed. "We get a few of the needles, dip 'em in the poison, Bob's your Uncle and we end up with a dead mining minister by nightfall!"

"Sounds like a great idea," Lee said as he took the berries and ground them with his pestle and mortar. The four men scripted their roles for the mission using crude drawings of the city streets on old receipt pads Jay used for his company.

"Is everything clear?" Lee asked. Everyone at the table nodded.

"Good. Everyone get some rest. We're going to need to be at full strength tomorrow," Lee said.

The men were restless as they tangled with the idea that they had plotted to assassinate a Minister. They tossed and turned while Lee turned to meditation when it became clear that he wouldn't sleep. Once the dawn hours came, the four men mobilized and took to the streets.

Deng sought out the acupuncture needles, Jay followed the Minister's procession while Lee and Zao searched for weak security points in the mines.

"Do you think Deng will come through? We both know he's

not the brightest star," Zao said.

"I know Deng will come through. He's by far the most reliable," Lee replied. "Calm down, everything is going to plan."

"What if it doesn't? What if none of this works?" Zao asked.

"We die. Just like we would've if we'd remained captured. There is no getting out of this alive Zao," Lee said, his voice laced with ice. Zao felt his heart flutter and his hands began to shake. The gravity of the situation began to press against his chest. In the back of his mind he always believed that there would be some way in which he'd make it out alive.

Lee stood up and place his hand against Zao's heart. "Steady your breathing. Dwell on your death. We are already ghosts. Let's haunt the Empire that killed us," he said.

Deng arrived at the mine entrance with the acupuncture needles. "Wait! How're we going to get Deng in there? His bald head makes him stick out!" Zao asked.

"Get him a helmet," Lee replied as he ran off into the midst of the crowd.

"Huh. Good thing we've still got our mining uniforms right Zao? Ol' Lee seems to stick out a bit don't he?" Deng asked as he picked up an abandoned helmet and put it on his head.

"Yeah. Great," Zao replied. He searched for Lee in the crowd, but lost track of him. He swallowed hard when he heard the foreman's scream which signaled that the Minister of Mining was on his way. The miners cleared out and stood at attention, while Zao tasted bile crawling along his throat.

Zao looked across the crowd and noticed that a mining foreman spotted him. The foreman approached, while Zao kept his face pointed towards the ground, hoping that the foreman would walk past.

He didn't.

The foreman honed right in on Zao. He felt every muscle tense and every instinct scream for him to run, but with the surrounding miners he couldn't budge from his position.

"Who do you think you are? Showing up late to work again?" The foreman screamed at Zao. Zao looked up and saw

Lee's snarling face under the yellow helmet. As he reprimanded Zao for being late in the native tongue, he palmed the vial of poison to Deng who dipped three needles into the vial and handed them to Zao.

Zao caught onto the act and handed Lee the three acupuncture needles, who slid them up his sleeve. Lee continued screaming at Zao until Diang's men were right behind him.

"Do not be late again, or I cut your rations for the next month!" Lee finished screaming. He turned around and collided with one of the Tingchia. The soldier glared at Lee, who profusely apologized and lowered his head in shame.

"Minister Diang, I beg for your forgiveness. If you would allow it, I would be honored to escort you to where you'll be speaking," Lee said.

Minister Diang looked at the crowd and nodded. Lee marched forward and escorted the entourage to the podium, where Diang would give his speech. Lee climbed onto the podium and tested the microphone. Satisfied, he walked down the steps and posed for a picture with the minister. After the picture the Minister rubbed his side and gave a quizzical look at Lee. However, the press came in and directed Minister Diang to the podium. Lee meanwhile, went behind the Tingchia guards and stood at attention.

"Miners! You are the iron will that moves this world!" Minister Diang said as he tried to rouse the crowd. The faces of the miners didn't show any emotion from the Minister's words since they knew he only said what he needed in front of the cameras. As long as he acknowledged the miners, they would continue to work.

Diang began to sweat as he spoke. His words slurred and his pauses became more frequent. Lee saw the Minister begin to lean on the podium and slipped off of the main stage as quietly as he could. He weaved his way through the miners, nobody questioning his movements since he was in the uniform of a foreman.

As he came across Zao and Deng, he gestured that it was

time for them to leave as well. The Minister wobbled against the podium and collapsed. There was an audible gasp from the crowd as they rushed forward, but the Tingchia screamed for all of the miners to stay back.

Lee, Zao and Deng exited the mines to find Jay waiting for them in a speeder. The three men climbed in and Jay drove off before the mass of people spilled out of the mines.

"Now we've got to get the word out on who was responsible. Congrats Lee, you're going on camera!" Jay said.

"Oh, no I'm not," Lee said.

"Yes, you are my friend," Jay replied. "You need to claim responsibility for the attack, otherwise the Empire will cover it up. We can't rely on gossip for this one."

"I told you, I'm not going on camera," Lee said as Jay propped up a camera.

"C'mon, your fans are waiting for you," Jay replied. Lee glared back but Jay was unfazed.

"Fine," Lee groaned. He took a seat in front of the camera while Jay adjusted the settings. "What do I say?" Lee asked.

"Just ramble off some of that guff about you terrorizing the Emperor. I'll edit the footage if we need it," Jay replied. "Alright, camera's set."

"Wait!"

"Nope! We are rolling!"

Lee stared at the camera for a moment. "Emperor Yiu Mei. You don't know who I am, but three years ago, a squad of your soldiers came into my home and executed my family before my eyes. One of them was my three year old daughter Ju, who carried this doll with her everywhere she went," Lee said as he held the doll up to the camera before tying it back onto his belt.

"For years you have held us under the heel of your boot in the name of 'security.' You wield your political influence on Earth to steal us from our homes and bring us here to harvest the coal which fuels only your wealth and influence. You subjugate us to beatings and arrests at night, pin neighbor against neighbor in the name of your 'terror,' the Xiongbu. I'm here to tell you that your reign is coming to an end. We are the ghosts of your Xiongbu and we will dismantle your Empire brick by brick. We started by eliminating one of your most trusted advisers, Minister Diang. We take full responsibility for his death and are here to inform you that more are to come. Your Xiongbu is in its final days Yiu Mei. My name is Xing Ming Lee and I'm the man who will end it."

"Perfect! Nothin' to it right?" Jay asked. "Now we send it out to the networks-"

"Where they'll suppress and bury it," Zao snipped.

"That's why I'm uploading it to some chaps I know who will provide coverage. They're a good group of blokes who'll help us out in a pinch."

"Who're they?" Deng asked.

"They're a group known as The Grid. Buncha old freedom fighters and techies who profit from chaos," Jay explained. "I've been sending the fellas a bunch of cries for help for weeks now."

"Well, let's hope they get the message since the Emperor controls the satellites too," Zao said.

"Cheer up Zao, it'll work. Just watch," Jay replied.

"Hey! Hey guys!" Zao said. "The Emperor's making an announcement!" The three other men rushed to watch the newscast.

"A terrorist has struck deep in the heart of our Empire," Yiu Mei proclaimed. "He operates to sow the chaos we suffered upon the arrival of this planet when we were part of the Core. He seeks to drive us back into the wilderness before we banded together under one flag and proclaimed ourselves a united and free Ophridia! Minister Diang Xia gave his life for the glory and the strength of our Empire. This terrorist seeks to destroy your safety! He seeks to erode the protections that I have worked so hard to put into place!" Yiu Mei screamed as he slammed his fist onto the podium. There was silence everywhere as the world held their breath for his next line in the speech.

"The Anarchist Xing Ming Lee seeks to eradicate the peace that has prevailed on Ophridia!"

"I am not an anarchist!" Lee hissed.

"Shh! Let's see where he's going with this," Jay said.

"He seeks to erase the peace that I have provided to this world! The peace that I kept on our planet while the rest of the Core waged their vicious civil war. While brother fought brother we united under one banner and built this world from scratch. We built this world through strength, through unity and through security! We will not be intimidated by a lone criminal who seeks to take that all away from us! As a result, I am placing a bounty on his head which is worth...whatever you wish it to be. Whosoever brings me the anarchist Xing Ming Lee will be granted any one wish that I as Emperor can grant."

"Let's see your reign of terror top that," Zao said.

"Bee-jway!" Lee snapped. He looked around and felt the walls closing in. He felt surrounded on all sides as though the entire planet had turned against him in an instant.

"It's not over my boy. You just need to lay low for a couple of weeks. I'll go into the streets and see what the word is on ya," Jay said.

"Yeah Lee. Don't worry, we'll keep you hidden right Zao?" Deng asked.

"Yeah...of course," Zao replied.

Lee nodded. He knew that the best course of action was to keep quiet and lie low like Jay had suggested.

"There anything you'd like?" Jay asked.

"Got any books?"

"I can find some. Bit of a collector myself."

"Good. Bring me some books, and I'll occupy my time," Lee said.

"...And together, we will emerge a stronger and more united Ophridia!" Yiu Mei screamed into the microphone and held both his arms high in triumph.

The weeks flowed as the four men navigated through the populace and set small bombs inside of government buildings. The empire rumbled and shook as the blasts consumed Yiu Mei's employees, with each retaliation from the Emperor more swift and brutal than the last. People were arrested in the dead of night as the Xiongbu consumed Ophridia's children just like the story of the ancient serpent. Lee and his men attacked the Tingchia who dared come out to make the arrests, and left the bodies of the soldiers in the streets. Rumors of the ghosts of the fallen who would protect the innocent from the Emperor's wrath.

"Good news lad," Jay said as the men convened just before midday. Lee read inside the converted office with books scattered all over the floor. "Blimey, you're at a loose end."

"What?" Lee asked.

"Doesn't matter," Jay replied. "Good news is that talk about you is gone. Murmurs and gossip are about the Tingers. There's no love for them right now. We eliminate one of those blokes, two more take their places."

"The chusheng zajiao de zanghuo!"

"Well I don't know how much they fornicate with livestock but-"

"Bee-jway!" Lee snapped. "We're not breaking the Emperor's men! I need the Tingchia to fear my knives more than the Emperor's guns!"

"What'd you have in mind then?"

"We need everyone to see. A sight nobody on Ophridia can miss. We string the Tingchia up on the streetlights by the hundreds! Thousands even!" Lee shouted. Zao and Deng walked into the warehouse. Zao carried in a box of grenades and set them on the floor. He grabbed three, then tossed a few to the others.

"Bringin' on the heavy stuff I see," Jay said.

"What're you ranting about?" Zao asked.

"We're going after the Tingchia. We make them more afraid of us than the Emperor."

"Yeah, the Tingchia need to be rooted out for what they did

to Bai, Ai Fen, and Ju. Make them bleed for all the loved ones they've taken from us. How're we gonna do it?" Deng asked.

"We'll need to start small. We attack a small squad on patrol, steal their uniforms and attack their stations," Lee said.

"They'll see our attack on the cameras. What'll we do when they swarm us?" Zao asked.

"We need to get to the Ministry of Information's headquarters and turn off all of the cameras," Lee replied.

"Oh, even better! How do you suggest we get in there then?" Zao asked.

"What if we don't have to risk our necks getting into the MoI?" Jay asked. "I'll bet we could outsource the task of making the Emperor blind."

"To who?" Lee asked.

"Those blokes at The Grid. They're big fans of ours, I'm sure I can talk 'em into givin' us a hand. They can navigate their way through all these computers and I can tell 'em which companies belong to Yiu Mei that run cargo to Earth. That'll keep 'em satisfied," Jay said.

"Good. Let's get to work on a plan," Lee said.

For hours Lee explained in crucial detail his plan of action of how to attack the Tingchia soldiers on patrol. The men deliberated on the best approach of achieving this objective until Jay broke the debate by going to his printer which held a stack of papers.

"What're those?" Lee asked.

"Posters," Jay replied.

"Of what?"

"You, Lee," Jay said as he revealed the poster. Lee met his own stern gaze and the word 'Resist' was inscribed on the bottom in Mandarin.

"While you blokes attack the Tingers, I'll spread some propaganda."

"Great. While we attack the soldiers, you decorate," Zao hissed.

"Don't worry lad. I'll help you with the Tingers and shut off the cameras. I'll even place the bombs on their speeders."

"That'll work," Lee said.

Lee waited until he saw the red light on the camera go off.

"And...go!" Lee whispered. Zao, Deng and Lee moved like ghosts through the streets until they were on top of three Tingchia soldiers. The men didn't have a chance to scream before their knives were buried in their throats. The sickening splash of blood on the streets caused Zao's stomach to lurch, but he swallowed the bile in silence.

"C'mon! Let's string them up!" Lee ordered. They stripped the soldiers of their clothing and despite the blood, put them on. Jay came out of the shadows with the posters he'd had made with Lee's stern gaze on them. He covered his fingers in ink and inscribed two characters on each of the soldier's bodies:

抵抗

"What're you doing?" Lee hissed.

"Branding," Jay replied. " 'Resist' may as well be your trademark on this world. All your posters say it, people gotta know you did this!"

"Hwai. C'mon, let's go after the station," Lee said.

Lee rammed the butt of his rifle against the keypad, which caused the doors to become bolted shut. Zao climbed onto the roof and dropped a grenade down an air duct. The grenade exploded and the soldiers inside scrambled to get away from the blast. They opened the front door but Lee and Deng were waiting and executed them on the spot. The pair moved in and shot the remaining soldiers inside, while the communications network came alive with captains demanding to know what was going on.

"What do I tell them?" Zao asked.

"Tell them everything is under control. Tell them we've secured the perimeter," Lee replied. Zao fed the information to the Captains, who seemed skeptical, but accepted his response. Lee found Jay on the side of the building painting the two characters on the police station.

"Perhaps instead of finger-painting you can have your friend shut down the communications for the Tingchia," Lee said.

"Are you mad?" Jay asked. "Then they'll know something is wrong."

"Then we should at least cut the emergency channels from here."

"That my dear chinaman, I can agree with."

Lee's squad moved to the next police station. There were only three throughout the entire city of New Peking, while the rest of the Tingchia resided within the Imperial Compound. They executed the soldiers in the second station just like the first, except this time they cut off the emergency beacon. The Tingchia had no idea that their brothers were being slaughtered within their own station.

At the third station, they executed their strategy to the letter, save the Captain who remained at the building.

"I will deal with him," Lee said as he drew his knife. "Tie him up!"

Zao and Deng rushed in and tied the captain to a chair. The Captain protested in Mandarin, and told the two men he would give them anything they wanted if they turned on Lee right now.

"I want you to get your precious Emperor to end the Xiongbu!" Deng snarled. "Can you do that? Huh?"

"Tsao ni zuzong shiba dai," the Captain snarled.

"Manners Captain," Lee replied in a calm tone. He waved Zao and Deng away as he drew his knife.

"The Emperor will kill you for this," the Captain spat.

"The Emperor tried to kill me once. He failed then, and he will fail now. None of you can kill me, I am the ghost of the Xiongbu," Lee hissed.

"You will all be shot like dogs!" the Captain snapped.

"You're not in a position for threats Captain," Lee said as he held the blade to the Captain's neck. "How do I get into the Imperial Palace?"

The Captain tightened his lips. He wasn't going to say a word.

"Good," Lee said. "I'd hoped that you'd make this difficult you hwoon dahn." Lee grasped the knife and stabbed the Captain's thigh. The Captain screamed out an array of curses at Lee.

"How do I get into the Imperial Palace?" Lee asked.

"Zao ni de xing!" the Captain screamed. Lee took hold of the knife and pulled the blade against the Captain's thigh muscles. The Captain spat and drooled in pain. His eyes lost focus and his head drooped.

"Lee, stop this!" Deng mumbled.

"Tzao-goa! How do I get into the Palace?" Lee howled. The Captain groaned through his teeth, but didn't break.

"The Emperor will stop you," The Captain said.

"I love true believers," Lee replied as he lifted the knife out of the Captain's thigh and plunged it into the other one. The Captain screamed in agony.

"Lee, please! Stop this!" Deng protested. "We're better than this! This is what they did to Bai!"

"Then it's time this hundan gets the payback they deserve," Lee said.

"No! Not like this! We can't become them Lee!" Deng screamed as he grabbed ahold of him.

Lee turned and held his knife to Deng's neck. "Do not touch me like that again!" Lee hissed. Deng stumbled backwards in horror at the sight of what Lee had become.

"This is what terror is! This is what I must do!" Lee said.

"You're no better than them!" Deng cried as he ran out of the police station. Lee turned back to the Captain and drove his blade back into his thigh. "How do I -"

"It's biometric!" The Captain confessed. "The Imperial Palace has a biometric lock, you can't get in unless you have access!"

"Do you have access Captain?" Lee asked. The Captain remained silent, but his gaze told Lee everything he needed to know. He dived for the Captain's hand while the Captain closed his eyes.

"Whoa, whoa whoa!" Jay screamed as he got between Lee and the Captain. "We can synthesize his fingerprints without taking this poor bloke's hand."

"Then do it!" Lee snapped. Jay untied the Captain and hoisted him over his shoulder and carried the man into the control room. Lee propped himself against the wall while he waited and wiped the blood off of his knife onto his uniform. Zao's eyes darted around the room and he swallowed hard at the grisly spectacle in front of him.

"What are you, some kind of ji bai?" Lee asked.

"Bee-jway!" Zao hissed. "You're the hundan who got us mixed up in all of this! You threatened Deng, the only one who was willing to stand up for justice!"

"You've been a weak little dairuomu ji since I came down from the mountains."

"You've been a ben tiansheng de yidui rou since you came from the mountains. Before then, you kept your head down, sought to do your part and return as a botanist on Earth. Now you synthesize poisons and torture captains."

"Better to be a monster than to die like a dog," Lee said. The moment the words left his mouth a hard blow cracked against his jaw. Lee fell to the ground while Zao wiped the blood off of his knuckles.

"I'll show you death like a dog," Zao said as he drew his pistol. He walked into the room where Jay was and executed the Captain at point blank range.

"Bloody hell!" Jay screamed. Zao holstered his pistol and left the police station. Jay came out of the office. "What in the hell did you do?"

"Are the prints done?" Lee asked as he got up off the floor.

"Course they are. Here," Jay said as he handed Lee the synthesized fingerprints. "Where's Zao?" Jay asked. "Did you piss him off too?"

Lee glared at Jay, which answered his question. He put on the synthesized fingerprints.

"Where do you think you're going?" Jay asked.

"I'm going to finish this with the Emperor. Tonight he dies," Lee said and left the police station.

Lee raced through the streets beneath the darkened sky and the dim lighting of the streetlamps. He came to the Imperial Gates, where there were scores of soldiers prepared to defend the Emperor. They stood at attention to guard against any threat.

"Rough night on patrol?" One of the guards asked, motioning to the blood on Lee's neck.

"Yeah, this stupid guy tried to resist, so we had to beat him to within an inch of his life, but he drooled a lot," Lee replied. He placed his hand on the biometric scanner and waited. His heart thundered in his chest until the light switched to green.

"That sucks. Have a good one," the guard said.

"You too," Lee replied. He searched the walls and palisades for every available weakness. He mentally noted every aspect of the structure and took in the entire Imperial complex. Behind the walled forcefield it looked like another city, with the imposing Palace at the top of the hill. Lee made his way with a strong march and nodded to every Tingchia he came across so as to not draw attention.

The Palace Guard were armed with weapons native to the Core, which were far superior than what those outside of the complex wielded. They were trained from the Core wars, which made an uprising even less likely.

Many guards intervened to stop Lee on his quest to the Emperor, but he kept pleading with them, stating that he had vital information on the whereabouts of Xing Ming Lee. Each time he mentioned his own name to the enemy, they let him pass.

The palace was dominating, ornate and made to appear ancient. The Emperor appreciated antiquity and marveled at the Chinese Emperors of Earth's past. He sought to emulate their grandeur for himself. Every tapestry, painting, and piece of furniture was picked for this reason, to make Yiu Mei into a Chinese Emperor.

Lee approached what he believed was the Emperor's

bedroom. Two guards stood outside with stern gazes that didn't look like they were capable of smiling.

"I have news for the Emperor. It's about Xing Ming Lee," Lee said. There was a moment of awkward silence that hung in the air. It soon became clear that the guards wouldn't allow admission.

"Go on, tell us," One of the guards said.

"It is for the Emperor's ears only," Lee replied.

"Nobody is permitted past this point," the other guard said.

"If I could just -"

"You stop there!" The first guard hissed as both men pointed their rifles at Lee. Lee halted, raised his hands and begged for an audience with the Emperor. One of the guards creeped up to Lee to make him walk away, but Lee grabbed ahold of his wrist. He spun the guard around and held him as a shield from the second guard's blaster. Lee grabbed the dead guard's blaster and fired back, killing the second soldier.

Lee threw the guard aside and pushed open the doors. The bedroom was barely lit while the golden light from the hallway flowed in. Lee drew his knife and creeped across the room to the sleeping Emperor before him.

"Now you die," Lee whispered as he raised the knife above the Emperor.

Lee drove the knife down but a searing chill gripped his thigh, which turned into a burning sensation. He smelled smoldering flesh and then realized too late when his leg gave out from underneath him that he'd been shot. Lee fell to the floor and saw a squad in the doorway. A man came walking in and Lee noticed the scar on Quan's chin. He saw the lines that crossed his face and the memories of watching Ai Fen and Ju die came flooding back.

"Quan," Lee whispered to himself.

"You're a decent enough assassin Lee, but you're still an amateur. You're reckless and desperate. Deadly combination for a man who is seeking to cut the head off the snake," Quan said as he signaled with his hand. Within seconds the entire bedroom flooded with Tingchia, all guns pointed at Lee.

"Quan! Explain to me how this...this thing made it to my bedside and stabbed my pillow!" Yiu Mei screamed.

"He overreached my liege. I let him have a small victory and he found himself caught in my snare," Quan explained. Two Tingchia reached down and pulled Lee up from the ground.

"Best put a mouth guard on this one, he has a tendency to bite," Quan said in condescension. Lee sneered at him while the soldiers put a black hood over his head.

"You're lucky I don't have you executed along with him Quan! That was too close!" Yiu Mei screamed as Lee was dragged down the stairs of the palace.

"My liege, you were not in any danger. I will take care of everything from here," Quan replied. His tone was calm, but forceful. The Emperor fell silent.

Lee felt the chill of the morning air as he was dragged outside and heard the rumbling exhaust from a hovertruck that waited at the base of the Imperial steps. He guessed that the truck was armored and that he was going to be taken to his execution. The soldiers dragged him into the truck and the doors slammed shut behind him.

"Where are you taking me?" Lee asked. His question lingered in the air, almost like he was alone, but the presence of the soldiers was hard to ignore as they bandaged up his leg.

"You know Lee, you've become quite an asset to me," Quan said.

"Why's that?" Lee asked.

"Because the Emperor needs to know that he's weak without me!" Quan snapped. "Killing peasants was becoming quite routine until you came along. You're a challenge. A true threat." There was a hint of admiration in Quan's voice.

"The Emperor seeks to make an example out of you. Execute you in the public square. I think this is foolish. I think it'll make you a martyr."

"Why do you carry out his will then?"

"I have my reasons," Quan replied. "Your friends won't last very long. They've certainly made their mark. Let him see," He ordered. One of the soldiers pulled Lee's hood off. Outside in the streets, hundreds of soldiers hanged from the streetlights. Posters brandishing Lee's face were everywhere. Crude signs dangled like rustic necklaces from many of the soldiers, each bearing the two characters that had risen to become his symbol.

抵抗

"Resist," Quan spat. "None of this would've happened without my help."

"Cho yade."

"Call me names all you want Lee, one of your own has collaborated with me to ensure your attacks go through. I know all and I see all. That's why I'm known as the 'Hunter.' "

"You're a liar! What do you gain from my attacks? They hurt you just like they hurt the Emperor!"

"You'd think that wouldn't you?" Quan asked. A pigeon landed on the window behind Lee. It carried a small handwritten note around its ankle.

"Get down!"

The pigeon flew away, and Lee dived for the floor. An explosion rocked the truck and sent it careening into a concrete building. Quan shouted orders at the soldiers who were disoriented from the crash. Lee rose to his feet, charged at Quan and pinned him between the truck and his shoulder.

Quan winced in pain as the door opened. Jay was there and waved with his hand for Lee to come out. Lee stumbled out of the truck while Zao and Deng swooped in to provide cover fire.

"I can't walk!" Lee said. Jay wrapped his arm around him and hoisted him up. Deng came in and grabbed the other arm. Deng and Zao provided suppression fire on the truck, while Quan hid behind the door. He aimed his pistol, fired and hit Deng in the shoulder. The impact drove Deng to the ground, taking Lee and Jay with him.

Zao unleashed a volley while Quan closed the door. Deng, Lee and Jay scrambled to get to their feet while several crimson soldiers closed in from the side.

"The Tingers are flanking us!" Jay screamed as he opened fire against the incoming men. Lee tried to run, but the muscles in his thigh refused to cooperate. Zao kept firing on the truck while Deng and Jay shot at the Tingchia trying to flank them. All four men sprinted down the streets, each of them wondering how they'd get out of this.

"We're done for! They've seen our faces!" Zao screamed.

"Why did you guys come for me? You could've kept fighting them in secret!" Lee yelled.

"Never leave one of your own behind!" Deng shouted. "That's why we came back for you!"

"I don't see a way out of this," Lee replied.

"All we need is to get to the warehouses. My diplomatic immunity will protect us there."

"No Jay. We won't make it to the Warehouse District in time," Lee said as he looked to the mountains. "We have two options. We can go to the mines and hope that the miners aren't interested in taking the Emperor's bargain." A bullet exploded into the concrete the men were hiding behind and rained dust on them. Another bullet tore through Deng's chest.

"Deng!" the men screamed.

"He'll never survive in the mines!" Zao hissed. "What's our other option?"

"We run into the mountains and take our chances in the wilderness," Lee said.

"No." Deng replied as blood flowed from his lips. "We can't abandon these people. We cause all of this terror and then leave them to deal with the fallout? No, we can't do that to them."

"Deng we-"

"I said no Lee!" Deng snapped. "We need the help of the people in this fight. Only if all of Ophridia unites against Yiu Mei will we have a fighting chance!" He turned and looked out at the encroaching Tingchia and then ran towards them.

"Deng! What are you doing?" Lee asked in a panic.

"Go for the mines! Convince the people of Ophridia to join us!" Deng screamed as he charged off towards the Tingchia.

"Deng!" Zao shouted. He stood speechless, unable to cope that his friend just ran off into the maw of Yiu Mei's elite.

"Right, we don't need you dying too," Jay said as he pulled on Zao's shoulder. "We shouldn't waste what we've been given." He ran up to one of the coal haulers from the mines, finagled with the wires and got the truck rumbling to life.

Zao picked Lee up and carried him into the truck where the three men drove off towards the mines. The Tingchia shot at the coal carrier, their blaster bolts making contact but not slowing the vehicle down. Jay radioed the guards on the tower ahead, but they'd already sealed off the gates.

"Zao! Shoot out the terminals that power the gate!" Jay screamed. "Otherwise we're going to know what it feels like to run into a brick wall!"

"What? Are you crazy?" He asked.

"It's our only chance!" Jay screamed.

Zao peered out of the window and fired at the terminal, which sizzled and crackled. Blaster bolts tore through the hood of the truck, but Jay kept driving.

"Almost seems like it'd be easier to surrender," Zao said. Lee and Jay both glared at him, their eyes full of daggers.

"Only a thought," He said as he leaned back into his seat. Lee's thoughts swirled inside in his head over Quan's words of how one of those in Lee's inner circle belonged to him.

Jay raced through the bleak and unending desolate Ophridian landscape until the Tingchia had given up pursuit.

"They finally caved. Unrelenting lot dontcha think?" Jay asked.

"They let us go," Lee said. "Quan won't stop hunting. He'll use drones to search for us out here."

The men rode in silence through the Ophridian darkness. Lee looked up to the mountains and thought of the sunlight. He imagined the glow as he meditated on the side of the mountain, where he saw his visions of terror, where this all began. Now he'd been shot and one of his best friends had been killed to ensure his escape.

The men circled back and abandoned the truck less than five kilometres away from the mines. They arrived to the mines a ragged bunch, but this made them blend in with the miners effortlessly. The three men stole some mining uniforms and tried their best not to call any attention to themselves.

They labored in the mines for three days. Every eye that crossed their path threatened the sign of recognition. Fraternizing with other miners took on a tactical role, one in which the three terrorists needed to solicit information of what was happening in the city. Every interaction was planned to see who knew what, yet they had to appear uninterested enough to only be soliciting gossip.

During the three days Lee's leg was in constant pain. His leg muscles strained from the burden, but he never ceased moving for the sake of the mission. In the back of his mind, he knew the three men would get caught, but their goal was only to last long enough.

"Word through the mines is the men are quite sore about their homes being disrupted by the Tingers," Jay whispered as the three men met for their daily meeting. Lee sat and stroked the hair of Ju's doll, imaging it back in her hands.

"Yeah, that's what I'm hearing too," Zao said.

"Why aren't they reacting?" Lee asked. "Why aren't they putting a stop to it?"

"Think about it Lee. The blokes are all out 'ere. Nothing they can do for their families."

"That's it. It's because nobody sees," Lee replied. "The Xiongbu. It's all done in secret, hidden away from the eyes of the public. Yes people are sad about the loss of their loved ones, but they don't see any of it. Nobody's outraged because nobody knows where the bodies go," Lee explained.

"You're right," Jay said. "If we can get the Tingers to overreact and lash out at the public, then they'll see. They'll resist against him."

"Yeah well it won't take much. Quan is uprooting everyone to find you," Zao said. "He and Yiu Mei have gone mad in their search for you."

"Then it's time those hwoon dahn find me," Lee said. "Jay! Rally these men!"

"Nope. This is a Chinaman's war. I'm an outsider. You need to rally them."

Lee winced, but he accepted. He climbed onto a ledge until he towered above all of the miners. Murmurs spread across the crowd while the foremen shouted for him to get down.

Lee cleared his throat and the miners looked up at him. "My name is Xing Ming Lee. I am the Anarchist of Ophridia, the one the Emperor blames for all of your suffering on his nightly newscasts. You have lost family members and friends. Every one of us has lost someone we hold dear. I lost my wife and daughter who were shot right in front of me by that duh liou mahng Quan Sito! For seven years the Emperor has waged his Xiongbu in secret. He has attacked all of us in the shadows, forced us to turn on each other with bribes and promises of riches for those who turn on their neighbors. I'm certain that many of you are thinking what you'll ask for when you bring the Emperor my dead body."

Lee paused. A wave of shame swept through the crowd, while the foremen marched at him with pistols drawn. Still, he continued. "We rejoiced when Yiu Mei kept us out of the Core Wars, but in secret he sent his own forces to fight. They came back hardened, trained and became the backbone of who we know as the Tingchia. We did not realize that our desire for peace became a weakness. I am guilty of this. I came here with the hope that I could serve China, work through my service in lieu of being in the military, but all it did was make me a target. One person named me in anonymity, most likely through torture and as a result my family was targeted. I was to be arrested and carried away in one of Yiu Mei's black bags, but I fought back and fled into the wilderness. While in exile I realized that somebody had to stand up to the Emperor, to cause him to feel the same terror that we feel every day. Now I can barely walk, let alone attack the Emperor. That's why I need your help. I need you miners to join me in rising up to stop Yiu Mei's reign of terror. He has sent his military after your families, uprooted you from your homes and he does so while you work here so that you don't see any of it! All of his attacks are in darkness, in the depth of night. We fear the night and the words 'curfew' for we know that those who go into the dark don't come back. Miners! March with me back into the city and let us put an end to Yiu Mei's reign!"

The foremen closed in, but the miners drowned them out in shouts of dissent. The foremen threatened to shoot, but the miners took them out.

Lee hobbled down from his position and walked through the civilians. One by one the miners dropped their equipment, and marched back for the city.

"What is going on?" One of the guards to the city asked.

"It's the miners! They're marching on us!" The other guard said.

"Quick! Radio General Quan!" The first guard said. The second guard got on the comm and explained the situation to the General.

"Let them through," he replied.

"Sir?"

"Let the miners through," Quan insisted. The two guards looked at each other, but they shut down the forcefield and stood at attention while the miners marched on the city.

Lee stopped and looked at the gate. His instincts told him that something was wrong, but the miners kept marching. Lee pushed forward, but stayed on high alert.

The miners walked through the civilian sector of New Peking, but it was as quiet as a ghost town. From what he'd heard, Lee expected there to be Tingchia forcing people out of their homes or executions in the streets. Instead there was nobody. The miners dispersed through the streets to check on their homes.

Whispers from the miners spread as a wave of fog washed

into the crowd. It was a sickly yellow color and it was heavy. It flowed like a river around their legs. They figured that it was another Ophridian fog until the men started coughing and gagging.

"It's poison! The Tingers are gassing us!" Jay screamed at the top of his lungs. Another cloud of gas poured in, the mob scrambling away from each other in full panic. Jay pulled on Lee and Zao by the arms and lead through a channel of alleyways into the warehouse district. Lee felt the gas get into his throat, which burned and made him cough. His breathing became constricted, and his vision blurred. Jay kept waving him and Zao ahead until they made it back to their hideout.

Inside, Lee and Zao couldn't stop coughing. The three men choked from the fumes they'd inhaled. Jay ripped a canister of pure oxygen out of a container and supplied Lee and Zao with a mask for them to breathe through. The two men inhaled until they'd recovered enough to breath on their own.

"I can't believe it," Lee said. "Yiu Mei...he gassed his own people. The miners, women, children…" He reached down and thumbed Ju's doll, a stunned silence settled on the room like a heavy blanket. "Where could he even get chemical weapons?"

Silence echoed through the room.

"Jay! I'm asking the importer, where could Yiu Mei have gotten these weapons?"

"Must've been from an old military stockpile. I think the company that made 'em was called Chemron," Jay said.

"Then after I kill Yiu Mei, I'm going to hunt down whoever developed those weapons," Lee said. He looked around the room and then started tearing through all of the supplies in the warehouse.

"What're you doing?" Jay asked.

"I'm going to end this and kill Yiu Mei once and for all or die trying," Lee said as he grabbed a fresh set of clothes, several knives and an air mask. "You two, go after Quan."

"Y'know Lee I'm not really sure if we-"

"We will," Zao said. "They all need to die. This regime falls today." His voice was as sharp as a dagger and steeled with conviction.

"Good. There is little chance that we'll come back from this," Lee said in an even tone.

"As long as some of them die with me, it doesn't matter," Zao said as the two men shook hands. Lee turned to Jay.

"Right. Been a part of this since the beginnin'. Good luck in there, you're gonna need it," Jay said as he and Lee shook hands.

Lee snapped the oxygen mask onto his face, took a deep breath and then bolted out of the warehouse. The air was still heavy with the clouds of weaponized chlorine which included materials that ate away at the tubes connected to Lee's oxygen tank.

"Ai Ya!" Lee cursed to himself as he sprinted through the fog towards the Imperial Gates. He had no plan of how he was going to get into the Imperial Palace, but he would adapt. He knew deep down a way would reveal itself.

Back inside the warehouse, Zao looked out the window and saw the gas clouds descending onto the streets. He took off his oxygen mask and looked at Jay.

"Come on, let's go," Zao said as he rose from the floor. He coughed out a heavy glob of bloody saliva, then shouldered his rifle.

"You sure?" Jay asked. "You got hit pretty hard from that gas."

"Oh well I guess. Not like I expect to live past this mission, may as well take some of the soldiers with me," Zao said.

Jay swallowed hard. "Alright. Where to?"

"The gas attack came from here in the warehouse district, that's why there wasn't much of a gas cloud. Come on!" Zao said as the two ran through the alleyways in between the unadorned cube-shaped buildings. Zao moved with a new sense of zealotry, propelled by his conviction to end the monsters who preyed on the miners of Ophridia.

Zao followed the trail of smoke until they came to the water treatment facility.

"Bloody hell! They stopped all the water flow in the sewers and released the chemicals through the water grates!" Jay said.

"Glad you caught on," Zao said. His eyes were watery and red, poisoned from the gas that wafted through the air.

"If we can get the water restarted, that'll negate the effect of the gas," Jay said and paused for a moment. "How did *you* know?"

"I figured it out," Zao said as he slammed the butt of his rifle against the door handle and kicked it open.

Zao walked in, rifle poised to fire. The two men came upon a heap of discarded chemical canisters. "Here are the canisters the Emperor used," Zao said. "Jay, where did these come from?"

"Buggered if I know. Someone must've brought them off world," Jay said.

"Now is not the time to play ignorant," a voice said from the doorway. It was Quan holding a pistol. Zao aimed his rifle at him, but a squad of Tingchia flooded into the room.

"What're you talking about yanse lang?" Zao asked.

"Your friend here is the one who brought the cargo offworld," Quan said as he gestured to Jay.

"You brought those weapons here?" Zao snapped and pointed his gun at his friend.

"Zao, I can explain," Jay said as he held his hands in the air. "I'm a respectable contractor who knows the planet well. I was told not to ask any questions when I received the shipment."

"Perfect," Quan muttered to himself.

"You brought the weapons that killed thousands of innocent people!" Zao screamed.

"Zao, I swear I had no idea! I coulda just dropped the shipment and left, but I didn't. I stayed here and fought with you. I've bled with you!"

"Not enough," Zao replied as he cocked his rifle.

"Zao! Quan is turning you against me!" Jay pleaded. "He's making you believe I intentionally brought those weapons to Ophridia!"

"Interesting thought isn't it? One in your party starts a terrorism campaign while another brings it to an end," Quan said.

"See Zao? He's using your anger and turning you against me!" Jay said.

"I'm hardly turning him against you. He just has a clearer idea of who is for and who is against this revolution," Quan said. "And I've allowed this insurrection to go on long enough."

"What? Allowed?" Jay asked.

"Yes. You think your friend would've gotten anywhere without my help? I allowed him to spread terror and weaken the Emperor. I allowed him to get inside the Emperor's Palace to show him how weak he is. My time has come to be the new Em-

"Bee-jway! We're not going to listen to this!" Zao hissed. "The entire Ophridian regime must die!" He screamed as he revealed an antimatter grenade from beneath his clothes and pulled the pin.

"Shoot him!" Quan ordered. The Tingchia fired round after round while Jay leaped through the window of the warehouse, into the street and ran away like he was escaping the maw of hell itself. He looked behind and saw the warehouse fill with a bright light followed by a sonic wave that sheared through the metals walls. Shards of metal went in all directions as the warehouse collapsed into a pile of rubble.

Jay crawled out of the dust-soaked area, coughing from the debris in the air. From the ground he looked up and saw the lights of the Core ships descending upon Ophridia. Someone got his emergency beacon. Jay picked himself up and ran for his warehouse. Inside he tuned into the Core comm frequencies and listened to the instructions being given to civilians on the ground. He then overheard about the chatter said onboard about Yiu Mei.

"I gotta get to Lee pronto!" Jay said as he dropped the comm device.

As Lee ran through New Peking, he was surprised by what he saw. The trap the Tingchia had set for the miners had backfired on them. All of the miners were in full revolt and attacking the crimson soldiers who'd tormented them for so long. Smoke rose from the city and cries of the dying loomed everywhere. A group of miners were attacking a platoon of soldiers who were in control of an artillery cannon. Lee had an idea.

He opened fire on the Tingchia, killing several of them and assisted in the brutal execution of the remaining soldiers. The miners looked to him with tired faces, but they were relieved that he'd helped them.

"I need to get into the Imperial Palace. Use this to fire on the forcefield protecting it!" Lee ordered.

"Yes sir!" One of the miners said as they saluted him. The miners turned the cannon, Lee adjusted the angle and they fired upon the forcefield. The cannon rumbled with a shattering boom and the force field in the distance rippled from the impact.

"Perfect! Keep firing!" Lee said as he ran off. The miners wished him luck and kept up their assault on the forcefield.

Lee moved block by block, the resistance from the Tingchia growing more fierce. He fought tooth and nail against the soldiers, doing his best to ignore the pain in his leg. As he moved closer to the Imperial City, he kept watch on the forcefield. More ripples. All he could do was hope that once the miners had control of the guns, that they'd keep control of them.

The miners kept advancing. There weren't many of the Tingchia left, all of the Imperial Guard were hidden behind the forcefield. Some of the soldiers broke rank and ran to the gate begging to be let in. They clawed like mad, but it was no use.

The last of the Tingchia resistance broke, and they retreated to a line in front of the forcefield.

Lee and the miners picked off the remaining Tingchia until the forcefield fell. The soldiers screamed and rejoiced at being let in, but Lee couldn't discern why they dropped the forcefield now.

Lee found his answer as he saw two starships rise from within the Imperial Compound. Two of them fired off, circled around and dropped bombs on the civilians.

Lee cursed under his breath. The third ship loomed in the air, waiting for the appropriate target. He knew that he had to try to get past the gate. He sprinted for the gate to the Imperial Compound, but was rebuffed when the airship opened fire with its gatling turret on the nose of the ship. Lee darted behind a building, but the blaster fire carved through the concrete like a hot knife through butter.

"C'mon, think of something, anything!" Lee told himself. He looked around the corner of the building, but the blaster bolts burst through the wall he was hiding behind. The wall was ready to collapse on top of him.

A fiery comet streaked across the sky and slammed into the ship. The ship spun out of control in the blaze of a falling star. Lee looked behind him and saw the smiling faces of the miners still in control of the artillery cannon.

Lee saluted them and took off into the Imperial Compound. Now that the Emperor was wielding bombers against the citizen revolt, the only way to stop the massacre was to go after the Emperor himself.

As Lee navigated through the Imperial Buildings, he could hear the orders of officers being shouted as well as the marching boots of the Tingchia. The Emperor's personal guard had been called out to quell the uprising and judging the fact that most of them were carrying Xeclian disintegration weapons, it was by any means necessary.

Lee looked back and saw that the miners wielded their cutting torches and lasers like weapons, but they didn't have a chance against such advanced weaponry. He looked at the gateway and saw two guards still at attention. He took out his rifle and shot both of the guards, then sprinted across the open pathway to the gate's terminal. Without any grace or subtlety, Lee ripped out the internal hardware, which brought down the entire forcefield protecting the Palace.

Lee knew that he'd never survive a direct encounter with

the guards inside of the palace. He knew that dropping the forcefield would've triggered some kind of alarm so he looked for an alternative route.

The outer steps featured elegantly carved tigers and dragons who served as guardians of the palace. Lee leaped onto the tiger statue in front and then jumped onto the dragon which curled around a pillar and led to the roof. The pain from the jump made him black out for a moment, but he knew that he had to keep moving. He took it all in, and used it as a focusing point of the harm he wanted to inflict on the Emperor.

From ledge to ledge along the roof Lee jumped and maneuvered around the slippery shingles until he made it to the window of the Emperor's bedchambers. He had to walk along the wall and make one last jump to the ledge. Below him was a fall over several hundred metres to a grisly death against stone. His leg was on fire and begging him to stop, but Lee stomped his foot to feel the pain and use it to drive him forward.

He made his final leap of faith to the ledge, smashed the window and crawled inside. Several shards of glass impaled his arms and abdomen as he spilled onto the floor from exhaustion. He looked around the room but noticed that nothing and nobody was there.

"Of course, he would've long since changed his bedroom," Lee whispered to himself. He went to the door and opened it a crack so that he could see what was going on inside of the palace.

What he saw surprised even him. There were only a handful of guards remaining to protect the Emperor behind a door across the main room. Lee took out his rifle and checked, only three shots remained. He had to make them count against the remnants of the Emperor's guard.

Lee took aim and fired the first shot, which dropped the Imperial guard, but the others retaliated by firing their disintegration rifles at him. Lee rolled away as the wall and doorway were blown to bits. He waited on the floor for the Tingchia to come, but after a few minutes, they never did. He crawled into a corner where he could see them.

"Wangbadan won't leave their precious Emperor. Fine by me," Lee said as he aimed at another Imperial Guard. They were searching around for him, but by the time the guard in his sights noticed him, it was too late. Lee shot the guard and rolled away. The last of the wall protecting him was obliterated in the next volley.

The last of the guards rallied in front of the door. Lee was down to one shot and he knew that at best he could take out only one guard. He wracked his brain for a way to finish off the remaining soldiers.

Out of the corner of his eye Lee noticed that the opposing wall was standing strong and that it was thick. Much thicker than what seemed appropriate for the building. The soldiers outside fired on the room, which took out large sections of the floor. The floorboards groaned at the stress and the room began to collapse. The wood creaked and groaned while dust threatened to choke Lee out.

The dust in the air flowed into a crevice within the wall. In that moment, Lee understood why the wall had held for so long.

"The hwoon dahn has a secret passageway," Lee whispered to himself. He leaped across the chasm, tumbled along the floor and sought out the door handle. He heard the click from the inside and the hidden door in the wall swung open.

The passage was a tight fit, but Lee managed to squeeze through. The passageway was lined with torn cobwebs, which was a sign that it was put to recent use. The deeper he went, the more it felt like the passages were closing in. There were tangents and side halls, but Lee kept walking straight.

"Ta ma duh, hwoon dahn must want me to run his little maze," Lee whispered to himself.

He heard the soldiers screaming on the outside, but there was a presence in the passageway. Someone entered, and Lee was closing in. He snaked through the corridors until he seized the shoulder of the man he was trailing.

It was Yiu Mei, the Emperor himself.

"Convenient how you live, sniveling dog," He hissed as he tried to point his pistol at Lee.

"Gunkai you fay-fay duh pee-yen!" Lee screamed as he snapped the Emperor's elbow. "You will answer for what you've done Yiu Mei! You're lucky that I don't carve you open and force feed you your worthless guts! Now surrender!"

Yiu Mei whimpered in the dark hall, the lines on his face deepened by the glow of the light from the other rooms. He looked like a harmless middle-aged man, not some sinister genocidal monster.

"Surrender!" Lee screamed again. Yiu Mei lowered his pistol to the floor and kneeled down.

"Make it quick," Yiu Mei said. Lee put his rifle to Yiu Mei's head. Up close, he noticed that the Emperor's eyes and face looked...familiar. It felt as though he recognized the man, but where?

Lee realized where he'd seen that face before.

"The Hermit from the mountains," Lee whispered.

"You know him?" Yiu Mei asked.

"Yes, how do you?"

"He's my brother," Yiu Mei replied.

Lee stared through the darkness in disbelief, but in hindsight realized the truth. He was to bring terror to the Emperor's heart. It was not up to him to execute the Emperor, that would be for the miners to do.

"Call off your troops! Call off the bombers!" Lee screamed as he pulled Yiu Mei to his feet, keeping his rifle placed firmly in Yiu Mei's back as he pushed him through the palace.

The two men walked out the front doors to see hundreds of crimson Tingchia standing in the courtyard.

"Tell them to surrender. Tell them it's over," Lee whispered into Yiu Mei's ear. "Snipers included."

"Lay down your weapons my warriors. I shall throw myself upon the mercy of the Core Senate!" Yiu Mei screamed.

The entire courtyard was aglow from the Core ships. The soldiers inside poured out in a tidal wave and ordered the miners to stand down. They saw the condition of the miners and made the Tingchia surrender all of their weapons.

Jay came across the mob in the courtyard. He tried to scream at Lee, to tell him to execute the Emperor then and there, but his voice was drowned out by the shouting mob.

Another ship landed, and a wave of civilian reporters and camera drones spilled out, searching for the Anarchist of Ophridia. The thousands of lights from the cameras threatened to overwhelm him. The normally sleepy, quiet courtyard had become a hive of activity within a matter of seconds.

The entire galaxy watched as Lee, the Anarchist of Ophridia held the toppled Emperor Yiu Mei on the edge of the palace.

Soldiers surrounding a Chinese man shouted at Lee to drop his weapon. This man was in a fine suit and approached the edge of the palace. "Hello Mr. Lee. I'm Core Senator Mao. We can take Colonial Governor Yiu Mei from here." His tone was too calm, too even.

"Colonial Governor?" Lee screamed. "Do you have any idea what this man has done to us?" An eerie quiet settled over the crowd except for the clicks from the cameras.

"He's murdered us! Tortured us! Held us under heel as slaves!" Lee screamed.

"We're all very aware of the alleged atrocities committed by Yiu Mei. Please, allow us to take him into custody so that we may proceed with a proper trial," Senator Mao said.

Alleged atrocities. That was how this representative of the Earth Core government saw the Yiu Mei situation. Earth wanted due process, which would take decades. Each passing year was one more year Yiu Mei would sit in protective custody, until the atrocities on Ophridia were long forgotten by Yiu Mei's prosecutors.

Lee saw only one option left. He looked to the doll that dangled from his belt and remembered Ju as she giggled when she came running across their dining room floor into Ai Fen's arms.

He kicked Yiu Mei behind his knees, forcing him to kneel and shot him in the back of the head. A collective gasp echoed across the crowd as the body of the fallen emperor tumbled down the palace steps.

Lee tossed his rifle away and kneeled down on the ground while the soldiers swarmed him and Senator Mao glared at him.

Lee and Jay were held in isolation for over a year while the Core compiled evidence on whether to hold a trial for the two men alleged as terrorists. The legal evidence was murky since Ophridia had been cut off in Yiu Mei's illegal secession from the Core.

One day, the holding cells were unlocked and the guards escorted Lee and Jay into an interrogation room telling them that they had a visitor. They gave each other a puzzled look.

"Maybe it's those bloody vultures in the media. Should we tell them to sod off?" Jay asked.

"Either that or tell them tsao ni zuzong shiba dai."

A black man wearing a gray suit and a black tie, neither of which fit quite right walked into the interrogation room. He adjusted his tie as he loaded up a dossier about Lee and Jay.

"How is it that a botanist-turned miner and a humble shipping merchant come to overthrow the most ruthless dictator in the galaxy?"

"Well you see now we-"

"It was a rhetorical question," the man said as he cut Jay off. "Now, you two have just executed one of the most well connected leaders in the Core. A lot of people were involved with keeping Yiu Mei in power for better or for worse and are going to find their pocket books getting a lot lighter. In short, people are going to come after you for this. Prison is going to be a very dangerous place."

"Get to the point hundan," Lee snapped.

"Yeah, I was told that you've got quite a potty mouth Lee. Look, I'm here to offer you two a third option. My name is Colonel John C. Henry and I'm building a team…"

—The End—

Horsemen United

PART FIVE

The First Horseman

Jabal climbed inside of his finished Chamber device. He saw his reflection in the screens surrounding him. A shaven head, beaked nose, and deep brown eyes, he always believed he was descended from Persian nobility. A cursor blinked in the corner, but then a vast array of jarred text filled the screen. Within seconds he was surrounded by code which he could manipulate at will. His customized bracelet controllers allowed him to physically move inside of his Chamber, the latest computer device which submerged their owners into a reality of their choosing. The Chamber was dome shaped, with a chair in the middle. When activated, the chamber darkened on the outside, protecting the systems from light interference. Inside, the world came alive as the screens projected the clearest images the human eye could recognize. Each of the screens were touchable, providing an interactive environment for gamers, coders and of course, hackers.

"Now I've got you," Jabal said as he waved his arms and zoomed in on a corporate account. It was a no-named shipping business located on Aurelius Prime, a planet known to house rebels, scoundrels and wealthy men who sought to hide their credits.

"You're no match for me." Jabal pulled up his holographic keyboard and typed a chain of script. His lightning-quick fingers were nimble and thin, honed from years of typing on invisible keys.

He set a timer and raced himself as he typed a series of commands. The company's virtual service code flooded before his eyes, his usual tricks no match against the strengthened security.

"Hmm, not bad bankers. Guess I'll send in my Wrecking Crew after you," Jabal said as he pulled up three windows.

"Hello Jabal, what data may I gather for you today?" A mischievous voice echoed within the Chamber.

"Hey Loki, take the Wrecking Crew and penetrate the server defenses here. It's time we test this ransomware we've been working on.

"I'm getting us into position for an assault on their security systems," Loki said as he evaporated into the code and went into cyberspace. Jabal had spent years developing multiple artificial intelligence programs which were capable of targeting any dataset he wanted and would find all the information he needed about it. Typically he performed small theft, but now there was a chance for a big score which held virtually no risk.

He had become obsessed with shipping companies that rarely traveled within Core jurisdiction. They would only service the outer reaches where the Coalition government reigned, and they kept encrypted shipping documents or cargo lists that were obviously falsified.

Arms dealers.

They wouldn't turn to the Core authorities, their sworn enemy in the midst of the Unification Wars, and the newly formed Coalition Government didn't have the resources to deal with cyber warfare.

Loki returned. "Sir, we've located the organization's servers. Millions of shipping records with destinations located in the Outer Regions beyond Core Space, right in Coalition territory."

"Perfect. Are Eris and Laverna in place?" Jabal asked.

"Yes sir they are," Loki replied.

"Perfect. Let's threaten to shut this place down," Jabal said. He typed out his demands to ransom the shipping company and threatened to destroy everything if they didn't agree to pay. His heart pounded in his chest, and his breathing grew shallow. He had never done anything on this scale before, but he did his research, and everything was in place. All that was left was to execute.

"Go!" Jabal shouted with glee. He issued his demands for ransom payment, put the Wrecking Crew on standby and waited for the owner to write back.

The reply was simple: "Do your worst."

Jabal grinned from ear to ear. "Loki, Eris, Laverna, overwhelm his servers," He commanded. The four issued millions of commands in seconds, unleashed the ransomware and waited for a response. Jabal could see the company's servers collapse one by one like a series of dominoes.

Another reply came through: "Fine! Take the damn money!" Jabal waited until he saw a deposit for over one million credits into his account, a sum most people wouldn't ever see in their lifetime.

"Loki, call them off," Jabal said as he shut down the ransomeware. He was interrupted when the Chamber door was thrown open.

"Jabal Amir! You should not be using this evil machine!" Abdul screamed.

"Father, there is nothing evil about this machine!" Jabal hissed.

"Of course these machines are evil! Young men spend all their time watching pornography or..." He paused as he saw the logo of his son's bank account on the Chamber dashboard. It was a notification of acceptance of over 1.3 million credits.

"Stealing?! *My* son, a thief?" Abdul screamed.

"Father, I wasn't stealing, it was a...um..."

"That's what I thought! In ancient times they would cut off the left hand of a thief like you! Son of a cleric indeed! You don't deserve to live here!"

"You know why you became a cleric father? It's because you're nothing! You're jealous of my talent for computers and you're pissed off that you don't have any skills other than getting on your knees five times a day!"

"How dare you speak to me like that! You think you're so smart to hide here in the basement of the mosque, but we found you because your machine uses up all of the electricity! The lights flicker when you turn this contraption on! I will not have this device of thievery in this sanctum," Abdul said and turned to a group of followers. He issued a orders to them in Farsi. All of them pulled out a steel rod and walked towards the Chamber.

"Father! You can't do this!" Jabal pleaded. He lunged for the Chamber, but his father stepped in and blocked him.

"Get out of my way! I paid for all of it! I built it! It's mine!" Jabal screamed, but Abdul held him firmly in place. His followers approached the Chamber and smashed it to pieces. In that moment Jabal watched his life's savings destroyed before his eyes.

"Get off of me you savage!" Jabal screamed as he shoved his father away. Abdul's eyes were set ablaze.

"Savage?!" Abdul hissed. "You shall honor your father!"

"You should honor your son, yet you just destroyed my life's work you mindless brute!"

Abdul seized Jabal by the collar. "You're life's work was wasted on these machines!"

"I said get off of me!" Jabal screamed as he socked Abdul in the jaw. Abdul released his son and covered his nose where blood was gushing out.

"Get out!" Abdul screamed. "Get out of my house and never come back! I never want to see you again!"

"With pleasure! I don't need you and your mysticism! I have all I need here!" Jabal said as he grabbed his comm device and ran out of the mosque.

The air was fraught with a heavy moisture as the sky above threatened to split. Jabal wandered the streets amidst the screaming merchants haggling with one another over the prices of their wares.

"Nothing like a day at the market on Planet Alexandria," Jabal whispered to himself.

A chill settled in through the market, while Jabal checked

his comm device. A tightness gripped his chest and he became light headed when he saw his screen.

His bank account was at zero.

Over the course of the next week, Jabal wandered the streets scrounging for food wherever he could find it. He slept in alleyways, his clothes becoming ragged and rotten from the rain. He tried his usual tricks in cyberspace, but it felt like there was a force preventing him from cyphering any money into his account. Feeling defeated and abandoned, he was able to use his comm device to create falsified identity papers and sell them in the back alleys. His hustling paid off, and the first thing he wanted was to buy a hot meal at The Djinn Palace, a local restaurant. He walked in, smelled the rich Alexian coffee, and sat down in a booth.

The crowd was full of lively discussion, and he didn't notice when a well-worn droid entered the restaurant. It was a brown, skeletal model with only the bare essentials but it had a nimble grace in each step. What drew attention to this unit was the fact that it had an oversized shawl tied around its neck. The droid paid no mind to most of the patrons as it scanned the room, searching for its target. The unit also had a rifle strapped over its shoulder which was against regulation, however enforcement had collapsed due to the Unification Wars.

There was a human male with his back to the droid. His description matched what the droid was searching for, but it needed to be certain. It walked through the restaurant in a casual stride until it passed the man in the booth.

Jabal tapped on his communication device, refining his artificial intelligence programs. A pair of rusty red mechanical legs slipped by him, until he felt as though he was being watched. He looked up, and saw the soulless eyes of a droid staring at him.

Jabal leaped up from his booth, but the droid shoved him back in with ease. It drew a pistol and slid into the booth, pinning Jabal inside.

"What do you want?" Jabal asked.

"For you not to panic," the droid replied. "My master wishes to speak with you."

Jabal's throat went dry and his heart thundered in his chest. This was no doubt about the money that he'd stolen. He tried to push out, but the droid drove him into the wall.

"Will you come willingly or do I need to tranquilize you and bring you in?"

Jabal huffed in frustration. "Will he kill me?" He asked.

"If my instructions were to kill you, you'd be dead," the droid replied. "No, you captured my master's attention and he would like to meet you face to face."

"So he sent a droid?!"

The droid groaned. "Humans. Always focusing on the obvious. He's a private individual. C'mon, up you go now," the droid slid out of the booth, pulled Jabal up, and then shoved the pistol into his back. Jabal felt his breathing constrict. He wanted to cry out for help, but even if he received help, the authorities would likely arrest him for inquiries into past cyber crimes. The droid shoved him forward with its pistol and out of the restaurant without anyone noticing.

The droid escorted Jabal to a small ship on the edge of the city. "Do you know how to fly?" It asked.

"No," Jabal replied.

"Good. That means if you attack me during the flight, you will plummet to your death."

"You...you can't just go kidnapping people like this!" He screamed.

"Go ahead, call the authorities," it replied. "I am fully compliant and posses papers stating my business. Non-falsified *legal* papers."

Jabal sneered at the droid. How could it have possibly known?

"That's what I thought," the droid replied.

The flight was a quiet three-week trip to a world beyond the fringes of Core space where sand dominated the landscape. Jabal was escorted to a warehouse where a man with short white hair and pitch black goggles stood out front. His face seemed as though it were chiseled into a permanent scowl with burn marks where fire had raked his cheek. He lifted his left hand to adjust the goggles, and revealed a metallic arm with white plates lining the entire limb. The dusty winds whipped against his simple tan clothing and over sized shawl.

"Bring me a present, Red?" He asked.

"Here he is master," Red said with a bow. Jabal shivered from fear, despite the heat of the desert. Goosebumps spread across his skin and he felt lost.

"Let's talk inside," the white-haired man said.

Jabal was frozen in place, too scared to move.

"C'mon now, he said inside," Red said as he waved his pistol.

Jabal felt his stomach swirl with bile. He wanted to crawl into a hole, bury his face in the sand, do anything other than face the man who had ousted him. Of all the people in the galaxy he could've stolen from, he picked the one man who would have him brought to an isolated desert where he could murder him and let the sands erode his memory.

The white-haired man sat at the table while Red and a towering silver droid flanked him. The silver droid was nearly twice as big as a human, its fists as large as the man's head. It had slivered red eyes, but there was a gentleness in its stare. A golden disc glowed in its chest, but he couldn't tell the purpose of the device.

Jabal crept into the room and took a seat.

"What do you want with me?" Jabal asked in a broken voice.

The white-haired man glared at him through his goggles for what felt like an eternity.

"What do you know?" He finally asked.

"Excuse me?" Jabal replied.

The man kept his scowl fixed on him. He tapped his fingers on the table, but didn't utter a word.

"I...don't know anything," Jabal said to break the silence.

"Bullshit. You're the first one to break through my defenses, to shut down my network. What do you know?"

"I only did what I needed to in order to get the credits. I didn't steal any information!"

The boxy silver droid leaned down next to the man and whispered something.

"Sol here says that based on your micro expressions you're telling the truth," the man said.

"Damn straight I am!" Jabal snapped. "At least I didn't take your life savings!"

"Cost of learning a life lesson," He said. "Your artificial intelligence programs are clunky, but effective."

"Thank you-"

"I wasn't done," He snapped. "What I need to know is: Why did you target my organization?"

"Nothing personal," Jabal replied. "Shipping companies like yours operating outside the fringes of Core space typically deal in smuggled goods or arms. I knew you wouldn't run to the Core for help, and the Coalition doesn't have a cyberdefense program yet. Seemed like the perfect target."

The old man's face held his embedded scowl. "Could you break through the Core government's system and steal their information?"

"Absolutely!" Jabal cheered. "Most systems utilize blockchain security, but the government still houses servers in a centralized location, making them extremely vulnerable to attack."

"Excellent, you can start on that immediately."

"What? But I-"

"When Red tracked you down, you were living hand to mouth like a common street rat. Are you saying you want to go back?"

"You're willing to hire me? I don't even know your name."

"We only use code names," the man replied. "You can refer to me as 'Houston.' The droid that brought you in is Red and the silver one here is Sol. What do you want us to call you?"

Jabal pondered for a moment. "Call me Hacker."

"Really?" Houston replied. "That's an incredibly stupid and cliché code name. Why in the hell would you pick that?"

"Get with the times old man! All of the computer guys are called Cyphers, Chainbreakers or Chainers now. Hacker is a throwback to the old days when programming meant something, not like today where it's a race to build a new cryptocurrency."

"Whatever, it's your code name, even if it is stupid," Houston said as he rose from his seat and turned to leave the room.

Hacker leaped to his feat and followed Houston. Down a set of stairs was a vast complex with some of the most advanced droid technology in existence. Discarded parts lay everywhere, processing chips were scattered, and wires dangled out of human-shaped metal casings.

"If you're to be any use to me, I'm going to need you to start probing the Core's information and defense mainframes. I want to see what we're up against," Houston said.

"Do you have a Chamber?" Hacker asked.

Houston turned to face him. "A what?"

"A Chamber. They're a computer device that submerges the user into a virtual reality that utilizes the palms, fingertips and eyes as inputs. They're the most effective computational device in existence! How can an organization like yours not have one?"

Houston chuckled. "I always called them 'sperm coffins' because too many boys forgot to eat while watching porn."

"That's not all they're used for! They're devices which allow us to write program chains we can barely comprehend! You of all people must understand the capability of these devices! Imagine if you could upgrade Red or Sol with nothing more than a tap of your finger!"

Houston looked over at his two droids who gazed back in blank stares.

"Kid, sometimes it's better to do things in the real world. Get your hands dirty. Stick to reality. Less inclined to warp your mind. Do you need one of these chambers to infiltrate the Core Cyberdefense Networks?"

"I don't *need* it, but it would certainly be a lot faster. Why?

What's in the CCN?"

"Have you ever heard of a little thing called the 'Core Invasion?'" Houston said as he climbed into his speeder. The two droids piled into the back seat while Hacker raced to the front.

"You mean the 'Unification Wars?'" Hacker asked.

"Depends on who you ask," Houston said. "Now, let's go get you one of those sperm coffins."

The only sound in the speeder during the ride was the subtle whirring from the processors of the droids in the back seat. Sand lined every edge of the horizon, as if there wasn't a single drop of water on the planet. Hacker's attention was drawn to Houston's mechanical limb.

"I lost it in the skirmishes that lead up to the Core Invas... er...Unification Wars," He said. "Gouged some guy's eyes out, but he got lucky with his knife. Stabbed me in the shoulder, tore all the ligaments and tendons out, needed to be amputated."

"You were a soldier for the rebellion?" Hacker asked.

"They didn't teach you shit in school, despite being what? Eighteen?"

"Nineteen."

Houston sighed. "I got this in what we call the 'Skirmishes.' The skirmishes were a series of battles where the first planets began to secede. They didn't believe they were getting a voice within the Core government, and one night, some representatives all quietly came in and signed the Articles of Secession. Next thing you know, the Core is sending armadas full of trained soldiers to put down what they saw as a peasant revolt. They didn't count on us being armed like we were. The combination of early victories and the Core's violent reaction drove the fringe planets into signing the Articles and creating the Coalition Government based on Centaura. Now we're in year six of a war that has no end in sight," He explained.

"Why do you need me to infiltrate the CCN?" Hacker asked.

"Since the War has dragged on for this long, the Core has

turned to droids to fight this war for them. They want machines to spare them the casualties that the war was inflicting. Fewer deaths means higher morale for new recruits. The Coalition also wants droids, the only difference is that they don't possess the infrastructure to produce them on a scale to wage an intergalactic war. Until the Coalition can get more foundries operating, they hire men like me to go in and steal droids to supply their war machine, pun intended."

"What does that have to do with the CCN?"

"I'm getting to it, don't interrupt," Houston snapped. "The CCN keeps a registry of their mech reserves. We can use that registry as a shopping list of the droids we target, steal them, and deliver them into the Coalition's hands."

"Do you believe in the Coalition's cause?" Hacker asked.

"Used to," Houston replied as he held out his mechanical arm. "What I know is I'm really good at fixing and programming droids, which allows me to charge a premium to a group of people who're in dire need of my services."

"Have you always worked on droids?"

"No, I used to be a mathematician. You wanna see wasted talent? There's a career path for ya. I made it work, but a more practical trade, hence fixing the droids. You've asked a lot of questions for today kid, no more till we get home."

"But Master, the art and science of asking questions is the source of all knowledge."

"Can it Sol," Houston snapped.

Houston landed the shuttle and met with a dealer who claimed to possess a Chamber device. He negotiated for a while, and then came back to the shuttle.

"What is the purpose of this machine?" Houston asked. "Why do we need it to infiltrate the Core Cyber Networks?"

Hacker sighed. "The device submerges the user into a virtual reality that can be altered at will. Think of it as being able to manipulate the Internet in three-dimensional space. It exposes more of the gaps that exist within the programming of a web page, a server, or a block chain."

"Figured," Houston said. "Just expensive as hell."

"I could even use it to design some smart contracts for your shipping company," Hacker said.

Houston nodded and flashed a devious grin. "It's funny, every time the technologists create something new, they believe it's their key to freedom, the key that will unlock their chains. In reality, all they've done is created a program those in power can use to oppress," He said. "All technological advancements started out with the intent to decentralize and flatten our world. In the end, all they do is consolidate and increase power for those who can wield it."

"How do you figure?" Hacker asked.

"Well take the smart contracts. They were supposed to execute everything perfectly, except what people forget is they're coded by humans. They don't see how they're being skimmed a little bit off the top or how he who wrote the contract has ensured that he gets the best deal."

"Wow, hadn't thought about it that way," Hacker said.

"Oh, here's the next bit: all of that database security and encryption created from multiple users instead of a single entry point? How do they compete against data miners? Especially when the data miners are all bots that can target all of the entry points at once?"

"It's an effective tactic," Hacker said. "My bots are really just modified data miners with some extra features I've refined over the years."

"My point exactly. Take something that was designed for smarter advertising and use it to crush mainframes." Houston grew silent as he let the thought sink in. A large droid wheeled out a Chamber device into the freighter ship, and the crew headed back to base.

The orbital-shaped computer was set up in the midst of scattered droid parts. Hacker spent days configuring his Chamber to the specifications he'd need to take on the CCN.

"There," Hacker said.

"Good afternoon sir," Loki said.

"Word up," Laverna replied.

"What can we do for you Hacker?" Eris asked.

"It's just good to have my Wrecking Crew back."

Once he had the programs he wished to use, Hacker climbed in and was bathed in the soft blue light of code swirling around him. He manipulated and maneuvered the scripts to serve his needs until he reached the CCN. He'd probed the network a handful of times, but never to the scale Houston wanted him to. Still, Hacker was determined to come away with a registry of droid foundries within the Core.

Hacker spent hours using every trick he knew, implementing his AI programs he managed to recover since his exile from home. He was able to upload a keylogger deep within the CCN's archives and from there, he could track everything they were doing. More importantly, he'd retrieved a registry of the foundries the Core had contracted to manufacture their droid army. He printed off his list, stormed up to Houston and shoved it into his chest.

"List of contractors manufacturing droids for the Core military."

"That sperm coffin may have just paid for itself," Houston replied.

"Wait, you're doing what?" Hacker asked over the comm device.

"We're going to infiltrate a droid foundry on a world called Solomon IV," Houston replied.

"Hey! That's my name," Sol said.

"That's a coincidence," Red replied.

"Coincidence is the word we use when we can't see the levers and pulleys."

"Insightful," Houston said. "Now's your chance to prove yourself kid. Red, Sol and I are going to infiltrate this mech factory and we'd really appreciate coming out of it alive. I've left you behind to handle their security systems. You overtake, I overcome."

"If I may sir, wouldn't it be more beneficial if Sol or I simply plugged in and took down the mainframe ourselves?" Red asked.

"You're smart Red, but Hacker claims to possess multiple AIs that are designed for this task," Houston said as he landed the ship. He leaped out and tossed a pair of rifles to Red and Sol, who stacked up against the doorway.

"You ready kid?" Houston asked.

"I'm in," Hacker said. "Door's unlocked."

"That was too easy," Houston said. "Be on high alert."

"I will, I will!" Hacker said.

A blaster bolt ripped into the doorway past the entrance as Houston and the droids approached. "Damn it!" Houston cursed as he cocked his rifle. "Told you there was something else! Kid, why didn't you see this?"

"What?" Hacker asked as he searched the lines of code that surrounded him.

"We're being fired upon!" Houston screamed.

"That's impossible!" Hacker snapped. "I shut down all of the interior defenses located at that facility!"

"Well you obviously missed *something* because we're being shot at!" Houston hissed.

Hacker searched the source code. "Let me get eyes on you through the cameras."

"Good," Houston replied.

"Should I shut them down or would it be less suspicious to find footage from the past few hours, play that on autofeed and-"

"I don't care!" Houston snapped. "You don't need me to hold your hand!"

Hacker grew silent from the outburst. He tried not to take it personally and pushed it to the back of his mind. He focused his eyes on the screen to see where the source of blaster fire was coming from. It was a giant mech wheeling towards Houston and the droids.

"Large mech approaching," Hacker said. "On wheels, canon on one side, gatling on the other. Built heavier than Sol."

"Shit, that's a *Gladiator* class unit," Houston said. "Kid, I need that mech deactivated now!"

Hacker searched the source code for the entire complex. He

found several files for defenses, but none of them contained anything about mech units being on patrol.

"C'mon kid I didn't ask for a dark matter formula!" Houston hissed.

"I...can't find its source code. There's no record of this mech existing here in the foundry!"

"The kid's losing the foundry," Houston said.

"No I'm not! I just need help finding this fucking droid!" Hacker screamed as he activated his three AI programs.

"What is it Master Hacker?" Loki asked.

"Find that droid and shut it down," Hacker commanded.

"Hacker," Eris interrupted. "We've already tried that. The droid you pointed out was written in a language that is highly classified and we cannot find a connection with the unit."

"That's what I thought," Houston said. "Sol, hunt it down." The droid rushed to the counsel, plugged in an uplink, and then powered down.

"No! You can't do this!" Hacker pleaded. "I can figure this out! Loki - find what language that droid has been coded in. Eris and Laverna - find out where that mech is being controlled from!"

"Sir, it appears that this droid was composed using the Kaleidoscope script," Loki said.

Hacker gasped.

"One of the evolving scripts that mimics consciousness," he said

"That doesn't mean anything except that this unit has a longer battery life," Houston replied.

"Houston, it seems the 'Wrecking Crew' is correct," Sol said. "That particular *Gladiator* unit is not connected to this foundry's mainframe and I'm not detecting a wireless signal of any sort. You're going to have to defeat that unit on your own."

"Damn it all to hell," Houston snapped. The mech fired off several rounds of blaster fire while Houston and Red hit the ground. Red returned fire as Houston pulled an electromagnetic grenade from beneath his shawl.

"Sir, is that a…?"

"You bet Red. Best run away."

"Appreciate the warning sir," Red replied as he scurried off. Houston lobbed the grenade, which flew and latched onto the mech's outstretched arm. Tendrils of electricity spread from the grenade throughout the mech's body, but the machine still kept moving.

"Damn it, damn it, damn it!" Houston cursed as he retreated back to Red. "EMP-proofed."

"Oh, drat. Sorry to hear sir," Red replied. "What should we do?"

Houston searched the room. A gleam of light reflected off of his polished arm, which captured his attention. He looked up and noticed Sol in the next room, who was still powered down.

"Red, I need you to get me something off of Sol."

"Hacker, we've managed to find gaps within the code and have provided you with the credentials needed to log into the system," Eris said.

"Perfect! Now we're Calvin Anders and I can-"

"Hey dude, I managed to find this," Laverna said. Hacker clicked on the window and sent the file to Houston.

Houston's comm device beeped. "Bout time you got the map of this place kid, but we're tied up at the moment. See if there are any other threats in the building."

Hacker expanded his view inside the foundry through the cameras. He flipped through all of the rooms only to find another hurdle in the way.

"The cameras are frozen in place!" He said.

"What?" Houston snapped.

Hacker watched in horror as his entire Chamber locked up. A security agency within the Core had isolated him and locked him out.

"We're still flying blind. I've been locked out," Hacker said. He'd never felt so useless in his life. The Chamber was closing in around him as his computer struggled to keep up beneath the onslaught unleashed by the outside coders.

"Useless," Houston grunted under his breath.

Hacker winced as he heard the words echo through his comm.

"Here it is sir," Red said as he handed a compact device to Houston, who was in the middle of disassembling his own arm. Houston took the device, slapped it into the joint where his forearm and wrist connected and screwed his hand back in.

"Does it even fit?" Red asked. "Perhaps not the wisest plan to integrate the parts of random droids into your own sir."

"You're right Red. I need to standardize my droid army. I'll make a note," Houston said as his fingers coiled to life. The glass disc on his wrist shined like the sun.

"It works!" Houston screamed victoriously. He willed his energy cell to power the device, and a half dome was projected from his wrist. He stepped into the fray as the mech fired relentlessly at him, but the shield absorbed all of the blaster bolts.

"Flank 'im Red!" Houston ordered as he marched for the mech. It stumbled backwards, but continued firing, not knowing what else to do.

Red creeped along the floor like a shadow. Houston closed in on the mech's arm and prepared to make a huge gamble. From behind Houston, Red leaped off a side wall and onto the mech's shoulders.

"Shall we try to recruit him sir?" Red asked.

"My power cell is at 15% Red, we don't have that kind of time," Houston replied.

"Very well then," Red said as he reached down and ripped the energy cell out of the mech's left arm. It's attention was drawn to its shoulders, but the moment it stopped firing on Houston he powered down his shield and grabbed ahold of the right arm.

"Hop down Red," Houston said as he jerked the arm out of his way, and fired at the mech's processor at the base of its metal skull. A short burst from his rifle silenced the war machine.

The lumbering mech collapsed, smoke rising from its neck. Red retrieved the processor and plugged it into his mainframe to learn how these droids operated.

"How many more of them are there?" Houston asked.

"I'm still flying blind!" Hacker screamed. He didn't know what to do. Every trick and tactic he'd utilized before had failed here. He had nothing left.

"Seriously?" Houston snapped. "Red, you're up. The kid can't do it."

"Sir if I may finish my task at hand," Red replied.

"Hurry up," Houston growled. "How do they communicate?"

"They seem to be on their own private security network which they access only twice a day."

"Mmm. Fascinating. How does it see?" Houston asked.

"Visually? It appears to be infrared. In fact, I speculate that they can see you right here sir."

"Then let's do something they won't see coming. Sol, fire up the new recruits."

Hacker tapped all over the screen. He was frozen in place, broken images flickering in and out of existence. He tried to reestablish a connection with his Wrecking Crew, but he couldn't hear anything.

"They want to keep me out? They'll have to try harder than that. It's time to burn down the forest," Hacker said as he pulled a chip out of his pocket. Despite the frozen screen, he could still open local files, and he clicked on one called 'Forest Fire.'

"Red, let's go after the other bastards," Houston said. The two followed the map Hacker had provided until they reached the warehouse. There was another *Gladiator* class mech waiting for them along with thousands upon thousands of battle droids powered down and hanging off the racks.

"We didn't bring a big enough freighter ship sir," Red said.

"Yeah, there's a few more than I anticipated," Houston replied. He activated his wrist shield right as the mech opened fire on the intruders. Red leaped down onto the floor, but the mech was onto him. It sprayed the room with it's gatling gun, going after Red.

Houston jumped over the stair railing, but his legs jolted in pain as he landed. "Shit, I'm getting too old for this," He cursed. He marched forward, firing at the mech's skull. The droid blocked the assault with its shoulder pads. It's yellow eyes became fixated on Houston while Red flanked in from the side.

Houston noticed movement out of the corner of his eye. The racks lit up and the claws opened. Human sized droids fell from the racks and set their sights on the *Gladiator* fighting Houston.

"All units converge on the assailant," One of the droids said. They cocked their rifles and opened fire, but the mech activated its orbital shield just in time.

The blasterfire looked like pebbles being thrown into a small pond. Only tiny ripples shimmered off the surface.

The mech realized that it was being surrounded. Houston could see the confusion as the processors were determining whether it should attack the units that it was sworn to protect.

It gave Houston the moment he needed.

Hacker weaved a tapestry of commands as he raced to issue his program. The security agents moved fast, too fast to be humans. He had to be battling a block chain run by AIs. They were attempting to overwhelm his servers and they were proving successful. However, Hacker's program hadn't failed before, even in the face of an AI block chain.

Hacker opened the file's script and issued the commands he needed to activate his program. Once activated, the script surged through a series of windows and commands at blinding speed, a system that he could barely control. It was a dangerous program, and he knew it.

The program named 'Forest Fire' tore through the block chains and rooted out the AI from their systems. One by one, the groups hold on Hacker's system was torn asunder, and there was nothing they could do about it. Once he was able to communicate with them, Hacker ordered the Wrecking Crew to assist in his malware assault against the enemy.

As his malware attacked the AIs, Hacker's chamber unfroze, and he was able to see the entire foundry in real time. He saw that a third mech was coming for Houston and Red. As he searched the screen, a tiny notification caught his eye. It was a timer for when the mech was to connect with the private security server and receive updates.

Hacker realized that this was the key to bringing the mechs down.

They may not be connected with the foundry's servers, but their timers are. If he could change the timer to notify the mech that it was time for an update, that would open the mech's ports and make it vulnerable to his attacks.

When he looked back at the screen, Hacker saw the humanoid droids attacking the mech and assisting Houston.

"What are you doing Hacker?" Sol asked. His voice became raspy and cracked.

"Oh no!" Hacker shouted. "My program is going after them isn't it?!"

"It seems so," Sol replied. "I have to go now."

"No! Sol, help me!" Hacker pleaded, but it was too late. Sol had already retreated back into his body and left the cyberrealm.

Hacker attempted to terminate his forest fire program, but it had already reached the battle droids on the ground.

Houston reached through the mech's shield and tore out the energy cell which powered its defenses. The humming came to a stop, and the shields fell. However, the battle droids ceased firing as they looked to each other in confusion.

"What the hell...?" Houston asked.

He watched in horror as all of the battle droids collapsed, inert on the ground.

The mech's hideous eyes focused on Houston.

"Shit."

The mech swung its massive arm, knocking Houston back almost 30 metres. It felt as though there was an explosion in his chest, and the edges of his vision blurred. The mech wheeled up, intending to finish him off.

Just as the mech reached Houston, a behemoth of metal landed in front of him.

"Sorry Master Houston, but I'm going to need to borrow this. My batteries are far more efficient than yours," Sol said as he removed Houston's hand and retrieved his shield unit.

"Go for it," Houston replied weakly. Sol put the shield device back into his chest and activated it as the mech opened fire on him. Sol lunged forward, striking the mech with his massive fists, knocking pieces out of the war droid. The mech's guns proved unwieldy in hand to hand combat, which is where Sol excelled. The mech tried to retreat, but Sol grabbed the gatling gun. He pulled the mech in, and unleashed his pneumatic arm, which pancaked the mech's face into a pile of scrap.

Right as Sol finished the mech off, another one charged in. It launched a missile at Houston, but Sol jumped in the way.

Houston felt the wave of heat as the missile slammed into Sol's shields. He flew back into the wall, his shield generator sparking from being overwhelmed.

The mech wheeled forward and pointed its gatling gun at the group. Houston closed his eyes as he steeled himself for the end.

A hissing noise broke the silence. Houston opened his eyes and saw the mech convulsing, until the unit finally powered down before him, as if bowing in submission.

Hacker cheered. "I got 'im! All of the droids are down! The foundry is yours!"

Houston groaned as he felt the pain in his ribs worsen. His breathing was shallow, and his torso was becoming black.

"Red, see if you can get Sol running again," Houston ordered.

"Yes sir," Red replied, who tended to the fallen golem.

Houston reached down and ripped off the mech's head lying on the ground and crushed the metal skull in front of the camera.

"That's what I think of your programming!" Houston

hissed.

Hacker felt a wave of shame overtake him. "I saved you! Why are you getting pissed at me?"

"We had this handled. Your interference caused me and Sol to get taken out!"

"But I was flying blind and-"

"Hacker, you need learn how to solve problems, not make more of them!" Houston snapped as he pulled the comm piece out of his ear. He walked to the droids scattered on the floor and began hooking them back to the racks.

Hacker shut down the Chamber and buried his face in his hands. Stomach acid swirled in his gut as shame and humiliation took hold of his mind. He wanted to help Houston, to make this better for him, but felt as though he'd made things worse. Houston was holding his side, but how could he have known what would happen?

The next three days felt like an eternity as Hacker mulled over the mission in his head. He felt like a failure, that he had no worth, that he was beyond redemption. He stewed in his misery, waiting for Houston's return.

The door to the sanctum groaned as it opened to receive a massive cargo ship lowering into the warehouse. The ship sat atop three cargo containers which housed the thousands of battle droids that Houston planned to sell to the Coalition Government.

A shivering nausea took root in Hacker's stomach as Houston walked out of the ship.

"Get the droids processed and reach out to our contacts on Centaura," Houston ordered.

"That's it?!" Hacker screamed. "That's all you have to say after three days?!"

Houston sighed. "Your mistake was in targeting a foundry where the security was run by AIs. Sure you seized access through one of their user profiles, but you should've targeted a foundry where the security was run by humans. Humans make mistakes with their coding, machines don't."

"Wait, you *knew* how to hack into the droid facility?" Hacker asked.

"Of course I do!" Houston snapped. "You think I haven't done this before? I was a mech runner when you were still wearing diapers!"

"Then why didn't you give me instructions on what to do?"

"Because I need a code breaker who can think for himself! Who doesn't need me to hold his hand every time he meets some resistance!"

"I *did* that and you got pissed at me!"

"It's a tough universe kid. Welcome to it."

"What makes you think you're so great at coding?"

"Well, for starters, I was one of the developers of the Atrium language."

Hacker gasped. "You said you were a mathematician! Not one of the developers of the most powerful AI language known to man!"

"There's a lot of math in robotics kid." Houston replied.

"This...this is incredible! How did you develop the language?"

"Look kid, there's nothing special about it. We designed Atrium to be one of the hardest languages for techies to learn, but it still sparked an AI arms race. Within a year there were a dozen AIs all streaming through cyberspace. Some went and exterminated villages, others are as docile as Red and Sol here. All depends on who wrote 'em."

"How advanced did you get with Atrium?"

"It was a dead end. Just like every other attempt at consciousness with machines. Red was my first. Good servant, excellent strategist, but can't think for himself. Sol was the second attempt utilizing one of the offshoot evolving scripts like what you saw in those droids. Came close to full consciousness with my philosophizing droid, but in the end, all he does is recite old quotes which makes him sound deeper than he is.

"One head cannot hold all wisdom," Sol said.

"Yeah, yeah. We get it," Houston replied.

"What happened to the Atrium project then?" Hacker

asked.

"The Core marked us as terrorists!" Houston screamed. "We unleashed a technology they couldn't contain! People had been trying to develop a working model for customizing AIs that mankind could control and we were the ones who succeeded! The Core hunted us down one by one, destroyed all public copies of Atrium and then utilized the program in their droid foundries. My compatriots are all gone now, and I'm forced to hide out in shit holes like this one, fighting for a cause I don't believe in, to kill a bunch of kids I don't know to finish a war I didn't start."

Hacker wanted to say something, but words failed him. Houston seemed like a man on a mission, but with no allegiance to anyone or anything. He was a zealous mercenary, a man driven by an paradoxical ideology even he couldn't define.

For over three years, Hacker studied under Houston as the two became the most infamous mech runners in the galaxy and the Core's most wanted. Their skill was unmatched by anyone within the Core as they hijacked supply ships and foundries that sought to replenish the Core's droid forces. Despite their help, the Coalition forces were being driven back to the edges of known space.

On Centaura, Hacker was socializing with some of the Coalition freedom fighters, listening to their ideas of liberty, trade and freedom. They were die-hards ravaged by war, but they would give all they had to ensure their families would have a better future. Hacker wished them well and was chuckling to himself as the two men sat down for dinner.

"These guys are something," Hacker said. "Their conviction is astounding, I only wish there was more we could do to help them."

"Now you know the most dangerous weapon known to man: ideas. There's nothing more we can do for them. If anything, we're going to pull the plug on this operation."

"What?! Why?"

"Because they can't win this war. It's time to focus our

efforts in preparation for a Core victory and to ready our assets to be protected when that happens."

"How do you know the Core will win?"

"I knew the Core would win the moment they issued their bombing run on Calliope. Once the Core started attacking unarmed civilian worlds, it was all over."

"The Coalition could still win!"

"Don't let your ideologies cloud your logic Hacker! The Coalition won't attack civilian worlds, which means they can't break the Core's morale. The Core on the other hand, doesn't care about public opinion and will do whatever it takes to win this war. Someone needs to tell those boys that close only counts in horse shoes and hand grenades."

The rest of their dinner was eaten in silence as Hacker mulled over Houston's words. He hated to admit it, but they made sense. However, Hacker didn't believe they were as powerless to influence events as Houston did.

"What if we turn to economic terrorism?" Hacker asked.

"Huh?"

"We use our AIs to target the Core markets. Their financial system is designed to keep people distracted while this war is going on. Nobody on Earth realizes they're fighting a war. What if we cause a market collapse and make them *feel* the pain of going against the Coalition?"

"It's a bold plan I'll give it to you, but it's too expensive, too much time, too much effort and most importantly: too late. As I said, let's focus our efforts towards the end of the war. I've secured a base on the last Coalition stronghold and-"

"No! I'm not ready to give up!" Hacker snapped. "This is a good plan, you just admitted it!"

"Kid, this is our reality. I stole the schematics for a droid foundry the size of a small moon that the Coalition has been building. When the Coalition loses, it will be destroyed or handed over to the Core as reparations. However, if a private individual were to make this foundry disappear, the Core wouldn't dare come after them since it would churn out more droids in a year than soldiers they can recruit. A person in control of a foundry like this would be untouchable, and I intend to be that person."

"Listen to you!" Hacker hissed. "You sound more like a mob boss than a freedom fighter.

"I'm a realist who only backs the winning side!" Houston snapped. "I was on the losing side once! I do not intend to be on that side again!" He screamed as he held up his arm. He rose up and stormed off, putting an end to the conversation.

Hacker stewed in silence. He had to prove Houston wrong, that his ideas were worth pursuing. He left the table, went inside the Chamber and brought up the Core news feed about the markets. He summoned his Wrecking Crew, and went to work.

"Stupid Core. They think their trust and stability in the economy will keep them safe? That they can ignore the Coalition's cause? They'll pay attention now," Hacker sneered as he minimized his script and turned to the newscast. The indices gauging the Core markets began to blink. What was once an array of green upticks ceased, and morphed into a band of red downticks. The charts held their apex for a moment, the teetered downward. Within seconds the descent turned into a freefall. The news anchors stopped in mid newscast as they watched the indices fall by the hundreds, and then the thousands. They sat by in horror, and silence reigned on the screen. Hacker smiled with his hands clasped in front of his face.

He watched as billions in wealth evaporated in seconds, and was mesmerized when the anchors were forced to report that they had no idea what was happening to the markets.

Hacker shut down the Chamber and exited. Houston stormed right towards him.

"What the hell did you just do?" Houston screamed.

"You said it'd be too long and too expensive. I infiltrated the biggest investment firms, coded an AI to go in, issue a 'Sell' order on their biggest holdings, and then repeated. All at a cost of a few minutes of time and bandwidth."

Houston groaned. "It won't take them long to recover from

that! Your attack generated a little media buzz, but those traders will reverse everything you've done! You didn't accomplish anything, you set them back maybe a day or two."

"What is it then?!" Hacker snapped. "What should I be doing? I've been here for three years and you don't instruct me on how to do anything! I learned only by watching you and your only capability seems to be in relentlessly criticizing my work!"

"Look kid, you've shown some promise I'll give you that-"

"Then tell me that! Give me something to go on!"

Houston sighed. "I have been a mentor and a teacher to you. A harsh one perhaps, but you came here looking for a father, and that's not what I am."

"I didn't expect you to-"

"That is *exactly* what you want me to be!" Houston snapped.

Hacker was taken aback, but words failed him. He didn't know what to say to Houston, and deep down a part of him was wounded.

"Focus on the mission Hacker, and I'll teach you whatever you want," Houston said and then walked away.

Hacker stepped into the Chamber and secured the plans as well as the title for ownership to the moon-sized droid foundry that the Coalition was constructing. Each line of script he typed twisted his stomach into a knot. He felt like he was betraying the fighters who had given so much in their cause against the Core. Hacker instructed the Wrecking Crew to go back and destroy all original files that mentioned the droid foundry.

"Sir, we've managed to track them to this location. You were right, the AI was more than helpful."

The Colonel looked up from the tablet and his sinister eyes made the soldier uncomfortable. A sadistic grin spread across his lips.

"Of course I was," He said. "Now let's pay those war criminals a visit."

As Hacker exited the Chamber, Red was searching the complex, calling out for Houston. His voice was raised in alarm.

"Red, what is it?" Hacker asked.

"Hostile ship approaching. I must inform the master."

On a countertop screen Hacker switched to the outside cameras. A gunmetal ship descended towards the complex which bore the new insignia of the Core. It showed Earth encircled by two rings of stars, showing which planet was truly triumphant in the Unification Wars. The turrets rotated towards the complex and opened fire.

Explosions rocked the facility. Hacker and Red searched for Houston, who came out carrying an assault rifle.

"Master, there is-"

"I know," Houston replied.

"Who is it?" Hacker asked.

"Remember when I told you about how during the skirmishes I gouged a man's eyes out?"

"Yeah."

"Looks like he's coming to dole out some payback."

"Who is it?"

"His name is Colonel Hawkes, and he is one of the Core's best men at hunting runaway criminals like me," Houston said as he grabbed an assault rifle and threw them to the droids. Hacker stood with his hands open, but Houston fixed his usual scowl.

"What? Give me one!"

"No kid, you're getting out of here. Go ready the escape ship."

"I'm not leaving you!" Hacker snapped.

Houston looked at Hacker and took off his sunglasses. Concealed beneath were a pair of dark mahogany eyes. He stared in silence for one last time, his mind searching for the right words.

"Sol, carry him out," He finally said.

Before Hacker could react Sol scooped him up and threw him inside of his metal belly. He charged for the exit as Red and Houston prepared to make their final stand.

Core soldiers stormed the complex, creeping along with fixed rifles. A man with demonic black and red eyes marched in victoriously. His armor rustled against his uniform, and the same sadistic grin was still spread across his face.

"It seems that I've found you," Hawkes said. "Still dragging along that rust bucket?"

"You'd be surprised how tough Red is," Houston said.

"Thank you Master Houston," Red replied.

"Houston now is it?" Hawkes asked.

"I gotta say, those implants sure look sinister."

Hawkes chuckled. "A gentle reminder of the new vision you've given me," He said. "A vision where outlaws like you have been hunted down and order is restored to my galaxy."

"See that's the thing," Houston said. "Remember the tiger back on Earth? They said you shouldn't ever back it into a corner. Well that's especially true for a droid mechanic whose workshop you've just swarmed. Lotta unstable reactors in here."

Sol entered into the escape shuttle and emptied Hacker onto the floor. He programmed a destination for the shuttle and then turned to Hacker, who was trying to crawl out.

"A journey of a thousand miles may begin with a single step, but right now I need your butt in the seat," Sol said as he dragged Hacker to a chair and strapped him in.

"I'm going back," Hacker snapped as he unbuckled his restraints.

"Impossible," Sol replied as he refastened them. "Patience is a virtue."

"Houston is in danger!"

"To err is human, but to forgive is divine."

"What does that have to do with-" As Hacker finished his question, Sol struck him in the head, knocking him out.

Sol finished putting in the coordinates and as he exited the ship, there was a rattling in his belly. He opened up and reached inside, pulling out a memory stick that must've fallen out of Hacker's pocket.

He turned around, but the shuttle had already blasted off. He looked at the memory stick and plugged it in.

"The droid foundry schematics. I must get these back to Master Houston!" He said. Sol turned to the workshop where a massive explosion tore the building open, with dark plumes of smoke rising into the sky.

"The strong don't put others down…they lift them up," Sol said, and charged off towards the explosion.

Hacker awoke in a daze, almost a mile in the sky. He looked around in panic and checked the cameras, where he saw his home smoldering below. He broke down in a sob as his shuttle reached for the sky, determined to take him into the unknown.

"Happy Twelve-Year Anniversary Hacker!" Rick screamed as he burst into the office. Hacker leaned back with a hot mug in his hands and savored the scent of fresh, warm coffee.

"Y'know, there are caffeine pills which can take care of that for you. Much more efficient," Rick said.

"But then I would not have the pleasure of smelling this delightful aroma and savoring the rich bold flavor provided to us by humble Ethiopian coffee farmers. Are you saying we shouldn't support them?" Hacker replied.

"I still can't believe you accepted all of those stupid beans as payment."

"Hey, that tip they provided us was more than worth it. Blocking that merger between the coffee producers by leaking the slash and burn photos raked in millions for us."

"And made it easier than ever for the Diallo regime in Africa to nationalize that coffee plantation!"

"Like it'll do them much good with this raging three-way continental civil war," Hacker said as he took a sip of the rich, velvety drink. "That's a nasty fight. Core won't get involved because they don't want to be on the wrong side of an ethnic cleansing accusation."

"Right?"

"So, what do we got today?" Hacker asked as the two men walked towards the Command Center.

"Rumor is circulating of a mega-merger between the seven biggest scientific research and development companies. The proposed name for the new company will be 'Ionics' short for..."

"Rick, I'm not really concerned about the new corporate name. Do we own shares in any of them?"

"Any of what?"

"The seven companies in this mega merger. Do we own shares?"

"I'll ask Akio. You're letting the merger go through?"

"Why not? It's for the betterment of science. May as well make a few credits off the deal. What's really amazing was Chemron's recovery after that mysterious explosion which wiped out the entire board over ten years ago."

The ground floor was a hive of activity as people coded inside their Chambers. They switched between monitors, live feeds, made calls and shouted orders at one another. The massive projectors aligned on the ceiling provided newscast feed from every corner of the Core. The Chambers below were armed with search bots that dived into the deep sea of the intergalactic web and fed Hacker all of the data that wasn't being reported by the news. Every shred of information within the Core made its way through the servers inside *the Grid*.

"Sir," A young woman said as she came by and handed Rick a comm piece. Rick took it and accepted the call.

"Who is it Gabby?" Hacker asked.

In a low whisper Gabby replied: "A Senator from China who is worried about the Ophridia situation."

"Senator Mao wants us to dig up a bunch of incriminating information on a rebel causing trouble for Yiu Mei," Rick interjected. "What should I tell him?"

"Tell him that if he ever calls here again I'll see to it that his human trafficking secret gets leaked," Hacker said.

"He's not involved in human trafficking," Rick replied.

"We can manufacture some evidence that says otherwise," Hacker said. "I will not support that bloodthirsty tyrant. In fact, let's help the rebel guy. Kevin, Gary and Arjun you three are my Ophridia task force! Let's take Yiu Mei down," Hacker said.

"Yes sir," the team replied. Rick finished speaking with the Senator's office and Gabby took the comm piece from him.

Rick shook his head. "The Senator must've been desperate, calling here. His voice was a whisper: 'Yes, the Grid? I need your help.' Can't believe him," Rick mocked.

"Well, contact with us is punishable by treason, insubordination, conspiracy. There's an entire legal manual to deal with us," Hacker replied.

"Yeah, but Senator Mao will never see prison time."

"No, he won't,"

"Still can't believe it. 'The Grid.' What kind of name is that anyway?" Rick asked.

"What's wrong with 'The Grid?'"

"It's only the most unoriginal name ever," Rick berated. "Seriously, 'Hacker?' 'The Grid?' Where did you get your naming skills?"

"Well, when *you* create your own network of information dealers, *you* can name it whatever *you* want," Hacker said.

"Fair enough," Rick replied. "Oh! We're wanted on the floor, Donald is waving us down."

"Alright," Hacker replied as he sipped on his coffee. "Anything else of interest going on?"

"The Angkor colony has been given the go-ahead by the Minister of Exploration." Rick said as the pair got into the elevator.

"That was fast. Oh well, have someone keep an ear to the ground. Colonization stories are always interesting, but Angkor is pretty run-of-the-mill right now," Hacker replied.

"Should we be concerned that the safe zone declaration was a rush job?"

"Nah, it get's everyone's minds off the war. If we're expanding, we're united. Maybe something will come out of it, like one of those viral mutations that occur on colonies." Hacker replied as the two stepped out of the elevator.

"Is that something we should wish for?"

"All I'm saying is someone's bound to screw it up. When someone screws up we can run 'em through the wringer," Hacker said as one of the technicians held out a tablet for him.

"You really don't trust the Core do you?" Rick asked.

"Call it more of a grudge. The Core may have won the war, but I wage my own war every day."

"Nothing like stolen secrets sold on the black markets to old revolutionaries," Rick said. "What would you do if the Core finally found all of this?"

"I'd just rebuild the place from the ground up. Speaking of that we should schedule an uproot."

"Already have some guys scouting out a new locale. Should we acquire permits or make some?"

"No, get legitimate permits. Details matter and it's trivial things like what which get people caught," Hacker said.

"Will do sir. That's all I got for ya."

"Great. Thanks Rick, I'll be in my office," Hacker said as he wandered through the maze of Chambers on the central floor. All of his technicians greeted him, honored to be in the presence of the freedom fighter still waging a cyber war against the Core. Hacker saw these technicians as allies in his ever-expanding network of information dealers.

Hacker walked into his office, closed the door, and turned on his Chamber. He pulled up the newscast feed which had two major stories going on. One was about the assassination of Ophridia's Minister of Mining. The newscast alluded to the possibility of an insurgent, but they wouldn't mention them by name. The other major story was of an erupting three-way civil war for control of the continent of Africa.

Hacker felt his blood rise. Tyrants, this was their pastime. Relentless suppression even when the media echoes the cry for help. With information came power, and Hacker was going to wield it against the Goliaths of the galaxy.

"Where is my Ophridia task force?" He asked. A couple of windows popped up on his screen.

"Find out who this rebel leader is. Learn his name because I want that name on the lips of every news anchor within one hour. Second, probe Ophridia's media networks for weaknesses. If these guys have a message, I want everyone to hear it!" He barked.

"They have a poster sir!" Kevin cried out.

"Bring it up." The newscast was replaced by the stern gaze of a Chinese man with two characters written in mandarin next to his face. The computer translated out one word: 'Resist.'

"Does our friend have a name?" Hacker asked.

"Says here his name is Xing Ming Lee sir," Gary replied. "He's even issued a statement!"

"I want this poster and his face pasted on every drive of every computer on every news network! Get this poster viral and make it spread to every corner of the Core! By the end of this week, everyone will know the name 'Xing Ming Lee,'" Hacker said.

"Yes sir!" Gary replied.

"Finance team: short every business that has a direct line of transport to Ophridia. The Emperor is paranoid, and he'll start shutting people out. Let's give our friend here every advantage we can! This is the kind of chaos we live for!" The technicians cheered as they launched their crusade against the Emperor Yiu Mei. Hacker patched Rick through.

"Yes sir?" Rick asked.

"Make Ophridia our top priority for today. Put together a team to keep an eye on Africa. The newscasters may ignore a bunch of Africans killing each other, but we won't."

"Yes sir," Rick replied.

"This is what I live for. The ability to wield all of this power through information! My vision, my dream, come to life! I can create new identities, disrupt stock markets, and topple entire governments! Anything is possible, for I have every shred of information that passes through the Core at my fingertips!"

"It really is something sir," Rick said.

Over the course of several weeks, the Grid remained a hotbed of activity. Hacker's will was executed on every front of every news story. The Grid dealt out information hand over fist in exchange for more information, credits, or insider deals. They were the black market for every source of ill-obtained digital media, but Hacker couldn't resist making policy alongside selling bootlegged content.

"What's on tap for today?" Hacker asked Rick as he clutched his coffee.

"I found this interesting," Rick replied as he turned on the newscast. "Remember that Angkor colony you had someone keep an eye on few weeks ago?"

"The rushed colony job?"

"Yes sir," Rick said. "We received emergency transmissions from the colony's-"

A news reporter interrupted Rick. "Analysts are unclear as to why the Angkor colony has gone dark, but one thing is certain: the military has issued a statement that they will get the colony back up and running as soon as possible," the reporter said.

"So the rushed colony has gone dark," Hacker said as he took a sip of coffee.

"Worse than that. We have emergency broadcasts from the colony's Chief Biologist has said that they're suffering from alien attacks every night, and routinely finding people who've been dismembered," Rick said.

"Ugh, disgusting. Who's the Chief Biologist?"

"Dr. Adam Sulture," Rick replied as he played the video feed. They watch a man with slick black hair begging the viewer for help. He was grimy and covered in sweat, each plea more desperate than the last.

"Why didn't anybody come to me with this sooner?" Hacker snapped.

"We just received a backlog of transmissions today. We tried sending several messages, but they got bounced."

"Fair enough. Get a team on it, the military is covering something up. Keep an ear on all emergency channels in case they get through. Backchannels, uplinks, comm delivery packages, hell use goddamn email if we have to. Something is going on at Angkor and I intend to find out what."

"Will do sir. Here's another interesting story: In Africa, Diallo has taken a decisive lead in the three-way civil war. We have video of his right hand man nabbing a highly skilled weapons specialist who is designing all kinds of deadly devices."

"Of course they did. What's the weapon designer's name?"

Rick pulled up the video. "His name is Jackson Warrens, but that little woman right there that the other guy is dragging along? That's his grandmother. Judging by the way this guy is holding a gun to her head…"

"Diallo takes the man's grandmother hostage and forces him to work on designing weapons," Hacker said, as he finished Rick's train of thought.

"Exactly."

Hacker sighed and stared at the video. "Keep an eye on this man. Follow him, but don't do anything. No contact, no assistance, nothing. If we try to help now, Diallo will kill both of them. He's a bloodthirsty ego maniac. Keep me posted on the situation. I'll say when and how we can help."

"Got it. Next up, the Yiu Mei regime has unleashed a slew of new propaganda on our man. They're referring to Xing Ming Lee as the 'Anarchist of Ophridia.'"

"That's got a good ring to it. It'll spread like crazy, even faster than the propaganda we're manufacturing. Play on that. Turn Yiu Mei's message against him. I mean, how's it going to look when he's struggling to defeat an Anarchist?"

"It's going to look bad sir."

"Precisely. Radicals stand out, they get attention, so whoever does the propaganda for Yiu Mei screwed up big time. If they'd stomped this guy out early he'd be long forgotten. Instead they branded him for us."

"I'll get the Ophridia guys churning some news stories after this meeting then. We've also got a resistance movement brewing on Alcyone. A secessionist movement that has accused the Core of bombing the planet to turn it into a personal private luxury resort for the rich."

"I'm not surprised by the Core's attempts to get a real estate deal, but I am surprised by Alcyone starting a secessionist movement. They're a peacenik world without any weapons or bases. Still this reeks of Core corruption. Let's provide media support. They're going to need all the help they can get. Anyone we know there?" Hacker asked.

"Uhh...there are these two pilots I'd hired to deliver some parts a few months ago. Apparently they joined up with the locals."

"They any good?"

"Oh, they're the best pilots in the galaxy. They're just...different sir."

"How so?"

"Well, one is always waiting to make a 'Your Mom' joke and the other is as jittery as a chihuahua."

"Ugh, I'd hate to be stuck on a ship with them. What's next?"

"Well turns out we're in the news too. Conspiracy tabloids have referenced the Grid as an omnipresent arm of the Core government and the mysterious leader Hacker: Stealer of Secrets as the right hand of the Ministry of Information," Rick said as flicked the article to Hacker's computer screen.

Hacker's grin widened. "I like that, run with it. Feed the conspiracy guys some goodies. Make me omnipresent," He said as he took another sip of coffee.

"Done. Also, the technicians are asking for another demo of how to get past the Ministry of Defense's firewall. They did a security upgrade last week and it's causing some headaches."

"Schedule it for after lunch. I'll configure some probes. What is the status from those real estate scouts on finding us a new location?"

"Still looking. I'm putting a lot of pressure on them."

"Tell them they have a week. If they don't find us a new location, they're out and I'll find an agent who can find us a new base by then."

"Will do sir. Why the rush?"

"We're way overdue for a move. The Core is beginning to

get a trace on our location. Schedule a look over of security protocols and have everyone scale back 30% on any government intrusions outside of my MoD probes. Let's make today's firewall demo the last breach for a few weeks," Hacker said.

"Isn't that a bit overzealous?"

"Secrets are meant to remain secret."

"Until *you* get ahold of them."

"Hey, I don't talk until the right price is paid."

"Sir, you need to see this," Rick said as he burst into Hacker's office. "It's that weapon maker Jackson Warrens. He uploaded a data string onto our servers...I've never seen anything like it!" He said as he brought the file up inside Hacker's chamber.

Hacker skimmed over the lines of code. He noticed the anomalies and the idiosyncrasies within the data that led him to one conclusion.

"This...whatever it is, it's technology we've never even comprehended before. The coding is beyond advanced, the layering is so thick that it would take most people weeks to unravel it."

"I'm guessing you've solved it?" Rick asked.

"Let me try something..." Hacker said as he ran a few simulations. He studied the matrices and the results of his computations.

"Unbelieveable. If my math is correct, then this is what is known as fourth dimensional metal."

"What?! How would metal have code?"

"Until now, it's existence was only a theory, but in the fourth dimension, an object such as this would exist in all states at once. Whether it be a shard of ore, or an advanced weapon of integrated circuitry, 4D metal is both of them at the same time. Coding is the means for the lower dimensions to control the object."

"But...*how* can *metal* have *code*?!"

"It was just...created like that. It's part of the item's state of being. It could've been put there by a superior intelligence as a gift to us or it is the means of us being able to control it. It'd be like giving a stick man on paper a pencil."

"How do you suppose he got ahold of it?"

"Dunno, but fact remains our friend has it. What I do know is that we have the most complicated code in history right in front of us, and I'm the one who gets to master it!" Hacker said with a grin. He expanded his script page and keyed in dozens of lines of code.

"What're you doing?"

"I'm going to give our friend some options. Get the casting engines ready, we're going to create a device which can control this amorphous metal."

"Do you think this is even possible sir?" Rick asked.

"I will make it possible. I will master this program, regardless of the complexity involved. I will turn the tide of this African war and bring it to an end!"

Rick paused for a moment as he mulled over Hacker's words. With all of their time hidden behind screens watching the events of the galaxy unfold, it was easy to forget about the people involved. Hacker thought he could end a war as easily as he could manipulate script. Rick knew it wasn't so simple, but he also knew better than to argue with Hacker.

"I also received this update from Akio. It's a statement issued by General Hawkes against us," Rick said.

Hacker froze. "The Ministry of Information's attack dog?" He asked.

"That's him," Rick said as he started the video.

Hawkes was standing at a podium, poised to issue a statement. "Rest assured citizens of the Core that I will hunt down The Grid to the very ends of Core space. They are a cancer on our society, traitors to our cause, and sowers of dissent. I will not allow this group to contaminate the ideals of order and civility within the Core. I have procured the resources I need from Minister Philips to launch my manhunt and put an end to The Grid once and for all. Praise be to the Core for order restored. I shall bring credibility back to our information sources," Hawkes said before Rick stopped the video.

"So, another one launching a crusade against us?" Hacker asked.

"The men are scared of him Hacker. Hawkes has a history of making people...disappear. Y'know, Blackhat Hawkes?"

"I know all too well of what Hawkes can do. He won't catch us. We'll outsmart him."

"I sure hope so sir."

A quiet 18 months passed as the Grid kept quiet under the Core's watchful eye. They kept their distance from the events which transpired, but intervened whenever they believed it would clearly benefit those they watched. The Grid was cautious, but wary. They treated every mission with special care in the hopes that they would never get caught.

"Hacker, sir. Do you have a minute?" Gabby asked as she tapped on Hacker's door.

"Of course! C'mon in."

"Sir, I need your help," She said as she closed the door and took a seat. Her deep blue eyes met his. "Sir, I'm in deep. Really deep with some bad people..." She mumbled, then burst into tears.

"Gabby, what's wrong?" He said as he got up to console her.

"It's...my boyfriend and I..." Gabby sobbed. "We needed money so we turned to some of those instant credit dealers, but we couldn't keep up with the payments. They threatened to send someone after us to 'collect.'" She buried her face in her hands.

"Shh, Gabby, it's okay," Hacker said as he patted her on the shoulder. "I will help you with this. But, we've got to do it legally, we're in a precarious position right now."

"Sir, if it was legal, I wouldn't be asking you."

"I would love to Gabby, but the Ministries of Commerce and Treasury are watching for suspicious transactions. I can't do it."

"Please? Not even for me?" She pleaded.

Hacker sighed. "Once we do the uproot, I can do it then. No guarantees either, the Core is watching everything now."

"Oh Hacker! Thank you, thank you!" Gabby said as she hugged him tight. She kissed him on the cheek, and he found her vanilla perfume impossible to ignore.

"How can I ever repay you? Oh! I know, can I buy my hero a drink after work?"

"Umm, are you sure?"

"Of course! You've saved our lives, it's the least I can do!" Gabby said.

The afternoon flew by as Hacker finished and sent off his device to control the fourth dimensional metal. As he walked out he noticed that Gabby was waiting for him outside. The two shared pleasantries and small talk as they walked to a bar called "The Ram's Head."

"Order whatever you want, my treat," Gabby said as she sat down to the bar.

"That's very sweet, but unnecessary," Hacker said. Gabby smiled and turned her attention to the drink menu.

"Whiskey," Hacker said as he closed the menu screen.

"I'll have the same," Gabby said. The barkeep moved in graceful silence as he grabbed the bottle by the neck and poured the two a shot.

Hacker and Gabby raised their glasses in a toast. They swallowed their drinks and as the glasses clattered on the bar, Gabby signaled for two more.

She turned her attention to Hacker. "Sir, I can't thank you enough for all of your help, it means a lot to me."

"Oh, Gabby, it's nothing. Could take it from a Core Senator's campaign fund, that would be hilarious," He said as he threw back another shot.

Gabby let out a giggle. "Sir, you're so smart and talented and…" She trailed off as her hand caressed Hacker's thigh.

"What was it like being a mech runner?" Gabby asked.

Hacker's brow furrowed. "I don't talk about it," He said.

"I did some research. Who was Houston?" Gabby's voice

became as soft as velvet, and her fingers glided across Hacker's shoulders.

"I said I don't talk about it," He said as he downed another shot.

"I know that he was distant. That he used your unique talents for his own personal gain."

"He was a heartless critic who got what came to him!" Hacker snapped as he threw back another shot.

"Aww, poor thing. He didn't deserve a son like you," Gabby said as she got in close and breathed in Hacker's ear. Her hot breath sent shivers down his spine. He turned and stared into Gabby's big blue eyes. His mind roiled in rage over her calling him his son, but his anger melted in the vast oceans within her eyes.

He felt a pinprick on his leg and realized he'd felt the slight sting of betrayal.

Then his world went dark.

The hood was ripped off, and a bright light seared Hacker's corneas. The burning rays of the lamp left his face feeling singed, and the dry heat raked his skin. Sweat dripped down his scalp, and his mouth was parched. He gasped for a breath, but the air was barren too. He felt the binders that held him down. The walls were closing in. Panic squeezed his heart.

Hacker noticed three men standing in the dark half of the room, and he put two and two together. Through the darkness he saw a pair of red eyes watching his every movement.

"At last we meet Jabal Amir. I am-"

"General Hawkes," Hacker said as the General stepped into the light. "A blind man could see *you* coming." Hawkes was covered in the scars of burn marks, remnants from his assault against Houston.

"Such fire," Hawkes said. "Yet you *didn't* see me coming. Just like your mentor, you have witnessed my persistence. I will hunt a terrorist to the furthest reaches of the galaxy. And with access to the Ministry of Information, nothing is out of my reach." The General's words carried an air of surgical precision, each syllable a razor born from the methodical approach to hunting coders.

"Some would call me a freedom fighter."

"You live to sow chaos and dissent. I will not have this galaxy spattering wild ideas that will throw us back into another civil war."

"What's wrong with a little chaos?"

"As long as I breathe there will be order!" Hawkes snapped, then cleared his throat. "Come to think of it Jabal-"

"That's not my name anymore!"

"Indeed. Defiant just like your mentor. You want us to believe that you like to sow chaos, but it is no match for what stirs inside you is it?"

"You've lost it Hawkes."

"I don't believe I have. All you've ever done in your life has been some desperate search for Daddy's approval. You couldn't get it with yours, so you sought out another figure, Houston. And he too, proved elusive with his affections."

Hacker steeled himself against the General's words.

"Ah! Must've hit it right on the nose. All this chaos because a handful of words never said. Let's rectify that shall we? Colonel Henry, bring in the source of the dissent."

Hacker looked around in confusion as he heard the metal doors open. Horror gripped him as he watched the bulky Colonel Henry push a man in a wheelchair into the interrogation room. His balding head was covered in beads of sweat, his hands bound to the chair and a dirty sock dangled from his mouth.

"Get up," Hawkes said as he kicked the chair. Abdul jumped in his chair and looked around the room. When his eyes met Hacker, he could see sheer terror in them and muffled cries lay stifled beneath the dirty sock.

"Why are you doing this Hawkes?"

"To bring the pup to heel."

Abdul looked up at Hacker. His eyes were red and swollen. He looked puffy and weak, as though the wheelchair was his only means of movement.

"It's a shame isn't it Jabal?" Hawkes asked. "All you've ever wanted was to hear four little words from your father. Do you remember what they were?"

"How do you know this?" Hacker hissed.

Hawkes sighed. "For years you've been using the same three artificial intelligence programs to interfere with my work. 'The Wrecking Crew' you called them. I had my best analysts create a virus which would turn one of your programs against you. It wouldn't even realize it was against you, it would merely supply us with all of the information about you I needed. I learned your strengths and your weaknesses from your own creation!"

Hacker felt a knot in his stomach. He couldn't believe his oversight, the negligence on his part for allowing this to have happened.

"From your data dumps, I was able to piece together a pattern that stems from a common root. Four words to be precise. Do you remember what they were?"

Hacker glared at Hawkes and swallowed hard. Words couldn't form in his mind.

"Perhaps it's been too long then," Hawkes said as he walked up behind Abdul. "Abdul Amir, you really should've been a better father."

"Shut up!" Hacker screamed.

"You should've applauded his achievements, showcased his abilities, instead you condemned them with your mysticism and blind faith!"

"Get away from him or I will kill you!" Hacker howled.

"All you had to say was: 'I'm proud of you.'" Hawkes screamed as he raised his arms in triumph. "I'll bet you would've liked to have heard that hmm Jabal?"

Tears spilled from Hacker's eyes. He looked down at his father, a round man who'd only sought to cleanse his soul. Their eyes met and filled with tears. Abdul's eyes were filled with regret and sorrow. In them, Hacker saw all that he needed.

"Too bad you never will," Hawkes said as he ripped the

sock out of Abdul's mouth.

"Jabal I'm sor-" A pair of mechanical arms from behind the chair seized Abdul's face, forced his mouth open and sliced out his tongue. The man gargled on blood as he leaned forward and spat it out. He wailed in pain, his eyes desperate to say something to his son.

"You son of a bitch!" Hacker cursed as he leaped up in his chair. Hawkes kicked him down to the floor.

"Luckily for you, the Ministry wants you alive, but they didn't specify about any of my other prisoners."

"Sir this is not-"

"Shut up Colonel Henry!" Hawkes snapped. "Your sympathy for these derelicts has cost me quite enough!"

Abdul dropped to the floor and crawled to Hacker. He wrapped his arms around his tethered son who cried uncontrollably.

"Dad, please believe me, I didn't want any of this to happen. I'm sorry for everything," Hacker said. Abdul wailed and groaned, but blood kept flowing from his mouth.

"It's okay Dad. I forgive you for everything. I know what you're trying to say and it's-

"So heartwarming," Hawkes interrupted. He shot Abdul in the back who died instantaneously, still clutching his son in his arms. "Now you've failed to save both of your fathers."

"You arrogant, pompous mother fucker!" Hacker shouted. Tears flowed down his face, but he saw a sadistic grin form on Hawkes' lips. Hacker realized that he was playing into Hawkes' hand. If he was to have any hope, he'd have to unsettle him. He'd have to ignite the icy General.

"Y'know Hawkes," Hacker said between sobs. "It's kinda sad that someone of your pay grade chased after little ol' me for twelve years. Move on man."

"Nonsense. I quite enjoy the hunt-"

"I wasn't done," Hacker said. "The really despicable act was using my secretary to oust us. You couldn't even find me of your own volition. You had to rely on the intel of a ditzy secretary."

"I would think that you'd believe intel is intel Jabal. How I
-"

"Y'know Hawkes, considering that I hadn't moved my HQ
for almost a year and a half, I would've thought that any of
your chainers could've found us. Shame that a has-been like
you couldn't."

"I am hardly a has-been like you are Jabal. I-"

"Can't code to save your life, we know. And since you're
such a messed up sadist, you've been spending so much
quality time with me that the Grid has the time they need to
escape from you."

"The Grid will never escape-"

"They already have Hawkes! I've set the Grid up that if I'm
not seen within the first two hours of my normal arrival time
and I don't report my status, they dump everything and pull
out the electromagnets."

"You wouldn't da-"

"I already have. You've lost your cha-"

"THAT'S ENOUGH!" Hawkes screamed. "Cease
interrupting me or I will see to it that you suffer!"

"Suffer how? You just killed your only source of leverage! I
have nothing to lose!"

"It's time that I put an end to your talking Jabal. I tire of that
damn mouth," Hawkes said as he holstered his pistol and
drew a syringe filled with a bright orange liquid. He
approached Hacker when the click of a hammer echoed
behind him.

Hawkes turned around. It was Colonel Henry with his gun
trained on him. "This has gone far enough General," He said.

"John, you dare threaten me?" Hawkes asked. "Especially
with another guardsman in the room?"

"Good point," John said and then shot the other guardsman
before he could draw his pistol. As John turned his attention
back to Hawkes, he realized that he'd pulled Hacker in front of
him to use as a human shield.

"You dare side with these anarchists?!" Hawkes asked. "I
will have your head for this you traitor!"

"It's not about whose side I'm on General, it's about doing what's right."

"The right thing to do is restore order John! I punish those who sow chaos, and this one is the worst of them all!" Hawkes hissed.

Hacker elbowed Hawkes in the stomach, while Hawkes plunged the serum into Hacker's neck. Within seconds, the spot where Hawkes injected the serum burned, and started to spread. A chill as cold as ice flowed through Hacker's neck and shoulders, and then the rest of his body. But in an instant his entire bloodstream had been ignited as though it was rocket fuel.

As Hawkes stumbled back, Hacker managed to snag the pistol inside the General's' jacket and tossed it to John before he collapsed onto the floor.

"You traitor!" Hawkes howled as he charged at John. He tackled John to the floor, and knocked the pistol out of his hands. He reached into his jacket for another syringe, but John held the mad General's hands at bay.

The two wrestled on the floor while Hacker watched, helpless as his body felt like fireworks pummeled every nerve. The concrete floor clawed at his skin, and Hawkes intended to inflict the same torture to John.

John kneed Hawkes in the groin, rolled on top of the General and fought to twist his wrists until the syringe was pointed at him. John and Hawkes pushed with all of their might, the two officers locked in a feat of strength against one another.

"AAAHHHH!" John howled as he broke the stalemate and pushed the plunger, injecting the serum into Hawkes.

"Come on!" John screamed as he leaped up and held out his hand to Hacker. Everything burned, even John's hand felt like a Titan's grip. The vibration from walking felt like a hammer striking every joint in his legs.

"I'm not...doing so hot..." Hacker said.

"You have to move Hacker! C'mon!" John grunted as he hoisted him over his shoulders.

John weaved through the underground bunker to avoid contact with all other Core soldiers inside the complex as Hacker's body temperature rose.

"Did you think this all the way through?" Hacker asked.

"Somewhat. If I can get you to a medic-"

"No! No military doctors! Take me to the Grid. We have someone onsite who can cure me."

"This serum is experimental! Only the Core has an antidote!"

"You just shot another Core officer and injected the serum into a high-ranking General! Do you really think a medic won't say something?"

"Point made. I'm sorry about your father, if I'd known..."

"Saying sorry doesn't bring him back Colonel Henry," He said bitterly. He wished he could've taken it all back. The final words he'd said to his father before this encounter would haunt him for the rest of his days. He hoped that in those final moments his father had only kind words in his heart. Hacker certainly did.

There was no penance from this. No atonement for his sin of hubris. Hacker yearned to die. He believed this serum to only be the start of the endless pain he would endure. He deserved it. In fact, he believed that he got off easy, being saved by a stranger at a time when all he wanted was to goad Hawkes into pulling the trigger and end the suffering to come.

"My blood is on fire," Hacker mumbled.

"I know Hacker. I'm going to get you out of here. Mark my words." The two escaped the bunker and commandeered a small shuttle on the ground. John strapped Hacker in.

"I...don't think I'm going to make it..."

"You will. We'll get to the Grid before they do. I promise," John said. He ran around, jumped into the pilots seat, ignited the shuttle and took off.

"I think I'm going into cardiac arrest," Hacker said as his heart drummed inside his chest. He took a deep breath, but couldn't exhale. His heart raced, and the air in his lungs piled up.

"God damn it!" John cursed. Hacker watched John strike him in the thigh, and then his world went dark.

"I need a medic!" John howled at the entrance of the Grid. The door opened, while Rick and three other members came out with pistols trained on John.

"What happened to him?" Rick asked.

"Hawkes gave him an experimental torture serum. He refused medical help at the base, he wanted to come here," John said.

"Is he dead?" Akio asked.

"If you guys don't move it, he will be," John said. Rick holstered his pistol and took Hacker into his arms.

"Clear the way," Rick said. "We're going to need to draw some blood. Akio, get a doctor on the line."

John approached the doorway, but Donald held him at bay with a pistol pointed between his eyes.

"Donald, let him go. I don't think the infamous John Henry is here to arrest us all by himself," Rick said.

Donald glared at John as he holstered his pistol. The four men walked into the base. Technicians everywhere were pulling out electromagnets and frying their Chambers. The screens frazzled in a mix of pixelated images before going black, taking their secrets into an unrecoverable ocean.

"We got suspicious when we hadn't heard from him," Rick said. "We have the protocols in place to prevent anyone in the Core from capturing our operation, and we're never afraid to pull the plug."

John watched as this sea of information was being thrown away. Billions in storage space was being wiped out, likely uploaded and stored in some off site server far away. It seemed like such a waste. The Grid possessed the most archived scientific information in the galaxy, and if the right people accessed its libraries, there was no telling how many new discoveries could be made in the field of science.

Rick placed Hacker on a table. "His heart is going out. Donald, get me the defibrillator." He ran into an adjacent room and retrieved the device that would get Hacker's heart moving.

"I'm drawing a blood sample. Akio, is Dr. Stirge ready?"

"Yes, we have him on the uplink. He's awaiting the sample now."

"Perfect. John, be a pal and give this to Akio," Rick said as he handed John the tube full of blood. John waltzed over and gave Akio the blood who placed it inside a small box.

"Okay, now let's try to wake him up," Rick said as he drew a shot of pure adrenaline.

"No, don't!" John shouted, but Rick raised the syringe and stabbed it into Hacker's chest. He plunged the syringe, and waited for Hacker to wake up.

Hacker's eyes opened and he screamed. He screamed in such agony every technician on the floor froze and watched in horror as the Stealer of Secrets begged his friends for death. His screams echoed through the halls of the complex, sending chills down every spine. Even John, who saw every kind of war wound known to man had never heard a man scream in such pain.

"That's why I knocked him out!" John said.

"Rick!" Akio shouted. "The Doctor...he's never seen anything like this before. He doesn't understand these synthetics!"

"Oh, shit," Rick replied. "Wait a minute! Get me that chemist I know, um...the professor on Titan! He'll know what to do!"

"Can we trust him?" John asked.

"Oh yeah, he's quiet. He once hired me to do a full scale identity wipe for him. Didn't make sense to me, but hey, he had the money and was more than willing to pay me to do it!" Rick said.

Hacker's throat became hoarse from his screams. His body writhed as he sought to escape the pain. His skin felt like it was being peeled off, then set aflame. His tears felt like branding irons being dragged against his cheeks. Existence itself was agony and torture.

"The pain...it's too much!" Hacker screamed. He convulsed on the table, his limbs flailing in all directions.

"The doctor said to knock him out! We need to put him into a medically induced coma if he's going to survive this!" Akio said.

"No! He just received an adrenaline shot to the heart, anything more will take his heart out!" John said.

Rick put his hand to Hacker's forehead. "He's burning up. What if we put him into an ice bath?"

"By the looks of it, we don't have much choice!" John said. "Get the ice!" He shouted. Akio and Donald ran off, but they could only find a few trays of ice in the freezer. John and Rick carried Hacker into the showers and turned on the water. They turned the knobs as far to cold as they could go, but nobody knew if it was going to be enough. Hacker whimpered as the water droplets splashed against his skin, each one felt like a pellet of molten steel raining down on him.

Akio ran in and held the ice against Hacker's chest and head. He screamed in agony again as the cold sting of the ice burned even more. He gasped for breath and rambled in whispers about his delusions. His eyes flickered as he snapped in and out of consciousness, the water and sweat cascading down his body.

"If we can't cool him down, his organs will cook!" John said.

"We need more ice!" Rick snapped. "Akio, go get some more from one of the local stores. Donald, has that chemist replied yet?"

"No sir, the sample hasn't even finished uploading yet. With the network down..." Donald paused.

"Son of a bitch!" Rick cursed. A crack of thunder roared outside. An explosion rocked the entire building and shook it to her foundations.

"Do I wanna know what that was?" Rick asked.

"The security cameras don't show anything...wait! They put our feed on a feedback loop!" Donald shouted.

"You! You led them here!" Akio hissed as he drew his pistol and pointed it at John.

"No...he didn't," Rick said. "Gabby did."

The technicians gasped in shock. "How do you know?" Akio asked.

"Because after an hour when I didn't hear from Hacker I looked at the footage. He left here with Gabby to the Ram's Head bar, where I was able to recover drone footage of her escorting Core soldiers in to pick him up. It was then that I issued the Phoenix Protocol to wipe out everything," Rick explained.

The room sat in silence while another explosion rocked overhead. "Seems that our luck has run out," Rick said.

"Maybe not yet. Do you have any comm lines open?" John asked.

"A few."

"Let me make a call. I'll try to get us out of this."

The door exploded, and a swarm of Core soldiers spilled into the building. Their guns were drawn, and the technicians saw no other choice than to surrender to the superior fighting force. The technicians kneeled on the floor, while the soldiers screamed for the others to get down. They attached zip ties to everyone on their knees, then moved to the lower levels.

Hawkes marched in triumphant at the top of the stairs. His face held a rosy hue, a mark that the serum hadn't been fully cleansed from his system.

"I should've known that my own John Henry would betray me for the leader of a renegade group of separatists. The war has been over for ten years, yet these miscreants insist on keeping it going...and you want to join them," Hawkes said.

"I did not betray you General. But you've made it clear that you don't intend on repairing the divisions here in the Core. Same with the other Generals. But there are those who do want the Core to heal, and one of them happens to be on my side," John said.

"What the hell are you talking about?"

"Madame Chairman Harris, I'll let you explain," John said as he turned on the communications array.

"General Hawkes, you are to cease and desist from the presence of this facility immediately!" Harris said.

"With all due respect Harris, you are merely a citizen of a very large company. And I am after a target that has stolen and sold state secrets!"

"General Hawkes, this facility is now under the ownership of the Ionics Corporation. We have procured their information sources regarding scientific research and advancement and quite frankly, you're trespassing," Harris said.

"I will not-"

"General, if you do not leave at once, I will personally contact Information Minister Philips about this infringement upon my property, without a warrant, and he will remove you from your position at once!" Harris screeched.

Hawkes pulled out a comm device, looked at the screen and then placed it back into his pocket. A snarl of defeat formed on his face.

"Release the prisoners," He ordered. The soldiers swept through the floor, cut the ties which bound all of the technicians and filed out of the facility. They left behind a massive mess of papers, overturned desks and smashed Chambers.

"Hacker's going to be pissed when he wakes up," Rick said.

"So Colonel, do I take that to mean you're accepting my offer?" Harris asked.

"Yes I am Lynn. I'll be there to sign the papers in a few days."

"Excellent. I'll see you then," Harris said as she cut the feed.

"Whew! That was a close one!" Rick said as he wiped his forehead.

"You will keep your end of the bargain right?" John asked.

"Of course. We'll sell Ionics all of our scientific data in exchange for our freedom," Rick said. "It'll take us a few days to compile all of it, but by the time Hawkes gets the warrant he needs, we'll be long gone.

"Yeah, Hawkes being on his feet was my biggest fear. It means the Core has an antidote for the serum," John said.

"Sir!" Akio shouted. "The chemist! He came through!"

"Perfect," Rick replied. "We can synthesize an antidote now."

Rick approached Hacker with a full IV bag and hung it on the stand.

"Time for your cure sir," Rick said.

"I don't deserve to be cured," Hacker said.

"Why not?"

"After what I did. To my father, to Houston, to all of you. I should've died. I deserve to die."

"Hacker, if you'd wanted to die, you would've. John said your organs would've cooked if we left you like that any longer. My contact came through and now I can dissolve that crap in your bloodstream."

"Not all of it. Leave some inside me Rick. Let it serve as a reminder of my ego getting in the way, so that I'll never forget the pain I inflicted on others."

"If you say so…"

There was a knock at the door. It was John.

"How're you feeling?" He asked.

"Everything hurts, but I'm getting used to it."

"Rick, may I have a moment?" John asked.

Rick bowed his head, and then left the room.

"I suppose you were wondering why I acted out against the Core and-"

"Not really," Hacker interrupted. "Colonel John C. Henry, rising star within the Core ranks for brave performance during the Core invasion. Spent the last few years directing contractors through the Ministry of Defense's regulations, believes that science is the key to mankind's salvation yet has no educational background in the field. A ravenous reader who likes to play dumb in front of others. Was offered a position within Ionics, a lucrative retirement job, but needed a few days to make his decision. Don't worry John, I do my homework."

John gave a knowing smile. "I knew you would. I also do

mine. We stand at a crossroad here in the Core. We're making the push into deep space but too many people don't know how to handle the dangers that exist out there. I want to put together a team that does know how to handle those dangers."

"And you want me to be a part of that team?"

"Well, yes."

"No," Hacker replied.

"And why not?"

"Should I ignore the fact that you sold a huge chunk of my organization in exchange for my freedom? That you traded one master for another?"

"Hacker, I suspect that deep down you and I both know that your time with the Grid is over. Your experience at the Grid has shown you the dark side of the black market information trade. You've seen what happens when you get caught, and everyone gets caught eventually."

"Still, I'm a lone wolf and you already played your get out of jail free card. I can take my skills anywhere I want."

"You're right Hacker, that's true. But remember, I saved your life."

"Really? Playing that card?"

"Seems it's all I got. How about instead of being a lone wolf you be a part of something greater. A brotherhood that will lay down their lives for each other."

Hacker felt a growing respect for John, his charisma eroding his gnawing loneliness. "I'm listening. What will you want me to do?"

"Once you recover, I'll task you with finding the rest of our members."

"You want me to track down a bunch of old soldiers who fought for the Core?"

"No. I want you to find me a team of scientists."

"You lost me."

"This program I'm developing, Core and Coalition soldiers are not who we want running around. I need scientists who will study the monsters we will face, learn their habits, and can kill them. I need scientists who can hold their own in a bar fight.

"That's a tall order. You're aware that there's *maybe* a dozen men in the galaxy like that?"

"I am aware. That's why I'm asking *you* to find them."

"Why do you want me on your team? I am an egotistical information dealer and failed mech runner from the war."

"Hacker, I'm giving you a chance to fight for something that you actually believe in. Instead of using your incredible skills to try and bring down 'the system' why not use them to help mankind? Granted it may not fix the current system, but more worlds in the Core means more voices, which will force the Core to see reason. We both know that the Core cannot decree their will forever. Let us help mankind outside of the system... because the system has failed both of us."

Hacker looked down at his arm where the IV was. He pondered for a moment, remembering all of the pain he'd caused. A part of him believed that this was a second chance, a chance to make things right.

"Running the Grid has become a bit monotonous. Hunting monsters would be an interesting reboot," Hacker said with a grin.

"Done." John said as he extended his hand. Hacker reached out and the two men shook, a new partnership born that night. John went to leave, but stopped at the door.

"Oh and Hacker," John said. "I'm proud of your decision."

Hacker looked up in surprise and struggled to hold back tears.

"This is your ship?" Hacker asked when he laid eyes on John's bulky behemoth. It was a freighter left over from the Core Invasion. A narrow nosed hulk with a massive engine system and had a large number of modifications which included a vast array of weapon systems. The two men climbed aboard the boat. Her hardware was in pristine condition, but the operating system was slow, buggy and had a habit of glitching.

"What's her name?" Hacker asked.

"The Enigma."

"Really?"

"You're criticizing *me* on names?" John replied with a smirk.

"Fair enough. However your OS is going to need an overhaul."

"Whatever you need to do to the operating system, do it. I want this ship ready for duty ASAP," John said. "On second thought, build my team first. That's far more critical to our mission."

"Will do."

Hacker flipped through the individual dossiers of the recommended Horsemen. He prepared their profiles for John so that when he approached these men, he knew everything he needed to know and could sell the idea that Ionics should buy their freedom. John was given a black budget to build his team, but Hacker couldn't quite pinpoint Ionics' gain from acquiring a team of scientists blacklisted from the scientific community.

First was the newly minted "Xenocidalist" Dr. Adam Sulture and his lieutenant Dr. Murph McGinnis, the heroes of the Angkor colony who kept them alive after the colony went dark and drove an alien species to extinction. As Hacker read the dossier to prepare his report, things became much clearer about the situation.

"Abandoned by the military, and 70% of the colony was wiped out. These guys weren't butchers, they were defending their homes and their neighbors. They didn't take it lying down either, that's why the Core is so pissy," Hacker mumbled to himself as he flipped to the next dossier.

"He included the 'your mom' pilot and the shrieking co-pilot," Hacker said to himself. "Still, Curly-haired led the Alcyone air resistance and brought down a battleship using nothing more than an enemy star fighter. Maybe there is hope."

Hacker smiled to himself when he saw the Anarchist Xing Ming Lee, who'd just been placed under arrest by the Core for executing the dictator Yiu Mei. He swiped along, adding him to the list.

Hacker gazed at the next profile. "It's the mechanic!" He said as he watched the news feed. "Looks like he put the Coeus design to good use. Managed to bring peace between the three armies and he...let the weapon... Why...Wait! NO! What is he doing with the weapon?" Hacker cursed as he added Jackson Warrens to the roster.

Finally, Hacker compared the profiles of two chemists. "Hmm, one who's valiantly fighting and mixing chemical bombs against alien aggressors on the fringes of Core space. Or a has-been chemistry professor at Titan University. Why did Rick even inclu-" Hacker paused as he reviewed the Professor's profile one more time.

He set the tablet down on the table. The name 'Silas Godfrey' flickered at the top of the screen. A small note left by Rick explained his decision: "Client saved Hacker's life."

Hacker looked at his hand and felt the fiery serum course through his veins. He clenched his fist and felt his blood burn. He stared at the screen and wondered who would be the better choice.

"The Professor gave me a second chance. Seems like he could use one too."

—The End—

Epilogue

Epilogue

"You let them get away," Hawkes said. "Just like that mob boss over a decade ago."

"I did," the man in the shadows replied.

"Why? What good will these miscreants do in tearing up the galaxy?"

"They won't tear anything up Hawkes. You worry too much. Henry will keep them in line."

"You don't worry enough! Henry has a mind of his own!"

"True, but Henry is an idealist with good intentions. And we both know where the road paved with good intentions leads to…"

"Well said sir."

"Besides, now that I own the Grid, consider all of its resources at your disposal. The only ones you can't hunt are Henry and his 'Horsemen'. I want them to have free reign."

"Dominic I must-"

The man held up his hand. "The Horsemen serve me. That is all you need to worry about."

PART SIX

Thanks for Reading!

A special thanks to you for reading! This has been an arduous project, one that I loved every minute of. If you can, please submit a review on Amazon - they're the lifeblood of all authors. Also, if you're interested in more stories and special deals with upcoming books, please visit www.benjaminshartman.com and sign up for my official newsletter!